KERRY WILKINSON

THE WOMAN IN BLACK

PAN BOOKS

First published by Kerry Wilkinson 2011

This edition published 2013 by Pan Books
an imprint of Pan Macmillan, a division of Macmillan Publishers Limited
Pan Macmillan, 20 New Wharf Road, London N1 9RR
Basingstoke and Oxford
Associated companies throughout the world
www.panmacmillan.com

ISBN 978-1-4472-2567-6

3 5 7 9 8 6 4 2

A CIP catalogue record for this book is available from the British Library.

Typeset by Ellipsis Digital Limited, Glasgow
Printed and bound by CPI Group (UK) Ltd, Croydon, CR0 4YY

Visit www.panmacmillan.com to read more about all our books
and to buy them. You will also find features, author interviews and
news of any author events, and you can sign up for e-newsletters
so that you're always first to hear about our new releases.

THE WOMAN IN BLACK

Kerry Wilkinson is something of an accidental author. His debut, *Locked In*, the first title in the detective Jessica Daniel series, was written as a challenge to himself but, after self-publishing, it became a UK Number One bestseller within three months of release. Kerry then went on to have more success with the second and third titles in the series, *Vigilante* and *The Woman in Black*. His new book, *Think of the Children*, will be available in both paperback and ebook soon.

Kerry has a degree in journalism and works for a national media company. He was born in Somerset but now lives in Lancashire.

For more information about Kerry and his books visit his website: www.kerrywilkinson.com or www.panmacmillan.com

By Kerry Wilkinson

LOCKED IN

VIGILANTE

THE WOMAN IN BLACK

THE WOMAN IN BLACK

1

Detective Sergeant Jessica Daniel swept the strand of long dark blonde hair away from her face and looked down at the object in front of her before saying the only thing that came to mind. 'Well, it's definitely a hand.'

The man standing next to her nodded in agreement. 'Blimey, nothing gets past you, does it?'

Jessica laughed. 'Oi. It's just you never know what you're going to get, do you? When I was in uniform I got sent out because there were reports of a dead animal blocking a road and it was only someone's coat. For all we knew, this "severed hand" could have been part of a kid's doll.'

Detective Inspector Jason Reynolds looked at the scene in front of them, nodding. 'You're right but this ain't a kid's toy.'

The appendage was greying in colour and blended with the patch of concrete it had been left on. Jessica thought it looked fairly hardened, as if the fingers would be stiff and awkward to move, even though the digits were splayed and it was flat to the ground. Given the clean-looking cut where it would have once been connected to someone's wrist, Jessica was surprised there was no blood. She didn't want to touch it but stepped closer and crouched, peering towards the small stump where the person's ring finger had been neatly sliced off. It looked as if the area had been burned after the amputation to stop any infection and she wondered if the finger had been removed before or after the rest of the hand.

Jessica stood and stepped backwards out of the small white tent into the heat of the morning sunshine with Reynolds just behind her. The inspector was a tall black officer who had an outwardly friendly demeanour but, when he wanted to be, was as tough as anyone she knew. She walked towards the edge of the police tape surrounding the scene, stopping before she got too close to the nearby uniformed officer who was preventing passers-by from getting too good a look. 'What do you reckon happened to the missing finger?' she asked.

'Who knows? It looks as if it was cut off as cleanly as the hand itself,' the inspector replied.

'Do you think the person it's from is dead?'

Reynolds blew out through his teeth as he squinted into the sun. 'Probably. We'll have to check the records to see if there have been any remains found in the past year or two that are missing a hand. There's nothing to say it would definitely be from a body from our area, so we'll have a bit of work to do. The way it's been preserved, it could be an old victim or someone brand new. Whoever left it has been very careful.'

'Not much to go on, was there?' Jessica said. 'No tattoos or anything.'

'I know. Given its shape with the wider fingers I'd bet it was a man's hand but that could just be minor decomposition. It looks as if whoever cut it off has kept it carefully.

We're going to have to wait for the forensics team to see if they can find anything.'

'Yeah, you've got to *hand* it to the lab boys, they do a top job.'

Reynolds looked at Jessica, eyebrows raised. 'I really don't think stand-up comedy is the career for you.'

Jessica grinned back. 'Oh come on. Just because you've been promoted, it doesn't mean you have to stop laughing at my jokes.'

'I don't remember ever laughing at your jokes.'

'All right, fine, be grumpy. What are we going to do next?'

Reynolds looked around at the buildings surrounding them. 'The thing is, this is the centre of Manchester, the second or third biggest city in the country. Just look at the cameras.' He pointed out the CCTV units mounted high on the shops, hotels and flats nearby. 'This is Piccadilly Gardens. You couldn't have picked a more public spot if you tried. Whoever left this wanted it to be found.' He paused, as if pondering what he wanted to do. 'If you take a constable and look through the footage from last night, I'll start working through any missing persons reports to see if there have been any bodies found without a hand nationwide. By the time we've gone through all that, we might have some test results back to give us a gender and age for the victim.'

Jessica looked to the areas the inspector had pointed out. Piccadilly Gardens was one of the main meeting points in the centre of Manchester. The middle part was a mixture of grassy park areas surrounded by benches and fountains, along with concreted and paved sections for people to walk. One side was dominated by a bus and tram station, another lined by a wide walkway and shops. Looming over the top of the area was a hotel and a road with more shops edged along the final side.

Jessica looked back towards the area the hand had been found in, just underneath one of the fountains next to a bench. Unless someone had dropped it, which made some very odd assumptions about the types of thing people carried around with them, it seemed clear the hand had been left purposely.

Jessica could see at least seven security cameras scanning the area, one of which was swivelling high on a pole around fifty feet away from where she was standing. Three other similar cameras were placed around the square. She knew they were linked into a set of other CCTV cameras throughout the city, the images feeding back to a central security point that was manned twenty-four hours a day. Most people thought the cameras were constantly watched by police officers but the operators were a private security firm paid for by the council.

As she scanned around, she could see two other cameras attached to the hotel and a further one high above a shop front. She figured footage from those would be kept somewhere on their respective sites.

Jessica felt the warmth of the June sun on her arms and thought about spending the rest of the day indoors watching camera footage from the night before. 'Whoever left it could have at least picked a rainy day,' she said to no one in particular.

Jessica slumped back into her chair and sighed. The office she was sitting in belonged to the private security firm who monitored the city's cameras. It felt small, lit only by a fluorescent strip on the ceiling above her and the bank of monitors she was facing. She leant forward to press a button on a control panel, stopping the video images she had been watching, then pushing back in her seat again and peering at the woman next to her. 'Bored of being in CID yet?'

The female officer slouched back in her own chair and laughed. 'We've only been looking through the tapes for an hour.'

'Exactly, an hour; we could have been out doing all sorts. Someone with a name like yours shouldn't be stuck inside on a day like this. You should be in a rock band or something.'

'"Isobel" isn't that strange a name.'

Jessica nodded. 'Maybe not but "Izzy" sounds cool. Especially "Izzy Diamond". It's too good a name to be wasted on the Greater Manchester Police force.'

'It wasn't so "cool" when I was at school. "Dizzy Izzy", "Isobel-End", "Izzy A Bloke?" and all that.'

'That's quite original bullying,' Jessica said, trying not to sound too impressed. 'At my school, I just got called "Dan the Man" for ten years.'

Detective Constable Izzy Diamond had only joined

Manchester Metropolitan's Criminal Investigation Department six weeks before. The division's detective chief inspector, John Farraday, had given up his job almost seven months ago but stayed on for a short while to help guide his successor into the post. The new incumbent, Jack Cole, had previously been a DI and, with his promotion, Jason Reynolds had been elevated from detective sergeant to inspector. Jessica had previously spent just over two years sharing an office with the then DS Reynolds and the pair's relationship hadn't altered much despite his change in job.

Because of the reshuffle and the fact one of their colleagues, DC Carrie Jones, had been killed the previous year, two new constables had been hired. DC Diamond was one of the fresh faces and Jessica had chosen to take the new girl under her wing. There was very little between them in terms of age, with Jessica in her early thirties and the constable less than a year younger.

Jessica glanced away from the monitors to look at the officer. 'Did you have that colour hair when you were at school?'

Izzy ran her hands through her long bright red mane seemingly without thinking about it. She let it drop to her shoulders then tied it into a ponytail with a band she'd had around her wrist. 'Nope, it was a type of browny dark colour then. I've only been red like this for the past year, since I got married. I fancied a change after we got back from honeymoon.'

Jessica nodded. 'I think it's pretty cool.'

'It scares off the older guys at the station so that's a

bonus. I think most of them think I'm a vampire or something.'

'What's it like?'

The constable grinned and had a twinkle in her blue eyes. 'What, being a vampire?'

Jessica laughed. 'No, being married.'

Izzy bit her bottom lip. 'Marriage is fine. My husband, Mal, would like to start trying for kids but I want to do this for a few more years at least before I think about that. I'd rather try the vampirism.'

Jessica looked back towards the monitors and pressed the button that started the footage at double speed. She kept her eyes on the screen, continuing to talk. 'Is Mal short for Malcolm?'

'Malachi.'

'Wow, you two have the best names ever. You did marry him just for the last name though, didn't you?'

Izzy laughed. 'Of course. Who could resist "Diamond" as a surname? I used to be "Isobel Smith", which was way more boring.'

Jessica had worked on a few minor things with the constable since she had been appointed but the mystery over the severed hand was by far the most serious case Izzy had been involved with. Jessica hadn't been told by anyone she had to go out of her way to work closely with any of the new recruits but had done so anyway. It felt strange because she was Izzy's supervisor but, in some respects, she felt inferior to her. Jessica lived in a flat on her own, the constable was married and owned a house. It wasn't that Jessica was desperate to have a boyfriend or settle down but they were roughly the same age and Izzy seemed like the proper grown-up to her. While the constable would do a full day at work and talk about hosting dinner parties and the like, Jessica would spend her evenings either in front of the television or on the Internet while eating microwaved food. The fact the woman next to her could even contemplate having children nailed her down as a genuine adult. Jessica couldn't stand other people's kids – let alone think about having any of her own.

'My mate's getting married,' Jessica said.

'Someone from the station?'

'I do have other friends too!'

'Sorry, I didn't mean . . .'

'It's all right. She's my oldest friend actually, Caroline. We lived together for ages but grew apart. We've only been back in regular contact for the last couple of months or so.'

'Let me guess, the job came between you?' From her tone, it sounded as if Izzy spoke from experience.

'You don't know the half of it . . .'

Two years previously, Jessica had been trying to find a serial killer. The trail ultimately led her to Caroline's boy-friend Randall, who tried to kill her. He was currently in a secure hospital and, as far as Jessica knew, hadn't spoken to anyone since his arrest. After that things hadn't quite been the same between the pair.

'Is it something you want to talk about?' Izzy asked, apparently sensing Jessica's discomfort.

'Not really. She phoned and asked if I'd be a bridesmaid for her.'

'Are you doing it?'

'Of course. We didn't fall out and I'd still call her my best friend. I'm glad she asked but I'm not so sure about the whole big event thing. I don't really do dressing up and all that.'

Izzy peered down at the light brown trouser suit she was wearing, fingering the thin lapel on her jacket. 'Don't you ever get bored of these suits every day?'

Jessica glanced away from the screens at her own grey suit. 'I used to, maybe a couple of years ago. I don't really think about it now. She's not picked the dresses yet. I'm worried it will be some sort of pink or yellow monstrosity and I'll be left living with those horrific photos until the end of time. If anyone from the station sees them . . .' She drifted off, contemplating how she would struggle to live down those potential images.

The constable laughed, glancing up at the screen Jessica was watching. 'I think my bridesmaids were worried about the same thing. We all chose together and went for something relatively plain and cream.'

'Caroline's favourite colour is purple, so I'm hoping she's kind.'

There was a short pause as they both watched the monitor. There wasn't much to see but every now and then a person or two would walk across the shot. After a period of silence, Izzy leant forward. 'Do we have any idea what time this hand would have been left?'

Jessica slowed the footage so it was playing at one and a half times the regular speed. 'Presumably after it went dark. It was found a little before eight this morning, so sometime between half-ten last night and then.' She pointed at the screen. 'There's a blind spot during this night footage because of where the street lights are.'

'What do you reckon's going on with the hand?'

Jessica made a humming noise. 'I don't know. Jason thinks whoever left it wanted it to be found.'

'You don't sound so sure.'

'I agree with him actually but I'm always worried by people who go out of their way to get attention. Most people we deal with don't want to be caught and do everything they can to avoid it. A handful are genuinely sorry and admit to what they've done in order to clear their conscience. Then you get a very tiny minority who want to show off. They're the ones who are unpredictable but know what they're doing. Maybe they want to be caught at some stage but not before they've made their point.'

'I'd never thought of it like that.'

'You don't until you find yourself in the middle of things.' Jessica reached forward and set the speed back to double. They sat in silence watching the images slowly lighten in front of them as the sun began to come up.

'Not bad quality, is it?' Izzy said.

'Most of the CCTV you go through isn't this good. Half the shops with cameras only have these grainy setups where you can't figure out who someone is even if they're looking directly at the camera,' Jessica replied.

'I've had a couple of those when I was back in uniform. It's ridiculous when you put the pictures out in the papers and you can't even tell if it's a man or woman.'

Jessica reached out and paused the footage, putting her

finger on the screen in front of them. 'What's that?' she said.

The constable turned to face her as Jessica scrolled the action back a few seconds and let it play at regular speed. The light was still dim but the video clearly showed the back of a figure wearing a long black robe walking across the paved walkway in between the fountains. The figure in itself wouldn't have necessarily been out of place but, aside from someone sleeping on one of the benches, they were the only person in shot. As the shape moved out of the frame, Jessica flicked the controls to change the angle to one of the other central cameras.

'Is it someone wearing one of those religious robes? A burqa or niqab?' Izzy said.

Jessica's fingers flicked across the controls as she spoke. 'I don't think so. Look.' She pointed towards the new screen that had appeared. 'There's no facial cover, it's just a robe, like a dressing gown. Let's see if we can zoom in.' She ran her hand over a dial and the images refocused closer in.

'Is it a man or a woman?' Izzy asked.

'Probably a woman. You can see she's wearing low heels and has that way of walking as if she's comfortable in them. It's the way she's moving too.'

Izzy clearly agreed. 'I doubt there are many men out there who can walk so comfortably in heels. I'm not great myself.'

'There are no clear images of the person's face. You can just about tell they're white but nothing more. She knows where the cameras are.'

Jessica pressed buttons to cut from one camera perspective to a second, then a third, before continuing. 'Look at the angle of her face. She's deliberately looking down and across because she knows there won't be a clear view of her.' She scrolled backwards through the footage to reinforce her point. 'She's turning ever so slightly as she walks to keep the angle and is wearing gloves too. This person knows what she's doing.'

Jessica moved the footage forward, switching between cameras until the hooded figure neared the base of the fountain where the hand had been found. Jessica slowed the stream down to regular speed, watching as the cloaked figure stopped by the edge of the fountain and crouched. She reached across herself, stretching into an inner pocket of the robe and taking out an object that had to be the hand, before placing it on the ground. It seemed as if the figure was deliberately spreading the fingers into the correct position, before nudging it towards a nook between the bench and fountain. Then they stood, walking back the way they came.

Jessica started to ask a question but Izzy got there first. 'Who the hell is that?'

2

Jessica peered down at the officers in front of her, waiting for one of her colleagues to speak. She was in Longsight Police Station's incident room in the basement, standing on a slightly raised platform next to DI Reynolds and DCI Cole. On a giant whiteboard behind them was an enlarged photo of the hand that had been found as well as stills from the video footage. In front of them was a selection of officers, some in uniform, as well as other members of CID.

Cole was someone Jessica had a lot of respect for. Although she'd had differences with each of the previous two chief inspectors, she had worked closely with him when he had been an inspector. He had covered for her on numerous occasions and she trusted him implicitly. Her only concern about his promotion was that he knew her a little too well. As an inspector he had given her a little leeway in the way she acted but Jessica wasn't convinced the same would apply now he had more responsibility.

It was Cole who opened the briefing. 'Following yesterday's discovery, I know we have some quite serious business to go over but, before any of that, I'd like to welcome a new member to our team.' He indicated for a woman near the front to come and stand next to him on the stage. Jessica had met her the previous week but it was the new person's first official day in the job.

As the woman reached the front, Cole continued, 'It's unfortunate the way timings have worked out but Louise Cornish will be taking the sergeant role vacated by DI Reynolds. She's new to the area so be nice. I've already filled her in about which ones of you are the trouble-makers.' He pointed at a couple of the officers in front of him to a mixture of laughs, cheers and boos.

Jessica didn't know much about DS Cornish but was aware she had asked for a transfer to the area from some-where around the Midlands, and that she was married with children. The sergeant was somewhere in her mid-forties and had short brown hair that was swept backwards. If Jessica had had to give one word to sum the new recruit up, it would have been 'mumsy', harshly thinking the woman had a shape that looked as if she'd had children but hadn't lost all of the weight.

Cole continued to speak after the shouts had quietened down. 'I'm positive you'll all get to know DS Cornish in time but, for now, let's crack on. A severed hand was found on the edge of Piccadilly Gardens yesterday morning.' He pointed behind him at the enlarged images from the CCTV cameras. 'These are the best images we have of the person who left it. As far as we can tell it is a white woman who is around five foot six or so. As you can see, there isn't an awful lot to go on.'

He looked towards Jessica, raising his eyebrows. She took the hint, explaining they were pretty sure the person had scouted the location and was most likely local to the area, given their apparent knowledge of the camera pos-itions.

Reynolds spoke next. 'We spent large parts of yesterday compiling a list of murder victims around the country who had been found with only one hand. There weren't many and nothing matched the right hand we discovered so we moved on to lists of missing people. Obviously this was pretty long to start with, even just locals, but we had some initial lab results through yesterday evening that helped narrow things down. We now know the hand came from a man likely in his late twenties or early thirties. Aside from indications it had been frozen before being left, we don't really have much else to go on in terms of who it came from. There are almost sixty names of men between the ages of twenty-five and thirty-five from this area who have been reported missing in the past twelve months. The only way of matching anyone from that list to the actual hand is by contacting one of their family members and asking for a swab so we can test the DNA. For now, this seems pretty impractical and an enormous drain on resources so we're going to go through the media first.'

Cole picked up again, strolling across the stage and then walking back to his original position. 'Our labs are still doing tests and we might get more results at some point today or tomorrow. From the camera stills, you can see the hooded person who dropped it was wearing gloves, so we're not expecting any fingerprints. Given the planning that seems to have gone into the choice of location, I don't think any of us are expecting much more in the way of evidence we can work with from forensics. As Jason said, we don't have the resources to contact family members of all those missing people at the moment. It would be a long shot anyway, given we would be assuming it belongs to someone local who has been reported missing. For now we're going to release these stills to the media and ask for a hand . . .'

He was cut off as the assembled officers collectively started to laugh.

He raised his voice to talk over them. 'All right, all right. You know what I mean. We don't have a clear facial image but perhaps someone will recognise something about the outfit? I've already been in contact with some-one from the BBC and they think it will make it onto the local news this lunchtime. The press office are drafting a full release that can go to the others.' He paused and looked at Jessica and Reynolds to see if they had anything to add. When it was clear they didn't, he spoke again. 'Does anyone have any ideas?'

Jessica knew some of the best leads they'd had over the years had come because of random suggestions from offi-cers in briefings such as this. Some senior detectives would prefer ideas to be brought to them in private so they could take partial credit but Cole wasn't one for pecking orders. As it was, everyone seemed as baffled as they were. There were a few questions about the finger that was missing from the hand and a couple of thoughts about what could have happened to the rest of the body – and whether the person it came from was still alive – but no one really knew anything.

When the ideas had dried up, Cole shushed everyone and spoke again. 'I have to remind you about the com-munity engagement programme.' He stopped as a groan sounded from the floor. Jessica wanted to join in but just about stopped herself. 'All right, calm down. Don't shoot the messenger. This has come from a lot higher up than me. I know there have been a few emails going around but, with the summer upon us, things are about to move fully into action. Essentially the idea is for us to get more involved with local projects in order to portray us all in a better light.'

There were more complaints from the floor as the DCI struggled to speak over the top of people. He eventually stopped, standing with his hands on his hips waiting for people to quieten down. He reminded Jessica of an old geography teacher she'd had who would stand and wait for silence. Her class had once wasted twenty-five minutes of a lesson as the teacher did nothing but glare at them in silence from the front of the room.

Finally the chatter dropped and the chief inspector continued. 'As I was saying, the idea is to place us more centrally in the community. Before the schools break up we will be attending a couple of careers days to talk to the students. There's also a summer fete-type event where we'll have a stall and be available for people to chat to, plus we're upping the number of community meetings we hold. There's a volunteers sheet outside my office so if anyone wants to get involved then put yourself down. If there aren't enough people interested, I'm going to have to assign people myself.' As more complaints sounded out, he finally lost his temper, raising his voice. 'All right, shut up. The next person to speak instantly gets volunteered for everything.' He paused, lowering his voice. 'I know it's not ideal but it might not be a bad idea, given the publicity we've had in recent years. Now stop moaning and wait for your jobs.'

Jessica could think of a few stories in the local press over the past two years that hadn't exactly painted them in a good light. She had no intentions of signing up for anything but wasn't convinced anyone else would either, given the apathy around the room. With her position there was every chance Cole would tell her to get involved whether she wanted to or not. It wasn't that she was against the overall idea behind the policy but she wasn't massively keen on associating with the general public at the best of times, let alone when she would have to act as some sort of representative.

The chief inspector divided people up into various teams and then sent everyone on their way. Jessica first went to help the press office but, after speaking to two different television stations, things had gone quiet. Her own office was on the ground floor near to the canteen. When she first moved in a couple of years before, DS Reynolds, as he was at the time, occupied it and had done for a while. After he moved into his own office a couple of months ago following his promotion, Jessica had enjoyed the large room to herself.

As she walked through the door, DS Cornish was in Reynolds's old chair closest to the entrance. Jessica's own desk was at the back of the room and, as usual, the items she was working on were scattered around the floor, the tops of filing cabinets and her own desk. Her messiness was well-known and ridiculed around the station.

The woman was typing on her keyboard but quickly stood as Jessica opened the door. She turned to face Jessica, speaking quickly and offering her hand. 'Hi, it's DS Daniel, isn't it? I hope this is okay? The chief inspector told me this would be my new office and the desk was free.'

Jessica shook her hand. 'It's fine but call me Jess. I'm not big on formalities.' She could see the sergeant had already made her mark. There were family photos placed in perfect rows on the desk and the keyboard and monitor had been moved so they were exactly perpendicular to the edge of the table itself.

The woman was wearing glasses, which she hadn't been earlier, but took them off and placed them on the desk. 'Nice to meet you, Jess, I'm Louise.'

Jessica walked across to her side of the room and shoved a stack of folders away from her keyboard, trying not to knock anything onto the floor, then sat down. 'It's not always as mad as this.'

Cornish laughed. 'I'd hope not. I didn't move up here for the quiet life but I wasn't expecting something like this on my first day.'

Jessica turned around to face her office mate. 'Where did you come from?'

Cornish was watching her closely. 'My husband James originally came from around here but we had been living in the Coventry area for almost ten years. I was a DS there but James's father has been really ill over the past few years. We've got two kids and we both wanted them to get to know their grandfather before he gets too sick. I put in for a transfer over a year ago but it's taken this long for things to work out.'

'How old are your children?'

'Nine and five. James looks after them while I go to work.'

Jessica realised she must have inadvertently pulled some sort of face because the woman instantly defended herself.

'It was his decision . . .'

'Sorry, I didn't mean anything.'

The sergeant looked away, clearly annoyed, leaving Jessica to feel uncomfortable. Her reaction wasn't deliberate but she realised how offensive it could have seemed. She didn't have any strong feelings about child-rearing but there weren't too many female officers who worked while their partners stayed at home with the children and the situation had caught her off-guard.

Cornish started typing on her keyboard and Jessica knew there wasn't much more she could add. Within a couple of minutes of properly meeting her new office mate for the first time, she had put her foot in it.

Jessica turned back to her computer and logged into the system, bringing up the Internet browser and loading a couple of news websites. The ones she looked at were already running the still of the woman in black along with their contact number – a good sign – while the first TV news stories should have been aired within the past half-hour or so.

As she read, Jessica could sense a tense atmosphere in

the office, the silence only broken by the tapping of keys on the two women's respective keyboards, the odd click of a mouse and a faint hum of activity from elsewhere in the station.

Jessica logged out and stood. 'I'm off to the press office if anyone comes looking for me,' she said. Cornish nodded, mumbling an acknowledgement as Jessica left the room.

On the station's basement level was the main incident room, some general-use computer terminals, the cells and a few private rooms for lawyers and others. The ground floor was where the main reception area was, as well as the senior officers' offices. Jessica and Cornish's was near the canteen, with Reynolds's just down the hallway. The interview rooms and other private meeting areas were also on the floor along with the press office, Human Resources department and separate press conference room. Upstairs was Cole's office as well as rooms visiting officers could use and a vast storage area.

As she made her way along the corridor, Jessica could hear a woman's raised voice coming from the reception area. It wasn't necessarily a surprise as most days involved at least one person getting angry in their entrance. Often it was someone with a relative that had been arrested who wanted information or sometimes it was just a person who had been picked up for being drunk and was about to be stuck in a cell for a few hours to sober up. Jessica couldn't hear anything specific but had to walk through reception to get to the press department.

As she moved, she tried not to catch the desk sergeant's

eye but he called her name out. 'DS Daniel here might be able to assist you . . .'

Jessica looked at the officer as if to offer a sarcastic 'thanks' and then walked across to the woman who was next to the main reception desk. She was red in the face and looked somewhere between upset and angry. She was in her fifties, short with greying shoulder-length brown hair and wearing clothes that were far too tight for her. Jessica offered a thin smile in an effort to partially placate her. 'Is everything okay?'

'I've been trying to get someone to listen to me,' she replied with a sigh. 'I drove straight here after watching the lunchtime news. I know who your woman in black is.'

3

Jessica's first thought was that the media had only been given a telephone number to pass on, not the address of the station. She guessed the reason the desk sergeant hadn't immediately contacted either her or Reynolds was because he was trying to figure out if the woman was genuine or another in a long line of attention-seekers.

'How did you know to come here, rather than call?' Jessica asked.

'I didn't really,' the woman stammered. 'This is where I came when my son first went missing. I've been in a few times since but there are never any updates. When I saw the news today, I knew what had happened.'

Jessica tried not to appear too puzzled. 'Okay, right. Do you want to follow me to a more private place?' She turned and led the woman down a hallway towards one of the station's meeting rooms. It was where they let witnesses who weren't suspects sit before they were formally interviewed. Sometimes family members would be allowed to wait in the area. Jessica still wasn't convinced the woman would have any useful information so wanted to talk to her first before deciding whether they would need to take a full statement.

The room was bright because of the overhead strip light but, despite the heat outside, it felt cold. Jessica opened the door and could hear the air-conditioning unit overhead working noisily. She tried not to shiver and offered the woman a seat. 'Do you want a cup of tea or something?' she asked.

'No, I just want someone to listen to me.'

Jessica nodded, closed the door behind them and sat opposite the woman. 'What's your name?'

'I'm Vicky Barnes, my son is Lewis and I think it's his girlfriend January who's your woman in black.'

'Why do you believe that?'

The woman spoke quickly. 'Lewis went missing around a month ago. He used to phone or text me every day but I've not heard from him. I went around to the flat they shared but January at first told me he was out. Then she changed her mind a few days later and said she hadn't seen him either. I reported him missing to you lot but no one's done anything. I always knew that druggie bitch was involved and then I saw her on the news in that cloak thing of hers.' Jessica saw the woman's bottom lip start to tremble. The last few words were barely audible. 'Oh God, does this mean . . . ?'

With the reports talking about a severed hand being found, it was a fair assumption the woman would now be contemplating the fact her son could be dead.

'Mrs Barnes?' Jessica put a hand on the woman's shoulder.

There were a few tears running down her face but she was fighting to stay in control. 'Yes?'

'Why do you think the person in the black cloak is your son's girlfriend?'

Vicky was trying to compose herself. 'On the news they said the hand belonged to someone between twenty-five and thirty-five. Lewis is exactly thirty. January's one of these Goth-weirdo types with long black hair and all that. She's always wearing a hooded top thing that's exactly like the one that was on the news. When Lewis went missing I just knew it was her.'

Jessica could see the woman was beginning to get angry again. 'Mrs Barnes, what I'm going to do is ask an officer to come and sit with you for a bit. I'm going to check our files to see what we have on your son Lewis and his partner. Then I'll come back and we'll take a formal statement. Is that okay?'

The woman took a tissue out from the bag she was carrying and blew her nose. 'Yes, thank you.'

'Can you tell me the full name of your son's girlfriend?'

'It's January Forrester.'

Jessica also took the couple's address and was about to leave the room when the woman called her back. 'Sorry, I forgot. Look, I brought this to show you.' She reached into her bag and took out a photograph, holding it out for Jessica to take. It was a picture of a young woman in heavy make-up clinging to the arm of a man. She was wearing a long black robe with a hood that looked a lot like the one from the footage. It was even the same length, the bottom ending just above the woman's ankles. Both people were smiling widely and it seemed as if they were in a park of some sorts.

'Is this Lewis and January?'

'Yes.'

After arranging for a uniformed officer to sit with the woman, Jessica returned to her office. Cornish was sitting in exactly the same place she had been when Jessica left and didn't move to acknowledge her colleague's re-entry. Jessica sat at her desk and logged back into the system, muttering 'come on' under her breath as the computer took its time. Eventually she got through to the area she wanted and searched for 'Lewis Barnes'. Everything his mother had told her was true – she had reported him missing in person four weeks ago to the day. From what Jessica could see, aside from the name being logged, very little else had been done other than someone scanning a photo into the system which had been uploaded onto the force's website.

She closed the record and searched for 'January Forrester'. The woman was twenty-six and had a criminal record. Jessica could see there were two thefts when she was still a teenager, a drunk and disorderly from two years previously and then, twice within the past year, charges of domestic violence that had been dropped before getting to court. Both incidents involved her hitting or scratching Lewis. From experience Jessica knew a lot of domestic violence cases never got as far as court whether it was a man hitting a woman, as most people would think, or the other way around.

Some people wanted to forget it had happened and went back to their partners, others were keen to move on with their lives away from the attacker. A few would take things as far as they could legally but, even with protection of witness programmes and being able to give evidence behind a screen in court, those were still the minority. Jessica was surprised no one had cross-referenced the missing persons report with the fact Lewis's girlfriend had recent charges for domestic violence but things like that did sometimes slip through the net.

Jessica again turned the computer off and left the room to tell Reynolds what had happened. At the absolute least she thought they could bring January in for questioning and take a mouth swab from Mrs Barnes that would be tested to see if the hand belonged to her son.

The inspector wasn't in his office so Jessica walked back through to reception where the desk sergeant pointed her towards Cole's office. She made her way upstairs and instantly saw both the DI and DCI in conversation through the glass windows of the chief inspector's room. As Cole noticed her, he waved her in. Jessica sat next to Reynolds across the desk from their boss. She started to tell him what had happened but didn't get the chance as he spoke first.

'I was about to come get you. Have you seen the news?'

'The woman in black stills?'

Cole sounded concerned. 'Not that. It's George Johnson.'

'The MP George Johnson? What about him?'

'Yes, the Member of Parliament – his wife has gone missing. It's the top story on the breaking news channels.'

'Why didn't we hear about this before?'

Reynolds answered. 'He's friends with the superintendent and went straight to him. It's only just filtered down to us but he spoke to the cameras before anyone took a proper statement. The news crews are outside his house now and have started phoning here but we don't have anything to tell them because we didn't know ourselves until twenty minutes ago. We don't even know how long she's been gone or if they were separated or anything.'

'Where does he live?' Jessica knew he was the MP for the Gorton constituency which covered the Longsight station where they were based but that didn't mean he lived in the area. Even if he was their representative, it wouldn't be their case if he resided elsewhere.

Her hopes were instantly dashed as Cole spoke. 'You know those giant houses on the edge of Platt Fields Park set back from the main road?'

'Bollocks, so it's ours then?' Jessica replied.

'I wouldn't have put it quite like that but yes.'

In the years they had worked together, Jessica had never heard the DCI swear and rarely known him to raise his voice or shout. The incident in the briefing that morning was one of a single-digit number of times he had even looked like he might lose his temper when she had been around.

With the news about George Johnson's missing wife, Jessica had almost forgotten why she had come upstairs in the first place. It came to her just as the chief inspector was about to start speaking. 'Sorry, I remembered why I was here. A woman walked into reception, claiming she knows who our woman in black is. She says her son went missing a month ago and that his girlfriend has an identical cloak.'

Jessica took the photo out of her jacket pocket and slid it across the desk. Cole picked it up and looked at it then turned it around for Reynolds to see. 'Do you think she's genuine?'

'I have no idea but the son's girlfriend has a record for DV. It's probably worth bringing her in to speak to and taking a sample from the mother to see if the hand really does belong to her son.'

Cole leant back, exhaling loudly. 'You're probably right but Superintendent Aylesbury is obviously very keen on us at least trying to find Johnson's wife.' He paused, thinking through his options.

Detective Superintendent William Aylesbury had been the DCI at the station until a year and a half ago. Jessica hadn't always got on with him but had just begun to see how good he was at his job when he had been promoted to the higher position. It meant he was no longer based at their station, instead overseeing the whole district.

The chief inspector leant forward in his chair. 'Okay. Jason, can you go and deal with Mr Johnson? Take Louise with you and it will at least look like we've got two senior people working on things. Jessica, pick a constable or two and do what you have to. Take a sample from the woman downstairs and get it off to the labs before you do anything. Regardless of whatever's in the girlfriend's past, it's pretty much irrelevant if the hand doesn't belong to the woman's son. After you've got that, go and bring the girl in. It can't do any harm to talk to her, especially as we've got a missing person anyway.'

Jessica and Reynolds nodded in agreement before leaving. 'I'm not sure who's got the shortest straw here,' the inspector said as they walked down the stairs together.

'Definitely you,' Jessica replied. 'While all the TV cameras are focused on what you're up to I can just go about my business.'

They separated at the bottom and Jessica went to sort out the saliva sample from Mrs Barnes. After the woman's swab had been passed on to the labs it was going to take until the morning at least before they knew whether the hand belonged to her son. Jessica told the woman one of the other officers would take a statement because they were going to pick up her son's girlfriend. Usually they would have spoken to the mother properly beforehand but if January did turn out to be involved in some way, the news coverage could have spooked her and the last thing anyone wanted was for her to disappear. Jessica already had the basic facts as well as January's criminal record, which at least gave them a reason to question her.

Mrs Barnes seemed delighted they were going to pick up her son's girlfriend and Jessica had to make clear they weren't arresting January, merely bringing her in so they could ask her questions about Lewis's disappearance. She checked the address they had was still valid and then walked through to the main floor. The person she was looking for was at a desk by himself so she walked around out of his eye line, creeping behind before cuffing him across the rear of his head with the back of her hand.

'Oi!' he yelled.

'All right, Dave. Fancy a road trip?'

Detective Constable David Rowlands spun in his chair, holding the back of his head. He had turned thirty just over six months ago and was a little delicate over it –

especially as the string of girlfriends he'd had over the past few years had started to slow down. He liked to maintain an air of being young, free and single but Jessica wasn't sure the last two were by choice any longer. She was an only child and considered Rowlands her best friend in the force, even if he was more of an annoying brother-type than anything else. They had been good mates before but, if anything, had become even more so since the death of their colleague and friend Carrie Jones the previous year. Both of them had been close to her and, in some ways, hadn't got over her death. Their way of coping was by constantly winding each other up. Regardless of that, Rowlands was one of the few colleagues Jessica was happy to spend time with away from the station.

'What did you do that for?' Rowlands said. At first he'd had an angry scowl on his face but, once he saw who it was that had hit him, it turned into an aggrieved grin.

'I was just flattening down a sticky-out bit of hair for you.'

'Is this because I signed you up for careers day duty?'

'You did what?'

Rowlands seemed surprised, then his smile widened. 'Oh, you hadn't noticed?'

'Did you really sign me up?'

'Erm, maybe. You know the DCI would have sent you anyway. This way you come off looking positive about things. You should thank me.'

'You do know you'll never beat me in this escalating war. I outrank you so you sign me up for careers day, I get you to work your way through that giant pile of freedom of information requests no one else wants to do.'

'Oh come on. That's playing dirty. What did you want me for anyway?'

Jessica explained they were going to collect January Forrester for questioning but they weren't going to arrest her. She chose two uniformed officers to go with them just in case and the four of them set off in two marked cars.

January lived in a flat above a row of shops in the Abbey Hey area. There were far worse districts in Manchester but, as they arrived, Jessica could see a grubby rank of stores with a dirty-looking and smelly pizza shop, a hairdressers and a convenience store. Each shop was separated by a single door leading to three upstairs flats. From what they could see, there was no back entrance to the properties, only loading areas for the shops.

Jessica rang the doorbell as Rowlands and the two other officers stood behind her. They had parked the cars in the alley which led to the delivery yard in order to not be too obvious.

There was no answer so Jessica rang and knocked again.

'Did Lewis's mother tell you if January worked?' Rowlands asked.

'She said she'd never known her have a job and that she was always in.'

'It doesn't bode well if she's gone missing, especially with everything that's been on the news.'

'She could have just popped out to the shops.'

Jessica turned, leaning against the store's window next to the front door. The other three officers were looking at her but Jessica saw a swish of long black hair out of the corner of her eye behind them. Someone had been walking towards where they were but quickly turned around. The person was moving quickly but not running. It was clearly a woman and, despite the ongoing June heat, she was wearing knee-length black leather boots with a short black dress. The woman reached the corner where the shops met the first house of a row and her head disappeared behind a hedge.

Jessica started walking quickly in the direction the woman had headed. 'I think she was just here,' she said as the three detectives followed her.

They got to the corner and could see the woman walking quickly away from them. As she moved, the girl turned and noticed the police officers, breaking into a run.

Jessica started sprinting too. It was a warm day and she didn't think her dark grey work suit was really the best attire to be running in. The other officers followed, one of the uniformed constables bolting past her in pursuit, weaving in and out of the other people on the pavement. Jessica was trying to watch where she was going while also keeping an eye on the woman and officer ahead.

The figure in front dashed across a patch of grass but Jessica could see the constable was right behind her. She gave another half-look backwards and, when she saw how close the man in uniform was, stopped running, turning around and holding her hands to the side.

Jessica slowed as she neared them.

'Are you January Forrester?' she asked as she came to a stop, trying not to sound too exhausted.

'Yeah, what's it to you?' January didn't seem out of breath but the officer who had caught her had barely broken sweat. Jessica thought she would remember his face if she ever needed to take another team out with her.

The other uniformed officer had kept pace with her while Rowlands finally arrived at the scene and instantly bent over with his hands on his knees, sweat drenching his forehead. Jessica tried not to smile. She wanted to give him a 'where were you?' look but he was staring at the ground trying to catch his breath.

Jessica took out her identification and introduced herself. 'Why did you run, January?'

'No reason, I run a lot. I didn't know you were chasing me.' She pointed at the officer who had caught her. 'As soon as I saw this guy, I stopped.'

'Do you always go out for a run in knee boots and a dress?'

The young woman sounded defiant. 'Sometimes. Why, is that a crime?'

'No but we're here to talk about your missing boyfriend.'

'Did you find Lewis?' January's voice had raised an octave. She could have been putting it on but it did sound as if there was hope in the tone.

'Not exactly, no,' Jessica said.

January rolled her eyes. 'Oh, right. His cow of a mum has been to see you, hasn't she? What is it this time?'

Jessica explained that they didn't want to arrest her but would really like it if she came with them to the station.

'We want to ask you about your boyfriend's disappearance, that's all.'

January pointed out that she'd already given a statement but, after some swearing, she finally agreed to go. Jessica didn't want to arrest her but they were allowed to keep people without charge for up to twenty-four hours. If she caused them any more hassle in the interview room, given the fact she had run as well, Jessica had half a mind to see if the custody sergeant would keep her in the cells in the hope the forensic results from the hand would be back before the time was up.

Jessica put January in the car with the two uniformed officers and let Rowlands drive her back to the station in the other vehicle.

'I didn't realise you were so unfit,' she said as the man drove.

'You guys got a bit of a head-start on me, that's all.'

'Rubbish. You were stood next to us. Are you sure it's not your age?'

'You're older than me.'

'Yeah and look who got to January the quickest. I'd already dialled nine and nine on my phone. I was waiting for you to drop to the floor before pressing the final nine and calling an ambulance.'

'It was all an act to get her off her guard. If she'd started to run again I'd have been right on her.'

'If she'd started to run again I don't think you'd have even noticed, considering you were bent over double trying not to throw up,' Jessica laughed.

'You're obviously not familiar with how we trained athletes work.'

'In perpetual agony by the looks of it.'

The afternoon rush-hour traffic was beginning to build up as the two cars pulled into the station. The pair of uniformed officers took January through the front entrance to be processed while the two detectives went to move past them to set up the interview room. As they were walking, the desk sergeant held out a hand to catch Jessica's attention. He was already dealing with a member of the public over the counter, so she waited as Rowlands carried on through.

Once the sergeant had finished speaking, he turned back to Jessica and reached under the desk.

'This arrived in the afternoon post van. Dunno who should open it really. I didn't want to send it upstairs to the DCI but the inspector is out and he's taken the new girl with him.'

He took out a thick padded brown envelope and passed it to Jessica. The station's address had been printed out and taped to the front while it was simply addressed 'Senior Detective'. Jessica turned the parcel over to see if there was any return address but there was nothing. It felt fairly light in her hand and she couldn't make out the shape of anything bulky through the packaging.

'Why didn't you put it through to the mail room?' Jessica asked.

'It only came half an hour ago or so, I haven't had time. You should be all right to open it, shouldn't you?'

'I guess . . .'

Jessica tore along the strip at the top, placing the envelope on the edge of the counter as she opened the flap. She couldn't see what was inside so turned the package upside down, emptying it onto the reception desk until an object dropped out and landed on the table top. Jessica looked at it and then glanced up to meet the desk sergeant's horrified eyes.

The neatly severed finger rolled along the edge of the desk and fell to the floor with a soft plop.

4

It seemed like an age before anyone moved. Jessica eventually put the envelope down on the counter then told one of the uniformed officers to get some evidence bags. The desk sergeant stood next to her, shielding the finger from January's view. The girl was still on the other side of reception and had seemingly not noticed anything untoward.

Jessica tried to keep cool. The finger itself was fairly shocking and she felt a little sick looking at it but she couldn't react with other people present. Jessica knew she had made a mistake; her fingerprints would be all over the envelope, which was bad enough, let alone the finger being allowed to fall to the floor. Jessica crouched to look at the object, which had already attracted a few bits of grit and dust from the ground. It was hard to tell for sure without touching it but it looked as if it had been frozen, starting to thaw as it had gone through the mail. There were drips of a clear liquid she assumed was water that had a faint trace of blood in it.

She stood back up and looked at the envelope. Using the end part of her sleeve to prevent getting any further fingerprints on it, she turned the packet over so she could see the front. The postmark was smudged and it was stamped, not franked, meaning there was a good chance it had been put into a post box, as opposed to being sent via a post office. The date was just about visible through the smeared ink and Jessica noticed it was yesterday's. That meant it had been collected the previous day, so it could have been sent anytime between the night before that and roughly late-afternoon yesterday; a period of twenty hours or so. In other words it was posted within a few hours of the rest of the hand being left and found.

The constable arrived back with the evidence bags and Jessica sealed everything up. January had begun to get annoyed behind the counter at having to wait but Jessica knew she couldn't have seen the finger from the angle she was at and if she had noticed the envelope, she hadn't reacted.

Discreetly everything was taken away and Jessica went up the stairs to see Cole while January was processed. She told him about what had happened and admitted she had made a big error in picking up the envelope. He wasn't too impressed at the finger falling into the dirt but was as calm as he usually seemed to be. He made the point that whoever had sent it was unlikely to have left any obvious clues, so a few careless fingerprints probably wouldn't cause too much harm, except for making more work for the forensics team.

'Is there any word from the labs about whether the hand belongs to Lewis Barnes?' Jessica asked.

Cole shook his head. 'They only got the sample from his mother an hour or so ago. I spoke to someone over there who said the result will be in by the morning.'

'They're going to have the envelope and finger to check now too,' Jessica said. 'I'm assuming the finger is the one missing from the hand but we'll need confirmation. I'm guessing that will be a day or so as well. Did anything new happen with the MP's wife? I've not seen the news.'

'You've been lucky. Somehow, we've come out of it looking completely incompetent. George Johnson's wife Christine has been missing for forty-eight hours. Jason is at his house now taking a formal statement but he's already given an interview to the TV crews and the government have put out a statement of support too. Everyone seems to know more than we do and those rolling news channels have been implying we don't have a clue what we're doing. They're right but only because it hadn't been reported properly.'

Jessica shrugged. 'It all sounds a bit dodgy.'

If Cole agreed, he didn't give anything away. 'Maybe. These people live in a different world where assistants and helpers do all sorts for them. I guess when you live in the public eye sometimes the obvious answer – for instance calling us – is forgotten because you're so used to doing everything through the press.'

Jessica wasn't convinced. 'I guess. Something doesn't seem quite right though.'

The DCI was unmoved. 'From what the news said, they've been married for twenty-seven years and have a couple of grown-up children. They reckon he spoke to her on the phone a couple of days ago but returned from Westminster to find she wasn't at their home. None of their children or friends apparently knows where she is and their bank accounts haven't been touched. She's just vanished.'

Jessica couldn't hide the disbelief on her face. 'He told all of that to the news stations before talking to us?'

Cole shrugged. 'I know. There's not much we can do now except take his statement and get moving. The superintendent didn't seem too fussed about how things had come out but the bad publicity hasn't gone down well.'

Jessica didn't know if she was better off in the middle of a media storm that wasn't her fault or dealing with sliced-off fingers in the station's reception area. Neither was particularly appealing. 'I'll talk to January then speak with you again afterwards,' she said.

'Do you think she's involved?'

Jessica shrugged. 'I don't know. She ran at first but maybe she's had a bad experience with us in the past? It's hard to tell with some people.'

'Did she actually try to escape?'

'Not really. She saw us from a distance when we were at her front door. She didn't resist but there's something going on between her and Lewis's mother.'

'You could ask the custody sergeant to keep her in overnight while you wait for the results on the hand to come back. If they are a match to Lewis it would be better to have her downstairs rather than risk her running. Whether he'll agree or not is another matter.'

'I was thinking that. It seems a bit harsh if the hand comes back as someone other than her boyfriend's but, with the media already thinking we're useless, it wouldn't look too good if we bailed someone who ran that ended up being our prime suspect.'

Cole nodded in agreement but there was little else to

say and Jessica returned downstairs. With bail rules the way they were, if magistrates gave them permission, they could keep January for up to ninety-six hours in total which could be used a few hours at a time spread across weeks or even months before having to charge. If they kept her in overnight, that would take at least ten hours out of that period so it had to be weighed up whether that was worth it.

The reception area was quiet, with officers beginning to leave as the day team switched with the evening shift. Jessica could have gone home herself but CID timekeeping was always flexible, even if you rarely got paid for the hours of overtime you worked.

Jessica made her way through the corridors to the interview room where Rowlands was already sitting.

'Where have you been?' he asked. 'I thought you were going to be just behind me?'

Jessica explained about the finger and having to talk to Cole.

'You let it drop on the floor?' the constable said.

'Not on purpose.' Jessica wanted to change the subject, feeling conscious of her mistake. 'It's chilly in here, isn't it?'

Rowlands nodded to the air-conditioning unit above them. 'It always is when it's boiling hot outside. You end up wanting to wear shorts when you're outside and a thick coat when you're inside.'

January had been taken downstairs to the cells where she was given access to a phone so she could speak to a duty solicitor. She wasn't under arrest but would be cautioned for the interview, meaning she was entitled to legal advice. If a suspect had their own lawyer, that guidance would obviously come from them but, for most people, it meant they ended up talking to the duty. In serious cases it would be in person but, in a lot of instances, it was simply over the phone.

As they were waiting for January, Jessica read through the statement Vicky Barnes had given to another officer while they had been out. It was fairly standard information, revolving around dates, but she did claim January had threatened to kill both her and her son in the past. Given the girlfriend's record of domestic violence, it gave them another reason to keep her in overnight until they knew whether the hand belonged to Lewis.

After a few minutes there was a knock at the door and a uniformed officer led January into the room. With the chase Jessica hadn't had much of a chance to look at her properly. As she sat in front of them, Jessica could see the woman's long black hair wasn't looking as straight and clean as it did in the photo she had seen of her. The heat of the day plus the run and wait around the station were clearly having an effect and it was exacerbated by the bright white fluorescent bulb overhead. January went out of her way to make herself up to look pale, with dark eyes matching her hair that contrasted sharply with her skin. It had begun to wear off, with a few spots around her chin that she had attempted to conceal. Her skin seemed blotchier now it wasn't quite so caked in make-up.

Despite that, Jessica thought she was a very attractive young woman. Her hips and waist were thin and her arms tiny. Jessica found it hard to believe someone with a frame so small could be capable of killing someone and hacking off their hand so cleanly but she had learned not to be surprised by what some could be capable of.

January said that she and Lewis had lived together for around six months before he went missing. The timings she gave pretty much confirmed what was in Mrs Barnes's statement.

'Is it true you first told Lewis's mother he was out?' Jessica asked.

January nodded. 'Yes but it wasn't really like that. It wasn't the first time he hadn't come home for a night. Every now and then he stayed with his friends after being out drinking; sometimes he texted me, sometimes not. You don't know what his mother's like, always calling and messaging him. She never gave us any peace. Plus she would try to get in the middle of us because she didn't like me. When I realised he actually had gone somewhere I did tell her.'

Jessica thought that sounded plausible. 'You don't seem too upset he's gone.'

January's eyes widened. 'Why? Because I'm not crying my eyes out? What do you want me to say? I gave you a statement when he first went missing a month ago and you haven't done anything since then.'

'What about the allegations you hit and scratched him?'

The woman looked away. 'I don't want to talk about that. I was never taken to court.'

Jessica knew that, if the duty solicitor had done their job properly, they would have told January not to talk about previous charges that had been dropped. Jessica couldn't push it given they hadn't had enough evidence last time, let alone now their only witness, Lewis, was missing. If it turned out the hand did belong to him, it would be a thread they'd come back to.

'Why did you run from us?' Jessica asked.

'I told you I didn't. I often go for a jog. As soon as I saw you, I stopped.'

She fidgeted in her seat and Jessica caught a glimpse of what looked like scars from old cuts on her arms. They had largely healed but there were still a few marks that clashed with her skin. To Jessica they appeared to be self-harm scars but January must have seen the officer's wandering eyes because she turned her arms back over so the blemishes were facing down.

Jessica didn't push the point or mention the marks, reaching into her pocket and taking out the photo Mrs Barnes had given her. 'Can you tell me about the cloak you're wearing here?'

January shrugged. 'What about it?'

'We're looking for someone who was wearing a cape very similar to it.'

'What's that got to do with me?'

'You tell me.'

January spoke defiantly. 'I have no idea what you're on about. I've been wearing that "cloak" as you call it since I was at school. The only reason I didn't have it on today was because it was so warm.'

'Where were you the night before last?'

'In bed watching TV and sleeping.'

'Can anyone else confirm that?'

From the woman's outraged reaction, Jessica realised the question hadn't come out how she meant it. The girl pushed away from the table, raising her voice. 'Do you think I'm some sort of slag? My boyfriend's missing.'

'I didn't mean it like that.'

'Oh piss off.'

For the second time that day, Jessica realised she had given someone else the wrong impression about what she actually meant. She tried to ask more questions and re-engage but any cooperation had been lost and January reverted to one- and two-word answers. The only time she showed any further emotion was when Jessica said they wanted to keep her in the cells overnight. January swore, hammering the table with her fists, which gave the officers a first-hand look at how aggressive she could be. She was led back downstairs by two uniformed officers as she launched a string of swear words towards Jessica.

'I don't think she likes you,' Rowlands observed dryly.

Jessica couldn't think of anything witty to say as she knew he was right. She told him he could leave for the day and then went to tell Cole they had come up with very little. He was waiting for Jason and Louise to arrive back from George Johnson's house but told Jessica she should go home herself.

Because she had stayed later than she had to, the roads were relatively quiet for Jessica's journey back to her flat. The sun was still warm on her arms through the driver's window and she listened to a talk radio station as she drove. She had been so busy, she hadn't seen or read the news that afternoon but the story about the MP's missing wife was getting coverage high up the national news bulletin. The report ended with the line, 'A police spokesman said they would be making no comment at this time,' which wasn't exactly encouraging but couldn't be seen as a total disaster either. As the news ended and the presenter started taking calls from listeners, Jessica changed the station to something playing music.

Her small car was over twenty years old and just about got around. It had limped through its last MOT and the work it needed doing to pass cost more than the car was worth but Jessica paid the money anyway without really knowing why. Now she had been a sergeant for a couple of years she did earn enough to upgrade to something far more reliable but there was something about her red Fiat Punto she wasn't quite ready to part with. It was the only car she had ever owned and had some sort of sentimental hold over her, even though she didn't feel too kindly towards it when the weather was colder and it wouldn't start.

As she pulled off the main road onto the estate where she lived, Jessica heard her phone ringing. She reached into her pocket and took the device out, glancing quickly towards it and seeing it was Cole. She pulled the car over and pressed the answer button. 'Sir?'

'Jessica, hi. Sorry for disturbing you, it could have waited until tomorrow but I figured you would rather know – January Forrester has been bailed.'

'Why, what happened?'

'The test results came through on the hand and it's definitely not Lewis Barnes's.'

The killer wasn't completely sure but thought the initial part of the plan had gone as well as it could have done. The first hand had been left in exactly the right place and all the scouting had really paid off. Timings were the easy bit; now it was almost the longest day of the year, the sun came up nice and early. It meant there was plenty of light in the early hours but not too many people around to actually witness anything. Most of those who were in the area were either drunk or semi-conscious so there was no real worry.

With the timing aspect not a problem, it then came down to the location. The hand had to be left somewhere as public as possible so it would be found quickly but that had to be balanced with the obvious concern of not being caught. It had taken journey after journey from all directions to finally get a grasp on where the CCTV cameras were. Most were obvious but there were others that belonged to hotels and shops which could have proven tricky. Those scouting trips had taken place during rush hour when hundreds of people poured from the trains and trams into work and back again during the morning and early evening. It was easy to get lost in the crowds and no one would notice someone paying greater attention to the particular security arrangements.

Ultimately, coming up with the list of locations hadn't been anywhere near as hard as the killer feared – all it took was planning and time. The tougher part was tracking down all of the targets. The first two people were by far the easiest: unassuming and weak and the killer knew exactly where to find them. Not everyone was going to be quite that straightforward but the plan had to be put in motion in order to drive the others out into the open.

The disguise had been a bit of an accident. They had known something would be needed to conceal their identity from the cameras but it had been hard to judge exactly what would be appropriate. Some sort of fancy dress didn't seem quite right, while anything that covered the face could prove troublesome if something did go wrong and a quick escape needed to be made. The key things were being able to see where you were going and wearing comfortable shoes to run in. The low heels chosen were perfect: comfortable but, given years of walking in them, surprisingly easy to move in. The long black hooded top had been an old favourite hanging in the wardrobe. It seemed so obvious afterwards that it was the ideal outfit and that had been proven by the coverage it had received.

After leaving that first hand, the killer had watched the television, listened to the radio and kept an eye on the major Internet news sites for two whole days. Things had gone pretty well. A bit more prominence would have been nice but perhaps that would come in time. The key thing was the police didn't have a clear picture; they had a good enough image to get them excited and put the photos out to the public but nothing specific to go on.

It felt so satisfying when all the hard work paid off. The endless mornings and evenings of mingling in all those crowds had worked out. The practice runs of walking through the square, gently angling away from the various cameras, had been worth it. The killer thought that if all the other locations turned out this well, they really would be in the clear.

The killer picked up the evening paper and looked at the enlarged CCTV image on page five. Even the nickname was brilliant.

'The Woman in Black'.

The killer thought it was almost a shame that wasn't what they had christened themselves. A calling card would have been good with that name written on it, although perhaps it would have been overkill. Using a put-on American accent, they played with the words. 'The Woman in Bah-lackkkkk,' they said out loud, extending the final word. A big grin appeared on the person's face; it really was a terrific moniker.

It only took a few moments for the smile to fade and the killer quickly felt sickened by their own flippancy. There was a real purpose to everything that had and was going to happen. The coverage had so far been decent and the nickname was a massive bonus but that was no reason to forget the reason behind it all.

Annoyed with themselves, they put the paper down and opened the lid of their laptop. Sending the finger had been a late addition to the scheme. At first they had just thought leaving the hand would be enough but the plan needed something a little extra to really draw the police in.

It would have helped in advance if the killer had known which officer to send the finger to but hopefully it would have arrived with the right person.

The killer skimmed through the same news sites as they had that afternoon looking for a name. Most of the places directed witnesses to call a number but that was far too general. It took a while but eventually the name of a specific officer was found; Detective Sergeant Jessica Daniel had spoken to a radio station about 'the woman in black' that afternoon and her quotes were now on the news section of their site.

Using a search engine, the killer looked up Sergeant Daniel. There was a photo of her on the police's website and a few interesting articles from the past few years. She had certainly been involved in a couple of interesting cases. Nodding as they read, the killer knew this woman would be their main point of contact from now on. There was something quite nice about it all – this woman up against 'the woman in black'. As long as the plan was stuck to and all the other locations were scouted as extensively as the first few, the killer knew there was only ever going to be one winner but it should be interesting. They hoped Ms Daniel was up to the task of unravelling all the information she would need to. From everything the online news archives said about her, she certainly seemed capable.

With everything in place, the killer closed the computer down and stood. They walked upstairs to pack the right shoes and the outfit and then made the journey to the storage unit that was such an integral part of the plan.

The trip didn't take too long and the killer had been

careful to visit regularly even before any bodies had been left there. The routine was important just in case the security officers present actually paid attention, which they never seemed to.

After entering the unit, the killer opened the lid of the large chest freezer. The size of it had initially been important just in case entire bodies needed to be kept in there but it had been easier than the killer thought to dispose of the bits that weren't needed; the heads and torsos would never be found.

As the steam rose from the ice, the figure gave a slight shiver as they reached in with their gloves to pull out the frozen hand. The finger had already been removed and sat snugly next to where the appendage had been placed. That would go in the post to Ms Daniel in the next day or so but, for now, the hand had to be left and location two was an absolute belter.

The killer thought of Sergeant Daniel and remembered the reason everything was happening. 'See you soon,' they said to no one in particular.

6

Jessica sat in Cole's office for the morning briefing trying to listen to what he was saying but constantly finding her mind drifting. It had been twenty-four hours since a second hand had been found in St Peter's Square, again with the ring finger missing. Whoever was leaving them was going out of their way to find Manchester's most public spots and Jessica couldn't figure out what was going on.

'Jessica? Sergeant?' Cole was speaking.

'Sorry, I don't . . .' Jessica mumbled.

'Are you okay?'

'Yes, I was just thinking about the hand.' Jessica didn't want to admit it but the finger that arrived in the post had troubled her more than she wanted to let on. At the time she had been so engrossed in having January in reception and trying to shield the object from view that it hadn't really sunk in what had happened. Someone had cut a human hand off and left it in a public place, then sent them a finger as if to emphasise the point. Then, within days, a second hand had been left. Jessica had dreamed of the finger for two nights in a row and the squelching sound it made as it fell to the floor. She generally thought of herself as having a strong stomach for the job but, for whatever reason, it was getting to her.

Cole was sitting behind his desk with Jessica, Reynolds and Cornish in three chairs across from him. The office hadn't changed much from when DCI Farraday had occupied it the year before. Two of the walls were glass-fronted, the others decorated with various photos, awards and certificates.

'Are you sure you're all right?' Cole added.

'Yes, no worries.'

'Okay, well, I know Jason and Louise have been elsewhere so I wanted to catch everyone up to where we are. Our resources are pretty stretched at the moment. Jessica?'

Reynolds had just told the room that the investigation into Christine Johnson's disappearance was going nowhere. They'd had no useful tip-offs and no idea where she had gone. The media attention her case was getting was detracting from Jessica's and she wasn't sure if it was a good thing.

'Yes, sorry,' Jessica said. 'As you know we discovered a second hand just outside of the town hall on St Peter's Square yesterday. There were no fingerprints or anything else found on the first hand and we're still waiting for any results back on the second. We have no idea who either of them belong to. Each hand had its ring finger cut off. The finger belonging to the first was mailed here but we're yet to receive anything from the second.'

Jessica paused for breath. The DI and DCI were both watching her but Louise was looking at the frames on the wall. 'Our only lead is CCTV images of the person who left it,' Jessica continued. 'We know it was someone wearing a black cape who, given their height, shape and the fact they were wearing low heels, we're pretty sure is a woman. We have no clear photos of the person's face but it seems obvious whoever it is knows where the cameras are.'

'When are the test results due on the second hand?' Reynolds asked.

'Any time now, I guess. I thought it might have been this morning. I'm not really expecting much though – whoever left these knew exactly what they were doing.'

'Any suspects?' he added.

'As many as you've got for your disappearing act,' Jessica replied with a wink. 'There was a woman, Vicky Barnes, whose son Lewis went missing a month ago. The mother reckons her lad's girlfriend, January, owns a black cape like the one in the camera footage. The girl has a record for DV but the hand didn't belong to her boyfriend. She's been bailed but there's no reason to associate her with anything really.'

'What about the finger that arrived?' Reynolds asked.

'All we know is that it belonged to the first hand. There were no fingerprints or skin samples or anything on the envelope. Well, except for mine.' Jessica looked sideways towards Cole but he didn't react. 'We know it was sent through a local post box but there was no saliva or anything on the stamps.'

'Were they those self-adhesive ones?' Cornish asked, acknowledging Jessica for the first time.

'Yes, Royal Mail have really screwed us with those things. At least with the old lickable ones, the stupider criminals would give themselves away. Either way, we have nothing. The address was printed out. We've asked the labs to look into specific types of ink and printers, which they've said they'll do but the guy I spoke to said there's very little chance of finding anything that could be unique. We . . .'

Jessica was interrupted by the phone ringing on Cole's desk. He held his hand up to indicate for her to stop talking and then answered it. Jessica thought he was as disconcertingly calm on the phone as he was in the field. All she could hear from the one half of the conversation was a series of 'yes', 'okay' and 'I see' responses. It could have been his wife calling to ask what he wanted for tea or the Prime Minister phoning to talk about a serious domestic terrorist incident. Either way he kept a perfectly straight face.

When he put the phone down, he scratched his chin and looked directly at Jessica. 'That was your test result.'

'Did they find anything?'

'Actually they did but I'm not sure it's what you would be expecting.'

Jessica felt her heart jump slightly. 'What?'

'The second hand belongs to Lewis Barnes.'

Jessica was speechless for a moment. She stared at her boss, who met her eyes. 'Really? How do they know?'

'They already had a swab from his mother to test the first hand. The person I spoke to said the DNA samples were stored in the same file so it automatically threw up the match.'

Jessica pushed back her chair and stood quickly, confused and excited in equal measures. 'We're going to have to go and pick up January. We let her go but she's the only suspect we've got. She's even got the bloody cape.'

She knew she was speaking too quickly. All she could think about was the fact they had let the girl go. It wasn't anyone's mistake as they had no reason to keep her but the media and ultimately the public wouldn't see it like that if it turned out January was involved. A lot of things didn't make sense, such as the fact she would have been released and then gone back to the streets to leave the hand, but that could all be figured out once she was returned to custody.

Cole's demeanour hadn't altered and Jessica struggled not to be frustrated by his steady voice. She wanted to shout as if it would make things happen quicker. He was perfectly calm as he spoke. 'If you take a team to her flat to pick her up, I'll apply for a warrant to search her property. Bring her back for questioning but leave an officer there to wait for the Scene of Crime team to arrive.'

Jessica didn't need telling twice. She turned and raced down the stairs two at a time, feeling the adrenaline flowing through her. Once they had January in the cells they could try to connect her to the first hand, even though they didn't yet know who it belonged to.

Jessica dashed through to the main floor and first found DC Diamond. 'Iz, are you busy?'

'A bit, not really.'

'I need you to start looking at something. On our list of missing persons is the name "Lewis Barnes". Find out what you can about him – where he's worked, where he went to school – that type of thing, then check that information against anyone else registered as missing. The second hand belongs to him and I'd be stunned if there wasn't a connection to the first.'

Izzy took the request in her stride. 'Is there anything I'm looking for specifically?'

'A man between twenty-five and thirty-five. Lewis was thirty, so anyone he went to school with would be the same age. Don't worry about women and don't worry about former or current workmates who are much older or younger. Use whatever officers you need as long as they're not trying to track down Christine Johnson. That's the priority around here but anyone else is fair game.'

Jessica had only worked with her for a short while but knew Izzy was the type of officer who would get things done. After the conversation, she grabbed Rowlands plus some uniformed officers who were milling around, including the one who had chased down and caught January a few days before. They again took two marked cars to the woman's flat but, unlike their previous visit, this time they used the sirens and flashing lights.

Jessica sat in the passenger seat as one of the uniformed officers drove but barely waited for the car to stop before opening the door and dashing towards January's flat. Members of the public who were visiting the adjacent shop stopped to watch as she hammered on the front door. The other officers caught her up as she knocked aggressively for a second time.

Rowlands caught her eye as he arrived. 'Bit of déjà vu, this.'

Jessica ignored him, taking her phone out from her suit jacket pocket. 'Come on, answer,' she muttered irritably as it rang. Cole soon picked up. Before he could say anything, Jessica jumped in. 'Did you get the warrant?'

Cole spluttered slightly at her abruptness. 'Not yet.

We're talking to a magistrate now, it shouldn't be long. What's going on?'

'She's either not in or not answering.'

'Well, stay there, it won't be long, I'll call you back.' Jessica hung up.

'Can we go in?' one of the uniformed officers asked.

Jessica didn't think twice. 'Yes, break it down.'

She had no doubt the warrant would be granted but didn't want to wait the ten minutes it might take. She could feel Rowlands peering at her but didn't move to meet his stare, instead standing back to give the officer room. If the door proved to be a problem they would request a tactical entry team, who would bring tools such as a battering ram to help them enter. From their first visit, Jessica had seen the door was made of thin wood and didn't think they'd have any issues getting in.

The man who had previously chased January took a step back and hammered his boot through the midsection close to the lock. The timber splintered and imploded, the door swinging open after just one blow.

Jessica told two of the officers and Rowlands to wait as she entered. Behind the door was a staircase that had a thinning patchy red carpet running up it. She walked up the stairs with the officer who had broken the door down behind her. At the top was another door. Jessica knocked loudly again.

'January, are you in there?'

The door felt as thin as the one downstairs. Jessica knew she had already broken procedure, if not the law itself, by not waiting for the warrant.

The officer looked at her, eyebrows raised as if to ask whether or not he should bust through this door too. Jessica nodded. The constable didn't have as much room but was as brutal with the second door as he had been with the first, smashing through the thin wood with barely a grunt. Jessica was impressed at his athleticism.

'Wait here,' she said to him, walking through the shattered remains of the timber into the flat. Her instincts told her January wasn't home and she didn't want anyone else potentially disrupting the scene, seeing as the place would have to be searched by a trained team.

The front door led directly into the living room. Aside from a television, the rest of the room was fairly empty. It looked lived-in though, a few books and odd items of clothing littering the floor. The randomness of the objects reminded Jessica of the way she lived. Frequently she found items of clothing or things like her phone charger in places around her flat without knowing when she had left them there.

'January?' Jessica called but everything was quiet. She jumped slightly as the silence was broken by her phone ringing. From the caller ID, she could see it was Cole.

'Sir?'

'We've got the warrant,' he said. 'I've requested two of the lab team to come and assist you too.'

'Thanks. She's not answered her door yet.'

'What does her flat look like?'

The comment confirmed her one fear about someone she had been close to professionally being promoted. When he was an inspector, Cole had seen exactly the way she worked and would have had a good idea she was going to get access to the flat as soon as she could.

'Now we've got the warrant, I'll get one of the officers to break through,' Jessica replied, figuring there was little point in confirming his suspicions.

Cole paused for a moment. 'Fair enough. If anything changes, let me know. If she's genuinely missing or made a run for it, we're going to have to get a photo of her out to as many media outlets as possible as soon as we can. The longer we wait, the further she could get if she has run.'

Jessica hung up and continued to look around the apartment. There wasn't much to it but she did make a point of carefully opening the wardrobes in the bedroom to see if the black cloak was present. Almost all of the clothes were black, making it hard to differentiate one item from the next without actually touching them.

There was no sign of January anywhere.

The kitchen was the worst-looking room by far. Jessica rarely used her own, except for the microwave, but it looked as if January's was almost untouched. Dirt lined the bottom of the white skirting boards, with cheap brown linoleum peeling away from the edges. A once-white cooker was in the corner but was covered in red and brown stains and the worktops were littered with empty food packaging. Jessica didn't want to venture too far into the room but could see a faded red stain more or less in the middle near a small dining table. She walked carefully towards it, crouching to get a better look. She didn't know for sure but it looked like dried blood someone had tried to clean. Given the state of the rest of the kitchen, it could be something as innocent as spaghetti sauce or gravy but its position in the centre, away from the cooker, worktops and the dining table, stood out.

Jessica returned to the front door, thinking she would mention it to the lab team when they arrived, although they were professional enough to spot it anyway.

The officer was still waiting for her on the stairs outside. 'Not in then?'

'Not unless she's a contortionist and hiding in the fridge.'

The reason for January not being in could be innocent but Jessica seriously doubted it. The fact the hands were being left in public places showed whoever was leaving them was trying to play games. Being arrested and then placing the hand of her boyfriend to taunt them seemed the type of thing the person might want to do but Jessica had looked into January's eyes in the interview room and it was hard to imagine her being that cunning.

She led the constable outside to where Rowlands and the other officers were standing. A small crowd had gathered not far from the shop's doorway. Jessica shook her head at Rowlands to indicate she hadn't found anything and then sent him and one officer back to the station. 'Izzy's looking to see if there's a connection from Lewis Barnes to anyone else reported missing,' she told the constable. 'Give her some help. I'll be back soon.'

Jessica waited with the other two officers for the lab team to arrive but phoned Cole to ask if January's photo could be released to the media. The picture of the woman in the cape alongside Lewis provided a good up-to-date likeness.

When the Scene of Crime team arrived, Jessica mentioned the substance she thought could be blood in the kitchen, then left the two officers with them. The constables would remain for a while in case the woman did arrive back. Someone would have to stay until the lab workers had left and the property could be boarded up and secured.

Jessica knew it was a bit cheeky but asked the officers if they minded her taking the second car. They didn't have a lot of choice but she felt a little better about asking rather than telling them she was going to drive back to the station. They would either have to phone into the base to get a lift, or take a bus. The pair didn't seem overly pleased but didn't object.

It was lunchtime and the sun was again warm on her arms as she drove but Jessica had barely pulled away when her phone rang. She pulled over to the side of the road and answered.

Jessica recognised the voice as Diamond's. 'Sergeant Daniel?'

'I've told you before to call me Jess,' she said. 'I've sent Dave back to help you.'

'He's not here yet but we think we've got something.'

'What?'

'We started with Lewis Barnes' school records given the age thing. There are so many names but we found someone he left sixth form with when he was eighteen. There's an "Edward Marks" listed as finishing at the same time as him, then an "Ed Marks" on our list of missing people. I don't know if it's the same person but they're the same age. I've got a contact number for his brother who reported him missing.'

Given it was a family member who had told them the man was absent, Jessica knew a simple swab would be able to tell them if the brother's DNA was a match for the first hand.

'That's brilliant work, Iz. I'm on my way back now. Call the brother and I'll go pick him up.'

The woman at the other end of the phone paused for a moment. 'There might be a problem with that . . .'

7

Jessica's heart sank. 'What's wrong?'

Izzy spoke confidently and fluently. 'The man who's missing is Ed Marks and it was his brother Charlie who reported it. Ed comes from around this area but, according to the notes we have, Charlie lives in London.'

Jessica knew the news wasn't as bad as it could have been but it meant the chance of picking Charlie up and getting a swab off to the labs to potentially identify the first hand wasn't going to happen that day.

'It's fine, Iz. That's really great work. I'm on my way back now. Can you leave Charlie Marks's details out for me and keep looking – there could be somebody else with a similar connection. I'll call the brother when I get back and we'll set him up to visit a police station near to him.'

Even if the man lived in London, he could give a DNA sample locally that the labs down south could process and send through.

As Jessica drove back to the station, she couldn't help but be impressed by the almost ruthless efficiency of Izzy's work. Some officers complained and stomped their feet when given tasks, others tried to delegate as much as they could, but the new recruit just got things done. Once again, Jessica found her colleague's competence and attention to detail almost intimidating.

Back at Longsight, Jessica walked briskly through to her office. DS Cornish wasn't at her desk and Jessica assumed she was out trying to track down Christine Johnson. Because of the intensity of her own case, she hadn't been involved in the hunt for the missing MP's wife but that seemed intriguing too.

On Jessica's desk was a printout of Edward Marks's missing persons report, which she read. The man's brother Charlie did live in London. He had been unable to contact Ed on the phone and called the police to report him missing approximately a month ago. Give or take a day or two, he had disappeared at the same time as Lewis Barnes.

Jessica picked up the phone on her desk and called the contact number they had for Ed's brother. The man answered on the second ring.

'Hello, is that Charlie Marks?' Jessica said.

'Yes, who's this?' said a man's voice.

'My name is Detective Sergeant Jessica Daniel and I work for Manchester's Metropolitan CID division . . .'

Before she could continue, the man cut in. 'Have you found my brother?'

'That's what I'm calling about, we're not sure. It's a bit complicated.' Jessica felt a little stuck because the first hand might not belong to Edward Marks and the fact he had been to the same school as Lewis Barnes and had gone missing at roughly the same time could be a coincidence. She didn't want to jump in and tell Charlie they might have found his brother's severed hand without having more to back it up.

'I don't want to say too much,' she continued. 'I wondered if you might be able to visit your local police station in the next day or two? If you tell me which one it is, I'll make the arrangements so you can just go in and out.'

'Why do you want me to do that?'

Jessica sighed. 'I don't want to talk out of turn but we'd like to take a mouth swab from you. It gives us DNA we can check . . .'

The man cut her off mid-sentence again. 'Have you found a body?'

Jessica tried to keep her voice as level as possible. 'Mr Marks, I know this is hard but I don't want to tell you things that could end up not being true. I promise that, if you can work with me, I'll tell you everything once we've tested your sample. I'm aware you don't know who I am but if you can trust me on this it will be better for everyone.'

Charlie's voice had been a little high-pitched throughout the conversation but the tone lowered slightly as he replied. 'Okay but I'm actually in the process of moving back to Manchester. It's been on the cards for a while. I've been selling off the bigger items I own down here and just have a few suitcases now. I'm catching a train in the morning and that's it, I'll be back in the north permanently.'

Jessica felt lost for words, stumbling over her reply. 'Right . . . um, would you like us to pick you up from the train station?'

'Have you moved into taxi services now?' The man gave a nervous-sounding laugh as he spoke.

'No, I just meant we could . . .'

For a third time, he cut her off. 'No, it's okay, I know. I

think I would rather drop my cases off if that's all right. It's an early train anyway. If you tell me where your station is, I'll be there by lunchtime.'

Jessica had little choice but to accept; it wasn't as if he was under arrest, he was helping them out. 'Yes that's fine, just ask for me on reception.'

Charlie asked her to send him a text message with the address of the station so he had a record he could look at, rather than something verbal. She tried not to use her personal mobile phone for police business but sometimes it was unavoidable, especially as the force consistently seemed to be a few years behind the real world when it came to technology.

Almost a day later and Jessica was sitting back at her desk. Things hadn't moved on since the identification of the second hand. Izzy and Dave were both trying to find a second link from Lewis Barnes to anyone else on their missing persons list. So far no other names had matched. Meanwhile, there had been no sign of January Forrester. She hadn't returned to her flat the previous day and there had been no sightings of her. It didn't help that even the local television channels and newspapers were fully focused on Christine Johnson. If it wasn't for that, the press office might have been able to push to get January's photo somewhere high up the news bulletins or near the front of the papers. As it was, the search for her was barely mentioned. January's photo had been put on the force's website and posted on social media networks but Jessica knew hardly anyone looked at those. She had once jokingly suggested in a meeting a few months ago that the best way to get the public to visit their website was to have a pornographic image at the top of each page. The idea hadn't been warmly received.

If that wasn't enough failure for one twenty-four hour period, the Scene of Crime team hadn't found the black cape at January's flat and had come away with little other than the slice of linoleum which might have a blood stain on it. Jessica spoke to one of the scientists the previous evening but they told her it would be hard to get a solid match given someone had tried to clean it and it would have likely been walked on many times since. If they could get something conclusive from the cutting, it wouldn't be in a hurry.

Jessica was contemplating the state of everything when the officer on reception phoned to tell her Charlie Marks had arrived. At the front desk, a man she didn't recognise was standing to one side, nervously moving from one foot to the other. He wasn't very tall but his frame was lean and tight, as if it were mainly muscle with little fat. The mini heatwave was somehow still lasting and Jessica thought the checked shorts and T-shirt he was wearing looked a lot more comfortable than the suit she was in. He had short sandy hair that was tousled in a just-got-out-of-bed way some men seemed to prefer. Because of the shade, she couldn't tell if it was bleached or his natural colour.

She held her hand out for him to shake. 'Are you Charlie?'

'Yes. Detective Daniel?'

The two shook hands and Jessica asked if she could take the swab. He had no objections and she passed the sample to an officer who would arrange for it to be taken across the city to the laboratories to be tested. Because Jessica had known a day ago they would be getting the saliva, she had already spoken to one of the scientists to tell them to expect it. With the first hand having already been tested, the person assured her it wouldn't take very long for Charlie's DNA to be compared to it.

Charlie was standing around looking a little lost and Jessica felt bad about bringing him in for something that had taken just a few moments. As with Vicky Barnes, she figured she could at least get as much information as possible from him to go with the missing persons file. Even if it turned out the first hand didn't belong to the man's brother, at least she would have done something.

Jessica invited him through to her office. With Louise seeming to be constantly out of the station, it seemed as good a place as any. Jessica wheeled the absent sergeant's chair around to the other side of her desk, offering it to her guest, before moving a few stacks of paper from her table so they could see each other. 'Do you want a cup of tea?' she asked. 'It's only from the machine and tastes a bit like washing-up liquid but I'll go get you one.'

'Were you a salesperson before you took this job?' Charlie replied, smiling.

Jessica grinned back. 'Yeah but I only sold coffee.'

'I think I'll be all right, it's too warm for a hot drink anyway.'

She fully agreed but could never hear anyone saying

that without thinking of her mother claiming a hot drink was the best thing to rehydrate you on a warm day. It sounded suspiciously made up but she had never bothered to look into it to know for sure.

Jessica rarely took notes herself nowadays, which was something that came with seniority. She hunted through the drawers of her desk to find a notepad and a pen and, for the first time in a while, started to write.

'I've read the report about your brother's disappearance but I was hoping you could tell me a bit more about it. When exactly did he go missing?'

Charlie shrugged slightly. 'I'm not sure. Obviously I've been living down south and he's been up here. We've only been back talking regularly recently and even then not more than once or twice a week. It was only when I'd not been able to reach him for a couple of weeks that I got in touch with you.'

'Why have you only recently been back in regular contact?'

Jessica thought she saw Charlie shiver a little but it was likely because of the air-conditioning unit buzzing away over his head and the fact he was dressed for a summer's day.

The man sighed, looking at the floor. 'We had a big falling out and didn't speak for something like five years. He got in contact a few months ago and it was only after that we started talking again. Things were going well and it's partly why I was moving back here.'

Jessica could see he was looking a little upset but trying not to show it. 'What did you fall out about?' She knew the answer was likely one of two things – a woman or money.

Charlie hesitated for a moment before replying. 'Our mother died when we were young but our dad passed away five years back. He raised Ed and me on his own. I'm the oldest by eighteen months and I guess I thought what he left would be shared out between us. Back then I had been working around the country but Ed had been looking after Dad as he was getting ill. It turned out Dad left the house and pretty much everything else to him. Ed said he'd earned things by being a full-time carer while I had gone off to pursue a career. There was this big row not long after the funeral and that was it – I went to London while he stayed here.'

Jessica had heard similar stories many times before. There was nothing quite like a will to get families falling out.

'Is it just you two?'

'Yes, we don't have any other family. I suppose it's why the disappearance is so hard to take. We had just made things up after all this time and then he's gone.'

Jessica could see he was looking a little emotional. 'Is all of this why you were moving back?'

Charlie nodded. 'Sort of. I was looking for a new job anyway. I work in publishing but wasn't enjoying it any more. It was more going through the motions and getting paid each month. Ed was an artist and the one with real talent. He phoned my office out of the blue three or four months ago. I didn't know how he got my number at first but he said he had looked me up on the Internet and found my name on the company's website.'

'Did you actually meet or just talk on the phone?'

'We met once. He came down to see me and gave me a key for the house, saying I was welcome any time. Eventually, with that and the fact I was after a new job anyway, I decided to move back. Ed lived in our house – Dad's house – ever since he passed away. He told me he wanted to sign half of it over to me and that I could come and live with him. I didn't know if I wanted it to be a permanent thing. The place is massive out Alderley Edge way but I think I've got a taste for city centres after living in London.'

Jessica knew the type of houses he was talking about. The area was just across the Cheshire border on the south of the city with many properties belonging to famous footballers and other celebrities. Even the smaller houses were enormous and, given the money involved, she could see why one brother had been so aggrieved at being written out of the will.

'What did your father do?' she asked.

Charlie knew what she was getting at. 'Oh, the house? We weren't rich or anything, it's complicated. Our mum died because of a medical mistake and our dad got a large payout; that's why he had a house in that area. Apart from the gardens, I don't think he ever really liked it. He was more hands-on and worked as a gas-fitter before that. With all that money he took up gardening and that was pretty much his only pleasure. I think the money just depressed him. Given the choice between that and Mum, he would have picked her every time.'

Jessica could see a picture of a very complicated family life emerging. She picked up the missing persons file that was still on her desk and read the address out. 'Is that where you're going to be living now?'

Charlie rubbed the stubble on his chin as he nodded. 'I guess. It's not as if I have anywhere else to go. I was only renting down south and the furniture was all theirs. I had a few bits to sell off but everything I arrived with this morning is all I have.'

Jessica felt an idea forming. 'Did your brother ever sign the other half of the house over to you?'

'No, he was going to do it when I moved back. I don't know what's going to happen now.'

Jessica had a reasonable inkling. It would probably take a while to go through the legal hoops considering Ed was missing, not confirmed dead, but the house would eventually become Charlie's in its entirety. Given the earlier rivalry between them, she wondered if the wounds hadn't entirely healed – people had killed for less in the past. If the test result on the first hand didn't come back as a match, it might be worth looking into the circumstances regarding Ed's disappearance and any possible connection to his brother. If Charlie's swab did show the first hand belonged to his brother though, it could give them a lead, albeit one with many unanswered questions.

There had been a brief pause in the conversation and Charlie spoke next. 'Can you tell me what you needed a sample for? Do you think he's . . . ?'

He didn't finish the sentence but Jessica didn't jump in too quickly, watching him closely to see if there was any reaction she wouldn't expect. Charlie looked a little upset. His eyes were slightly red and he had his arms crossed tightly. Jessica figured she was going to end up telling him one way or the other within the next few days, so informed him about the hand they had found. She left out the woman in black – if he wanted to check the news, he could find that out for himself.

'So you think the hand could be Ed's?' Charlie asked.

'We don't know. Your sample will help us find out one way or the other.'

'Why do you think it might be his?'

Jessica didn't give the full details but said someone he previously went to college with had also been missing and it was a shot in the dark. Charlie nodded along.

'Can I give you a couple of names and ask if you know them?' Jessica asked.

'Sure but I've not lived here in a while.'

'Do you know a "January Forrester"?'

Charlie shook his head. 'Never heard of her. I'd probably remember someone with that first name but I don't even recognise the surname.'

'How about Lewis Barnes?'

The man screwed up his eyes. 'I don't think so. It rings a vague bell but maybe that's just because the first and last names aren't that uncommon? I can have a look in the house if you want? All of Ed's photos and papers are still around – there might be something in those.'

Jessica wasn't sure what to make of his reaction. It seemed genuine and perhaps she was being overly suspicious because of the complicated family setup. He hadn't really done anything to alert her. 'Okay, that would be good. Do you still have my number?'

'Yes, I'll call if I find anything.'

She knew it was a little premature as there was every chance the first hand didn't belong to Ed but extra information couldn't do any harm. Jessica glanced at the clock above the door, realising they had been talking for over an hour and a half. After making sure there was nothing else Charlie wanted to ask and assuring him she would let him know the results from the hand as soon as she had them, Jessica showed the man back out of the station, asking one of the officers to give him a lift home.

The rest of the afternoon was spent typing up her hand-written notes for the missing persons report. Jessica was a quick typist but reading her own writing was proving tricky. She was holding the paper a few inches from her face, squinting, when the phone on her desk rang. 'Daniel,' she answered.

'Hi, I'm calling from Bradford Park with the results you wanted from this afternoon's sample,' a man's voice said.

Bradford Park was the central hub where the force's forensics work took place.

'That was quick. What have you got?' Jessica asked.

The person at the other end gulped. 'I'll email you over the confirmation but the swab came from a "Charlie Marks", correct?'

'Yes.'

'That first hand comes from a direct relation of his.'

8

Jessica was in her office, with Izzy sitting on a chair across from her and Dave perched on DS Cornish's desk. She had already told him once not to disturb the neat rows of photographs her office mate had laid out but was keeping a close eye as her colleague's backside edged ever closer to the other sergeant's family pictures.

'What is going on with the heat?' Rowlands asked, undoing his top button.

'Er, funny story, that,' Jessica said. 'It was a bit chilly in here yesterday so I asked someone from admin if I could alter the thermostat. Unfortunately, a bit broke off.'

'So the station's entire air-conditioning system has stopped working because of you?'

'No, because whoever installed it didn't do a very good job,' Jessica said defensively.

'But it was you who broke it?'

'It's not like I wrenched the dial off, it just snapped. The engineers were in this morning and reckon it's not just the dial. Apparently there was some knock-on effect and the whole thing has to be turned off.'

The constable took off his suit jacket, placing it across the desk while being careful not to nudge the various knick-knacks. He rolled his shirt sleeves up. 'Brilliant, so we've all got to walk around sweltering because you're bumbling around like the Incredible Hulk breaking things.'

'You can't blame me for the heatwave. Anyway, what the hell's that on your arm?' Jessica pointed to a tattoo on the constable's inner forearm she hadn't seen before.

'It's just a tattoo. I had it done a few weeks ago.'

Jessica stood and stepped forward to get a closer look. 'What does it say?'

Rowlands didn't seem too keen to talk about it. 'It's Chinese lettering,' he said. 'I picked it out of the guy's folder. It means "Warrior".'

Izzy giggled from her chair and Jessica glanced over to her, raising her eyebrows while re-taking her seat. '"Warrior?"' Jessica said. 'How is that appropriate? Do you go cage fighting in the evenings?'

'Sod off, I just liked the shape of it.' Rowlands twisted his arm around so he could see the marking.

'Are you sure it doesn't say "knob" or something like that?' Izzy asked in between giggles. Jessica joined in the laughing.

'All right, all right,' Rowlands said, pointing at Jessica. 'You've been hanging out with her for too long. What's this, some sort of harem with the two wicked witches ganging up on me?'

'In your dreams, mate,' Jessica said. 'Besides, from what I've heard, this is the most female attention you've had in months.'

Rowlands didn't seem amused. 'Why are you so obsessed with me? I know I'm charming and dazzlingly good-looking but your infatuation is almost worrying.' Both women were openly laughing now. Dave nodded towards Izzy. 'What's with the bright red hair anyway? Are you a secret ginger?'

The two women exchanged amused looks. 'What's wrong with being ginger?' Izzy asked.

'Nothing, Ginge. You're the one trying to cover it up.'

Jessica was grinning but knew it was time to get to business. 'All right, as I'm sure you've noticed, a lot of the officers around here are stuck failing to find Christine Johnson. Jack let me pick who I wanted to work with and, because I'm losing my mind, I opted for you two. We've got uniform support when we need it but, for now, it's just us. You know the first hand belongs to Ed Marks and we already knew the second comes from Lewis Barnes. Now it's down to us to connect the dots.'

Despite the jovial atmosphere moments before, Jessica knew the two constables were professional enough to switch on when they needed to. The banter got them through the day and Jessica enjoyed it but they did have a job to do.

'First things first,' she continued. 'We don't actually know if these two are dead yet given the fact we've not found the rest of their bodies. Obviously the first issue is whether we're looking at a murder investigation or a missing persons one. Given the length of time they've been gone – and having spoken to Jack earlier – I think it seems sensible to treat this as murder.'

The two officers were nodding as she spoke. 'Dave, can you write this down? This is what we have to try to answer. First, are Lewis and Ed connected in any way other than going to the same college? Were they even friends?

It seems too much of a coincidence for them to be total strangers. Second, can we connect January Forrester to Ed in any way? She's still our only formal suspect but finding her isn't too easy given we have hardly anyone else to help.'

Jessica looked to Izzy, who was playing with a strand of her long red hair as she spoke. 'The calls have slowed to a stop. I spoke to the press office yesterday but they said the main media aren't interested in publicising January's photo. We've had a few mentions but no major coverage. It's on the website for all the good that is but she's gone to ground.'

Izzy looked back to a nodding Jessica for approval.

'Exactly,' Jessica replied. 'Dave, find anyone connected to January you can and doorstep them. She could be hiding with a friend but someone must know where she's gone. I don't think she's the type to live on the streets. Take an officer in case you do stumble across her and she runs.'

She winked at him, struggling to contain a mischievous grin as she remembered how out of breath he had been during their last chase.

'Iz, I want you to carry on working from here. See if you can link Lewis and Ed or Ed and January. Just in case, see if we can get a list of everyone who finished sixth form at the same time as them. There's no way we can contact them all to say they could be in danger, not that we know they are, but at least we'll be prepared. While you fish around, you might find out they were all members of some school club or something.'

Izzy was making notes of her own and Jessica knew she was the right person for the job. 'Check in with me during the day. I'm going to look at Charlie Marks. He was feuding with his brother. There might be nothing in it but it's worth going over. He's a year and half older so would have been in a different year at school but if you see any reference to him, let me know.'

Jessica sent the two officers out for the day and then turned on her computer. She had become used to her office being empty as Cornish was almost never there. While she waited for her computer to boot up, Jessica walked across to the other sergeant's desk, checking the photos were still perfectly in line.

The missing MP's wife was huge news and officers from other areas had been called in with the superintendent taking an active part in the investigation. Jessica guessed it was down to political pressure but didn't want to get too involved herself.

The information they held on the Marks brothers was limited as neither of them had criminal records so she called someone she hadn't contacted in a while. Garry Ashford was a journalist on the *Manchester Morning Herald* newspaper. They'd had a fractious professional relationship in the past but he had certainly helped her on occasion, infuriating her on others. He had a dress sense that was a throwback to an age of tweed and long hair and, although she actually quite liked him, she would never have told him that.

He answered on the second ring.

'Garry, it's Jess. Have you got a minute?' she said.

'Sure.'

'Can you do me a favour?'

'It depends . . .' Jessica thought his tone of voice betrayed a slight amount of panic. She knew he was a little scared of her and liked playing up to it.

'It's nothing too bad. I was just wondering how easy your archives are to work with and whether you could check something for me?'

The man paused before replying. 'They're not brilliant. The company employed someone to start digitising everything last year but then sacked them four months into the job because it was taking too long and costing too much. Everything's very patchy so it's pot luck really.'

Jessica gave him the name of the Markses' father. She told Garry she was looking for a story about his wife's death that could be anything up to thirty years old. She was also after something about his own death from approximately five years beforehand.

'I might be able to find something on the man's death if there was an obit but there's no chance on the other one,' Garry said. 'The library might have something if you've got an exact date or you can come in and go through our archives yourself if the editor agrees. I'll have a look for the more recent one on our system and call you back.'

Jessica thanked him and hung up. She didn't have the time or inclination to hunt through newspapers and didn't know an exact date the father had died anyway. Without going back to Charlie Marks she was unlikely to get it and she didn't want to alert him to the fact she was checking his background. Twenty-four hours after meeting him, her suspicions had waned but she wanted to check all angles before ruling him out in her own mind.

In complete contrast to the previous day, Jessica's office was sweltering. She was trying to keep it quiet that it was her who had broken the air-conditioning system because the whole station was baking. It seemed typical that, in a city where it was consistently grey and wet, they were in the middle of a heatwave as their cooling system was broken. She hadn't told Rowlands but the engineer told her he would have to order a part and it could take weeks to get everything fixed again.

Despite the discomfort, Jessica continued to work as best she could before calling Rowlands in the middle of the afternoon. He had visited January's parents, who lived separately, as well as a few of her friends. Either no one knew where she was or they didn't want to say.

As for Izzy, she had compiled a full list of college-leavers and spoken to one of the old teachers who still worked at the establishment. Unfortunately, the person couldn't even remember the names, let alone tell her if Ed Marks and Lewis Barnes had been friends. Neither she nor Jessica could find any connection between the two victims, not to mention January or Charlie.

After a couple of hours, Garry phoned back but he could only confirm what Charlie had said. The father's obituary had been accompanied by a news piece which had a couple of lines saying the man's wife had been killed by a medical mix-up years previously. Garry said it sounded as if it had been a big story at the time but it would be too much work for him to go back through the archives. She thanked him but had a sinking feeling all of their leads were slowly drifting.

Cole was involved in various briefings because of Christine Johnson's disappearance so Jessica emailed him an update before leaving for the day.

Usually her drive home was a depressing tale of red traffic lights and commuters who didn't know what lane they were supposed to be in but Jessica had other plans for the evening. The steering wheel was far too hot for her to grip properly as she started her car's engine. Jessica cursed herself for parking where the shade had been that morning instead of where it had moved to by the end of the day. The weather had been clear and sunny for over a week now, something almost unheard of in Manchester. She often thought people got so used to moaning about the rain they didn't quite know what to do when the sun came out for longer than a couple of hours.

Jessica lived south of the city centre in the Didsbury area but travelled west crawling at an even worse speed than she usually did. One of the other side-effects of the good weather was that everyone was in a rush to get home and enjoy it. Drivers weaved in and out and Jessica saw at least half-a-dozen people jumping red traffic lights that she could have pulled over. She tried to keep her patience, eventually manoeuvring her way to Salford Quays. The area had been extensively redeveloped over twenty years and what had once been largely wasteland was now a thriving hub for the media industry, surrounded by posh apartments.

Jessica parked her car in an area dominated by vehicles that dwarfed hers both in size and value. She had only been to the area a few times in the past but knew where she was going and rang a nearby doorbell. A voice crackled through the speaker to ask who she was before a buzzing sound indicated the front door opening. Jessica walked up three flights of stairs and saw a woman holding the door open for her with a big smile on her face.

'Glad you could make it,' she said.

Jessica hugged her. 'Good to see you, Caz.'

Caroline Morrison pulled the door open the whole way and invited Jessica in. She had long dark hair and olive-coloured skin. Her appearance had barely changed in the sixteen or seventeen years Jessica had known her. She was wearing a short flowery white dress and Jessica felt under-dressed in her work suit.

'I've not had much time to clear up,' Caroline said. 'I've been cooking us tea.'

The flat looked pretty clean to Jessica. Certainly if this counted as messy, it didn't say much for her own apart-ment. The two had lived together for around ten years and it had always been Caroline who kept the place tidy. Jessica walked through the hallway into the main living room. It had large bay windows looking out over the Quays and the whole scene looked gorgeous on a sunny day like it was that day.

Caroline opened up the sliding door which led onto a balcony. 'You can sit out if you want? I'm just in the kitchen. Tom will be home soon.'

'Nah, I'll come and annoy you.'

Caroline giggled and the two women walked through into a separate open-plan kitchen. Everything was spotless and, even though she had seen it before, Jessica couldn't help but be impressed. When they had first moved in together it was to a flat far smaller than this one. They had carried on living with each other not because of any financial necessity but just because they liked each other's company. Caroline had a successful advertising career and could have moved into her own place whenever she wanted. She had been planning on moving in with Randall before Jessica discovered his true nature and it was only after that incident that they went their separate ways.

They hadn't had any sort of argument but had become different people. It was hard to meet without remembering what had happened. They gradually went from seeing each other every day, to meeting once a week, to talking on the phone, to swapping text messages. Before long those had dried up but, after over a year of almost no contact, Caroline had called to say she was getting married and asking if Jessica would be a bridesmaid.

It was a shock to Jessica given she didn't even know her friend was in a relationship but, from there, they had gradually come to know each other again. A lot of the back-and-forth had initially been wedding-related but Jessica was pleased they were beginning to talk about things as mates again. Neither of them had ever spoken about Randall and Jessica had no plans to do so. She had only met Caroline's fiancé Thomas once before and that was brief, so tonight her friend had invited her around to get together properly.

'How is Tom?' Jessica asked.

'Same old. He says he's excited about the wedding but you never really know with blokes, do you? He's started writing a book in his spare time.'

'What is it he does again?'

'He works in television production just over the water. He's only got a five-minute walk to work. All right for some, isn't it?' Jessica thought about her own commute and couldn't disagree. Before she could say anything, Caroline continued, 'What about you? Are you helping to find that MP's wife that's been all over the news?'

'No, I'm on something else at the moment.'

Caroline made a 'hmm' sound as she started to stir something in a saucepan that was simmering on the hob. 'Have you got a bloke on the go yet?'

Jessica didn't want to dwell on the issue. 'Not at the moment, I'm too busy working.'

Her friend glanced up from the saucepan, smiling. 'Come on, there must've been somebody?'

Jessica let out an involuntary sigh. 'There was this guy Adam but it didn't work out.'

'That's a shame. What happened?'

'Not much, just work things.'

A few years ago, Jessica wouldn't have hesitated to tell her friend everything but she didn't feel comfortable opening up yet, given their distance. The reason she and Adam had split was entirely down to her. She had been working on a case and made some terrible assumptions and mistakes. Her paranoia had got on top of her and she asked Adam to break the law for her. He had done it but at the expense of their relationship. Losing him and trying to reconcile the way she acted was something that had stayed with her in the seven months or so since. Every now and then she would get a text message out of the blue and hope it was him but he hadn't contacted her since and she had to respect his wishes.

Before Caroline could ask any further questions there was the sound of the front door opening and a man's voice saying, 'Hello'. Caroline called out, 'In here' and her fiancé walked into the kitchen.

'Hey, hon,' he said.

'All right?' Caroline replied.

'I was talking to your bridesmaid,' he said with a wink.

Jessica had first been introduced to him by his full name, Thomas Bateman. While the two women were both in their early thirties, Tom was in his early forties. The only thing that gave away his age was his greying hair. He was fit and athletic with a grin that made him look years younger. Caroline had always gone for younger men and this was the first time Jessica had known her go out with anyone older.

He leant in and kissed her on the cheek. 'Nice to meet you again, Jessica,' he said.

Jessica smiled back. 'Jess is fine.'

'Oi, where's mine?' Caroline said with a grin of her own, patting her lips. Tom walked over to her and kissed her on the forehead.

The meal itself was terrific – as it always was when Caroline cooked. As the three of them ate on the balcony looking out at the sun reflecting off the water, Jessica remembered how good her friend's culinary skills were. She had become so used to eating takeaways and microwaved meals and, while they sat, ate and chatted, Jessica realised how much she missed having a best friend. The sun stayed high and Caroline opened a bottle of wine that she shared with Tom. Jessica never had anything alcoholic when she was driving and turned down a glass. Caroline's fiancé was genuinely funny and had the two women giggling frequently. Jessica found herself warming to him greatly but couldn't help but wonder if Caroline had been drawn to him on the rebound. Ultimately she had been out of her friend's life for too long to know for sure but it had only been two years ago their lives had been torn apart by Randall and now she was on the brink of marrying someone else.

Jessica kept her thoughts to herself, trying to relax. The sun had only just begun to dip below the building opposite when her phone rang. She looked over at her two hosts to make sure they didn't mind her taking the call but Caroline gave her a thumbs-up.

'Hello,' Jessica said.

A man's voice spoke. 'Hi, this is Charlie Marks. I hope it's not too late to call you?'

'No, it's fine. What are you after?' She had phoned him the evening before to confirm it was his brother's hand that had been found. She had been wary about him having her mobile number and hoped he wouldn't be someone who constantly pestered her with how the case was going. As it was, she needn't have worried.

'You remember the names you gave me to look at yesterday, Lewis Barnes and January Forrester?' Charlie said. 'I think I've found a link to my brother.'

9

Jessica went directly to the Markses' home the next morning. From where she lived in Didsbury, Charlie's house was around ten miles away. There was little point going to the station then driving back out again, so she'd messaged Dave and Izzy to tell them she was going to be late. There was plenty for them to be working on in any case.

Her morning commute was a lot easier than usual as she was driving away from the centre rather than towards it. As she got closer to the address on Ed Marks's file, the size of the properties noticeably grew. There were lots of houses with large imposing gates at the front to maintain privacy and all of the homes seemed to have sprawling gardens. Jessica wasn't sure exactly where it was but there was an area locally known as 'Millionaire's Row' somewhere nearby where rich locals would buy patches of land and develop their own properties. The place she was visiting wasn't quite in that area but it wasn't far off and the obvious wealth was astonishing.

Jessica had checked directions before leaving but didn't own a satellite navigation system of her own. She was struggling to find the address, partly because of the large gaps between houses and partly because a lot of the properties had names instead of numbers. She pulled over to ask someone walking their dog but whoever the person was sped up and ignored her, clearly concerned about why someone with such an old vehicle would be driving in an affluent area. While she sat in her car, she tried to load a maps application on her phone but the signal was so poor, it took too long to work. In the end she continued driving before realising the Markses' house was on the opposite side of the road from where she had been looking. She had already driven past it three times without noticing.

Around two-thirds of the properties on the road had big gates at the front but she could pull straight onto the Markses' driveway. A large tree at the front of the garden obscured the view from the road and you could have comfortably fitted a dozen cars nose-to-tail on the drive given its length. The tarmac was flanked on both sides by long patches of grass that were turning brown and beginning to look a little overgrown. The drive was empty apart from Jessica's car, although there was a large garage at the end of it that, from the width of the door, could have comfortably accommodated three vehicles.

Before she went to the front door, Jessica walked around the side of the garage to the back of the house. If anything, the garden at the rear stretched farther than the one at the front. The surface was also beginning to brown after a couple of weeks without rain, the bushes running along the sides needing a trim. The only other thing noticeable at the rear was that an extension was half-built at the far end of the house. Because she hadn't been inside yet, Jessica didn't know what it was attached to but there was already a large conservatory, so she assumed it would offer another room both upstairs and downstairs. The brickwork appeared to be finished but there were holes where windows hadn't yet been fitted.

Jessica walked back to the front of the property. The style of bricks wasn't of the type used for most houses. Instead the building was made of much larger stones and somehow seemed both old-fashioned and state-of-the-art at the same time. The whole place was huge and she guessed it would have at least six bedrooms given the number of upstairs windows.

After Jessica had rung the doorbell, it took almost a minute before Charlie Marks opened it. He was bare-footed and wearing what seemed to be the same shorts from a few days previously, as well as a loose-fitting white linen shirt.

'Sergeant,' he said, welcoming her in. 'Did you find the place okay?'

Jessica couldn't be bothered explaining herself so just replied with: 'Yes.'

'I won't waste your time. As you can see, the place is pretty big and I don't even begin to know where to start. I've not touched many of my brother's things but there's still so much space. It looks like there are loads of Dad's things still in boxes upstairs too. After we talked the other day, I began looking through some of the photos and items upstairs.'

The man started walking away from her as he spoke and Jessica followed. While the entranceway had white stone flooring, the staircase was wide and covered with a red carpet. The stairs looped around, ending on a landing with a choice of doors and a varnished wooden floor. It was an odd mix of apparently being finished and furnished, with other areas that hadn't been touched in years. There were thin layers of dust on some of the surfaces and boxes stacked in a few corners.

'I've not checked through all of these rooms,' Charlie continued, pointing towards one end of the upstairs hall. 'I've been sleeping in the one furthest down there because the room seemed empty.' He turned around and pointed to the closest opening. 'That one there is full of boxes.'

He pushed open a door and led Jessica inside. The room had large windows directly opposite the door that looked out over the back garden. A four-poster bed was on her left but unmade and had a collection of random items on it. There were more boxes pushed to the edges of the room and a dressing table with a cracked glass top.

Jessica walked to the window, peering towards the extension. 'What's that?' she asked, pointing towards the structure.

Charlie had picked up something from the bed and came over to stand next to her. 'I'll show you if you want? It looked like Ed was having a swimming pool put in but it's not finished for whatever reason.'

'Why's everything in boxes? Was he looking to sell?'

Charlie shrugged. 'I don't think so, although he had offered to half-sign it over, so maybe. We've lived here most of our lives but it's always been a little like this. I told you before I don't think Dad really knew what to do with it all. He spent loads of time in the garden and conservatory. Some of this stuff was still in boxes when I moved out five years ago or so. I think you just get used to living in a certain way, don't you?'

Jessica knew that was true; she was always likely to be a little messy whatever happened to her in the future. 'Why did you call me over?'

Charlie offered her a framed photo he had been holding. 'Look.'

She took the object from him and turned it around. The frame was made of dark wood and the photo showed what Jessica at first thought was a football team. Something didn't seem quite right and she quickly realised there were too many people in the photo. Even though she had no interest in sport, she knew a football team had eleven players. She then saw an oval-shaped rugby ball resting next to a trophy at the front of the picture with one row of players kneeling and another standing behind.

The people pictured all seemed to be in their teens but Jessica couldn't recognise any of the faces. 'What am I looking at?' she asked.

'Turn it over.'

Stuck to the wood on the back was a note that had been meticulously hand-written. It had the name of the rugby team and then one by one listed all of the players' surnames. She skimmed through the list and saw the word 'Marks', then turned the photo back over and looked at the young man who must have been Ed. He was crouching in the front row and, now she was looking, she could see a strong resemblance to his brother. The hair was darker but he was a similar build and had the same smile.

Jessica flipped the frame back over and looked through the names for a second time. This time, her eyes were drawn to the name 'Barnes'. She felt a tingle of excitement as she again turned the frame over. The young man she assumed must be Lewis Barnes was directly behind Ed, towering over him. She didn't know rugby positions but was aware a team often mixed smaller lads with much larger ones.

'How did you find this?' she asked.

'By accident really. It was in a box of other photos. I'd started looking through them just because . . . well, because of everything going on. There were a few of Ed and me as kids and others of Dad playing football with us and so on. I saw that one and noticed the names on the back.'

'Did you play?'

'No, it was never my thing. I remember him playing for a couple of seasons when he was about sixteen or seventeen. It was one of the local clubs around here. I wouldn't have been able to tell you the name without that note, mind you.'

'Do you know any of the other boys in the picture?'

Charlie shook his head. 'No, I didn't recognise the faces or names. The only reason I noticed anything was because of the writing on the back and you'd asked about a "Barnes". I don't know if that's who you're after but the last name matches.'

Jessica nodded, thinking the match was unlikely to be a coincidence. There was an awkward pause as she continued to scan the photograph and names before changing the subject. 'What's it like being back up here?'

Charlie smiled. 'Different, drier for a start.'

'It's not usually.'

'So I gather. I'm not sure what to do with my time to be honest. I was planning to come up and look for a job. I've got some savings to get me by for a while but it feels weird.'

'Where did you work in London?'

'The publishers were called Bennett Piper. It was a family company at some point but not by the time I got there.'

Jessica tried to sound dismissive, as if only half-listening. 'Can you give me a few minutes? I need to make a call.'

'Sure, I'll go downstairs. Give me a shout when you want me.'

Charlie turned around and left the room. Jessica was going to phone Izzy at the station but didn't want the man to be around to hear her. She still wasn't entirely ready to discount him as being a suspect, even if he was only one in her own mind and not officially. Having now seen the extent of the house, it was clear the property was worth hundreds of thousands of pounds, if not more. If Charlie was interested in getting his hands on the place, cutting off his brother's hand, as well as someone else's, and getting someone to leave them in a public place seemed a very convoluted way of doing it.

Jessica took out her phone and dialled DC Diamond's extension. She asked the constable if she had a pen handy and then read out the list of surnames from the back of the photo.

After that, she explained about the picture. 'Can you call Vicky Barnes and ask if her son ever played rugby? Hopefully she'll remember but, if not, we could ask her if she can identify her son in the photo. Also cross-check the surnames with anything else we might have on record. The link could be the rugby team as opposed to the college but at least there are less people to contact if we start with the sporting angle.'

'Is there anything else?' Izzy asked.

'Can you get me a phone number? The Internet's not great on my phone.'

'Who are you after?'

'A publishing company in London called "Bennett Piper". Message me the number.'

Jessica hung up and looked through a few of the other items littered around the room as she waited for the number to arrive. The items in the boxes really were an assortment of junk, as if someone had gone to a car-boot sale and bought every item, then packed it all up and left it for twenty years. It did seem strange that the family had been in the house for somewhere between twenty and thirty years and were still living out of boxes. Jessica didn't find it as odd as some might, however, as she strongly suspected she would be exactly the same if she lived in a house this big. Her bedroom would have all the clothes she needed but everything else would be untouched until required.

The alert tone sounded on her phone and she pressed the buttons to load the message. Izzy had sent her the company's name and the number. Jessica thumbed the screen and put the phone to her ear as it rang. A secretary answered and Jessica introduced herself as a police officer, asking if she could speak to whoever was in charge. After a short wait, she ended up talking to a woman with a plummy-sounding accent.

Jessica again introduced herself but didn't elaborate on exact reasons for her call. 'Can I check that a Charlie Marks worked for you until recently?'

The woman didn't hesitate. 'Charlie? Yes, he was here for a few years. He quit a few weeks ago. It was a bit of a surprise really. He's not in any trouble, is he?'

'Not at all, I just wanted to check a couple of details. Did he tell you why he left?'

'Not really, something about returning to the north. I think there may have been a family member involved but I only know that from one of the other people who work here. He didn't elaborate when he gave his notice.'

Jessica thanked the woman for her time and then hung up, walking out of the room quietly. She wasn't deliberately creeping but kept to the edges of the hall in an effort to avoid obviously squeaky floorboards. She looked in a couple of other rooms which were very similar to the first in terms of random items. The fourth door she tried led into what was probably Ed's bedroom. Instead of boxes there were wardrobes that were open with clothes inside and shoes at the bottom. A four-poster bed was made and didn't seem as if it had been slept in recently and a huge window at the front of the room looked out over the driveway.

Jessica didn't know what she was looking for so made her way back downstairs. 'Charlie?'

He came out from a room opposite the front door. 'Are you sorted?'

'Yes, I passed on the names from the back of this photo so we can look into them.' She held up the picture of the rugby team. 'Do you mind if I keep this for a while?'

'No worries. Do you want to see some of my brother's work?'

Jessica didn't instantly clock what Charlie was asking her but then remembered he had told her his brother was an artist. She wasn't too fussed either way but was soon glad she'd accepted. Charlie led her into a wide circular room that led out to the back garden. Lining the walls were a series of paintings she was instantly drawn to. Each one was beautifully crafted in watercolour, showing various countryside scenes.

'They're brilliant, aren't they?' Charlie sounded genuinely impressed at his brother's work and, for the first time that day, Jessica felt something like sorrow in his voice. She guessed it was hard for him to grieve for someone he didn't know for sure was dead and hadn't known properly for years.

'He was always a decent artist but I didn't know about any of this,' Charlie added, pointing to a scene on the wall showing a vast green field with a stone bridge crossing a stream. 'We used to play football here when we were kids. It was converted into houses years ago but I guess he remembered it.'

Jessica walked around the room, taking time to look at each image. She had never been able to draw herself and had no interest in the art world. Her parents had visited from Cumbria a few years previously and insisted on taking her to the Tate Gallery in Liverpool. They had spent hours but she'd been bored within minutes. All she could remember was a broken men's urinal stuck to a wall and a basketball suspended in a box, neither of which had impressed her. Her father had jokingly called her a 'Philistine' because of her reaction to it all but the paintings mounted around the room genuinely impressed her.

'They're terrific,' she said. 'He's very talented.' She had almost said 'was very talented' but stopped herself.

'Pick one,' Charlie said. 'I'm sure he wouldn't mind. He never wanted to sell his work because he didn't need the money but he frequently gave pieces away when we were younger.'

Jessica thought about the offer for a few moments. 'No, they're absolutely beautiful but I'm not sure it would be right. I'd have nowhere to put it anyway.'

'Okay, well, the offer's there if you change your mind. Did you say you wanted to see the pool?'

Jessica hadn't said that exactly but followed Charlie out of the room in any case. He walked through a large archway down a passageway that looped back around towards the rear of the building. There was a white plastic sheet covering a doorway which he moved to one side and held open for her to walk through. Jessica slid sideways past him into the unfinished room. Sunlight streamed through the small gaps where the windows should be but all it showed was a large hole in the ground. Half of the space had been concreted, the other part under a sheet similar to the one at the door.

'I don't know why it was started but not finished,' Charlie said. 'I've been looking for paperwork because it's a bit silly like this. I don't know if someone's been paid to finish it, or if Ed changed his mind for whatever reason.'

Jessica nodded. 'It will be good when it's done, especially on a day like today.'

'I've got to try to get to grips with the house really. There's so much stuff and I don't know where anything is. If I find anything else that could relate to Ed going missing, I've still got your number.'

Jessica thanked Charlie for his time and the photo and walked to her car. She drove down the driveway then turned left. Before she could speed up, she saw someone in the garden of the house next door. The man looked past retirement age but was happily pushing a lawnmower up and down. Jessica parked her car and walked towards him. The wall that ran around his house was around three feet tall but the garden was landscaped to run to the top of it so she had to peer up at him.

'Hello?' There was no answer so Jessica climbed up onto the wall and walked across the newly cut grass towards him. 'Hi?' The man finally glanced up as she got closer. He seemed confused, removing a pair of earplugs and stopping the machine.

'Can I help you?'

'Hi, sorry. I'm Detective Sergeant Jessica Daniel from Manchester's Metropolitan CID. Can I ask how long you've lived here?'

The man didn't smile. 'Twenty-odd years. Why?'

'I was wondering how well you knew the Marks family next door.'

'Only in passing, people keep to themselves around here.'

'Do you know much about the two sons?'

The man shrugged, not thinking about his answer. 'The dark-haired one was the only one who's been living here as far as I know but I've not seen him in a little while. I saw someone yesterday with blond hair but I didn't want to be seen to be sticking my nose in so haven't been around.'

'Edward Marks, the younger brother with darker hair, has gone missing,' Jessica said. 'The older brother, Charlie, is the blond one at the property now. I don't suppose you've seen anything suspicious recently, have you?'

'No, like I said, you pretty much keep to yourself around here. You try not to stick your nose into other people's business. Every now and then there's a bit of banging and drilling but Edward said he was building a pool or something. It's nice to hear the other brother's back though. I remember them as kids, running around and booting balls into my garden. It was always the dark-haired one who'd come to my door because he said the other one was too shy.'

Jessica thanked the neighbour for his time and returned to her car. As odd as the family situation seemed, everything Charlie had told her checked out. She was naturally programmed to be suspicious but at least, on this occasion, she could put those to one side and re-focus on finding January.

She hadn't started her engine when Izzy's name appeared on Jessica's phone screen. She answered as quickly as she could. 'Hi, Iz, I'm on my way back. I've got the picture I gave you the names from. Did you speak to Vicky?'

'Yes, she said immediately her son was a rugby player. She insisted she'd come in to look at the picture but I'm not sure there's any need. That's not why I'm calling though.'

'What's up?' Jessica asked.

'Cross-checking these rugby players' surnames have been a nightmare. I've got first names for just over half of them because they went to the school too. They live all over but there's one guy who is definitely still a local. I thought you might want to visit him?'

Jessica was again impressed at the woman's speed and accuracy of work. 'I'll do it this afternoon. Is Dave with you?'

'Yes, he's right here moaning about how hot it is.'

'Good, tell him to keep working. I'll come and pick you up and we'll visit this rugby player. I think you deserve some time out of the station.'

10

Jessica drove back to the station mulling everything over. They now had a second connection to the rugby side as well as the school that linked the first hand to the second. She still had no idea how the woman in the black cape fitted into things – or if that person was January.

At the station Jessica parked her car and went to find Izzy. As she walked in, it was as if she was going through an invisible wall. The air felt heavy and, even though it was pretty humid outside, it was even hotter indoors. Luckily, the news hadn't spread too far that it was her that broke the air-conditioning system. If it had, she would have been given far more dirty looks as she made her way to the canteen where the two constables were. Rowlands had a moan that he was being left to work from the station but Jessica didn't pay his complaints too much attention.

Jessica and Izzy took a marked police car to see the rugby player. She didn't know what she expected to get from him but there could be something buried in the past which had seemed innocuous at the time that was causing everything to happen now. Sometimes taking an actual police car as opposed to an officer's own vehicle offered that little extra bit of encouragement for someone to talk.

Izzy was driving but happily chatting away as she followed the navigation device's instructions. 'How come you let me drive?'

Jessica shrugged, even though the constable wouldn't have seen her from the driver's seat. 'Dunno really, going soft in my old age.'

'Dave reckons you're the worst driver he's ever been in a car with.'

Jessica was outraged. 'The cheek of it. I'll remind him of that next time he's complaining about being left at the station.'

'He's not the only one; your driving skills are legendary.'

'Who says?'

'Everyone. When I joined and you started giving me bits to do, one of the first things someone said to me was, "Don't get in a car if she's driving".'

'Bunch of bastards. I'm not that bad.'

'One of the guys in uniform reckoned he was in the back seat when you mounted a kerb, did a U-turn, skidded between two cyclists and then handbraked it before jumping out of the driver's seat to chase someone down.'

Jessica hummed in agreement. 'That was only once and I got the guy. That was years ago.'

'He told me someone else had a week off with whiplash.'

'That guy was faking. He just wanted time off.'

'A whole load of people reckon they've seen you take the turn into our car park on two wheels.'

'I think they've been watching too many films.'

Jessica was trying her best to act outraged but all three stories sounded suspiciously close to the truth.

'Anyway, what's the deal with you and Dave?' Izzy said.

'Rowlands? What do you mean?'

'You have that whole angsty thing going on. It's like when you pick on someone at school because you secretly fancy them.'

'Er, no. It's just because he's a mate and it's fun to annoy him.'

'That's exactly what I mean. You joke around it but there's this whole flirty thing going on.'

'Flirting? Eew, he's like a brother.'

'Have you ever . . . ?'

'Ever what? Oh, God, no, of course not. Yuck. Only in his dreams.' Jessica wasn't comfortable with the questions but figured ducking them would make it worse.

'You've never even thought about it?'

'Get out of it. He tried it one time when I was still a DC but I sent him packing. Not my type.'

'So you do have a type then?'

'Yes, they have to be male and not a complete dick.'

Izzy laughed. 'So you'll take a partial dick as long as he's not a complete one? That's setting the bar pretty high.'

Jessica sniggered. 'Why the interest?'

'Nothing really, now I'm married I have to get my kicks from hearing about other people's fractured relationships.'

'If you go into marriage counselling, you should use that as your slogan.'

Although she rarely talked to anyone about relationships, Jessica found it hard not to like her colleague. As well as the constable being an excellent professional, they shared a similar type of humour. Jessica had a sudden inclination to take the woman out and get her absolutely hammered, if only to see how she acted then. Izzy was great fun to hang around with – but a little too good.

As their conversation fizzled out, Jessica checked the notepad the constable had given her. The former player they were visiting lived in the Droylsden area, around twenty minutes from the police station. Izzy had phoned and asked if the man could spare them a bit of time. He was currently working for a building firm renovating some offices around halfway between his house and their base. After checking with his boss, he told the constable he could take a late lunch and talk to them during that.

Jacob Chrisp was already waiting when they pulled onto the premises. He gave them a half-wave to indicate who he was and then started walking towards the car as Izzy parked. Jessica thought he looked as if he still had the build to play the game. He was wearing shorts and a vest with large muscled and tanned shoulders on display. There were spiralling tattoos running down the outside of both his arms and she afforded herself a small smile thinking how pitiful Rowlands's was in comparison.

The man shook their hands and asked if they wanted to talk to him indoors. Jessica wasn't bothered so the three of them sat on a wall next to the offices that were being cleared out. Given the clatter of furniture being removed it was a little noisy but Jessica thought that was outweighed by being able to sit in the sunshine.

'How can I help you two ladies, then?' Jacob said. From his tone of voice, Jessica could tell he was already looking to try it on.

Jessica slid the photo of the rugby team out of an envelope, pointing at one of the teenagers crouching down. 'Is this you, Jacob?'

He took the picture from her, peering closely as a large grin spread on his face. 'Yes. Wow, I've not seen this in years. Where did you find it?'

Jessica ignored his question. 'Can you tell me anything about the other players?'

Jacob blew out, scratching his head. 'Not really. We won the league this year, only lost one game. Do you know much about rugby?'

Jessica shook her head but Izzy spoke. 'Only Union, I don't follow League.'

The man smiled. 'Cool, a rugby chick. Nice.' Jessica was a little surprised her colleague was into sport but wasn't convinced the officer would be overly impressed by being called a 'chick'. She certainly wouldn't have been but the constable said nothing.

Jacob pointed to a few more faces in the picture. 'I played in the centre. This guy here played outside me and then Eddie and Liam were our two wingers.' He had pointed to Ed Marks.

'Can you think of anything significant away from the pitch that might have happened? I know you went to school with some of the players too.'

Jacob looked a little rattled for the first time. He handed back the picture to Jessica, screwing up his eyes. 'How do you mean?'

'You tell me? I'm a woman of the world; I know what groups of lads get up to.'

'We were only eighteen or nineteen.'

Jessica raised her eyebrows and made sure she caught Jacob's eyes. 'Sometimes that can make it worse.'

'I'm not sure I know what you're getting at.'

Jessica wasn't convinced. After having his arms open and being happy to eye them both up, he had now crossed them and was looking at the ground. 'Two people from this photo have been hurt,' she said. 'We're not sure why and we're talking to other people in it to see if there's a reason anyone might be able to think of.'

Jacob scratched his head, beginning to look a little nervy. Jessica noticed his dark tattoo circled all the way down from the bottom of his neck to the tip of his little finger. Even though she had never been much of a fan of body art, it was impressive.

'How badly were they hurt?' he asked.

Jessica didn't want to give too much away. If the man did know anything, it was better to keep him on edge. 'They were just hurt,' she replied coolly, trying to make Jacob look at her.

'I'm not sure what you want me to say. We were young lads but most of us could get served in pubs and we had a few good times. There's nothing wrong with that, is there?'

'Again, you tell me. Did anything go particularly wrong?'

'No . . . well, not really. The season after that we went on a bit of a tour. You know what it's like with boys having a bit of a laugh, not everyone likes it, do they?'

'Who didn't like it?'

'A few of the locals where we went drinking. One of the coaches ended up quitting too.'

'Why?'

Jacob stood, not wanting to talk any longer. 'I've got to get back. I did say I only had my dinner to talk.'

Jessica wasn't in the mood for being mucked around. 'You'll have to be quick then. What happened with the coach?'

'Nothing. Look, things just got a bit out of hand, some of the team were a bit drunk. They used to wind him up anyway and call him names. As well as coaching, he worked at the school. Anyway, he had that look, do you know what I mean?'

'No, what look?'

'You know, like glasses and that, like he was a paedo.'

Jessica tried not to roll her eyes. 'He looked like a paedophile because he wore glasses?'

'No, it wasn't like that. He had this limp too.'

'So because he limped and wore glasses, you and your friends accused him of molesting children?'

'No . . . well, yes.'

Jessica was finding it hard to disguise her contempt. Although Jacob was well-built, his frame had almost shrunk as he stood. He was slumped with his shoulders down and head drooping towards the ground, clearly embarrassed about what had happened at some point in the past.

'What did you do to this man on tour?'

'I told you, it wasn't me. Some of the lads were pissed up and we were staying in this giant hostel place. They stripped him then threw him in a freezing cold shower. After that they tied him to the roof of our minibus and left him overnight.'

'What happened then?'

'Well, it was the middle of winter. He ended up in hospital but no one owned up to it and nothing happened. He didn't grass or anything and everyone was really impressed but he didn't come back to coaching after that.'

'I wonder why.'

Jacob was suddenly angry. 'Look, I told you it wasn't me. We were only kids mucking about.'

'I'm sure that's how he saw it when he spent a night strapped to a bus in the freezing cold.'

Jacob sounded defensive. 'All right, it's not like it was yesterday or anything, it was ages ago.'

'Anything else you want to tell us about?' Jessica could see in his face that he wasn't going to say anything further, even if there was more to come. It was why she had tried to hide her contempt but the effort had become too much.

'I've got to get back to work.'

'What was his name?'

'Who, the coach? You can't reckon he's involved? He was only this little skinny bloke.'

'What's his name?' Jessica spoke firmly to show she wasn't in the mood.

'I don't know, it was ages ago. Mr Wright, something like that. Michael I think. Look, what's going on with people being hurt?'

'We're not sure yet but if you see anyone limping who wears glasses I'm sure you'll know exactly how to act.'

Izzy wrote the man's name down as they noted the school he taught at was the same one Edward Marks had gone to. If he was a former staff member, his contact details should be on record somewhere. The two women walked back to the car.

'Do you think we should have given him more information?' Izzy asked.

'No, we don't even know if the rugby team is the link yet. It's not as if we should be telling him or anyone to be vigilant because we don't know who the targets are – or if there's more to come.'

'What do you reckon about the coach?'

'Who knows? They sounded like right little shits.'

Izzy hummed in agreement. 'It's a bit of a long wait from then to now if it is the coach though, plus it's a pretty extreme form of revenge.'

'I know. I doubt it's him; it's a bit obvious. Still, it's someone else to go talk to. Anything that keeps us out of the station.'

'Well, if you hadn't have broken the air-conditioning, it wouldn't be too bad.'

'Oi, that sounds like something Dave might say. Just for that, I'm driving.'

When they were back in the vehicle, Jessica made sure to drive as steadily as she could. She didn't swear and was extra careful not to be angry with other drivers. While she drove, Diamond checked in with Rowlands. Jessica couldn't make out much from the one side of the conversation she'd heard but the constable sounded a little excited about something.

'What was that?' Jessica asked after the other woman had hung up.

'You remember the stain you told us about on the floor in January's kitchen?'

'It was either blood or gravy.'

Izzy laughed before composing herself. 'Dave says the labs have been on and emailed through some results. It's blood and it definitely comes from Lewis Barnes.'

11

The morning briefings were really beginning to wind Jessica up because her case was being treated as a distant second priority compared to the disappearance of Christine Johnson. Jessica wouldn't have minded quite so much if Reynolds and Cornish were actually getting anywhere.

Cole had told them all that the superintendent was on the brink of becoming personally involved in the hunt. Jessica knew DSI Aylesbury from when he had been DCI and didn't have a clue quite what he thought he could add by interjecting himself. She had drifted in and out of the talk but, from what Jessica had heard, they really didn't have any ideas what had happened to the MP's wife. In between the conversation with her husband on the phone and him arriving back from Parliament, she had simply disappeared. There didn't seem to be anything untoward in the couple's finances, none of their vehicles had moved, their cleaner hadn't seen anything and the woman's passport and other documents were still at the house.

Officers had looked at CCTV feeds from local shops and roads but had seen nothing, there was no sign of anything untoward in her phone records and the movements of the couple's children, as well as of the MP himself, were all accounted for. Jessica knew a small team of officers were quietly looking into George Johnson's background to see if he might have been having an affair or keeping other secrets that could have a bearing. Despite everything, and the massive amount of media attention the case had received, they knew as much now as they had when the woman first went missing.

Despite their initial falling out, it really was becoming a baptism of fire for Cornish, and Jessica felt sorry for the woman, watching her say nothing during the briefing and wondering if she was regretting the transfer yet. With such scrutiny and a lack of leads, even Cole was beginning to show a degree of strain. Outwardly he was still calm but Jessica knew him well enough to see the worry lines beginning to appear in his face.

By the time it was her turn to update them on her case, the other three officers seemed completely uninterested, not that Jessica blamed them. Cole had been interrupted during the meeting four separate times by his phone going off.

She managed to tell everyone about the rugby team, plus the coach and teacher Michael Wright, but even she had to admit she doubted it was him. By the time the chief inspector's phone rang for a fifth time, he ushered the other detectives out of his office, giving Jessica the fairly obvious brief that she should put her efforts into finding January.

If she didn't respect him so much – and if he hadn't been on the phone – she might have pointed out that giving her some other officers to work with might actually be a help. It wasn't that she disagreed with him but, while two senior detectives and two-thirds of the rest of the station's staff, along with other senior figures across the district, were trying to track down Christine Johnson, Jessica couldn't keep the hunt for January in the news for longer than the initial one day. After that, she simply didn't have the numbers to go door-to-door while there were still other leads to follow up.

It didn't help that everyone was on edge because of the heat and humidity inside the station. If Cole knew it was her fault, he hadn't said anything and she had no intention of letting on to Reynolds or Cornish. The engineer hadn't been in for two days, leaving a message with the admin department that he was waiting on a part.

After returning to her own office, Jessica called Rowlands and Diamond into sit with her. The two had a mini argument over who got the spare seat before Dave relented, sitting on the corner of the other sergeant's desk as he had done a couple of days before.

'I feel like I'm babysitting sometimes,' Jessica said, shaking her head. 'The DCI wants us to focus on finding January. He's so keen on that happening, he's given us no extra staff and zero extra resources. As usual, it means it's just us. The good news is we're all going to get out of this oven today. I'd like you guys to go back and doorstep everyone Dave spoke to the other day. If you can find any other friends or relations January may have, get onto them, else just harass the same people. We all know she's not started living on the streets somewhere – so someone knows what she's up to. Take some officers with you, even if you don't have a use for them. If we don't use them, they'll only spend the day around here being used by Jason and his crew.'

'Where are you off to?' Izzy asked.

'I'm going to go talk to this rugby-coaching-teacher guy. I doubt he's involved but maybe he'll know some other things the team got up to. I still don't know if the link is the school, the team or something else but I'm not going to sit around in this heat all day. Did you see the temperature on the news this morning? Twenty bloody nine degrees. They reckon it's the driest June for thirty years.'

'Typical, it rains eleven months of the year and now we've got a hosepipe ban,' Rowlands said.

'Why does that affect you? What are you doing with a hosepipe?' Jessica asked.

'Nothing, it's just the principle.'

The two women exchanged looks before Jessica continued. 'Right, you guys head off. Call me if anything happens and I'll check in later anyway. Iz, if Dave tries to flirt, you've got my permission to arrest him with as much force as you deem necessary. Dave, if she calls you a "knob" more than three times you can put in an official complaint.'

Rowlands had an outraged look on his face but Jessica knew full well he had been waiting for an opportunity to try it on with the fiery red-head, whether she was married or not. In some places it could be seen as some sort of sexual harassment but he was so clumsy with his words – and the female officers were generally pretty tough anyway – so it wasn't as if there was any harm done. Everyone knew there was a fine line between professional banter and something more serious and no one thought the constable crossed it.

After they had left, still bickering, Jessica checked the information she had on Michael Wright. Jacob had remembered the name correctly and Jessica suspected he recalled things a little more clearly than he wanted to let on. Izzy found his details the previous evening between a mixture of old school records and the electoral roll. Jessica called and asked if he was free to talk. She hadn't told him exactly what about but he said he was retired anyway and invited her over.

Jessica had spent large parts of the last few days driving around the city to visit various people and was getting tired of navigating Manchester's roads while the sun shone. Her car blowers were bad enough when it was cold and she needed the heat to clear the windscreen – but they weren't much better when it was baking hot and she set to cool. The device seemed to have three settings: off, really hot or really cold. Even on a scorching day, the 'cold' setting somehow managed to make things feel arctic but the heat of the sun through the window was too hot to switch them off. The weather forecasters had predicted no end in sight for the current heatwave and people didn't seem sure how to deal with it. When it rained everyone knew where they stood, that was just what it did in the city. A day or two of sun had everyone wondering why it couldn't be like that more often but, after two weeks without rain, Jessica thought the locals, including herself, seemed to be walking around a little bemused.

She didn't think she'd had one conversation in the last week that hadn't involved the weather in one way or another. Jessica's parents lived further north and she spoke to them once a fortnight or so. She had spoken to them the previous night but all they wanted to talk about was the weather. 'I like it hot,' her mother had said. 'But not *this* hot.' Considering her mum had spent large parts of the winter saying how cold it was, Jessica wondered if there was a magic temperature where it was just fine. Half a degree hotter or colder and it would be too far the other way again.

Before she knew it, Jessica had arrived at Michael Wright's house. She was familiar with the place as it wasn't too far from where she used to live when she first came to the city with Caroline. As she got out of her car, she realised that would have been roughly the same year the rugby photo was taken.

Jessica rang the man's doorbell and, before the chime had finished, the door was yanked inwards. Jessica thought of the way Jacob had described his former coach and, as much as she hated herself for thinking it, it was hard to disagree with the picture he had painted. Michael Wright was shorter than she was and wore black thick-rimmed glasses. As he stepped backwards to let her in, he had a clear limp, as if one leg were shorter than the other. He was completely bald and stammered as he spoke. 'Can I, I, I see your identification please?'

Jessica took her identification out from her jacket pocket and let him examine it. He held it close to his face and, for a moment, she thought he was going to lick it. Much to her relief, he didn't and handed it back. 'C-C-Come in.'

As much as you were trained to treat and judge people

on their actions and words, police officers were still human beings and made snap first impressions like anyone else.

The front door opened immediately into a living room and, as Jessica sat in the armchair the man offered to her, she could see why the team had picked on him. She remembered being at schools and in clubs herself and knew there was always one teacher or helper who the children targeted. For her there was the geography teacher who would stand and wait for the class to go quiet but, when she was younger than that, she remembered a form tutor dashing out of registration in tears because no one was listening to her.

Michael stood in front of her rocking slightly from one leg to the other. 'Can I get you a cup of tea or something?'

'If it's not too much trouble, that would be fab. No sugar though, just milk.'

Jessica didn't really want one but figured if he was in the kitchen, she could have a proper look around his living room. It was a trick one of the men she first worked with had taught her. He had told her off for turning down a hot drink and then, when she'd told the person she'd changed her mind, they had scuttled off and her colleague had proceeded to look at every photo, even opening a few drawers.

With Michael out of the room, Jessica stood and peered at a couple of pictures around the room. Nothing appeared to be recent. A couple of photos seemed to be of a group of people who looked like teachers. Jessica could clearly see Michael standing on the end, leaning slightly to one side. There were two even older photos of a couple getting married whom she assumed were the man's parents. The only picture that jumped out was on the mantelpiece behind another frame. She had to pick it up to see it properly but it was of a rugby team. She looked to see if either Ed Marks or Lewis Barnes was a part of the side but it didn't look like it. Jessica put the frame back down and returned to the armchair.

The whole room looked like a throwback to twenty years ago. The carpet, sofa and armchair all had flowery patterns, the wallpaper sporting an awful raised print design. It had been painted over and was flaking in some parts. When she looked properly, Jessica could see the windows were single-glazed too with flimsy looking wooden frames. It was the kind of house she had grown up in but even her parents had redecorated at least twice since.

Michael walked back into the room with two china teacups clinking on saucers next to a teapot on a tray. It didn't surprise her to see the crockery had a flowery pattern too. He put everything on the coffee table and sat on the sofa. 'I hope I didn't put t-t-too much milk in.'

Jessica took a sip just to be polite and assured him it was fine. 'Thanks for inviting me around, Mr Wright. I just wanted to ask you a couple of questions about some of your former students, if that's all right?'

'I've not taught for over ten years I'm afraid, I'm not sure h-h-how much use I can be.' He pushed his glasses up higher on his face but seemed far too nervous to actually look at Jessica.

'If I ask you about a couple of people, could you tell me if you recognise the names?'

He made something approaching a gurgling noise before saying that was fine.

'Do you remember a student called Edward Marks?'

The man's reply was instant. 'Yes, he took A-levels in English Literature, Communication Studies and Art. He had a brother called Charles.'

Jessica was a little startled. 'How do you know that?'

'If I've taught someone, I remember everything. Edward got two C's and an A for Art if I remember correctly. He played hockey and rugby too. He was a pretty quick winger from what I remember.'

Jessica noticed his stammer had gone and he suddenly sounded confident. 'How about Lewis Barnes?'

'English Literature, History and Geography. Two B's and a C. He also played rugby, open-side flanker, and was a keen swimmer.'

'Jacob Chrisp?'

'Government and Politics, History and Communication Studies. B, C, D. Inside centre.'

Jessica tried to remember one of the other names from the photo. Izzy had matched as many first names to surnames as she could and they had identified all but three of the players, although hadn't contacted anyone except for Jacob.

'How about Rory King?'

'No idea, not one of mine.'

'Timothy Davidson?'

The man shook his head emphatically. 'Nope.'

Jessica gave him a few more names; some of them he knew, some he didn't. 'I've got to ask again, how can you remember all this? It's astonishing.'

The man sounded nervous but somewhat proud. He had stopped stammering. 'It's just something I can do. If I've taught or coached someone, I remember things like that. Those names weren't too long from before I retired but I can go back a lot further.'

It almost sounded like a challenge. If he was involved in any way, surely showing off this kind of knowledge of the victims would be an odd thing to do in front of a police officer? Looking at him, she felt guilty herself for thinking he was a bit odd but he didn't seem capable of hacking off a hand. Her instincts were telling her he was just someone who had been caught up in something unsavoury a few years ago but was harmless enough.

'I understand you were a teacher and rugby coach?' Jessica asked.

'And hockey – plus I worked for the scouts for a while too.'

'Why did you stop?'

The man leant forward and picked up the teacup, taking two large sips and then returning it to the tray. His hand was shaking and the hot liquid spilled on his hand. He barely reacted, wiping it on the sofa. Still staring at the carpet he finally spoke. 'After I got out of hospital I couldn't face it any longer.'

Jessica suddenly felt awful; there was such pain in the man's voice. She didn't want to ask the question but the words came out anyway. 'Why were you in hospital?'

Michael drank some more tea before answering. 'An acc-acc-accident with some of the rugby players I was coaching. It wasn't the first time and things weren't right at the college either. They offered me some m-m-money to go and I took it and quit everything else too.'

Jessica didn't know what else she could get from the conversation. The man's stutter had returned and he was clearly upset. The picture seemed pretty clear without him filling in the gaps. Given years of bullying from the very people he had spent a career trying to help, he had finally reached the end of his tether.

'I've just got one last thing. Do you ever see your students out and about?' It wasn't the exact question she should have asked but she didn't want to upset him further.

'One of them was my postman for a little while b-b-but unless they're on TV or in the paper, I wouldn't really notice. I d-d-don't often go out.'

Jessica could have continued to talk to him but, despite his almost autistic knowledge of former students, he seemed a little pathetic. As he stood to show Jessica out, a thought occurred to her. Ever since they had looked at the first CCTV footage, they had been assuming the figure in the black cape was a woman. She didn't think the former teacher was involved but perhaps another male with his stature could be. If they were confident enough to walk in heels, she thought someone as short and slight as him could just about pass as female.

After saying her goodbyes, Jessica drove back to the station. Clouds had started to form and taken the edge off the heat. She walked through reception into her office which was hot and empty. Jessica was planning on running a few more checks on the former teacher. She suspected he may have had a breakdown at some point and, though the police didn't have open access to someone's medical records, there could be something in their system that could reveal more about him.

Her desk was messy at the best of times but there was a pile of post on Jessica's seat that would have been left by someone from the mail room. Although that was what the officers called it, it was essentially just a cubby hole connected to the admin and Human Resources department. She flicked through a couple of letters, before seeing an object that sent a chill through her. A large brown envelope with a printed name and address was at the bottom of the pile. Jessica could see it matched the package that had been sent to the station containing the severed finger but, unlike that one, this was addressed directly to her.

12

Jacob Chrisp downed the rest of his pint and looked across the table at the man opposite. 'Oi, Fred, your round, fella.'

'Who got the last lot?' the man asked.

'I got the first round, Stevo got his, Legs was next and now it's your turn. Get moving.'

Fred stood and stepped out from under the giant parasol that extended over the table they were sitting at. 'Same again, lads?'

The three men nodded. Jacob stretched out from under the umbrella to make sure the upper half of his bare torso was in the sun. 'Bloody lovely weather, this.'

One of the other two men rolled up the sleeves on his T-shirt to make it more like a vest, moving further into the evening sun. 'Aye aye,' he said, nodding his head towards the beer garden's entrance. The pub was the closest to the office they were clearing. It wasn't great but the beer was cheap and, with weather like they were having, the patio at the back was perfect for drinking after work.

Jacob and the third man glanced towards where their friend had nodded to see two women sitting on opposite sides of a wooden table a few yards away. One had short blonde hair and was wearing denim shorts with a small white vest top, the other had on a short skirt and bikini top.

'Whew, that is top quality,' Jacob said. He gave a low whistle and raised his eyebrows as the two girls looked over. 'Evening, ladies.' The two females ignored him, each lighting a cigarette and stretching their legs into the sun. 'Probably lesbians,' Jacob said, looking back to his friends. 'They look the type.' He coughed loudly. 'Dykes.'

The two men around him laughed. 'Who was the red-headed one you were with earlier?' one of them asked.

'Some chick from the Old Bill.'

'What did she want?'

Jacob didn't know what to think of the two detectives who had visited him and couldn't figure out what they wanted. Were they saying he could be a target because of something to do with his rugby team or were they just after information? Either way, he had no intention of telling his friends about it. 'I saw some car accident last week. They were taking a statement.'

'What were they like close-up? They looked tidy from a distance.'

'Oh, you definitely would. The red-head was a stunner but there was something about the other one too.'

Despite his bravado, Jacob had been a bit spooked by the officer with the dark blonde hair. Maybe it was the way she had completely dismissed him but he got the feeling there was something she wasn't telling him. The comments about two of the players being hurt were cryptic but he hadn't wanted to ask too many questions in case they had come back with more inquiries of their own. As far as he was concerned, the less said about the tours their rugby team had gone on, the better – and it was years ago anyway. Aside from the odd one, he hadn't seen any of the players for ages and, as for the two detectives, he had given them the name of the freak coach but knew they wouldn't get too much from him, even if they could find him.

Jacob's thoughts were interrupted by Fred returning with a tray of drinks. 'You took your time.'

'Yeah, just some bloke being a dick and trying to cut in line at the bar. It's heaving in there. I've never seen the place so busy.'

As he spoke a man walked across, standing behind him and putting a hand on his shoulder. 'You all right, fellas? I just wanted to apologise for jumping the queue inside. I don't want any trouble or anything. Can I get you all a drink to make up for it?'

Fred looked at the man and then glanced across to Jacob, who shrugged, thinking he had something vaguely familiar about him. 'No worries, buddy, we're all on lager here so a pint each and we'll say no more about it, yeah?'

'Sure, I'll be right back.'

The man disappeared back into the pub as Jacob and the other two men stared at Fred. 'What did you say to him inside?'

Fred seemed slightly confused. 'Nothing, I just sent him packing. I guess he saw us and figured he didn't want a scrap. Can't blame him really.'

Jacob took his fresh drink from the tray and took a large slurp. 'Better get these ones down if we've got more on the way.'

Fred nodded towards the two girls who now had their backs to the men. 'You seen those two?'

'Both lezzers,' Jacob replied.

The group continued talking and a few minutes later the other man returned with a tray of four drinks. He walked around the table putting a pint down in front of each man. 'Here you are, boys, sorry about the trouble.'

Jacob downed his pint and picked up the new one, shrugging at his friends. 'Free beer – we'll have to send Fred in to put the shits up people more often.'

'Aye, it's always the quiet ones,' one of the other men said.

They continued to talk and joke but, after finishing the fifth drink of the evening, Fred stood. 'Time for me to go, fellas, Suzie will be wondering where I am.'

One of the other men got to his feet. 'I should probably be off too. I'm driving and my copper mate reckons they have those random drink-driving stops after eight. I'm not getting done again.'

'Can I hop in with you?' the third man asked, also standing up.

'Yeah, but let's get going, it's already half seven.'

'You're all off?' Jacob said accusingly, though he could hear his own words slurring.

'Sorry, mate,' Fred replied. 'I've got to look after the kids tomorrow night too but we'll come back the day after that.' The other two men nodded in agreement.

Jacob wanted to protest but was feeling sluggish. The three men left via the gate at the back of the garden, rather than walking back through the pub. Jacob took his phone out of his pocket but the screen was too blurry to make out. He knew there was a taxi rank nearby but couldn't remember exactly where it was. The man picked up his T-shirt from the table and put it back on. For some reason he couldn't fit his head through and, as he heard nearby giggling, he realised it was because he was trying to squeeze it through an arm hole. Feeling stupid, he twisted the top around and finally managed to put it on properly. The two women from earlier were now looking at him, laughing openly.

'What's your problem?' he demanded but his words garbled into one. He felt very drunk but couldn't figure out why.

The two girls were still laughing. 'Think you've had too much to drink, you stupid prick,' one of them said.

Jacob stood quickly but stumbled on the wooden seat. He regained his balance but his head was spinning. He tried to shout some abuse at the women but his words blended into one, which just made them laugh even more. Trying to keep himself steady, he stomped past them out the back gate his friends had disappeared through minutes earlier. He knew where he was but, for some reason, his brain wasn't giving him the information he needed about which direction to go in. Jacob stopped, trying to focus on a spot across the road in order to clear his head.

The strange thing was he was thinking clearly enough to know he hadn't had enough alcohol to feel this drunk. He could remember the five drinks, which was only a little more than he might have on his own in an evening at home. He had only had a pie for lunch but that wasn't unusual either. One thing he was known for in his circle of friends was being able to put the beer away.

Jacob stumbled to his right, not knowing entirely where the taxi rank was but realising he had a fifty per cent chance of being correct. Before he could get to the junction he felt a hand on his shoulder. He started to turn but felt a blow hammer into the side of his cheek. His vision was spinning anyway but started to go black from the ferocity of the attack.

Jacob fought to stay standing, throwing a punch of his own, but he couldn't see where the blow had come from. His swing connected only with warm air as something smashed into the back of his head. He tried to stay focused and upright but a final blow was enough to make everything go dark.

13

Jessica was sitting at her desk, looking at the two constables in front of her. 'Where'd you get the chair from, Dave?'

Rowlands shrugged. 'Nicked it from downstairs. I figured that if we're going to keep meeting in your office, I should at least have somewhere to sit.' He looked accusingly at Izzy.

'All right, kiddies,' Jessica said, looking from one constable to the other, 'who wants to go first?'

Izzy flicked her hair back behind her ears and started to tie it in a ponytail. 'Me and the boy wonder have visited everyone we know that has any association with January. Everyone claims they don't know where she is, which isn't a surprise, I guess.'

Rowlands nodded, taking his colleague's cue to chip in. 'I reckon she's hiding out with a friend somewhere. There are a few people we think might know more than they're letting on but there's not much we can do. Aside from sounding a bit shifty we don't have any reason to suspect anyone specifically.'

Jessica knew he was right. 'Next time I see the super I'll ask him to get onto the Home Secretary about bringing in a law so we can arrest shifty-looking and -sounding people. Personally I'm all for it.' She again looked from one constable to the other. 'You both know about the package I was sent a couple of days ago. Because of the similarity in print on the front I didn't even touch it and the lab boys came to take it. I got a phone call and email with the results this morning. As I thought, it contained a finger belonging to Lewis Barnes.'

'Why do you think it was addressed directly to you?' Izzy asked.

'No idea really. The case has been in the papers and the details are on the website so someone could have taken it from there. Maybe it's someone like January we've spoken to who knows me? There weren't any fingerprints on the envelope so it's a bit of a dead end. The labs couldn't give us anything specific about printer or ink types but it was always going to be a long shot.'

'Are you okay with things?' Izzy asked, referring to the fact it had been Jessica specifically who had received the latest parcel.

Jessica was still having the odd flash of the first finger in her dreams and was relieved she hadn't opened the second package. If she was honest she was a little concerned that whoever was sending the parcels apparently knew who she was but she didn't want to show those feelings to her colleagues. Cole and Reynolds had both asked her the same question the previous day.

Jessica shrugged. 'Not much I can do, is there? Every piece of mail I get is being screened before it gets to me now. If someone could do the same with my bills at home I'd be laughing.' Her two colleagues exchanged a look as if to tell each other they knew she was putting a brave face on it. She pretended she hadn't seen it and changed the subject. 'Have either of you managed to dig up anything on Michael Wright?'

Rowlands and Diamond both shook their heads. 'Me neither,' said Jessica. 'I know you guys didn't see him but I think he's a bit of a red herring anyway. He didn't seem bitter to me, just sad. The poor guy loved the job and enjoyed his students' success. He's a little *unconventional* but nothing more.' Jessica had almost used the word 'weird'. Even though the man wasn't present it would have felt as if she was bullying him.

'Where does that leave us?' Rowlands asked.

Jessica puffed her cheeks out, shrugging. 'In a bit of a mess. The rugby players live all over the country and I'm not convinced that's our link anyway. If they all went to the same school, there's every chance they did other things together. I think we'll have one more day going back over what we've already got and then, after that, it's working our way through every name on that list of school-leavers. I don't think any of us want to be doing that. Iz, take an officer and go see Vicky Barnes. You know what she's like but keep her calm and see if she knows anything about where January could be. We know Lewis played rugby but what else was he involved with? Did he play any other sports or was he part of other clubs and so on?'

Izzy had taken her notebook out and was writing. Jessica looked to Rowlands. 'Dave, there are two other players from the rugby team who live in this area. I spoke to the pair of them on the phone but go and do your blokey thing with them. Take another male officer and try to get them off-guard. I'm not convinced Jacob told us all he knew. It's probably nothing but ask them about tours and celebrations and so on. See if anyone remembers Lewis and Ed being friends or find out if they're linked in any way aside from the rugby.'

'Anything else? Dave asked.

'No, when you're done talking you can both nick off but don't take the piss and rush. I've got some bits to do here but then I've got to leave early too.'

Rowlands grinned. 'Oh yeah . . .'

'You can take that smug look off your face.'

'What's going on?' Izzy asked.

Jessica went to speak but Rowlands cut in ahead of her. 'Tomboy Jess has a dress-fitting for that wedding today. It sounds bloody hilarious.'

'What's so funny about that?' Jessica said.

'Just you in a big fancy dress thing. I'd pay to see that.'

'You'd pay to see women in their underwear trying on clothes? That's not a surprise to anyone.'

'No, I'd pay to see your face. How long have I known you now? Four years? Five? I think I've only ever seen you in a dress a couple of times.'

'What are you, my stalker?'

'In your dreams.'

Jessica saw Izzy's knowing look but swiftly glanced away. 'Right, let's get going. The quicker we get all this done, the quicker we can all get home then come back tomorrow ready to wade through a list of over a hundred school-leavers.'

After they left, Jessica took her shoes off in an effort to cool down. It was still hot in the station but the weather that day wasn't as warm as it had been. For the first time since the case had fallen into her lap, she was beginning to feel a little stuck. They had spent a couple of weeks moving from one minor lead to the next but, aside from now knowing the identity of the victims, none of it had really advanced the case. They still didn't know if Lewis Barnes and Ed Marks were dead or alive, although she had been working from the assumption they were deceased. They also had no idea who was leaving the hands, or why.

The prominence of the case surrounding Christine Johnson's disappearance was both a stroke of luck and a total inconvenience. In relation to Jessica's situation, it allowed her to get on with things without too much scrutiny from above. The command structure where she would have to pass things through DI Reynolds to DCI Cole had been completely sidelined because both men were under huge pressure from DSI Aylesbury to get results. Although that suited her and left her with two constables she actually liked to work alongside, the downside was becoming apparent. Given their difficulties in tracking down January – or any other kind of lead relating to the woman in black or a connection between the two victims – their usual course of action would have been to get the media as heavily involved as possible. Unfortunately the journalists were only interested in one case and it wasn't hers.

With no other obvious ideas, she dialled Garry Ashford's mobile number and waited for him to answer. 'Hello,' he said gloomily.

'All right, cheer up, I could be calling to tell you some-one's handed in a hundred grand that was left on the street and it's your name on the envelope.'

'Have they?'

'No, but you didn't know that.'

'Sorry, it's just bloody hot,' Garry sighed. 'I've spent most of the last fortnight camped outside George Johnson's house. It's not as if he even comes to talk to us and your lot never have anything to say. I think I've got sun stroke.'

'Why don't you go back to the office then?'

'Christ knows. The editor wants someone here in case anything happens. There are about half-a-dozen of us sitting around in our cars like complete prats on the off-chance his wife comes home. I don't suppose you know anything, do you?'

'Naff all.'

'Can I quote you on that? "A senior police source said they knew 'naff all' about the case".'

'Take out the word "senior" and you've got a deal.'

'Hardee-har. What are you after?'

'January Forrester.'

Garry sighed again. 'I told you last week, the editor's not interested. You got the picture printed the day after she went missing but there's not much more I can do.'

'So it's only news if someone married to somebody a bit famous goes missing, not if someone who could be a serial killer disappears?'

'Do you think she's a serial killer?'

'That's not the point. She's a suspect who's gone miss-ing and we could do with help finding her.'

'Sorry, but it's not up to me.'

'Look, if I feed you a whole load of quotes on the record will you write something up for me? I'll email you the photos to go with it and you won't have to do very much at all.'

'What's in it for me?'

'My eternal gratitude?'

Garry laughed. 'Sod off. How about a future exclusive of my choosing?'

'Done. I thought you were going to ask for one of my kidneys or something.'

'Not with the amount of wine you can put away.'

Jessica tried not to but found herself laughing. 'All right, funny man. If I email you a load of information can you just take some quotes out of that for me? Fill in the gaps if you want but don't make me sound like a dick.'

'So you want me to make you sound literate? I thought you said there wouldn't be much work involved?'

'Yeah, yeah, just think of the juicy exclusive you'll have coming your way someday. How's Mrs Ashford anyway? A big spiky-haired birdie named Dave told me you had a girl-friend.' It had taken Jessica a few years to get him to admit it but Rowlands and Garry Ashford were old university friends. At first they had kept it very much to themselves with the constable acting as a source for his mate. Jessica had put a stop to that but kept the nature of their relationship to herself to prevent Dave getting into any kind of trouble.

Garry sounded a little embarrassed. 'She's all right. I don't know why he's going around telling people though.'

'I think it's sweet. Is she blind and deaf or just blind?'

'All right, sod off, do you want a favour or not?'

'Yeah, I'll get typing it now. I'll even run a spell-check just for you.'

'Cheers, I'll text you later to let you know if it's going in.'

Jessica hung up with a smile on her face. She didn't know many journalists directly but Garry would usually do things for her, even if she did have to threaten, bully or promise him things.

With the dress-fitting in the late afternoon, Jessica skipped lunch and continued working from her desk. First she sent Garry the information he might need, then started to sort the list of college-leavers. Even with the girls taken out and the rugby players crossed off who they had already spoken to, there were still just under a hundred names. Having to contact everyone individually was the last thing she wanted to do. It would no doubt be an enormous waste of time but if the two constables came back with nothing, they would have little other option.

Feeling bored and frustrated, Jessica eventually gave up and walked to the bus stop at the end of the road the station was on. Caroline had asked her a couple of weeks ago to keep the date free and said there would be free wine at the dress shop. With that in mind, Jessica had used public transport to get to work that morning. The buses and trams around the centre of Manchester weren't too bad in general but were always overcrowded at peak hours and, from her experience, had at least one idiot on board during others. Sometimes she would flash her identification to shut them up, others she would sit in silence with everyone else. From speaking to people she knew, most officers found it hard to reconcile their post with having a 'normal' life when they weren't working. When you saw someone acting unsociably, you were supposed to step in but it wasn't quite that easy when you were on your own. Her general rule was that she would intervene if someone was causing someone else distress, otherwise she would stay quiet.

The back of the bus had a group of kids playing music loudly through their phone but she did her best to ignore them as the vehicle moved slowly towards the city centre. Rowlands had struck something of a nerve earlier when he had spoken about her wearing dresses. He was right but it wasn't really a conscious choice of hers in quite the way he had insinuated. The idea of the fitting was for Caroline, Jessica and the other bridesmaids to collectively make a choice about what would best match the bride's dress. Realistically, having known Caroline for as long as she had, Jessica was aware only one person would be making that decision – and it had probably already been made.

The dress shop was staying open late specifically for them and as Jessica arrived at the store a couple of streets away from the Arndale shopping centre, she could see people hurrying to catch their buses and trains home for the evening.

She went through the front of the shop and was met by a woman in her late fifties. 'You must be the main bridesmaid, yes? Here you go, dear.' The woman offered Jessica a glass of wine then locked the door behind her. She then pointed to an area towards the back of the shop. 'Everyone's in there.'

Jessica walked through a curtain and almost gasped as she saw Caroline fully trussed up in her wedding dress. Even for someone who wasn't a fan of the pomp, Jessica had to admit she was impressed. The gown was white satin and fitted her friend perfectly. It wasn't too over the top in terms of frills and size but was just right.

Caroline gave a little squeal as she noticed Jessica. 'What do you reckon?'.

'Bit scruffy,' Jessica said with a massive grin. 'Aren't you getting dressed up?'

The two women laughed. Jessica gave her friend a gentle hug before being shooed away from the dress. She glanced around and, aside from the shop workers, she could only see one girl who seemed around thirteen and looked pretty grumpy, plus a much younger child of about five who was playing with some Lego on the floor. 'Where's everyone else?' Jessica asked.

'What do you mean?'

It suddenly dawned on her. Caroline had told her she was going to be one of three bridesmaids. For whatever reason, she had assumed that meant adults but instead it now looked like she was going to have to supervise these two children on the day. Jessica tried not to look too disheartened. 'Oh, er, nothing . . . so what is it you want us to wear?'

Caroline smiled broadly. 'I think you're going to like them.' One of the shop workers walked to a rail and picked off three light blue satin dresses. She handed one to Jessica and then beckoned the two children through to separate dressing rooms. The two adults were alone in the main area at the back of the shop. Jessica held her dress at arm's length. The colour was actually quite nice but she wasn't sure about the height of the neckline.

'What do you reckon?' Caroline asked.

'Not too bad. I'll try it on first.' Jessica put the dress on another nearby rail and sat down to start getting undressed. 'Who are the two other bridesmaids?'

'Tom's nieces. When we told his family we were getting married it was a bit of a blur and I ended up promising the youngest one she could be a bridesmaid. The oldest one's a typical teenage pain. I don't think she wants to do it but, because the other one is, she doesn't want to miss out on anything.'

Jessica couldn't disguise her thoughts any longer. 'Kids?'

'Sorry, I thought I'd told you.'

'You know what I'm like with children. I'll end up saying "fu—" . . . using the f-word in front of them or something. Do you remember when we went out to eat that time?' Jessica glanced sideways towards the changing room and lowered her voice. 'We were talking about . . . downstairs bits . . . and that kid's mother asked me to mind my language? I just know something like that's going to happen and I'll totally ruin your day.'

'You'll be fine.'

'"Fine"? Do you remember when we went to see your workmate's new baby? I accidentally told the woman her son looked like an alien.'

Caroline laughed. 'That was pretty bad. It's the kind of thing you think but don't say. You probably shouldn't have used the word "bug-eyed" either.'

'Exactly! This is a recipe for disaster. I thought it was a compliment but it came out wrong. The bloody kid just kept staring at me with those freaky big eyes while he dribbled. It was like that boy from "The Omen".'

'At least you didn't say that.'

'What do you even talk to kids about? I thought it was all PlayStations and violent movies nowadays. Do they still have dolls or is it just stabby things nowadays?'

Caroline threw her arms up, grinning. '"Stabby things"? Yes, kids still play with dolls. You could ask what they're interested in and take it from there.'

Jessica stood and took the dress from the rack, stepping into it then pulling it up before turning around for her friend to zip it. 'Yeah, but what if they're into, I don't know, horses or something? I don't know anything about animals. I'll probably end up going on about glue factories.'

Caroline burst out laughing as the zip reached the top. 'Just be yourself.'

'That's what I'm trying to tell you, I'm an idiot especially with children.'

'So you can interrogate any manner of criminal but two kids scare the hell out of you?'

'Yes, now you're catching on. What do you do if they start acting up?'

'I don't know. I'll point out their parents and you can tell them. What did your parents do when you were young?'

'They'd threaten to send me to bed. It didn't matter what time of day it was, Mum would tell me to stop mucking about or I'd go to bed. I'd bring that back actually. If you're performing badly at work your boss punishes you by sending you to bed for a few hours, that'd be brilliant.'

'Yeah, I'd rather you didn't send my bridesmaids to bed halfway through the ceremony please.' Jessica turned to face her friend. 'You look great,' Caroline added.

Jessica walked to a mirror and looked herself up and down. 'Yeah, I am pretty hot. Now we just have to sort the scrag bag bride out.'

'Oi, get out of it. Tom's mum cried when she saw me in this.' Caroline's own parents had both died years ago, which had helped draw her and Jessica closer together. It hadn't crossed Jessica's mind before but she suddenly realised that created a problem.

She didn't want to sound too insensitive or obvious so made sure she had eye contact with her friend as she spoke. 'Who's giving you away, Caz?'

Caroline smiled but it seemed a little forced. Being without both parents and especially her father on such a big day must be hard. 'I've been meaning to ask you.'

Jessica nodded and smiled. 'What if I want to keep you for myself?'

'Tough luck.'

One of the other shop workers had come back into the room. 'Ooh, that's nice,' she said, looking at Jessica, who wondered if the woman had ever slated a bridal party in her life. She figured that, even if the bride looked like a baby hippopotamus in her dress, the shop worker would still say she looked 'nice'. The woman started measuring around Jessica's body and making small statements such as, 'need taking out a bit there', and, 'not quite right in this bit' which Jessica largely ignored.

'All right, fine,' Jessica said. 'I'll give you away. I don't get trusted with rings or anything like that, do I? If you can give me as little responsibility as possible, that would be much appreciated.'

'His brother is best man and he'll have the rings. Don't you know anything?'

'Well, yeah, but it's not often your mate gives you away, there might be some sort of special rules or something. Do I have to make a speech?'

'No but you do have to bring someone.'

'A man?'

'Yes. I've already got you giving me away; if you bring a female, we're going to end up looking like a trio of predatory lesbians.' The shop worker measuring Jessica up giggled but tried to stifle it.

'All right, I'll find someone but I can't promise it won't be some bloke off the street.'

'As long as they've had a shave I don't care. Anyway, isn't there something else happening before the wedding anyway?'

'No.'

'Ooh, is that a little porky? I think it's someone's birthday.'

'Not me. I stopped having birthdays when I turned twenty-five.'

The shop worker stood, indicating to Jessica she could

take the dress off again. 'We'll get you back in a few days before the ceremony to make sure it all still fits,' she said.

Jessica started undressing again as the worker walked over to Caroline. 'It's time to take this one off again too, I'm afraid.' With the aid of the helper, the bride started to remove the dress.

'What are you doing for your birthday then?' Caroline asked.

'Oh, I dunno, hopefully catching this psycho who's leaving hands everywhere. If not that then maybe I'll go to the pub.'

'Rolling the boat out then?'

'Well, thirty-three's not a big one, is it?'

'What are you going to do when you hit forty?'

Jessica winced as she finished taking the dress off and put it on the hanger. 'Don't even think about that. I'm going to go out in a blaze of sex and drugs long before then.' The shop assistant looked over, a little confused. 'Sorry, I'm not really. I'm a police officer, I was joking.' Jessica caught her friend's eye as if to indicate comments like that were exactly why she shouldn't be trusted with children.

She sat back down and started to drink a second glass of wine that had been brought through and was in the process of putting her work suit back on when her phone rang. She picked it up off the floor, listening.

After hanging up, she hurried to get dressed. 'Sorry, Caz, I've got to go, work stuff.' She walked across to her friend and kissed her on the forehead then turned to the worker. 'Is the front door unlocked for me to get out?'

She left the shop, walking as quickly as she could to the location the person on the phone had given her. After an enjoyable time with her friend, her police brain had kicked back in. The crowds of people finishing work had thinned and the streets were relatively empty. She quickened her pace until she was almost running as she dashed past two giant department stores and the Old Wellington pub, seeing a cordoned-off area next to the cathedral with three uniformed officers standing with their backs to it.

She rushed up to the closest one who she didn't recognise and showed her identification. 'What's going on?'

'You got here quick,' the officer said, looking surprised.

'I was in the area. What's happening?'

'A member of the public phoned 999. We came down to check things then called it in. I guess that's why you're here. Scene of Crime are on their way but they might be a while because there's been a pile-up on the M60.'

Jessica skipped around the men, walking to an area on the grassy verge next to the main part of the cathedral. There was a white plastic sheet which she lifted, wincing at what was underneath.

Not only was it another severed hand with its ring finger missing but, given the tattoo that ran the length of the person's little finger, she knew it belonged to Jacob Chrisp.

14

Jessica had mixed feelings the next day. Technically, she wasn't quite senior enough to be heading an investigation and everything was supposed to be referred up. In practice, it might as well be her case. With anything like this, the next body or, in this case, hand, was met with dread and regret for the victim along with a twinge of selfish relief you had something new to work with. It was those types of feelings you could never talk about with a civilian. It wasn't that you looked forward to the next macabre find but sometimes it became the only way to get things moving.

She hadn't exactly warmed to Jacob Chrisp during their brief meeting but he surely didn't deserve what had happened to him? Jessica had returned to the station the previous evening and found a contact number and address for the man's parents. Someone local to them in Lancaster had gone to break the news, then, if that wasn't bad enough, they'd asked for a mouth swab from one of the parents to confirm for sure the hand definitely belonged to him. Jessica had no doubts what the results would show. Unless someone else had the exact same swirling tattoo along the side of their hand, she knew it would prove to be Jacob's.

That meant three players from the photo of the rugby

team had likely been killed and the priority now was speaking to every person in the picture face-to-face. She had talked to both constables the previous evening. Rowlands hadn't got anything of note from the other two rugby players he had seen that day. With the three dead players and those two, it left ten people she needed to speak to. There could be other squad members too but none of them were either in the photo or named on the back. Diamond hadn't come up with much from the previous day either, saying it was hard to draw Vicky Barnes away from blaming everything on January.

Rowlands was again working on contacting every member of the rugby team and getting full address details. Jessica was planning on visiting them all one by one, regardless of where they lived around the country. Diamond was juggling a few jobs. She was trying to see if January had a connection to Jacob while, much to Jessica's relief, talking to the media too. The discovery of the third hand had seemingly woken up the newspapers and TV stations, who were now coming to them for information.

Officers had been sent around to see if the coach, Michael Wright, had an alibi. Jessica hoped he did because she didn't believe he was involved and keeping him a part of their investigation would only end up wasting their time and perhaps causing him more hurt.

After directing where everyone should be, Jessica finally made her way to where she should have been first thing – the monitoring area for the city's CCTV cameras. She would have preferred to have either Dave or Izzy with her but, with everything now moving quickly, she didn't have that luxury. Instead she was in front of the bank of monitors with one of the members of the private security firm who operated the city's cameras. Despite not being her first choice, it was always useful to have two pairs of eyes to look over the footage.

The complicated thing was finding out when the hand had been left. It had been found in the early evening but, if it had been left in the daytime, it would have been completely different to the first two drops where the person in the black cape had appeared at sunrise.

There were no cameras pointing directly at the side of the cathedral itself where the hand had been left but there were only three ways to reach it. The first was from Victoria train station, another route was from the Printworks entertainment complex and the final cut-through was just off the main road. All three areas were huge public hubs and very well-monitored. Jessica was working backwards from the time the police had arrived on the scene.

Given she didn't know the person she was working alongside, she watched the footage at a slower speed than she might usually have done. Jessica began with images from the cameras leading from the train station to the cathedral. The thought occurred to her that, with no cameras directly watching the spot the hand had been left at, assuming the person knew their positions as well as they seemed to, there was every chance the hand could have been left undetected by pretty much anyone. Because of that, she specifically watched for people in dark clothing, especially those on their own. With the hot day, she thought it would rule out a lot of people before realising that a huge majority of people leaving the train station were wearing suits for work. She skimmed through the coverage all the way back until the sun had gone down in reverse without seeing anything untoward.

The second set of angles came from the main road. There was one camera pointing directly at the entrance to the pathway running alongside the cathedral and a second one monitoring the opposite side of the road. It gave her fewer people to watch but, aside from a few dangerous driving manoeuvres, she again saw nothing.

The final set of cameras were mounted around the Printworks complex. In the evenings the place was full of people visiting the various bars and restaurants and the cinema. There was a steady stream of pedestrians throughout the day but Jessica's eyes were feeling tired. She checked the time on her phone and realised she had been watching the videos for almost three hours.

She had also missed a text message from Garry Ashford: 'Got ur piece in. Did u see?'

She texted him back: 'Yes. Given latest find I reckon it wudve gone in anyway. Still deal a deal. X'

Jessica couldn't help but feel Garry had struck lucky. She had given him information his editor hadn't initially been bothered about but, following the latest hand being found, the media outlets were suddenly after information again and would have been looking to run a story about January in any case.

Jessica paused the footage and phoned Izzy. She told the constable she hadn't found anything so far and asked what had been going on.

'A few things,' Izzy replied. 'I've not found you anything from January that links her to the other players yet. Dave's got a list of addresses and phone numbers for you from the rest of the team. People are all over the country but you already knew that. He's been helping the press office.'

'What about Michael Wright?'

'Didn't anyone call you?'

'No, what's happened?'

'He's spent the last couple of days in hospital.'

'What with?'

'I'm not sure. One of his neighbours said he fainted on his doorstep. I spoke to someone at the hospital who said he's been on a ward the past two nights. They're doing tests.'

Jessica wondered if her questions had brought back too many bad memories that caused him enough stress to have some sort of breakdown. She hoped not but could at least take a tiny amount of solace in the fact he had an alibi and she shouldn't have to bother him any longer. 'How's everyone else?' she asked.

'Just busy and hot. Don't worry, I've not grassed you up for breaking the air-conditioning.'

'It wasn't me, it was dodgy workmanship.'

'Whatever. How long are you going to be?'

'No idea. There's no camera looking directly at the spot where the hand was left but I'm on the final set of angles looking towards it. Do we have the formal ID yet?'

'No. Jacob Chrisp's mother gave us a sample but it is being tested. Someone said the hand wasn't in a great state either.'

'Yeah, I saw it. It looked like it had been out in the sun for a while. I'll call you when I'm coming back.'

Jessica hung up and started the footage again. Her eyes felt a little rested after a few minutes away from it. The man next to her was clearly bored and jumped in his seat when she made an involuntary squeal. 'Look.'

The footage was almost back to sunrise but a little later than the times the other hands had been left. The angle she was watching came from a camera pointing at the corner of the pathway leading along the side of the cathedral. The device was across the road so the images weren't entirely clear because the shot was so wide.

Jessica rewound the footage and played it again as the man watched more intently second time around. A figure in a black cape emerged from out of shot and was walking across the road away from the camera. She paused and zoomed in as best she could. As with the previous footage they had found, there wasn't anything clear enough to get a precise shot of the person's face and the hood was pulled forward. She could see the same heels from before and, given the person's stature, it certainly looked like a woman.

'Is that who you're looking for?' the man asked.

Jessica zoomed out slightly and set the video to play again. 'I think so.' They both watched as the figure reached the other side of the road and then gasped at the same time.

'Did she just do what I think she did?' the man said. Jessica looked at him and his eyes were wide in disbelief.

Jessica scrolled the images backwards and zoomed in

again before pressing play. As it got to the crucial part, the man next to her started laughing gently. 'I can't believe it,' he said.

She paused the stream and pressed a button to store the screen grab. A printer at the back of the room hummed into action and she walked over to it, returning to her seat with a sheet of paper.

'They're waving at the bloody camera,' she said, barely believing it herself.

The rest of the footage hadn't been much use. After waving, the figure had walked out of shot towards the spot where the hand had been left, then returned the exact same way. There was a second camera which showed the person walking into an alley but the exit of that had no CCTV pointed at it. Other local cameras had shown Jessica nothing while the quality of the images and the way the person kept their hood forward, angling their face away from the recording devices, ensured there was no clear shot.

The hand had been out in the sun for the best part of twelve hours with no one noticing. It wasn't necessarily a surprise because it had been left slightly away from the main path on a grassy area and Jessica again thought the person who had left it must have known the district incredibly well. Their audacity was unbelievable.

It also proved beyond any doubt that whoever was leaving the appendages wanted them to be found. The blind spot in the cameras around the cathedral could have given them an opportunity to walk through in a crowd of people during daylight, break off to leave the hand and then walk back out again in another group of pedestrians. They hadn't done that though, going out of their way to show off. With the fact the person had sent her Lewis Barnes's finger directly too, she felt as if they were leaving her a trail, wanting her to find out why the men had been targeted. They obviously didn't want to give her too much information, presumably in case it implicated themselves.

The day after Jessica had gone through the video footage saw the local newspapers and television news bulletins lead off with the still-shot of the figure waving at the camera. Phone calls had started to come in from the public but there wasn't much to go on as the person's face wasn't visible. Jessica left a rather grumpy Rowlands to deal with those as she journeyed around the country with Izzy speaking to the other members of the rugby team.

Cole seemed convinced the rugby connection was key but the more she spoke to the players, the more Jessica began to think there was some other link they hadn't yet found. It became clear the team had got up to various misdeeds but, through the stories people told, Jessica didn't believe it amounted to much more than drunken stupidity and immaturity. A few players acted a little evasively as others seemingly spilled everything they knew. Some were married and wanted to meet away from their partners, others had no problems talking in front of them. Most of the players told her what had happened to Michael Wright and almost all of them seemed genuinely sorry for it. The two detectives told all of them that three of their teammates had been harmed and they should be extra careful and report anything suspicious immediately to the police. Putting all ten into protective custody was impractical, especially given the distance between them all.

Jessica and Izzy were sitting on a train back to Manchester after visiting the final player. It had been two and a half days of travelling, talking and then travelling again. Their carriage was fairly quiet and both women had tried to sleep without success.

'What do you reckon?' Izzy asked sleepily.

Jessica was in the seat opposite and couldn't stop herself yawning. 'I think we've done too much moving around this week.'

'Not got us anywhere though, has it?'

'No, most of the players were just a bit embarrassed. I always knew young men had dirty minds but I could have done without hearing about those strippers.'

'Yeah, some of the practical jokes were a bit extreme but none of it was too serious, was it? Nothing worse than what you'd see in some town centres on a Friday night.'

'Exactly. One or two might have been holding back but, between this lot, Jacob and the two Dave spoke to, I think we probably heard more or less everything. It's not as if there were any clear motives for someone external to be coming after them and I don't reckon any of the ones we spoke to were involved.'

'Did you speak to Dave?'

'Yeah. He was pretty pissed off at spending three days talking to members of the public but he'd also been out to talk to the friends Jacob had been with the evening he was last seen.'

'Did they say much?'

'Just that they'd been to the pub after work and that was the last they'd seen of him. The samples from his mother matched the hand too so we know for sure it's his. It would just be nice to get some closure for all these people. We've got his parents, Lewis Barnes's mum and Charlie Marks not knowing if their relatives are alive or dead.'

As she spoke, Jessica heard the text message alert tone on her phone and took the device out of her jacket pocket. They must have been in between good reception areas because she had two missed calls from the station even though it hadn't rung. There was a text message too. Izzy noticed Jessica's surprise at the content.

'What?' the constable asked.

Jessica gulped with surprise. 'January Forrester has handed herself in.'

15

Any tiredness Jessica had been feeling evaporated instantly. The rest of the train journey seemed to take twice as long as it actually did while she fumed each time it stopped. Jessica tried not to act too angrily when Izzy pointed out it was in fact running on time. When they finally arrived back in Manchester, a taxi took them to Longsight and Jessica almost forgot how hot it was as she hurried through the entrance. The humidity hit her as the desk sergeant said, 'Suspect's downstairs,' and she walked past him.

Before going to see the woman, Jessica took Izzy to find Rowlands. They eventually discovered him in the canteen with a full plate of chips in front of him. The two women sat in a pair of seats across the table from him. 'How's the diet?' Jessica said.

'What diet?'

'Exactly. You should be looking after yourself a bit better now you're the wrong side of thirty.'

'I need something to keep me going after all the shite you left me with. I can say this with total honesty – the general public are complete morons. We've had every type of maniac calling in over the past couple of days while you've been on holiday. Someone reckoned this black cape woman was living in their shed. There've been loads more calling in to say their wife, daughter or neighbour owns a cloak a bit like the one in the pictures. It's like the Salem witch trials or something.'

'Firstly, we've not been on holiday, we've spent most of our time sat on trains and in taxis. Secondly, isn't *The Crucible* a bit high-brow for you?'

Rowlands screwed a couple of chips into his mouth. 'I don't know why you're so surprised.'

'Maybe because you have potato stuck to your chin,' Jessica said. 'It doesn't give off a message that says "literary expert". Anyway, what's going on with January?'

The constable wiped his chin and swallowed his mouthful. 'It was a bit of a weird one. Everyone was working as normal and then a call came through from reception looking for you. There was hardly anyone around so I went through to the front and January was standing there with her arms crossed. The guy on the desk didn't even know who she was because she'd walked in asking for you.'

'What did she say?'

'Nothing, she just asked if you were around. I cautioned her then one of the guys took her to the cells. The DCI was upstairs but he said to wait for you, even if it took until tomorrow. She's downstairs with the duty solicitor. Do you want her bringing up?'

'No, sod it, she can wait a while.' Jessica looked at the woman sat next to her. 'Do you want something to eat?'

'Anything but chips,' Izzy replied. 'For some reason I've gone right off them.'

The three detectives sat and ate, catching up on news

from the past couple of days. Dave said DCI Cole had sent around an email the previous day reminding everyone about the community engagement programme that would be going on through the summer. Unsurprisingly not too many people had put their names down. Jessica didn't know when the careers day was but figured it couldn't be too far off with the schools breaking up soon for the summer. She hoped the chief inspector would realise how busy she was and forget all about it.

Jessica had to admit she was actually quite enjoying working with a small team of people. There was a good chemistry between her and the two constables and she figured they were performing as well as they could do. Any complaining was very much tongue-in-cheek and there was a lot of mutual respect, even if it might not be apparent to other people, given their bickering.

Dave ribbed Jessica about the bridesmaid dress she might have to wear, although she gave nothing away, while Izzy thought up more possibilities for what his tattoo might really say. Most of them seemed to involve words relating to various parts of the male anatomy.

After days of seemingly working non-stop, Jessica felt a lot clearer following fifteen minutes away from the job and, in essence, enjoying a laugh with her mates.

'I guess it's time to go see what January has to say for herself,' she said. 'Who's coming in with me?'

'You go, Iz,' Dave said. 'I've got some bits to finish anyway.'

'Great, I thought I was going to have to make you two paper, scissors, stone for it.'

Jessica and Izzy walked through to the interview room and asked one of the officers nearby to bring January up if she'd finished speaking to the solicitor. They had to wait a short while until there was a knock at the door and their suspect was led in along with her legal representative.

January looked remarkably different from the last time Jessica had seen her. She had no make-up on, while brown roots were beginning to appear, clashing with the rest of her long black hair. She wasn't wearing black clothes and instead had on a pair of jeans with trainers and a hooded top. Someone had set up a desk fan, which was rotating as it blew air around the room.

The woman didn't look up from the table during the caution and introductions. 'Are you all right, January?' Jessica asked.

'Fine.' There was a definite tone of resignation in her voice.

'Where have you been since we last saw you?'

'Around. With friends. I don't want to say.' Jessica thought that was probably fair enough. If people had really been hiding her, they hadn't broken the law because it wasn't as if she had absconded from custody and there was no real need to push it considering that wasn't a priority.

'Why did you hand yourself in?'

'I was tired of staying indoors. I've not done anything wrong but I realised the longer I stayed away the worse it looked. I know I shouldn't have disappeared.'

'Why did you?'

'All the stuff in the papers at first and after you spoke to me. I was scared because I know how it all looked.'

'How do you think it looked?'

January sighed. 'Well, Lewis had gone missing and the only stuff you had was about that person in the black cape thing. Obviously I've got one, so you were going to come after me. Vicky was calling me and I couldn't cope.'

'You should know, we found a sample of Lewis's blood on your kitchen floor.'

January looked up from the table to her solicitor and then finally met Jessica's eyes for the first time. She seemed on the brink of tears. 'I'm surprised it was only the kitchen. If you look closely enough there's probably some of mine around the place too. We didn't have the most normal of relationships.' She turned her arms over and rolled the sleeves on her hoody up, revealing the scars Jessica had seen a glimpse of before. 'The only reason I got charged for scratching him was because Vicky made him complain. He hit me too but I never said anything. It was just what we did. He'd tell you if he was here.'

Jessica nodded gently. She had no way of knowing it was true but, as she looked at the young woman's face, she believed her. She also realised there was a problem brewing because January hadn't been charged with anything and, given she had a pretty good explanation for why there was blood in her flat, she hadn't actually committed an offence. When she had been first arrested, she had been given police bail, which only meant she had to reappear at the station at a later date. Not answering that bail wasn't necessarily uncommon and, if the investigation was still ongoing, a suspect would usually just be sent a letter saying their bail had been extended. January hadn't turned up when she was supposed to but it wasn't enough to hold her for very long and, unless they were going to charge her with something relating to the disappearance of her boyfriend, they wouldn't be able to keep her for longer than maybe a night. The duty solicitor would have told her that.

Because she had surrendered they would simply have the usual length of time to hold her as they couldn't keep bringing her in for interview without the formal charge. Regardless of any of that, Jessica knew they had nothing on the woman because there was no law about staying with friends for a couple of weeks. Despite their best efforts, they couldn't connect her to the other victims and, aside from the blood on their kitchen floor, nothing to link her to anything untoward happening to her boyfriend either.

'I'm going to ask you about some names and show you some pictures,' Jessica said. 'Can you tell me if you know the people?' Jessica had up-to-date photos of Edward Marks and Jacob Chrisp but January said she didn't recognise either of them. Jessica again thought the woman was being honest.

Jessica re-checked the details of her boyfriend's disappearance but ultimately January had nothing to add. She either genuinely knew nothing or was very good at hiding it. She certainly wasn't evasive and when her solicitor went to step in on a couple of occasions, the woman bypassed him, answering anyway.

Jessica had reached the end of anything she could reasonably hope to get from the interview and January had replied to everything without complaint. 'Is there anything you want to add?' Jessica asked.

January shrugged. 'Just that I miss him.'

Jessica said nothing and the woman was escorted back to the cells.

'Are we going to charge her?' Izzy asked when it was just them left in the room.

'With what? Being in a mutually abusive relationship? Knowing someone who went missing? We can't prove she's done anything wrong.'

'So are you going to let her go?'

'I don't know. I'll talk to Jack but it's not as if we have anything to take to the CPS. Conspiracy to wear dark clothing isn't going to cut it.'

'Only with the fashion police. What do you think about her?'

'Wrong person in the wrong place at the wrong time who just happens to have a similar taste in clothing to whoever we are looking for. We already had her in without charge before she skipped out and we can't keep arresting her. She seemed happy to cooperate this time and we didn't find anything except that dried blood at her house. Considering the two of them lived together, it's not necessarily a surprise. If you're chopping carrots in your kitchen, accidentally nick yourself and drip blood on the floor, it doesn't prove much, does it?'

'So we're screwed basically?' Diamond said.

'Exactly. I'll go upstairs and see what Jack reckons, then

have a chat with the custody sergeant. You may as well nick off. The last few days have just blended into one. I don't even know what time it is.'

Jessica walked back through the station, taking her suit jacket off. After going from the interview room where there was a fan back into the main areas, the heat felt stifling again. She walked up the stairs hoping Cole hadn't gone home for the day. She could see through the window of his office that he was still sitting in his chair. As he waved her in, she saw in his face how things were weighing on him. The worry lines across his forehead seemed to have deepened and he looked older than he had a few weeks earlier. She thought all the years of staying calm whatever the circumstances were finally catching up with him. Sometimes everyone needed a sweary five minutes to get it out of their system.

He obviously knew January had handed herself in but they were both in agreement they had nothing they could take to the CPS to ultimately charge her with. Cole suggested keeping her in overnight on the off-chance anything else came in from the phone calls. The custody sergeant would likely agree, simply because she had disappeared, but they both knew it was unlikely something would turn up and they would end up releasing her in the morning anyway.

'Are you okay, Sir?' Jessica asked. The chief inspector looked very tired.

Almost as if on cue, he yawned. 'Yes, thanks for asking. Just lots of pressure from above because of Christine Johnson. We're really struggling, if I'm honest.'

'Anything I can help with?' Jessica didn't really mean it seeing as she was busy enough but it sounded like the right thing to say.

'Um . . . maybe.' Jessica's heart sank, realising she could have talked herself into more work. 'How about tomorrow, you spend the day with Jason. I know you get on well. Just go over everything. I'll get Louise to have a look over your things. Maybe it all just needs a fresh pair of eyes?'

Jessica wasn't overly pleased with the idea but thought it couldn't do much harm if it was only for a day. Maybe he was right and a new viewpoint on each case could get things moving.

'All right, I'll come in tomorrow and bail January, then trail Jason for the day. If anything happens, though, I want someone to call me straight away.'

'Of course. I'm not suggesting anything permanent. It's Friday tomorrow then we've got the summer fete thing the day after.'

'That's this weekend?'

Cole yawned again. 'Yes, I put it all in an email. Didn't you see it? The super's big on the community engagement thing. I said you'd all get the time back.'

Jessica tried not to sound too annoyed 'Isn't that the kind of thing we have officers in uniform for? No one's going to want to talk to me.'

'I don't know, you have all this crime scene stuff on television nowadays. I think you'll be surprised. Thanks for signing up for the careers day thing too.'

Jessica couldn't be bothered telling him it wasn't her who had done so. 'No worries. Will you pass all the messages on to Jason and Louise about plans for tomorrow?'

'Yeah, believe me I think they'll be grateful to have a change for a day.'

Jessica said goodbye and left. After the grind the week had turned into, she really didn't mind having one day to think about something else. She wondered how Louise might react to Dave and Izzy's bickering and sent them both text messages to let them know what was going on.

The next day she arrived at the station with a plan to check the phone calls from the night before and then put January out of her misery. A night in the cells would have hopefully taught her a lesson that she should cooperate with them in future. As she arrived, there was a small van parked outside reception belonging to the Scene of Crime team. They were a common sight at crime scenes but not usually at the station. Jessica walked into reception and asked the desk sergeant what was going on.

'DCI's down at the HR office.'

Jessica didn't need a fuller answer than that to have a pretty good idea what had happened. She rushed through the corridors until she saw a small crowd of officers at the entrance to the station's main admin room. Cole was there and saw her coming.

'Ah, I didn't want to call you in especially,' he said.

'We got another package, didn't we?'

'Yes.'

'Does it look like the other ones?'

'Yes.'

'Was it addressed to me?'

The chief inspector didn't say anything, nodding instead. Jessica felt a chill ripple down her back – someone had sent her a finger that most likely belonged to Jacob Chrisp.

'Have they opened it yet?'

'No. Someone from the department flagged it up and they're going to take it back to Bradford Park.'

Jessica thought for a moment. 'If it turns out to be something I bought off eBay, can I have it back?'

Cole burst out laughing unexpectedly. 'I'll ask.'

'Did you see from the postmark when it was sent?'

'Some time yesterday afternoon. It looks like it was put in a post box too like the others.'

Jessica nodded, knowing that was what he was going to say. 'That rules January out then – she was in the cells downstairs while whoever did this was mailing me a present.'

16

It was hard for Jessica not to feel targeted as twice now somebody had sent her a finger directly. She knew they could easily have got her name through the media coverage but that wasn't the point. One of the things drummed into you through training was not to take things personally but it was hard not to when someone was addressing body parts to you. She wondered if the person was actually watching her, or if they knew where she lived.

The one thing she did feel grateful for is that nothing had yet been sent to her flat. She wasn't sure how she might take it if something like that happened. One of the ways you coped with the horrific things you sometimes had to deal with was to try as best you could to keep a separate home and work life. If a person crossed that line it wouldn't be the kind of thing she would be able to put to the back of her mind. It seemed obvious whoever was leaving the hands and sending her fingers wanted her to put the pieces together to figure out whatever point they were making but, if that was true, why couldn't they make it more obvious?

Cole asked if she was all right and Jessica said she was, even though she didn't really feel it. It didn't take long for the lab team to leave with the package. The fact it had been sent while January was in custody didn't entirely show she had nothing to do with it as she could have an accomplice but, given everything else they knew, it seemed they could let her go and pretty much rule her out of their immediate investigation.

As January was being re-bailed, Jessica gave the woman her card and asked her to get in contact if she could think of any new information.

After the morning's events, Cole said Jessica didn't have to work with Reynolds if she didn't feel like it but, seeing as they would have to wait for results on the package from the laboratories in any case, Jessica figured not much else had changed.

First she went to talk to Cornish who was sitting in their office for the first time in what seemed like a long while. She still seemed a little frosty but they were at least cordial to each other. Jessica handed over the hard-copy files and showed her colleague where things were on the computer system. The sergeant thanked her, then Jessica went to Reynolds's office. Somehow he had managed to get himself a large fan that was propped up against a filing cabinet. Jessica thought the room must have been the coolest in the building.

'How'd you get your hands on that?' she asked, nodding towards the fan.

The inspector laughed. 'Pure and simple theft.'

Jessica reacted with mock horror. 'In a police station?'

'If anyone else asks, I'll deny it to my grave. Either that or pin it on someone else.'

'What's the plan for today then?'

Jessica noticed how tired her former office mate was

looking. He pointed towards a couple of files on his desk but there were visible bags around his eyes. 'I thought maybe read through these and then we'll go see George Johnson this afternoon. I'll show you what's on the computer system too. A lot of it is just cuttings though. There's not much in our files that hasn't been in the papers – he tends to do most of his talking through the media.'

'I've not really had time to see what's been on the news. I only know what's been said in our morning briefings.'

'Fair enough, maybe you'll see something we haven't?'

Jessica wasn't convinced. 'Does he know we're going to see him later?'

'I cleared it with his PA. I think he likes us visiting his house because a photo ends up in the paper. He asked us around last week even though he had nothing to say.'

Jessica had rarely heard of something so formal. 'You've got to go through a secretary to book time with him?'

'We could just barge in but we're never sure where he is. He's been in London a couple of times this week.' Jessica was grateful she didn't have to deal with him as barging into places was very much her style.

She sat in a spare chair and began to read but found it hard to concentrate. As much as she thought it a good idea to look at each other's cases for a day, she couldn't get her mind away from her own. Her eyes skimmed the words but she found herself drawn to the pictures, almost like a child pretending to read. As the inspector had said, a lot of the items in their dossier were simply cuttings from various newspapers. There were plenty of photos of the MP and his wife together grinning in a posed fashion for the camera. Jessica couldn't see a single picture that didn't look staged.

If she hadn't known who he was but had just been shown a photo of George Johnson and asked to guess what his profession was, Jessica's first response would always have been 'politician'. He looked exactly like she expected an MP to look. The man was somewhere in his late fifties or early sixties. He had silver hair that was constantly swept away from his face. Most of the images had him in a full suit but the odd one showed him in an open-necked shirt, presumably showing people he knew how to relax. None of it looked particularly real to Jessica, as if the man's life was lived through fake smiles and expensive clothing. She hated having her own picture taken but, even given that, there were plenty around of her with food dropped down her clothing and silly faces being pulled as someone took her off-guard.

Some people hated politicians just because of what they were but Jessica had never really shared that disdain for anyone because of their job. She judged people on the way they acted, not on what they did but, even without meeting him, there was something about George Johnson that didn't sit quite right with her. Jessica tried to put those feelings to the back of her mind as she didn't want to prejudice her opinion before meeting him but, having skimmed through the newspaper reports, it seemed clear the focus of a lot of what he had been saying was about himself, not his missing wife.

After lunch, Reynolds drove them to the politician's house. The area wasn't affluent as such, but the road

George Johnson lived on ran between Platt Fields Park and Birchfields Park in the Rusholme area of the city. It was covered by the Gorton constituency he represented and provided an odd mix of large properties set back from the road that were within walking distance of a notorious area where plenty of trouble originated from. As they pulled onto the street, a few teenage girls in school uniform walked past, sharing a cigarette between them. A private girls' school was on the edge of the park and Jessica figured their lunch break must be coming to a close. They were in a marked car and, as Reynolds drove past, Jessica saw one of the girls trying to hide the cigarette behind her back.

Although Jessica knew roughly where the MP lived, she didn't know exactly which house belonged to him. Reynolds parked just past where the girls had been walking and the two detectives got out of the vehicle. Jessica followed her boss further down the street but soon saw a familiar face sitting in a nearby car.

'Just give me a minute,' she said to the inspector, who carried on walking. Jessica knocked on the car's window, crouching to grin at Garry Ashford through the passenger window. The journalist opened his door and got out before coming around to where Jessica was now sitting on his bonnet.

'What are you doing here?' Garry asked.

'I couldn't let this new girlfriend of yours have you to herself. I'm here to declare my undying love for you. Let's go to Vegas and make it official.'

The journalist laughed. 'I'd rather pay for it.'

Jessica could tell from the look on his face he was

joking. 'Oi, I seem to remember you asking me out once upon a time. At a funeral, no less.'

'You must have misheard me.'

Jessica smiled. 'All right, get yourself a girlfriend and suddenly you're all confident. What's going on anyway?'

'Not much, still sat here waiting for something to happen. Even the editor is getting bored now though. Unless something comes out today, I'm back in the office from Monday. The TV cameras went home a couple of days ago and it's all winding down. Why are you here?'

'Job swap for a day seeing as none of our major cases are going anywhere.'

'Can I quote you on that?'

Jessica snorted. 'Piss off but thanks for that piece the other day anyway.'

Garry smiled. 'No worries. I'm just hedging my bets you pull your finger out and do your jobs properly so I can get my exclusive at the end of it all.'

'All right, don't worry about me. I'll see you soon – and say "hello" to Mrs Ashford for me. Hopefully she'll be released from that mental hospital sometime soon.'

Jessica stood up from the journalist's bonnet and followed the direction Reynolds had gone in. He was waiting for her around fifty yards down the road next to some huge metal gates at the bottom of a driveway. She saw a nearby photographer taking their picture as the inspector spoke into an intercom box and a side gate buzzed open. The drive arched upwards, looping around a perfectly manicured piece of garden. Parked in front of the property was a sparklingly clean black vehicle that Jessica would have guessed cost more than she earned in a year. The house itself wasn't as big as the one Charlie Marks was living in but still looked impressive. There was a wide mock-Tudor front door and the window frames were in the same style. Jessica noticed a man on a ladder trimming a hedge on the far side of the grass.

Reynolds led Jessica towards the front door and rang the doorbell. A woman answered after a few seconds and walked them into a downstairs room lined with hardback books. The two detectives were each offered leather-backed armchairs and the woman asked in broken English with an eastern European accent if they wanted tea. After the heat outside, Jessica found the house refreshingly cool but still didn't fancy a hot drink and they both declined.

As the woman walked away, Jessica met her boss's eyes and he answered the question she hadn't needed to ask. 'It's the maid. I think she does all the cooking and cleaning too.'

Jessica hadn't experienced a situation quite like this before. Usually when you wanted to speak to someone, whether they were a suspect or a witness, you simply did it. Making appointments and being welcomed by a maid was far from the norm.

'Have you interviewed the maid?' Jessica asked.

'Yes, her statement is one of the few things that hasn't ended up in the papers but she didn't have much to say. When the wife went missing, she was shopping.' Jessica realised she should really have read that statement earlier in the morning but Reynolds didn't seem to mind going over what would be old ground for him.

While they waited, Jessica heard her phone's text tone sounding. It was a message from Rowlands telling her the contents of the envelope addressed to her had been confirmed as a finger that came from Jacob Chrisp's hand. It was exactly what she'd expected but reminded her of the feelings of being targeted. Jessica sent him a message back to thank him, then put her phone on silent.

A few minutes later, a man she recognised as George Johnson swept into the room. He moved quickly and, even though he was in his own home, was still dressed in a sharp navy-blue suit with a matching tie. The two detectives stood and he offered his hand. 'Detective Inspector Reynolds,' the politician said as he shook hands with the inspector, then turned to Jessica. 'And . . .' he added, fishing for Jessica's name.

'DS Daniel,' Jessica replied, also shaking his hand. He squeezed hard, almost as if it were a competition. It didn't hurt her as such but certainly took her by surprise. Jessica had always been annoyed by people that took firm handshakes to the extreme. She had once worked with a lawyer whose grip bordered on common assault. Not only that but Jessica hadn't met a single person with a firm handshake who she'd got on with. In her mind there was a direct correlation between how hard you shook someone's hand and how much of a dick you were.

'Nice to meet you,' the politician said but he had already turned away to sit down, looking towards Reynolds. 'What is it you wanted me for?'

Jessica saw that the inspector met the man's gaze.

'Nothing in particular, Mr Johnson, we just wanted you to go over a few of the key details again.'

'Is this actually leading anywhere?' The politician wasn't exactly angry but he wasn't hiding his disdain for them either.

Reynolds kept a calm tone. 'I can assure you we're completely focused on finding your wife. Sometimes going over things witnesses have already told us can help clarify things in their own minds as well as ours.'

'You do realise I'm a very busy person?'

Reynolds started to speak but Jessica got in before him. 'You do realise your wife is missing?' Both the inspector and the MP stared at her but she defiantly met the politician's gaze. She didn't know why she had spoken but most people whose partner had gone missing could have only dreamed of the type of attention the man in front of her was getting. Jessica thought of Vicky Barnes and the way she had struggled to get the police to focus on her son's disappearance. George Johnson had almost their full department at his disposal and was complaining because he was busy.

He clearly wasn't happy about Jessica's tone of voice but, instead of showing any anger, he let his face fall. 'Of course, excuse my abruptness.'

She thought his change in approach seemed very forced but nodded, letting Reynolds pick the conversation back up, having felt his accusing stare after her outburst.

Although the two officers had shared an office, they had rarely worked directly on anything together. Because they had held an equal position as sergeants at the time, they tended to deal with their own cases rather than work with each other. She guessed he might have been regretting allowing her to come with him.

Reynolds went over most of the key facts of the case with the MP and Jessica figured a lot of it was for her benefit. The man reiterated that he had spoken to his wife while working in London but by the time he returned to the family home the following day, there was no sign of her. He insisted they'd had no fallings-out and had enjoyed a twenty-seven-year marriage and were very proud of their children. Any leads that could have come through the offspring were non-starters as one was at university in Paris, while the other worked for the European Parliament.

Given the woman had gone missing while the maid was shopping and her passport and other key documents were left at the house, there wasn't much else to go on. As the inspector had finished going over things, Jessica did have a thought. 'Do you have a private security system, Mr Johnson?' she asked.

The man hadn't acknowledged Jessica since her previous outburst but turned to face her. 'What do you mean?'

'I'm not sure – it's a big house. I'm sure a lot of people have internal video systems or alarms. I was just wondering if you had anything like that?'

Although she had only skimmed through the files, she hadn't seen anything mentioned about a security system being present on the property and hadn't seen any cameras herself. Given the obvious wealth on display, and the fact the man spent long periods of time away from the house, she thought there was a good chance there could be something. She noticed Reynolds lean forward in his seat, as if it was something he didn't know the answer to.

'We have an alarm but that's only set at night,' Mr Johnson said. As he spoke, the maid returned with a tray holding a large jug of water and three tumblers. She placed it on a table in between them.

'What about cameras? Even just one watching the entrance or the front gate?' Jessica asked.

'Not that I know of.' As the maid poured water into the glasses, ice cubes tinkled while she moved from one to the other.

'What other security measures are there?' Jessica went on.

She was taken by surprise as the maid looked at her and spoke. 'There is a camera.'

The three men stared at the woman who finished pouring and put the jug back down. 'I'm sorry?' Jessica said.

'What camera?' Mr Johnson added.

'A video machine that points at the gate.' The maid seemed confused, stumbling over her words with her accent more pronounced. 'The other Mr Johnson put it in?'

'My son?'

'Yes. The other Mr Johnson.'

'When? Why don't I know this?' Jessica couldn't figure out if the man was angry or just confused.

The maid continued nervously. 'Mrs Johnson was worried about who might come. I don't know when.'

'Where is your son?' Reynolds asked.

The politician seemed stunned, his calm demeanour

forgotten. 'In Luxembourg. He's been out there for five months now.'

'Why didn't you tell us this when we spoke to you before?' the inspector asked the maid.

The woman looked confused and shrugged her shoulders. She used her hands while she spoke, as if constantly searching for the correct words. 'You didn't ask. I didn't know important.' She looked back to her boss. 'Am I in trouble?'

The man shook his head. 'No, no, not at all.'

'Do you know where the camera is?' Jessica asked the maid.

The woman waved her hands from side to side. 'I don't know. The other Mr Johnson just told Mrs Johnson it was pointing at the gate. He wasn't talking to me.' She looked around at the politician and hurriedly added, 'I don't listen in to things.'

The man nodded and Jessica couldn't read his face. She looked to Reynolds. 'We're going to have to either talk to the son or get some electrical experts in who know more than we do.'

Her boss had already started to stand, clearly thinking along the same lines. 'I'll try to contact the son first to find out if the camera that's present actually stores the images.' He turned back to the maid who was standing next to the politician, addressing the pair of them. 'Do you know why the camera was placed? Is it there for you to see who's at the gate?'

The man was shaking his head as he stood. 'I have no idea. We have the intercom for people to say who's at the front. I didn't even know there was a camera. Until recently, I didn't spend much time here. I was either in our flat in London and we have a place in France where we usually spend the summer.'

Reynolds asked Mr Johnson to phone his son as Jessica went to look for the camera. The maid insisted she didn't know where it was so she was on her own. It seemed almost inconceivable there could be a camera on the politician's property he didn't know about. The maid said Christine Johnson had wanted it putting in but why would she do so without her husband's knowledge and, if he did know about it, why hadn't he told them?

Jessica let herself back out of the front door, walking down the driveway towards the front gate. When she reached it, she turned, looking for areas that would have a decent visibility of the opening. She peered at the large gateposts but there was nothing on top. Jessica walked back up the paved area, glancing from side to side. She couldn't see anything on the house itself and, even if there was, it would have had to be zoomed in significantly to have a clear view.

After walking to the house and back to the gate another time, she decided to have a look at a large oak tree that was sprawled on the edge of the garden. The main trunk was thick and must have been many years old but the branches themselves had been trimmed at some point not too long ago. Jessica squinted up at the top of the trunk and, in a large circular knot, finally saw what she was looking for. It was too high to reach but there was definitely some kind of metal-looking object angled towards the entrance.

She returned inside where Reynolds was standing next to George Johnson talking on a portable home phone. Not long after she entered, the inspector passed the phone to the other man and moved next to Jessica.

'I found it,' she said. 'It's in a knot of that giant tree out there. It's no surprise no one else saw it; you never would unless you were looking.'

Reynolds nodded. 'The son says he put the camera in for his mother because she was worried about being on her own a lot. He doesn't know if his dad knew or not.'

'Does it keep recordings?' Jessica asked.

'He said the camera is wireless and stores a still image once every minute. I didn't really understand it all but he said everything is recorded on a web server and, unless he specifically deletes something, everything is kept.'

'Why didn't he tell you this before?'

'Maybe he thought we knew? I have no idea. I'm going to talk to some of the computer team out at Bradford Park and get them to contact the son. The system only takes a photo every minute but, unless she jumped over the hedge or left in between snaps, hopefully we'll have something of her.'

17

With little more she could contribute, Jessica cheekily asked Garry Ashford for a lift back to the station as Reynolds was going to be a little while and would need the car. The journalist obliged and she told him he might want to make a check-call or two to the police press office a little later.

Back at Longsight, Cole already knew what they had found and had been in contact with one of the computer technicians to discover how long things would take. Jessica didn't understand the technical talk entirely but there was some sort of problem they were trying to sort out with George Johnson's son that wasn't proving easy as he was having problems accessing the Internet wherever he was.

Jessica checked in with Rowlands and Diamond, neither of whom sounded like they'd had a fun day. Cornish had made them talk her through each step of where they were up to in the investigation, telling them how she would have done things differently. Jessica thought it was a sign she had matured, even if only a little, that those revelations hadn't sent her into an instant rage. A few years ago it certainly would have done but she was at the point where, if someone thought they could do a better job, they were welcome to try – and have severed fingers addressed to them instead of her. Either way, it didn't seem as if they had got any further and, once again, it looked as if they were going to have to work their way through the full list of college-leavers in an effort to find anything to move the case forward.

That evening, Reynolds called Jessica at home. He thanked her for her help, refusing to accept her point that the afternoon's discovery was just luck and not much to do with her. From the tone of his voice, she figured a lot of the gratitude was simply down to relief that something had happened. She knew both the inspector and Cole were under a lot of pressure to make a breakthrough. He told her the computer experts had finally managed to figure out with the Johnsons' son what was going on with the stored images. There were tens of thousands to scan through and the naming of the files wasn't too efficient but, after hours of work, they had isolated three still-shots 'of interest'.

From the day Christine Johnson had gone missing, one image showed the maid heading out via the gate at the front which was presumably to go shopping as she had told them, leaving Mrs Johnson alone in the house. Twenty minutes later a faded red van pulled up outside the large double gates at the end of the driveway. The vehicle was in the next three pictures before disappearing, meaning it had been outside for less than four minutes. In the final image, the rear door of the van had been open and there was a faded logo visible which they were now trying to identify.

The bad news was that, with the gap in between the photos, no actual people had been seen but it did at least give them something to work with. With the high-profile nature of the case, experts were going to spend the week-end enhancing the images as best they could in order to release them to the media. Reynolds also said he was look-ing into either getting permission to go to Luxembourg to visit the son, or seeing if they could arrange for him to return home to be interviewed. The man insisted he had set up the camera at the request of his mother and assumed it was done with his father's knowledge. Given the lack of time his dad spent at the family home, it was plausible but certainly unusual.

When she woke up the next day, Jessica had almost for-gotten that she had to go to the summer fete as part of the dreaded community engagement plan. She had finally read Cole's email properly and it was clear a lot of it had been written under duress from people above him. Three separate times it mentioned that instructions had come down from the superintendent, presumably to stop the rest of the officers thinking too badly of him. The event was at Crowcroft Park, the recreation area closest to their station, and there was very little information other than the venue and a rota for the times they should arrive.

It was another scorching day and Jessica couldn't remember a longer spell of uninterrupted good weather since she had moved to the area. When she arrived, Jessica could see the park itself was parched with large areas of sand-coloured grass. A lot of people had come out seem-ingly because of the weather and the whole spectacle took Jessica back to a different age when she was young.

In the village where she'd grown up, there would always be a summer fair once a year. The whole population would descend on their local park where there would be a funfair, stalls selling homemade cakes and biscuits, various tables offering jumble-sale items for charities and all sorts of games going on. It was probably selective memory but it never seemed to rain on those days and she could remember her father with his big tanned arms carrying her around on his shoulders.

Jessica thought it was amazing how one thing could give you flashes of another. It was the smell of candyfloss as she walked through the park gates that most reminded her of the village fetes where she used to live. She couldn't even remember the last time she'd eaten any but the stall next to the entrance had a queue of children and she could almost see herself as one of the younger girls in line.

Jessica had arrived early and didn't know where the police's stall was so decided to go for a walk. She had her work suit on as it wouldn't have seemed right representing the force wearing her everyday clothes but she was feeling a little sweaty given the heat. A small ferris wheel was the obvious thing Jessica noticed as she strolled around. It was playing a cheesy fairground tune but the other noise that stood out was laughter. In doing a job that could be so dark at times, it was easy to forget the little things like this. Children weaved in between adults, running around excitedly as parents pushed empty pushchairs. A group of youngsters had started a game of rounders against a hedge and Jessica couldn't help but smile.

Her thoughts were interrupted by a tap on her shoulder.

She turned around and Izzy stood there grinning. She wasn't in her work clothes, instead wearing a long flowing white skirt and pale vest top. Jessica thought the woman's hair looked a brighter red, most likely because it wasn't tied back or perhaps because her clothes were lighter than usual. She was arm-in-arm with a man she introduced as her husband, Mal. He was a little older than her with greying patches of hair above his ears.

'You not on the stall today?' Jessica asked.

'Nah, just thought I'd come down and have a look at everything seeing as the sun's out.'

'Do you know where we're based?'

Izzy pointed towards an area on the far side of the park. 'It's over there. Jack's on the stall but not looking too happy. I think his wife and kids are around somewhere. It's mainly uniform but there are a couple of other detectives from the area there too. It's not just our lot.'

'Was it looking busy?'

'The press office team have got some games set up and are taking photos for the website. You can tell they're mad keen to make us look good in all of this. They'd just collared one of the local newspaper photographers too.'

Jessica didn't think it sounded her type of thing. 'I'll hide over here for a bit then. If they're looking for a good impression, the last thing they need is me telling off a bunch of kids.' Jessica remembered her colleague talking about the dispute over children she was having with her husband and saw what looked like an awkward glance sideways from Mal to his wife. 'I'll leave you to it,' she added.

Izzy said goodbye and the couple walked away still arm-in-arm. Jessica slowly made her way around the rest of the park towards the direction the constable had said their stall was in. The ambulance service and fire brigade had setups of their own and Jessica watched as the paramedics showed people how to perform CPR. She nodded at one of the workers she recognised and they shared a 'What are we doing here on a Saturday?' look.

The fire officers had a much larger stall and were showing people the dangers of chip-pan fires by deliberately pouring water on hot oil. Huge flames shot into the air and Jessica saw a group of gathered youngsters gasping at the heat. She wondered if the display was aiding awareness or simply putting ideas in the minds of potential young pyromaniacs. She concluded her suspicious mind was getting the better of her.

Eventually she saw the force's stall. Cole was handing out pencils to children and she could see the forced smile on his face. With the rota he had sent around, she was due to do a two-hour shift on the stall which would take them up to the day's end. He seemed relieved she was there, wiping the sweat away from his forehead as the line of children thinned.

'Are you all right?' Jessica asked.

'Yes but I'm glad you're here.' The man explained that press officers were running games of cops and robbers every half hour and there was a big pile of certificates for her to sign and give out to the participants. He said the day had gone well but his tired eyes told a different story. 'Did Jason call you last night? He said he was going to.'

'Yes, he told me about the stills from the camera. What do you reckon?'

Cole shrugged. 'I'm not really sure. The quality isn't great but the lab boys reckon they can enhance them. I guess we'll find out on Monday.'

'How is Jason?'

'Between you and me, I think he needs a day off. He's gone to the labs today just to watch.'

'Maybe he didn't want to get stuck here?'

The chief inspector knew her well enough to know she was joking and smiled back. 'I know it's a pain but the idea behind all of this is a noble one.' He nodded towards the children running around nearby. 'If we can get this lot not hating us from an early age it will be better for everyone.'

Jessica knew he was right. 'Are you off home now?'

'No, I said I'd help put everything back down later. The super was around earlier too. I'm going to nick off for a bit. My kids were definitely around here somewhere. I'll be back later, have fun.'

Jessica wouldn't have said she had 'fun' but the afternoon wasn't as bad as she thought it might have been. During a round of cops and robbers, two young boys collided with each other and the game had to be abandoned. It was the type of accident that would have health and safety officials filling in forms for the rest of the day but, with the ambulance service just a few stalls down, there was no harm done except for two bumped heads. At first, Jessica had to force herself not to laugh because of the comical way the youngsters had fallen over. They had both been racing in one direction while looking in another and run head-first into one another before bouncing and falling to the floor. There was an audible gasp from onlooking parents but Jessica was convinced she saw other adults trying not to laugh as well.

The DCI had been correct in that there were plenty of questions about her job from young people. The uniformed officers had the attention from the youngest children and they had a police car parked on the grass for people to sit in and look at the equipment they used. While the younger ones were drawn to the other officers, the teenagers who weren't hanging around in small groups pretending they were too cool to be there came to talk to her. One girl in particular wanted to talk about becoming a detective and although Jessica wanted to tell her the pay, hours and expectations were all terrible, she stayed on-message and gave a balanced assessment, telling her it was a hard profession that had its good days and bad days – but that the successes felt so good they outweighed everything else. Jessica wasn't sure if she believed it herself but it didn't seem right to go out of her way to put someone off just because she was feeling cynical.

After the accident, the head press officer decided to stop any further games. The idea of the day was to engage with the public and perhaps get a nice few photographs of the event into the local papers and, if they were really lucky, on the local television news. A picture of two boys crying with blood pouring from their heads didn't exactly give the right impression.

By the time it got to four o'clock, the crowds had started to dwindle. Cole returned and, along with some of the uniformed officers and the press office staff, began to pack the tables away. As they worked, the chief inspector broke away to answer his phone and, a few moments later, called Jessica over. He edged across into an area next to some benches where there weren't any members of the public.

'I've just had a fairly disturbing phone call,' he said.

'What's up?'

'Someone held up an off-licence on Stockport Road an hour ago.'

'Our end?' Jessica asked. Stockport Road was one of the main arteries in and out of Manchester city centre and ran for around five miles. Not far past the park they were in, it branched off.

'About a mile away. They had a knife.'

'Was anyone hurt?'

'No but they took a few hundred pounds.'

Jessica wondered why he was telling her. 'Why did you get the call? There must be someone at the station who can deal with things?'

Cole nodded. 'They had been. It wasn't because of the robbery that they called; it was because of the description of the person who did it.'

'What do you mean?'

'The robber was a woman wearing low heels and a long black hooded robe.'

18

Jessica was technically on a day off but didn't think twice about getting one of the uniformed officers to drive her to the off-licence in question. It was only a couple of miles away from the Longsight station and police tape was already set up around the premises, while Scene of Crime officers were on site.

One of the male forensics team let her into the shop and there was a beep as the front door opened. He led Jessica along an aisle which didn't interfere with the area they were inspecting, before she was pointed towards a door behind the counter. If it hadn't been for the presence of the officers and the fact she knew there had been a robbery, Jessica wouldn't have realised anything untoward had happened. The only sign was that, as she approached it, she could see the cash register open and empty.

The officer told her the shopkeeper owned the upstairs flat and was currently waiting there. 'Is there CCTV footage?' Jessica asked, nodding towards a camera above the door.

'Apparently but we haven't looked through it properly yet,' the officer said. 'The owner showed it to us so we could get an idea of the path the person took. We're going to take it back when we're finished.'

'Have you found anything?'

The officer shook his head. 'The robber was wearing gloves so we're not even looking for fingerprints but they didn't touch anything anyway. We're trying to isolate a few footprints. The video footage is going to be our best bet but we've got to get all of this done first.'

'Do you know if someone's taken the shopkeeper's statement yet?'

'I don't know. Someone is upstairs with him.'

Jessica thanked the man and walked through the door, finding herself alone in what looked like a storeroom. The overhead lights were on and a fan in the corner was blowing cool air around as it rotated. On her left were boxes of unopened crisps and chocolate bars plus a mop, bucket and a few other cleaning items resting against a wide chest freezer. There was another door at the back with a large bolt locked across while crates of beer cans and bottles were stacked underneath the staircase.

The stairs were old and wooden and each one creaked as Jessica walked up, holding onto the banister which rocked from side to side as she gripped it. There was a door at the top that appeared to be locked as Jessica pressed it, so she knocked instead. A uniformed female constable opened the door and they instantly recognised each other.

'I was wondering if it would be you they sent along,' the officer said.

'Yep, I'm the queen of short straws,' Jessica replied with a smile. The other officer went to turn around but Jessica continued, 'Has someone taken a statement? I was in a bit of a rush to get here and haven't come via the station.'

'One of the officers took it all down. It was only

midway through when he realised the connection because of the black cloak. He called it in for someone to pass on. It all goes a bit above us.'

The other officer turned again and led Jessica down a carpeted hallway into a joint living room and kitchen area. A man was sitting on a sofa but stood as she walked in. Jessica saw he was shorter than she was. He had slicked-back dark hair and didn't look as if he'd shaved in a while, with a tufty beard on his chin. The man was clearly still stunned by what had happened. A full cup of tea sat on a table in front of him and he nervously looked at the other officer as Jessica came into the room.

Jessica introduced herself, showing her identification. The man said his name was Victor Burnham and confirmed he owned and managed the shop. He appeared to calm down slightly, offering her an armchair opposite the sofa. The seat was uncomfortable and Jessica had to force herself not to wriggle as what felt like a series of thin wires dug into her back. As she looked around, she could see a lot of the furniture in the flat seemed dated. The sofa and the chair she was sitting in were a dirty cream with a mix of pink and purple flowers on the material. Everything from the carpet to the lights appeared covered in a thin layer of dust and, as she scanned around, she could smell a musty unclean scent too.

Perhaps because that was now in the front of her mind, but also because she didn't want to dive straight in and potentially unsettle the man, Jessica was careful with her first question. 'Do you live up here, Mr Burnham?'

He shook his head emphatically. 'No, no. Only when

there's a really early delivery. There's a bed just through there.' Victor pointed towards a closed door on the far side of the mini kitchen. 'I have young children and they have school and so on. It's not fair to wake them up at five when I have to get here.'

'So do you own this whole property?'

'Yes, I've got this and another shop a mile or so away then my wife and I have a separate house too. I manage this one and my brother runs the other.'

'Can you talk me through a normal Saturday?'

Victor nodded solemnly. 'I usually get here for around six, sometimes a little earlier. It's a big day with the papers. You have to sort out all the magazines and get everything onto the racks before we open at seven but there are the paperboys to organise too.'

'Does anyone help you?' Jessica asked.

'Only my wife sometimes, or my nephew. I guess . . .' The man tailed off and swallowed hard. 'I guess it's lucky my wife wasn't here today. We alternate Saturdays so we can each have time with the kids.'

Jessica allowed him a few moments to settle and made eye contact with the constable. The other woman went to the kitchen and returned with three glasses of water. Even though Victor hadn't touched his cup of tea, he drank from the glass and said 'thank you'.

'What else would happen on a regular Saturday?' Jessica asked when the man had re-settled.

'After the papers, we would open and there would usually be a bit of a rush before nine o'clock. It's not as bad as on a Sunday but we still sell a fair few newspapers on the weekends. Then it would calm down until lunchtime. On a weekday we get loads of people in for sandwiches and pasties. There's a cafe just down the rank but not everyone wants to stop. It's much quieter on a Saturday but we still get the odd workman in.'

'Can you tell me specifically about the incident today? I know you've talked to my colleague already and you don't have to go over things again if you don't want to.'

The man seemed weary but didn't object, finishing off his water. 'No, it's fine. It was around three o'clock and no one had come in for maybe fifteen minutes or so. I've got a little radio which sits under the counter. I was listening to the cricket and reading through one of the magazines. There's a buzzer security thing that goes off every time the main door is opened. I looked up and couldn't see anyone at first and glanced back to my magazine. It was just a moment but suddenly there was someone right in front of me.'

'What did they look like?'

'I don't know really. You know about the cloak, don't you?'

'Tell me.'

'It was a woman, maybe around my height, wearing this black robe thing. It had a hood pulled down over her face and I could only see her mouth.'

Jessica was hanging on his replies. 'How do you know it was a female?'

The man shook his head slightly as if it were a stupid question. 'The voice, it was a woman's voice. She was just so calm.'

'What did she say?'

'"Open the till".'

'That was it?'

'Well, she repeated it. It happened so quickly. You know when you think you've heard what somebody has said to you but it's not really gone in? It was like that. Then I saw the knife.'

Jessica knew she had to be careful with her words. 'What did it look like?'

'It was a kitchen knife, like something you might cut meat up with.'

'What did her voice sound like? Was there any type of accent?'

'I . . . I don't know. It just sounded normal, I wasn't thinking about it.'

It was what Jessica would have expected. 'Okay, that's fine,' she said. 'What happened after she repeated herself?'

'I just . . . it was like I was someone else. Have you ever felt like you're in a corner of a room watching yourself do something? It felt like somebody else was controlling me and I was just looking at things. I only know because I showed the people downstairs the video. I opened the register and stepped backwards.'

'What happened then?'

'She reached across and pulled the notes out. It's the one thing I clearly remember because there was a moment where she was on tiptoes stretching forward. It was just a fraction where I thought about . . . well, I don't know, trying to grab the knife or something. She was off-balance but it wasn't as if I really had time to think. As soon as it crossed my mind she had taken everything and moved away.'

Jessica could see he was starting to get a little emotional and there were tears in his eyes. He wiped them away and was almost shouting as he continued. 'It's not even the money but it could have been my wife, y'know? We've had our kids in here before . . . and I just did nothing.'

Jessica knew there wasn't much she could say. Even for a man who wasn't sexist at all, she guessed it would be hard to be robbed by anyone but perhaps the fact it was a woman made it a little worse.

'I'm sure there's nothing you could have done, Mr Burnham,' Jessica said as reassuringly as she could. The man shrugged, clearly fighting to stop himself crying. 'Did anything happen after she had taken the money?' Jessica added. 'Did you notice anyone else in the shop?'

The man shook his head again. 'I don't really remember. I think she just left.'

'Where is the camera footage stored, Mr Burnham?'

Victor pointed towards the bedroom door he had indicated before. 'It's in there, my brother put it in. The wires come up through the ceiling and it's all stored on a hard drive. Once a week I have to switch them over but it looks after itself apart from that. The system has been in for almost two years and this is only the second time I've ever used it. The first was just some lads nicking porno mags.'

'Did you report it?'

The man actually laughed a little as he answered. 'No, I knew the parents of one of them. I could've come to you but he was so terrified of me telling his mum, he paid for everything. I could've still reported him or whatever but what's the point? He's only fifteen or so.'

'Can you show me the footage from earlier?'

'Okay – I'm not very good with the equipment though.'

Victor stood, leading Jessica into the bedroom. It was a little larger than she would have guessed but shared the same stale smell as the rest of the flat. The bed was un-made, a duvet cover half on the floor and the sheets ruffled into the centre. The room wasn't very bright, the only illumination coming through one small window before the man turned on the lights.

A desktop computer was on a table with a large plastic-looking box next to it. Victor sat in front of the machine and pointed to the box. 'Those are the external hard drives,' he said, then indicated a set of wires running up the wall. 'It all connects to the cameras downstairs. The computer doesn't need to be on to record but it does if you want to watch anything back. I turned it on earlier.'

The man moved the mouse and the screen lit up, then he clicked around the screen to bring up a new window. 'I'm not brilliant with this but my wife's gone around to my brother's family's house so he can't come over. He'd be the best one to explain the system. I can show you this though.' After moving the mouse around some more, a new box appeared that had a still image looking at the front door of the shop from the inside. He then pressed a button on the key-board and the view cut to the camera that was over the top of the cash register looking down. He pointed out to Jessica which buttons moved the action forward and backwards and where she needed to press to change the camera angles.

'I'll let you look for yourself because you know as much as me now,' he said.

Victor stood and offered the seat to Jessica. He clearly didn't want to watch the footage again, moving across to the bed and starting to make it. Jessica sat as the constable stood behind her. It took her a few moments to get used to how everything worked and the thought crossed her mind that so much of what she'd been working on in the past few weeks revolved in one way or another around cameras.

The shop owner had left the video at the start of the morning's footage and, using the timestamps at the bottom of the screen, Jessica moved it forward to a little after half past two. She watched it at triple speed but there was only one visitor into the shop, a middle-aged man who didn't buy anything, before the timer clicked over to three o'clock. Jessica set the camera angle to the one watching the front door. At two minutes past, Jessica saw what she was waiting for. The door opened and a figure in a black cloak walked confidently into the shop. They shut the door behind them and turned into one of the aisles without looking up.

Jessica had to switch to the second camera angle and saw everything happen exactly as Victor said it had. It was chilling to watch the coolness the person moved with. There was no hesitation and not even a trace of anything that could be seen as emotion in the body language. If anything, the shop owner had underestimated the size of the knife. From the footage, Jessica could see it had been concealed in the wide sleeve of the gown and then taken out when they were halfway into the shop. It had a wide fearsome-looking blade and she could see why Victor had almost switched off mentally at the sight of it.

Jessica rewound the recording and watched it three times in a row, each time looking for different things. She tried to see if the gloves the figure was wearing looked like the ones that had been seen in the footage of the person leaving the hands. On the third viewing, she watched the shape of the robe and the way the person moved. The only time she could see the person's shoes properly was when they stretched across and snatched the cash, then walked away. There were only a few brief frames but they looked very similar to the style of low dark heels from the recordings taken in the city centre.

When she had looked for all she could, Jessica realised Victor wasn't in the room. She found him at the sink in the kitchen area washing up. 'Are there any cameras outside, Mr Burnham?'

He replied without turning. 'Not that belong to me. I've never noticed anything else.'

Jessica didn't know what else she could add. The forensics team would take the video and try to enhance some of the still frames in case there was a clear image of the person's face. From what she had seen, Jessica didn't think they would get one. The entire time she had been watching the video, Jessica had been looking for any sign to disassociate the robber from the person leaving the hands. When she had first heard about the robbery and throughout Victor's description, she had been thinking the person was a copycat.

Now, having watched the footage over and over, she just didn't know.

19

As much as she disliked the morning senior detective briefings, Jessica spent the rest of the weekend waiting for Monday's. It was largely because she wanted to hear other people's opinions about the robbery but also because she now felt she had a little invested in the disappearance of Christine Johnson after meeting the woman's husband.

If there was just one big case on the go, the briefings would usually be a wider affair where jobs would be assigned to other officers. Because of the way the squad had been split, the senior briefings had become a good way of sharing ideas before the respective detectives would talk to their own individual teams. There was plenty of news to exchange but, as before and despite the robbery, Jessica knew her case wasn't the priority.

A large fan rotated in the back corner of Cole's office as Reynolds, Cornish and Jessica sat across from the chief inspector. The DI took some printed sheets of paper out of an envelope and passed one copy to each of the people present.

'Sorry about the printouts,' Reynolds said. 'The computer image is a lot better but I don't have the best printer in my office.'

Jessica squinted at the image and wondered if it was just her who couldn't see anything other than a red blur.

She didn't want to appear stupid so nodded, doing her best to look as if she knew what she was peering at.

After everyone had looked at the pictures, Reynolds started to speak. 'An image-enhancement expert spent large parts of the weekend working on these. Considering what he had to work with, he's done a pretty good job. The one you're looking at is the final photo out of three we have from the Johnsons' security camera. We know there was a red van parked outside the gates for between three and four minutes at around the time Christine Johnson went missing. What you're looking at, we think, is an extremely faded Royal Mail logo.'

Jessica stared at the image and, now it had been pointed out, she could just about make out a crown and couple of the letters. The traditional bright red mail vans had yellow lettering but this one just had two shades of red.

Reynolds continued. 'We've been in contact with a few people over the weekend and, from what we can gather, the mail service sell off vans after a few years of using them. When they do that, they are quite often sold as a lot to local garages or other dealerships. It's uncommon for Royal Mail to sell directly to the public but not completely unheard of. The guy I spoke to said the yellow lettering is removed either before sale or sometimes by the garage themselves.'

'Is there anything else to identify it?' Jessica asked.

'Not obviously. There's no number plate we could see, which only really gives us the shape. We've got someone trying to give us a rough make and model which we can take back to Royal Mail. They should apparently have records of everything that's sold and who to – but the quality of that information would depend on the various areas of the country. All of that could be our biggest problem – the van could have been sold anywhere across the UK. That's a lot of vehicles and a lot of checking. Once we've got an idea of what model the van is, we'll get the image out to the media and see if people can help.'

'Do you think the van is going to be key?' Jessica asked.

Reynolds glanced at Cornish and they exchanged shrugs. 'We're not sure. It could just be workmen asking for directions, or someone else parking for a few moments. There's less than a three-hour window in between the Johnsons' maid going to the shops and returning and it was in that time Christine Johnson went missing. The security camera only took one still-shot every minute so there are odd flashes of people walking past the gates but, in the entire period, this is all we have of somebody or something directly outside for anything longer than a few moments.'

He paused and swallowed. It looked to Jessica as if he was thinking how to phrase what he was going to say. He soon continued. 'The other thing that's bugging me is if you think about the area and even the way you drive, you wouldn't usually park blocking someone's driveway gates. I know the image you have is zoomed in but on the full shot, you can see they are completely in front of the ramp that links the property to the road. Unless you knew the people, or were as bad a driver as DS Daniel here, it's just not the kind of thing you'd do.'

Reynolds winked at Jessica as he insulted her driving. Jessica pulled a face. 'This bad driving thing is just a myth and that's slander.' She pointed at the DCI and Cornish. 'You're my witnesses – I'd get myself a good lawyer if I were you.'

The chief inspector spoke. 'It's not slander if it's true.'

'You too? This is outrageous. It's not as if I've ever been in an accident.'

Jessica looked to Cornish as if hoping for a bit of fellow female support. 'I was warned in my first week not to get into a car with you,' the other woman said.

The other detectives laughed as Jessica did her best to look annoyed. 'This is harassment and workplace bullying.' She looked to Cole. 'Can I put in a formal complaint?'

'No.'

Reynolds grinned at her. 'All right, maybe you're not that bad. Either way, I think we can all agree that you wouldn't usually park across someone's driveway like this. You can just about see in the other shots that there is space both in front and behind it too, so it didn't have to stop where it did. We're not sure if it means anything specifically but it's not normal.'

Cornish actually smiled. 'We don't have anything else to go on either.'

Jessica hadn't heard the woman speak flippantly before and, perhaps because they were all surprised by her tone, or because she was a little too close to the truth, all four officers laughed gently.

'What about the Johnsons' son? Where is he living?' Cole asked.

'Luxembourg. He's working for the European Parliament. They break for summer recess very soon and he'll be back over here but, until then, he said he's struggling to get away. I've spoken to him over the phone this weekend and, in all honesty, I'm not sure there's much he can add. There does seem to be a lot of confusion over the security camera and whether or not his father knew about it.' He looked at Jessica. 'You were there, what do you reckon?'

She didn't know the inspector was going to ask for her opinion but it was clear the other three officers were interested. Cornish would have been updated about things over the past few days but the two women hadn't spoken in that time and even she looked expectantly at Jessica.

Jessica pursed her lips before speaking. 'I found him difficult to read – it's hard to get past the media training he must have had.' As she spoke she saw Cornish and Reynolds nodding in agreement. 'On balance, I would probably say he didn't know about the camera pointing at the gate but I don't know what that tells us. Maybe his relationship with his wife isn't as solid as everyone's been making out? You can understand why he wasn't at the family home much given his job – but you would've thought it'd be something they'd discuss?' She turned to address Reynolds. 'Did the son give you a proper reason for his mother wanting it? Was she actually scared of someone or something?'

Reynolds shook his head. 'No, I went through all of this with him. It's difficult over the phone but he just said his mum had been talking about security for a little while. The family setup certainly seems a little odd.' He looked sideways at Cornish. 'I think we're of the same opinion as you about George Johnson – he's very helpful on the surface but ultimately very hard to read.'

Cornish looked to emphasise the point. 'He's all about making eye contact and trying to look and sound as sincere as possible and he keeps his body language open. Obviously if you were talking to someone in the interview room, that's the kind of thing you'd look for but, with him, he's so used to doing it now, it's second nature.'

'Were you watching him when the maid told us about the camera?' Jessica asked, looking at Reynolds.

The inspector shook his head. 'No, I think I was looking at her.'

'There was something in his face, just a moment before he corrected himself. At the time I thought it was surprise but maybe there was a little more there.'

'Like panic?'

'Maybe? I don't know. It was only a fraction of a second he let his guard down. It could have been hope, I suppose. I think I'm just naturally suspicious of everyone.'

Jessica looked back at Reynolds, waiting for him to speak. 'There's not much else we've got at the moment,' he said. 'I'm hoping someone can give us a manufacturer for the van by lunchtime or so. If they do I can get onto the press office and we can get the photo out. Some of it has already leaked because we've had a few inquiries.'

'Can someone really give you a car make and model just from the shape of the roof and windscreen?' Jessica asked.

Reynolds nodded. 'Apparently. Who knows what these

people spend the rest of their time doing but if it can help us identify the vehicle I'm really not bothered.'

Cole looked to Jessica, raising his eyebrows, indicating it was her turn.

Jessica took a breath, then began. 'I'm sure you know by now. There was a bit on the news about the robbery but I only received the enhanced images back this morning.' She took some photos out of an envelope and passed them around. 'On Saturday at about three, there was a knife robbery at an off-licence on Stockport Road. They got away with a few hundred quid but, as you can see, our thief was wearing something very familiar.'

Jessica went on to explain the facts about the case, including that the laboratories hadn't found anything at the scene apart from a scuffed footprint in the dust showing the woman had size five feet. She talked about the female voice and similarity in the CCTV footage from the shop to the images they had from whoever was leaving the hands.

'Are you thinking copycat?' Reynolds said.

'I was, maybe still am. I don't know.' She indicated the pictures he was holding. 'If you look at the still frames you've got from the shop, they're a pretty high quality. The ones from the city centre are zoomed in from a distance and not as good so you can't compare like with like. All you can say is that they look . . . similar. They're around the same height and build and wearing the same type of shoes and cloak.'

Reynolds was nodding. 'It seems strange to go from cutting off hands to robbing shops.'

Jessica nodded. 'Exactly but then we don't really know what's going on with the hands in the first place. Are the victims dead? Is the person leaving them working alone or with someone else and so on? We don't know the motive, so maybe robbery is a part of it? It would definitely be odd but then so is leaving hands in the centre of a major city.'

'What are you going to do with it?' Cornish asked.

'I'm off to Bradford Park to go through the camera footage with one of the team there,' Jessica said. 'I watched it at the shop the other day but we're going to skim through a week of footage. The woman moves so quickly, it must be because she knew the shop layout. There's no hesitation about where the counter is, or where the cameras are, because they already know. We'll look to see if there's anyone in the past week or so who has been in that seems to be paying particular attention to the layout. If they really know what they're doing it will be hard to spot but I'm wary of getting all these photos into the media in case it is all unconnected and the robbery stills end up diluting people's memories for the other case.'

Jessica was well aware the previous chief inspector, DCI Farraday, had made a disastrous call some months before that had ended up linking one suspect's description to a much wider case the person wasn't involved with. It had ended up denting both cases and Jessica didn't want to repeat the same mistake.

'The press office have already put out a standard statement about the date, time and place of the robbery,' she added. 'We'll see if anyone comes forward for that while I go back over the videos. If we're struggling in a few days, it could be a time to release the new still-shots.'

With little else to talk about, everyone went their separate ways but Jessica did at least feel the tension between her and Cornish had thawed slightly, even if it had taken jibes about her driving to do it. After the meeting, Jessica updated Rowlands and Diamond and set them to work finding out which traffic cameras and other CCTV fixtures were close to the shop. The robber must have gone somewhere and, although there wasn't a monitoring device directly outside, there would be city-operated ones somewhere nearby.

Jessica drove to the Bradford Park station, which was close to Manchester City's football ground. The place operated not only as a local community hub but also provided a base for almost all of Greater Manchester Police's forensics team and other non-frontline staff, such as payroll and Human Resources. The shop's hard drive had been taken for analysis and image enhancement, which wasn't something they could do from the Longsight station.

She was led through the building to an area full of computers and introduced to a staff member who would be working with her. Together they began to watch the footage, starting with the Saturday itself and working backwards.

It was largely a tedious job but it did become easy to eliminate people. A lot of visitors to the shop clearly knew the layout already as they would simply walk in, pick up the newspaper or other item they wanted, pay for it and leave. Jessica realised that if the robber used the shop frequently, they would be hard to isolate. The process could still be useful if someone paid particular attention to the cameras.

Victor Burnham had been right about the Saturday-morning rush. As he opened the shop, there was a steady stream of customers who almost all picked up a paper, paid for it with near enough the right change, then quickly left. After the first couple of hours, the foot traffic dropped considerably and, after lunch, there were very few people who entered.

At the point the time code had moved on to half past two, Jessica knew that was where she had picked the footage up when she had viewed it the first time. A man entered the shop, as she knew he would, but this time she was watching properly. The scientist working with her saw exactly what she had and they exchanged a look before he rewound it to watch again. When the man walked into the shop, he glanced immediately upwards at the camera, holding the look for a fraction of a second longer than would have been normal. Switching from one angle to the other, they saw him do the exact same thing to the second camera before walking around the store. He picked up a magazine then put it back where it was and left the shop without buying anything.

They watched it back again and the man turned to Jessica. 'What do you reckon?'

'I believe the term is "casing the joint",' she said.

Jessica was annoyed at herself for being in a rush the first time and not spotting it. She had noticed the man not buying anything but completely missed his mannerisms. It could be a coincidence but, as it had happened just half an hour before the woman entered the store, it appeared unlikely. If the woman had an accomplice, it seemed all the more probable they had some sort of car, which made the work the other two constables were doing crucial.

Jessica checked in with Izzy, who said they were struggling with the various agencies that operated the cameras. She then got the contact number for the shop's owner. Jessica called Victor Burnham and described the footage before asking if he knew exactly which magazine it was the man had picked up. The angle of the camera wasn't the best but, with her descriptions, the owner narrowed down the possible titles to three or four. Because he had been shut on the Sunday, he was convinced none of the publications had been sold since the person picked it up. Jessica told him not to touch the rack as she would arrange for someone to come and collect the magazines. If they could isolate fingerprints, they could run it against their database to see if they had any record of the man.

While that was all going on, the scientist had managed to get some better definition printouts of the man looking at the cameras. Jessica took the hard copies and asked him to email the digital versions then drove back to the station. The jokes about her driving were definitely in the back of her mind as she was careful and stuck to all the speed limits.

As she was waiting to pull into the station's car park, three marked police cars raced out of the entrance, their sirens and lights going. Jessica parked and walked into the front reception area.

'Where were they off to?' she asked the desk sergeant.

'There's something going on in town. I'm not completely sure, it's been mad here this morning.'

As they were talking, Jessica's mobile phone started to ring and she saw it was Cole's extension. 'I'm downstairs,' she said as her way of answering.

After a short conversation with her boss, Jessica turned and ran back to her car – and this time she wouldn't be driving quite so carefully.

20

Given his twenty-one years of eating and drinking experience, Frank Rice was finding it hard to figure out quite how he'd managed to forget how to do something seemingly simple. In essence, he'd done everything right. He had picked up the cappuccino mug, put it to his lips and then, for some reason that utterly escaped him, breathed in the milk foam instead of sipping it.

The woman sitting opposite him asked if he was all right and, despite not being able to get a word out without coughing, he assured her he was. In actual fact, every time he breathed in, he could feel a tiny bit of liquid at the top of his lungs while his nose still tickled. He had also burned the outside of his right index finger trying to hastily put the cup down as the spluttering began and was pretty sure his eyes had been bulging at one point.

All in all, it wasn't the best impression to be making on a first date.

Frank tried to smile but the woman in the chair across from him had her head tilted slightly to the side with a puzzled look. 'Are you sure you're . . .' she started.

'Yeah, no worries.' Frank nodded as he spoke but felt his voice lurch down an octave as he struggled not to cough again.

The woman picked up a napkin from under her own cup and held it out towards him. 'Do you want a tissue?'

Frank reached out and took it before turning around, hunching over and letting out the most guttural heave he had ever managed without throwing up. He finally felt the liquid come back up his windpipe and swallowed it properly then turned back around to face the woman. 'Sorry about that.'

Kelly Stark was clearly trying not to laugh. 'I'm not saying I've been out with too many guys I've met on the Internet but you're definitely the first who's nearly choked to death.'

Frank didn't want to ask how many she had been out with – but she was his third Internet date and the first two hadn't gone too well. The first had been a little similar to the current one in that they had opted for an afternoon meeting in a cafe. After they sat down at a table, she'd asked him if he minded that she had asked to meet on an afternoon instead of an evening. His reply still haunted him. 'Yes it's fine – I'm not a sex attacker or anything.'

It had taken him a few days to figure out his own thought process. When he had first signed up for the dating website, he read the Frequently Asked Questions section. In that, it advised people to meet in public places, which seemed sensible. Frank had confided in only one friend that he'd joined the service and, after telling him he was all set for a coffee date with a girl, his mate had joked that the only reason she had asked to meet during the daytime was so he couldn't attack her.

With the mixture of his friend's joke and the site's FAQ

in his mind, for some reason he thought the best thing he could say to a stranger on the first date was that he had no intention of assaulting her.

There wasn't really anywhere to go from there.

The second date had definitely gone better and Frank was on the brink of asking her about a possible second meeting. That was until the woman's tiny dog had stuck its head out from her handbag. Frank didn't hate animals but he wasn't a massive fan either and he figured dogs just weren't meant to be that small. He felt a shiver go down his back each time the creature appeared and it was clear that wasn't going to work either.

When he had first seen the pictures of Kelly and sent her a message, he hadn't thought for a moment she would message him back. She had gorgeous long straight black hair and big brown eyes. He knew she was probably out of his league and his friend had put it best. 'She's an eight or a nine, mate and, if you're lucky, you're a five.'

As Kelly smiled across the table at him, Frank wasn't sure if she was trying not to laugh at him but the crinkles around her eyes and the way her dark eyes grinned with her lips meant marking her down as an 'eight' was definitely underplaying it.

'Sorry, I just sort of breathed the frothy bit in,' Frank said.

'I wondered why you'd gone purple.' Frank took a sip from his cup and managed to swallow it without choking. Kelly grinned widely and silently clapped him. 'Well done.'

Frank wasn't sure how to respond. He was used to feeling uncomfortable around girls but hadn't met too many who were actually friendly.

'So, why did you email me then?' Kelly asked.

Frank knew the answer was, 'Because I saw a little bit of cleavage in your picture, clicked to have a closer look and then thought you actually seemed quite nice' but didn't think that would be the best response. 'I just saw you liked the cinema and music and thought we'd get on,' he said.

Kelly took a sip of her strawberry smoothie and had a playful smile on her face as she put the glass down. 'I guess there aren't that many people interested in movies and music. What type of films are you into?'

Frank thought the look on her face showed she was teasing him and there was a definite hint of sarcasm in her voice. He tried to give himself a few moments by breathing deeply and looking as if he was thinking about it. He didn't want to say the wrong thing and was trying to remember his friend's advice about asking a question, then agreeing with the girl's answer rather than letting her do the initial talking. At the time it sounded like a ridiculously sexist notion but, as he weighed up whether to admit 'The Lion King' was his favourite movie, he saw the sense in it. If he had asked the question and she had named some subtitled indie movie, he could have agreed with her and sounded vaguely intellectual. Choosing a children's cartoon could either show he was endearingly sensitive or make her think he was tragically immature. 'Probably "Citizen Kane",' Frank said, thinking it sounded like a safe option, even though he had never seen it.

'Oh, that's a good choice. I wish I could say something

like that but I still like stuff like "Toy Story" and "The Lion King",' Kelly replied. Frank nodded along with her choices but was annoyed with himself for not being honest. 'What else do you get up to?' Kelly asked.

The man thought it was the time to tell the truth. 'You know I'm a student and am doing agency work through the summer but when I'm on days off from that, I just tend to play on the PlayStation, maybe watch a bit of wrestling on TV or football during the season, go to the pub . . . that kind of thing.'

'Video games and wrestling?'

'Not all the time.'

Kelly started laughing. 'No, it's fine. At least you're honest. Some guys will tell you anything.'

Frank screwed up his face slightly in his best look of disbelief. 'Really? That's just shameless.'

'Yeah, like you'll ask them what movie they like and they'll mention some classic just because it's in all those top ten of all time lists.'

Frank peered at her but she was smiling. 'How did you know?'

'I looked you up – I look everyone up. I don't just go out with someone based on their stupid dating website profile. Everyone looks like a decent person on there. I read the reviews you wrote on the uni's magazine website. I know what you're actually into, that's why I agreed to meet.'

'Oh, right. That's kind of clever. I didn't do any of that.'

Kelly grinned even more widely and Frank realised he really liked her. 'No, it's fine,' she said. 'Admittedly I didn't find anything that said you didn't know how to drink a cup of coffee but the rest of it seemed nice.'

'Sorry, I can usually drink without choking,' Frank smiled. 'So, er, what do you mean by "looking people up"?'

'Why, have you got something to hide?'

'No but . . .'

'Look, you're twenty-one and I'm twenty-three. When you're a young woman on a site like that, you get all types of weirdo wanting to talk to you. You get the older guys telling you how rich they are and that they'll look after you, then you get the younger ones sending you pictures of their six-packs as if it's supposed to be impressive.'

Frank must have glanced down at his own non-washboard stomach because Kelly giggled. 'Look, if it was only pictures of stomachs I got sent, I'd be fine.'

The man felt his eyes widen. 'Oh . . .'

'Exactly. By comparison, you're pretty normal. That's good.'

'So do you already know my favourite film?'

'Yes, you should probably change the privacy settings when you sign up to social networks.'

'Is it your favourite movie too?'

'Yes. I used to watch it over and over when I was a kid. I think it's kind of sweet you like it too.'

Frank didn't know what to say. He felt a little embarrassed but also slightly ill-equipped as Kelly clearly knew far more about him than he did about her. It did give him hope that he could just be himself rather than have to concentrate non-stop in an effort to try to be someone he wasn't.

He took another drink of his coffee while the woman watched him. 'Sorry if I sound a little stalker-ish but I've been out with a few dicks over the years and I don't have the time to invest in them any longer. You seemed nice.'

'Thanks, you seem . . . nice too. A little scary though.'

Kelly laughed. 'Yeah, I'm terrifying.'

Frank enjoyed the rest of the afternoon. Kelly was certainly different and didn't seem to have any kind of ego. Her intelligence shone through and, the more they spoke, the more Frank realised she had agreed to go out with him not because of his cheesy message to her on the website but because she had looked up the kind of things he liked and known they had a lot in common. She was happy to laugh at him without it being cruel and have him poke fun at her too. Her confidence was a little intimidating but, if that was her worst trait, he figured it was his problem not hers.

After they finished their first drinks and had another each, Kelly said she had to go because she had an evening shift on the reception desk of the hospital where she worked.

Frank was nervous about asking if she would go out with him again but she didn't give him any option by saying she'd message him to arrange going out on a Friday or Saturday evening. As they said goodbye outside the cafe, Frank stretched his arm out and they shook hands before going their separate ways. The woman had a massive smile on her face and giggled throughout the handshake and Frank could see how absurd it was. He cursed himself for not trying to hug her at the very least.

It was a fairly short walk home for the man and he spent

the journey thinking about little things he could have said differently and wondering how he could phrase a text message later that day to say he'd enjoyed himself. As he neared his flat, Frank decided to stop in the off-licence on the next road over to see if his friend was working.

He entered the shop and was delighted to see a familiar face. 'Hey, Sanj, how are you doing?' he said.

The young man behind the counter looked up from the magazine he was reading and grinned. 'Not bad, how are you, fella? We still on for Friday?'

'Definitely. Can I use your toilet?'

'Are you still waiting on a plumber?'

'Our landlord keeps saying he'll sort it but we still have to flush with a bucket for now.'

The man behind the counter pulled a face. 'All right, you know where it is but don't tell my dad I let you back there.'

Frank walked towards the rear of the store and went through the side door he knew led down a short corridor to the small bathroom. Someone had already left a newspaper in there so he skimmed through it while also checking the emails on his phone. He went to flush the toilet but, as he did so, thought he heard raised voices from the main part of the shop. He quietly opened the door and walked towards the voices. There was a curtain of beads that stretched all the way to the floor and Frank peered through the gaps, being careful not to disturb them.

Despite the warmth of the day, he felt a chill tingle down his back as someone in a black hood stood holding a knife at his terrified friend.

21

After the conversation with Cole, Jessica knew exactly where she was going. A call had come in from a man apparently in a back room of an off-licence just off Oxford Road saying it was being held up by a woman wearing a familiar-sounding black hooded cloak. He told the operator he was going to intervene and had not given the person time to try to talk him out of it.

Jessica had no idea what to expect at the scene because the man who called them had hung up. She could be going to a situation where somebody had been stabbed or to a shop where the person she was trying to track down had been stopped. As she pulled onto the side street where the shop was, her heart sank. Police had sealed off the area and there was a chaotic mix of officers trying to keep pedestrians away, others securing the scene, and an ambulance blocking one end of the road. She hoped the woman she wanted hadn't escaped but, above that, wanted to hear no one had been hurt.

Jessica parked on double yellow lines, half on the pavement, and bounded towards the officers. 'What's going on?' she said.

One of the officers recognised her and replied. 'There's a woman down on the inside and a paramedic with her. Two men have been separated and are being spoken to.'

'Is she badly hurt?' Jessica asked.

'I don't think so. I've been out here and it's been a bit crazy.' The officer broke off to tell a pedestrian who had come a little too close to back away. Jessica looked around and glimpsed a familiar-looking face among the small crowd of people. She didn't want to spook the person so continued looking around the crowd as if it was a natural thing to do. Jessica walked back towards her car as calmly as she could, then doubled around until she was at the back of the people watching the shop front. A few other pedestrians continued to walk by but Jessica kept her eyes on the back of the man. He was edgy and kept reaching towards the pocket of the three-quarter-length trousers he was wearing. Jessica hoped it was a phone or something similar but wasn't willing to take any chances.

Still out of sight of the man, she beckoned one of the larger male police officers over and whispered some instructions to him. The crowd had grown a little larger while she had been watching and while she might have usually acted on her own, it wasn't worth the risk with so many others around.

The officer crept forward quietly with Jessica following. They moved into position in the crowd so they were just behind the man and the police officer acted quickly, taking a grip of the man's wrists and handcuffing him. Jessica stepped around to look into the face of the person she recognised from the CCTV footage she had been poring over. He was undoubtedly the person who had picked up the magazine from the rack in the off-licence a few days previously and Jessica told him he was under arrest.

Moments later as the man was being led to a waiting police van, the noise from the crowd around the shop increased. Jessica turned and saw a woman wearing dark clothing being led out of the door by two officers. She didn't appear to be hurt and her hood was slumped around her shoulders. Her face was visible but it didn't belong to anyone Jessica recognised.

The rest of the day was a blur as Jessica lurched from one job to the next. Before going back to the station to talk to the people who had been detained, she persuaded the shopkeeper and the Scene of Crime team to let her watch some of the CCTV footage on site.

The camera system in the off-licence was more sophisticated than the first one and the young man who said his father owned the shop was much better at using it.

He skilfully manoeuvred through the screens, finding the exact piece of footage Jessica knew they would likely need at a later date. Forty minutes before the robbery had taken place, the man who had been arrested outside the shop entered. Much like on the first occasion, he looked around at the floor layout, made a few brief glances towards where the cameras were placed, then left without buying anything.

Jessica had no idea who the two people were but the plot seemed relatively clear. The man would walk in at a time mid-afternoon when they figured the shop would be quiet and familiarise himself with the layout. Then, at some point not long after, his accomplice would enter the store wearing the robe and carrying a large knife. Presumably the man would be waiting somewhere nearby with a car to make their exit.

Before she left, Jessica checked the buildings around the off-licence to see if there were any cameras around. As far as she could tell there weren't, which was consistent with the first target. The internal recording devices would be easy to avoid given the disguise but it would be much harder to conceal a car waiting outside if there were a camera there.

Back at the station, the two suspects were separated and put in different cells on the basement level. Neither had a legal representative so the process of them both talking separately to the duty solicitor was taking some time. Jessica didn't really mind as it gave her the opportunity to gather some evidence before the interview. She got new copies of the still-shots of both the man and hooded figure from the first robbery and harassed one of the computer team to send her through the images of the man from just before the second one. They would work on enhancing the pictures at a later time but it gave her a start.

She was pretty sure the couple were copycats and that the coverage in the papers of the woman leaving hands around the centre of the city had given them a convenient cover to commit crimes.

When the solicitor had finished, Jessica interviewed the man first. They found out his name was Jordan Benson and he had a lengthy record for thefts. He was in his thirties but had almost fifty convictions for crimes ranging from shoplifting minor goods not worth much up to street robbery and burglary. The interview had been a mixed affair which started with a stream of 'no comment's and ended with the suspect blaming everything on his partner.

According to his version of events his girlfriend, Erica Tomlinson, had planned the whole thing. She had chosen targets for them to rob then sent him in to scout the place out. After that, she would enter in disguise to get the money and they would escape together. Jessica believed the final parts but wasn't quite so convinced he played as small a part as he claimed. Because of his confession, the still images from the CCTV cameras and the fact they were likely to get fingerprints from the magazine he picked up in the first shop, Jordan was charged with robbery. That charge could be downgraded to conspiracy to rob before he got to court but it would be the Crown Prosecution Service's ultimate choice. If they felt they could prove he was involved in the planning of the crimes, he would be charged for the more serious offence. If he continued to insist his partner was the one to blame, it would be something their respective legal teams could argue between themselves in court. Jessica didn't even bother to question him about the hands as it was his girlfriend she was waiting to talk to and he could always be re-interviewed at a later time.

Erica was brought up to the interview room next. She was in her late thirties and had short blonde hair in very tight curls but otherwise seemed very plain except for a series of garish tattoos down her arms. The woman had a criminal record of her own, including a few thefts, but it was all minor compared to Jordan and most of it revolved around drug possession. As soon as they started talking,

Jessica realised the woman probably couldn't spell 'mastermind' let alone be one. After giving her name, Erica copied her boyfriend by answering 'no comment' to the first few questions.

'You do know Jordan just told us everything?' Jessica said. 'He talked all about how you planned the robberies and sent him in ahead.'

The woman stared back. 'No he didn't.'

'I'm afraid he did. If it wasn't your idea you should probably say so.'

'No comment.'

Jessica sighed and reached into an envelope, taking out a series of photographs. She selected the one from the CCTV camera in Piccadilly Gardens of the figure positioning the first hand they had found. 'Why did you leave this hand?'

The woman picked up the photograph and looked at it before angrily putting it down. 'It weren't me.'

Jessica handed her the other photos. 'What about these hands?'

'They weren't me.'

'It looks like you.'

'But it weren't.'

'Why were you caught robbing from a shop with the exact same outfit then?'

'No comment.'

Jessica sighed again and leant back in her chair. 'Do you want to go to prison, Erica?' The woman said nothing. 'Right, I'll assume that's a "no". Do you know the starting point for the type of robbery you committed is four years in prison? With some remorse, a confession and the return of the money you might get away with a year, maybe two on a suspended sentence so you stay out. If you've done time on remand you might not even get that. The reason I say "might" is because, if you don't start talking, Jordan's going to pin all of this on you and that's not to mention the issue of the hands. We've found three so far. Three hands, three people missing, no bodies. That could be three murder charges. That's life, probably with little chance of parole.'

Jessica knew the outfit on its own wasn't enough to link the woman to the hands and in their brief initial inquiries they hadn't managed to connect her to any of the victims as she was a different age and from a different area compared to the three people they had identified.

Erica stared at the table and spoke quietly. 'I didn't kill anyone.'

'Right and I believe that but, if you had nothing to do with it, you need to tell me why you've been stealing money while wearing a black robe that looks just like this one.'

The woman sighed and started to cry. Her solicitor passed her some tissues and she took a drink of water. 'It was Jordan's idea,' she said. 'He'd seen the pictures on the news of this woman in the cloak and reckoned if we robbed some places it would get blamed on whoever that was. I've had the outfit for ages because of this fancy dress thing a few years back but not worn it.'

'Didn't it cross your mind that, if you got caught first, those more serious crimes would be blamed on you?'

The woman continued to dry her eyes and shook her head. 'I didn't think of it like that. The first one went so well we didn't think we'd get caught. We thought it would be easy money.'

It was pretty much what Jessica suspected. 'So, just to be clear, are you saying the reason you went in with a knife was because you wanted us to think you were the same person that has been leaving hands?'

'Yes.'

'And is that why Jordan did the initial scouting instead of committing the actual robberies?'

'Yes.'

Erica's story was actually remarkably similar to her boyfriend's with the one key difference that she blamed him for planning the robberies, while he insisted it was her idea. Jessica didn't believe either of them was involved in the main case she was working on but a warrant had been granted for a search team to raid their house. Erica said the cash left over from the first theft was in a box under their bed, which seemed to back up the point neither of them were the sharpest criminals going. The car they had used had also been impounded as evidence after being found around the corner from the second scene.

In terms of the robberies, Jessica had worked on enough cases to know things should be fairly straightforward. Jordan's record would probably be enough to get him remanded, while Erica was likely to get the same treatment because she used a knife. The level of planning, albeit a little unscientific, would go against them too and Jessica thought the pair would spend the months leading up to their Crown Court date behind bars despite their confession.

Things would still need to be checked and compared to her main case. Their house and car were being searched while some officers had already begun to see if there was a link from either of them to the missing victims. None of the hands offered any forensic clues as to who left them, so the two suspects' DNA wouldn't be any use from that point of view – but they did at least now have time.

With a regular suspect, they would only have the usual period of questioning before they had to charge or release, which was the problem they had run into when January was in custody. Because the pair were likely to be re-manded, if anything unexpected did turn up when they were trying to link them to the victims, they would at least know where the duo were.

Jessica charged Erica with robbery and the woman was led back to the cells. The two would be appearing in the magistrates' court the following morning.

She went back through to the main area and found Dave and Izzy, who had been tasked with looking into the pair's backgrounds. 'Have you found anything to link them to the hands?' Jessica asked after they found a quiet corner.

The two constables shook their heads almost in unison and it was Izzy who spoke. 'Nope, neither of them are on our college-leavers' list and they're both too old anyway. Erica was brought up out of the area and seemingly only moved here a couple of years ago. Jordan comes from around here but we've not got anything that says he knows any of the victims let alone might have a grievance against them.'

Jessica nodded. 'I thought we'd probably struggle. There's no violence on either of their records and they don't seem the type. To be honest, they're too stupid.' The two constables exchanged knowing smiles and Jessica continued. 'You are going to have to keep working on this for a little while though. Check everything and let's make it official. I don't want us to miss something and end up looking like fools but I don't want to waste days looking into something we know is a blind alley either.'

'How are you anyway?' Rowlands asked. 'It's been a mad few days.'

Jessica nodded. 'You're right about that and, because of you, I've got to spend tomorrow morning at a bloody primary school talking about careers. I thought it was older kids until I read the email properly.'

'Can't someone else go?' Izzy asked.

'Are you volunteering?'

'No . . .'

'Jack says it can't be anyone working on the Christine Johnson case and he wants someone senior. He reckons the super wants it both ways. He doesn't want any officers taken from the Johnson inquiry but wants us to keep up this community engagement thing. Did you see the coverage the fete got in the paper the other day? They gave that more space than when we were trying to get them interested in the severed hands.'

'I didn't see you in any of the pictures,' Dave said.

'Yeah, sod that. Because I wasn't in uniform the photographer didn't realise I was involved. I went and hid next to some of the parents as he snapped away.'

The two constables laughed in unison. 'Do you have to give a speech tomorrow?' Izzy asked.

Jessica realised she had no idea. 'I bloody hope not.'

Their conversation was interrupted by a young out-of-breath constable in uniform arriving and tapping Jessica on the shoulder. 'Are you all right?' Jessica asked.

'Yeah, they want you back. It's something to do with the Erica Tomlinson woman.'

'Where is she?'

'One of the interview rooms. She's been asking for you but we weren't sure where you were.'

Jessica quickly retraced her steps and was surprised to see Cole sitting in the interview room as she entered. She looked quizzically at him but he simply nodded towards Erica, who was sitting next to her solicitor on the opposite side of the table.

'I hear you've been asking for me?' Jessica said.

'Yeah, you were saying earlier about being able to stay out of prison for cooperating and that?'

Jessica pursed her lips. 'Sort of, I said you might get a lesser sentence if you confessed and gave us the details. It wouldn't be up to us – you still robbed two places carrying a knife and that means you should go to custody.'

'What if I had information?'

'It depends what it was about.'

The woman looked nervously to her solicitor then back at Jessica. 'What if I told you who arranged for that politician's missus to go missing?'

22

One of the first rules of interviewing suspects was to give nothing away but, if it had been a game of poker, Jessica knew full well the whole room would know she had a flush. She wheeled around to face Cole, who had barely suppressed his surprise either.

'Sorry, can you repeat that?' Jessica asked.

'I know who sorted it for the politician's wife to disappear. I dunno if she's dead but I know who paid for it.'

'How do you know this?'

'I just know people. You hear them talking.'

Jessica was trying to stay calm. 'Who did you hear talking?'

'I'm not telling you that.'

'Okay, so what do you know? Do you know where she is?'

Erica continued to stare at the table. 'No, I don't know any of that. I don't know who took her either but I know who arranged it and why.'

'Do you have evidence or is it just something you've heard?'

'Something I heard – but the person won't be wrong.'

Cole leant forward and looked at Erica's solicitor. 'We're going to need a few minutes.' The two officers left the room, shutting the heavy door behind them and crossing into a nearby room they used for witnesses. It was stifling as they walked across the threshold. The air-conditioning was still not working and, although fans were cooling the interview room, the room they had gone into had none of that.

Jessica used her hand to fan her face as she spoke. 'What do you reckon?'

'She's never going to get what she wants regardless of what she thinks she knows. If she knew who took Mrs Johnson, why they took her and where the woman is, whether she's alive or dead, then maybe the CPS would talk about things. All she says is that she knows who arranged for it and she won't even tell us who told her. I think she's seen too much American TV. It doesn't work like that here.'

Jessica shrugged. 'Are you going to talk to the super?'

'Yes, let's go back and tell her she's got no chance first and see if she's got anything else to add. I don't know what her solicitor thinks he's playing at.'

The two detectives walked back into the interview room and sat down. 'I think there might be a bit of confusion here,' Jessica said. 'If you're going to confess to the robberies in court, they will sentence you. All we can do is tell the people prosecuting you that you've been extremely helpful. We've had a chat and, in all honesty, neither of us are convinced you've got any information you can help us with. Even if you knew where Mrs Johnson was, or who took her, we still couldn't drop the charges. It doesn't work like that.'

The woman glanced at the table then scratched her

head before nodding towards the solicitor sitting next to her. 'That's what he said.' Jessica looked at the DCI but, before they could say any more, Erica spoke again. 'It was the husband.' The tone was lower and softer than the woman's previous words.

'Sorry?' Jessica said.

'It was the husband who wanted rid of her – the one that's been all over TV. He paid some people to get rid of her. He's got some other woman somewhere.'

'Who told you?'

'I'm not saying. I don't know anything else, that's it.' She looked to her solicitor. 'Can I go back downstairs now?'

Erica refused to add anything else and, after she had been returned to the cells, Cole called both Reynolds and Cornish back to the station and told them what had been said. The information was nothing they could use as evidence but, at the same time, the robbery suspect had ended up giving it to them voluntarily. She didn't have a reason to lie as they hadn't promised her anything.

Jessica knew officers had discreetly been looking into a situation such as the MP himself being involved but hadn't come up with anything. It was an awkward thing to examine because they would need a warrant to look at items like bank records, phone logs or emails and, at least until the current moment, the situation hadn't reached that far. Even if they did get that paperwork, they all knew the politician would have had to be pretty careless to leave a trail. The chief inspector said he would ask DSI Aylesbury what he thought but even that was complicated as he was apparently friends with George Johnson. The priority was still to track down the red van that had been parked outside the gates. Reynolds said they had a likely make and model, which would be shared with the media, but that trying to go via the Royal Mail's own records of vehicles sold wasn't getting them anywhere as the files were so patchy across the different areas. All in all, the inspector was undeniably correct when he pointed out that everyone was struggling.

The following morning, Jessica had to go to the school for the careers day. She had found out the previous evening that she was expected to give some sort of talk, which might have been useful information to have had a few weeks ago.

It was a late-morning start at the school and, just before she was getting ready to leave the station, news came through via the desk sergeant that magistrates had remanded both Erica and Jordan. In the end, their legal teams hadn't objected to the refusal of bail, which meant there wouldn't be any appeal against the decision either.

While that had been going on, it had been more or less accepted that neither were credible suspects to have left the hands. Apart from the cash relating to the first burglary, nothing of note had been found at their house and no connection had been found between either of them and the missing victims. Jessica left Rowlands working through the list of almost a hundred college-leavers to find as much information as possible on each one. A lot of the basics had already been discovered, such as current addresses, but there were still a few they hadn't had time to look into.

The school wasn't far from the station and Jessica decided she would walk, hopefully giving her time to figure out what she was going to say. Her own primary school had been one of two in the Cumbrian town she lived in. All of the children on one half of town went to one, while the other school housed the rest. It led to some very competitive sports days but, as there was only one high school, they all ended up going to the same place in the end.

Jessica walked through the school gates into a reception area where a secretary told her she would have to have her identification checked for security purposes. Along with the huge metal railings that ran around the perimeter of the building, it was certainly a change from the school she had gone to. The district it was in wasn't one of the best in the city but it was nothing compared to some of the ones you read about. Despite that, there was still a metal-detecting gate just inside the doors and a table on either side where bag searches were carried out.

The receptionist finally put her phone down and gave Jessica back her identification. A few moments later a woman came into the area. She had short black hair and walked quickly, almost as if the speed she moved at had to be ruthlessly efficient. She was wearing a bright green cardigan, which clashed with a navy-blue knee-length skirt, and she stretched out a hand for Jessica to shake. The woman introduced herself as the deputy head teacher and led Jessica up a set of stairs to the staff room. The over-whelming smell of coffee drifted from the room as Jessica sat on a low material-backed chair, turning down a hot drink.

When she had made herself a cup of tea, the teacher sat opposite her and started. 'The students you're here to speak to are all in year six and in their last few weeks at this school. They head off to secondary school in September. They're all either ten or eleven years old so shouldn't give you too much trouble. They're at that age where they have enough of an attention span as long as you only talk for five or ten minutes but not at the point where the hormones have gone crazy.'

'What's with all the security gates downstairs?' Jessica asked.

The woman shrugged sadly. 'A sign of the times. Some year five pupil brought a knife to school eighteen months ago and threatened another child. I don't think he even knew the damage he could do. The governors decided every student should have to pass through a metal detec-tor on their way in now and we have to pay for security guards to stand around.'

'That's just . . . wrong.' Jessica meant the situation, not the fact the scanners had been put in but the teacher knew what she was getting at.

'I couldn't agree more but it's one of those things. It will be everywhere in a few years.'

'How does today work then?'

After another sip of her tea, the teacher continued. 'We've organised someone from a different profession to come in every day this week and again next week. There are around forty students. You just need to talk for a few minutes about what you do. Obviously you know the children are still quite young so please don't be too explicit. We had a fire marshal in yesterday and a journalist is coming tomorrow. The day after that, we've got a local author. We've got a doctor and a chef next week. It's not really to get them thinking about jobs specifically – more about the types of thing they like doing. They have to start choosing school subjects to focus on in a while, so it's just to give them something to reflect on over the summer.'

'That doesn't sound too bad actually. I didn't have a clue what I wanted to do when I left school.'

'We've been doing it for a couple of years now. Are you sure you don't want a coffee?'

'Have you got anything stronger?'

Jessica's attempt at a joke had clearly been missed and the deputy head looked fairly concerned. 'Er, no . . .'

'Sorry, I was joking. I know I'm an acquired taste,' Jessica said. 'I only usually drink before operating heavy machinery and driving.' The woman pulled another face. 'Shit, sorry, I make bad jokes when I'm nervous . . . and, er, swear.'

The woman didn't seem too impressed. 'Are you going to be all right to not do that when I take you through?'

'Yes, sorry. I'm a little nervy. I don't really deal with children very often.'

'It'll be fine. They only bite at the end of the week.' It was Jessica's turn to pull a concerned face. 'Sorry,' the deputy head added, 'I guess I make ill-judged jokes too.'

After a few more minutes, the woman stood, leading Jessica down a corridor into an empty classroom. Even though she couldn't have expected anything else, the height of the tables and chairs took Jessica by surprise. Each desk had four chairs placed around it that barely seemed higher than her knee. The whole room was a mass of colour with measurement charts, paintings and giant pictures of castles. In the corner was a carpeted area surrounded by low bookcases whose spines offered yet more colour.

'We're going to have a couple of classes joining into one for your talk,' the deputy head said. 'It's up to you if you want to sit or stand. I'll get you a chair if you want one.'

'Standing's fine. I quite fancy one of those little chairs anyway though. I'll put one in our interview room to confuse people.'

This time the teacher realised she was joking and laughed. 'If you want to settle yourself, I'll go and get everyone.'

Jessica put her phone on silent and turned around to have a look at some of the work pinned to the wall. There was a display showing various students' handwriting and she had to admit to herself that almost all of the examples were better than what she could have managed. With the way she delegated jobs and the fact most of the work she did was through a computer, Jessica rarely had to write anything down and, when she did, it was generally an untidy scrawl. She wondered if the children knew how little they would most likely have to use a pen as soon as they left education.

The sound of high-pitched chatter interrupted her thoughts and she turned to see a stream of youngsters walking through the door. Some of them were carrying chairs and by the time they had finished arranging themselves, the room was packed. Two other teachers stood at the back as the deputy head came to the front and introduced Jessica.

The students gave a resounding chant-like, 'Good after-noon, De-tec-tive Dan-i-el' that was more creepy than anything else. Jessica tried to keep things simple in her speech, talking about how a criminal could be caught by fingerprints or their blood and then saying how they could get a warrant to read people's emails or text messages. She didn't want to go into too much depth and there were clearly areas of her job it wouldn't be appropriate to talk to children about. After that, she reverted to the usual kind of speech a standard police officer might give, telling them about things like dialling 999 in an emergency.

When she began to see heads turning to look at the walls instead of her, she realised it was time to stop and let them ask questions. Jessica had been expecting the students to put their hands up but it was the deputy head that had the first query. 'Why did you want to become a detective?'

Jessica almost felt as if she were the subject of a dreary magazine article but explained it had never really been an ambition and that applying to join the police force was just something she had done when she wasn't sure what she wanted to do with her life. It was only once she was working as an officer in uniform, that she had decided to take the step up. She knew it didn't really answer the question but there wasn't a better explanation.

From the predictable dreariness of an adult's question, the children's queries were far more random and funny. The first, 'Have you ever shot anyone?' brought a few giggles from around the room and an apologetic 'sorry' from one of the teachers at the back. Jessica didn't mind answering and struggled not to smile herself. She told the young boy she hadn't shot anyone as there was a specialist firearms squad and she didn't carry a weapon. That brought the perhaps inevitable follow-up question, 'Have you ever wanted to shoot anyone?'

It took a little while for the youngsters to move away from questions relating to guns. Given the security gates below it could have been a little unsettling but there didn't seem to be any malice, simply kids asking about the things they had no doubt seen on television. She was asked the fastest speed she had ever driven at and whether or not she knew someone's dad because they were in prison along with a series of other things she couldn't have predicted.

The final question was the one that tripped her up the most. A young girl near the back asked how they could get away with a crime. Jessica didn't know if she was just talking about stealing sweets from a shop but either way she couldn't responsibly answer the question. 'You'll always get caught,' she said, not really believing it herself but at least feeling she might have put someone off committing a crime at such a young age.

After the children left for lunch, the various teachers thanked Jessica and she left to walk back to the station.

The last question had stuck with her because she knew the answer. If you wanted to get away with something, the best way was to make people like her think the crime was committed by someone else. If George Johnson had arranged for his wife to disappear, maybe that was where he had gone wrong? He had left them nothing to go on, instead of something misleading to follow up. With her case they had the woman in the black cloak from the very first day and Jessica wondered if that was where their problem lay? The hands were being left in public places for a reason and Jessica felt as if whoever was behind things wanted her to put the pieces together. There was definitely a degree of showing off, which the wave to the CCTV camera proved, but the full reasoning seemed beyond her.

As she walked, Jessica remembered her phone was still on silent. She took it out of her pocket and thumbed across the welcome screen, noticing she had a text message from Rowlands.

'Call me, urgent.'

She pressed the button to phone his mobile and the constable picked up on the first ring. 'Jess, are you on your way back?'

'Yeah, I'm walking. I'll be about five minutes.'

'Are you all right?'

'Why wouldn't I be?'

'Another finger has arrived for you.'

23

Jessica instantly asked the question she knew Rowlands wouldn't have the answer to. 'Whose is it? We've not found a hand.'

'We don't know. The forensics team have already been and gone. The envelope was exactly the same and the mail room staff got the DCI involved straight away.'

Jessica raised her voice. 'Why didn't anyone call me?'

Rowlands's tone sounded softer than usual. 'It was the DCI's decision. I guess he thought there wasn't much you could do anyway. None of us could because the science lot were called immediately. The finger and the envelope and all of that have been taken back to the labs.'

Jessica hung up without saying goodbye. She felt angry at not being called, even though there was nothing she could have added if she had have been. As she neared the station, she sat on a wall for a couple of minutes to compose herself. She realised the fury wasn't something she felt against her colleagues, more towards the person who was sending her body parts. Jessica felt targeted but figured the only way she could escape those feelings was to find out what it was the person was trying to tell her.

Once at the station she acted as calmly as she could as Cole gave her the information she already knew. He put a hand on her shoulder and asked if she was okay. Jessica nodded and replied she was fine.

She had already decided what she wanted to do. 'I know it's loads of work but I'm going to take constables Rowlands and Diamond with me to look through CCTV footage from the past few mornings. Before this, we've only received fingers after a hand has been found so perhaps it's still out in the open somewhere?'

'What exactly are you going to look for?' Cole asked.

'Our woman in black I suppose – someone leaving the hand. If things follow the pattern of the others in that it happens early in the morning in a public place, we'll hopefully come up with something. It's going to be lots of locations to search through and it could have been left any time in the last few days.'

Cole nodded in agreement. 'I have one other thing for you. The person from the labs who handled the package said the finger had a letter "A" tattooed just above the knuckle.'

Jessica crinkled her eyes in surprise. 'Like the "love–hate" thing people put on their hands when they're in prison?'

'Possibly. If it's a ring finger like the others, that could fit but the others were a right hand, so that would make it "hate" on the right hand and "love" on the left. It's usually the other way around.'

'You're right. It's worth looking at though. Can you spare me some officers?'

Cole shook his head. 'Not many. How many do you want?'

'Someone to update our missing persons list with anyone reported since the last time we went through it. After that, I want them to check the names against lists of former prisoners. It could end up being worthless but at least we're ahead if it does turn out to be from a prison tattoo.'

'Fine, you go do what you need to and I'll set someone on this and give them your mobile number.'

After checking with the private security firm that there was space for three officers to invade their offices for an afternoon at least, Jessica drove Dave and Izzy the few miles into the city centre. She drove very carefully given it was apparently open-season on her abilities but that seemed to amuse Rowlands even more. 'Who stole our DS and replaced her with my gran?' he asked.

When she wasn't having the mickey taken out of her, Jessica spent the rest of the journey briefing the constables about what was required. The company said they would set up three individual terminals so they could work separately. Between them, they put together a list of public spots in the city they would watch footage from. To start with, they were assuming the previous three locations wouldn't be revisited.

The plan was to look at footage from dawn until eight in the morning from the past four days and to work their way through the list of places one by one. If they came up with nothing, they could either go for other locations, a wider time period or even days from further back. Jessica feared the worst in terms of wasting hours and coming up with nothing but began to feel a little more confident as they arrived. She was going to examine footage from the bus and train stations, while Izzy had the outside of the arena, theatres and the remaining public squares. Dave would look at cameras covering the streets around the shopping areas.

Jessica felt sure they would find something – it seemed too inconsistent for the finger to arrive before a hand had been found. It broke the pattern and, considering the way the person had worked in the past, that structure had been consistent.

With no second person to check what she was doing, Jessica kept the speed of the footage at double and watched two monitors at the same time. Izzy worked on two other screens at the back of the small office they were in while Dave was in the room next door. The two female detectives chatted despite having their backs to each other.

'How was school this morning?' Izzy asked.

'Not too bad. All the kids just wanted to talk about shooting each other.'

The constable laughed gently. 'My brother was all about toy guns and football until he became a teenager, then he'd lock himself in his room and play computer games all the time. Well, that and moan about girls not being interested in him.'

'Maybe that was because he was in his room all the time?'

'That's what Dad used to tell him.'

Jessica had taken on one of the harder jobs because there were more people around the train and bus stations, even in the early hours of the morning. She stopped and scrolled back a piece of footage but realised the person who had grasped her attention was someone wearing a dark jacket.

'How are things with Mal? He seemed nice enough on Saturday,' Jessica said.

'He's still going on about kids. He ended up playing in this impromptu dads versus lads football game at the park while we were out. I think he was trying to make a point.'

'I don't know what to tell you. I'm terrified about being bridesmaid alongside two youngsters next month.'

'It's not just that,' Izzy replied. 'He wants to carry on working but for me to give all this up. I don't know if I want to do that at all – but certainly not at the moment.'

'Have you told him that?'

'Sort of, it's not easy. All our friends are expecting me to be pregnant soon as well. It's part of getting married I suppose.' There was a short pause before she added, 'You got anything?'

'Nothing. One particular cleaner who picks his nose and eats it but that's not a crime.'

'It bloody should be. The theatres I've been looking at have all had a homeless person sleeping next to them or in the doorways, even after the sun's up. Maybe they feel safer because people can see them? I don't know but I think I'm wasting my time with these.'

'Do you want to start on something else? We can always go back to the theatres, I'm just wary of time.'

'Yes, can you remember where that tech guy said the other feeds could be accessed from?' Jessica paused her screens and walked across to her colleague. She brought up a new window with a list of available footage. 'Thanks,' Izzy said.

Jessica returned to her seat. 'What are you going to go over?'

'Hotels are next on our list.'

Jessica knew the constable didn't mean every hotel but there were a handful around the city centre that had been converted from old buildings. The former Free Trade Hall on Peter Street was the site of a nineteenth-century massacre, as well as a place where famous musicians had given concerts and politicians made speeches. Others were actually listed buildings, while the tallest property in the city was also owned by a hotel chain.

All of that meant there were certain hotels that were almost as famous for the building they were in than for the brand. Jessica finished looking through the camera angles from outside the main Piccadilly train station and uploaded footage from Victoria instead.

'Did you hear Erica Tomlinson and Jordan Benson were remanded this morning?' Izzy asked.

'I caught it just before I went to the school. If they keep blaming it on each other, they'll both get sent down for robbery. I hope the CPS do him for it as well and don't downgrade the charges.'

'Did you see the statements about how she was actually caught?' Izzy asked.

'Sort of, it was a mad day. Some bloke hiding in the toilet, wasn't it?'

'Almost. I took the statements from the shopkeeper. The other guy who phoned us was his mate. His friend had let him use the staff toilet in the back and, on his way out, he'd seen the woman with the knife. He called us then shoulder-charged her.'

'Brave thing to do considering Erica had a knife,' Jessica said.

'He was called Frank something. The funny thing was he kept saying he'd never hit a girl before. I was telling him he wasn't in trouble but he was saying how he'd just got a new girlfriend and he didn't know how she'd take it if she knew he was going around bashing women.'

Jessica laughed. 'I think it's a bit of a special circumstance.'

'I told him that but he wasn't having it and the shopkeeper kid kept saying how he'd be in trouble with his dad for letting a non-staff member use the toilet.'

Jessica flicked a dial on the dashboard in front of her. 'People are strange, don't you think? We've got this one guy worrying about being a woman-beater because he tackled a female threatening his mate with a bloody great knife but, meanwhile, there's some lunatic cutting off people's hands seemingly without bothering about it.'

'That's the job though, isn't it?'

'That's the job.'

Jessica tried not to sound too disheartened but it was hard not to let things get to her considering whoever was responsible for leaving the hands knew who she was.

'What do you think about the rumours about the MP?' Izzy went on.

Jessica paused before replying, wondering how she should respond. 'We've got to keep it quiet.'

'Sorry, I wasn't meaning to . . .'

'No, I know. The minute something is supposed to be kept under wraps everyone starts talking about it.' Izzy didn't say anything and Jessica sighed before continuing. 'I wasn't telling you to stop, just that you've got to be discreet if it comes up at the station. I trust you and Dave enough to talk about it in front of you but it can't go beyond us.'

'What's going on then?' Izzy asked.

Jessica could almost hear herself from a few years ago, fishing for information and trying to learn the station's internal politics.

'What have you heard?'

'That we're now looking into George Johnson himself.'

'Who told you that?'

'Everyone knows.'

Jessica sighed again. 'It's supposed to be a secret. We got a warrant this morning to look at his bank records. We want to go through his emails too but don't want to let him know anything yet. We don't need to tell him to obtain a warrant but his emails are more complicated because they could contain sensitive information due to his position. I think Jack's hoping there's something in his finances because it's going to be too hard to keep things from him otherwise. The super's looking into how it all stands legally. There was even some talk about MI5 but I think that's just because no one knows the law.'

'What do you reckon?'

'Who knows? I think everyone automatically assumes it's the husband, wife, boyfriend or girlfriend. I really don't think he knew about the camera. At the time I thought the look on his face was surprise but perhaps it was panic because he had an idea of what might have been captured?' Jessica switched the footage she was watching onto another day and yawned. 'You bored yet?'

'Yeah, I wonder how Dave's getting on?'

'Probably zooming in on any women wearing a low-cut top.'

'Ha! He is pretty good, y'know?'

'I know. Why do you think I pick you guys to work with? Just don't tell him I said that.'

Izzy's voice suddenly raised in pitch. 'Hey, look.' Jessica stopped her footage and spun to look over her colleague's shoulder. 'I think that's her,' the constable added.

Jessica could see what she meant. There was a figure in the distance from one of the camera angles but it was hard to see. 'Where are you looking at?'

'One of the street cameras on the bottom of the road that leads to Oxford Road train station. It points down the side of the Palace Hotel.'

'Is that the one with the giant clock tower?' Jessica asked.

'Exactly.'

'Is there a different angle?'

Izzy clicked through a couple of windows and brought up some new footage, scrolling through it to get to the same time as the frames she had been watching. 'This one is pointing in the other direction,' she said.

They watched in silence as a figure in a long dark cloak walked into frame. Jessica said nothing but knew it was who they were after. It felt like the constable had read her mind as she slowed the footage, zooming in.

'She knows where the cameras are again,' Izzy said.

'I know. Where's she going though?'

The constable had learned the system quickly and was easily able to swap from one shot to another. They had the figure from three separate camera angles but there was a blind spot before they first appeared in the frame and any number of alleys or side streets the person could have emerged from.

Once they established they couldn't narrow down where the cloaked figure had come from, Izzy moved the footage forward again and they watched in real-time as the person walked along the side of the ancient building and bent down to place the hand under the canopied corner entrance. Given the thousands of people who walked past the spot on a daily basis, it was inconceivable no one had contacted them. The drop had happened two days previously. Jessica looked at the timestamp at the bottom of the screen. It was just after five in the morning and, though the streets were almost empty, people would have been around.

'Shall we phone it in and get someone to visit there?' the constable asked.

'Let it play through first,' Jessica said.

Izzy left one of the two screens focusing on the corner where the hand had been placed, while, on the second one, she switched to the camera that gave them the best view of the figure walking away. The figure started by returning the way they had come but then crossed the street – a different direction to the one from which they had entered the shot.

Throughout the footage, the figure moved in the exact way they had done on the other occasions. They kept their head angled away from the cameras, the robe dropping to just above their ankles leaving a little flesh and the choice of footwear, the low black heels, on display.

The person in the cloak disappeared out of the shot. 'Is there another camera watching that spot?' Jessica asked.

Izzy had already stopped the footage and was looking through the list of cameras available. She clicked through a few options but they weren't the ones she wanted. 'Do you know what that road's called?'

'No idea.'

They could have looked it up but it was as quick to use trial and error. Izzy continued to scan through the options until eventually they stumbled across the one they had been looking for. The figure in the cloak walked confidently down the street, moving past a couple of shops towards the camera which, from the angle of the images, was high up on the corner of a building. After passing the stores, they paused next to the entrance of an alley and, without turning towards it, gave a thumbs-up to the camera.

Izzy gave a little laugh in disbelief. 'I didn't expect that.'

'Unbelievable,' Jessica said. 'Right, we'll have to get someone else to clean this footage up and get us a zoomed-in still-shot. Let's find out what happened to the hand though.' She pointed at the first screen and asked the constable to speed the footage up.

Almost fifteen minutes had passed since the hand had been dropped and one person had walked past it completely oblivious to what was on the ground. The two detectives then saw why the appendage hadn't been found. A stray dog bounced down the street, sniffed the hand and picked it up before trotting down the road the person in black had first come from and disappearing into an alley that ran along the back of the hotel.

24

Jessica drove more loosely without the other two detectives in the car. She left Izzy and Dave to see if there was any trace of either the dog or their figure in black emerging from the alleyways. Someone was also working on enhancing the still frames they had.

She told the constables to contact the station as she weaved through traffic to get to the Palace Hotel. It wasn't too far from the offices of the security company who operated the cameras but the traffic was barely moving. She wondered if she would have been better walking as she hammered the horn on her car in protest at a driver who was indicating to change lanes, blocking her path. He flicked her a V-sign and shouted an insult that would have certainly made her pull him over if she wasn't in her own vehicle and in such a hurry. Regardless of that, he did finally move and she powered through an amber traffic light, swerved late to avoid a cyclist and parked on double yellow lines blocking the alleyway that not long ago she had been watching on the CCTV cameras.

Other officers hadn't yet arrived but the area would be taped off when they did. Her vehicle was causing an obstruction as it blocked half a lane of a main road and cars beeped their horns as they waited, before swerving around her. She ignored the protests and started to walk slowly down the alley looking from side to side. It was littered with rubbish but, despite the ongoing good weather and brightness of the day, the narrow walkway was completely in the shade.

Jessica moved a few boxes with her hands, scanning the verges on each side as car horns blared behind her. In the distance were police sirens, which she hoped meant her colleagues were on their way as opposed to some other major incident happening.

As Jessica neared the area where the hotel's large metal bins were, the smell of something rotting increased. There were scraps of food and a few takeaway wrappers on the floor but Jessica was struggling to breathe because of the stench. She took a few steps backwards and inhaled a large breath of clean air before moving quickly down the alley.

Her eyes darted from side to side before being drawn to an object just past a fire exit. She crouched and, although she didn't want to touch it, she could see clearly it looked like a hand. It had been badly chewed, either by the dog or, given its proximity to the bins, possibly by rats. It reminded her of an undercooked piece of steak she had once spat out in a restaurant: a mixture of lumpy soft meat. The only thing that really identified it as a hand was the fact three of the fingers and a thumb still had nails attached.

Jessica stepped away and made her way further down the alley to take another breath. She didn't know if the stink belonged to the hand or the bins and scattered take-away leftovers. With a fresh lungful, Jessica returned to the hand. The digits themselves were largely mangled but she looked closely to see if she could pick out any further letters on the skin. According to what the lab worker had told Cole, the finger that had been sent to her had an 'A' tattooed on it, which would be the second letter in whatever was spelled across the knuckles. There was definitely a gap where the ring finger had been removed and on one of the other fingers she could make out what she first thought was a 'W', before realising she was looking at it from the wrong way and that it was actually an 'M'.

She squinted to see if it was possibly an 'H', which would have backed up the love–hate theory, but it really did look like an 'M'. The markings on the other two fingers were difficult to work out because of the scratches and teeth marks. They could have been 'I's, 'L's, 'T's or possibly 'P's, or any combination of those.

Jessica stood, walking back towards her car. There were still plenty of vehicles beeping their horns but she could also hear police sirens very close too. In her head, she tried to work out what the word could be if it wasn't 'hate'. Without anything to write on, she struggled slightly but none of 'malt', 'halt', 'hail' or 'mail' made much sense, unless the victim had been a postman and was particularly proud of it.

As Jessica was trying to think, she could hear vehicles braking loudly and saw the flash of white as police cars stopped either side of her car at the end of the alley. A few uniformed officers started to look at the Fiat Punto but Jessica emerged from the alley showing her identification. 'It's mine,' she said. The officer nodded. 'Are the Scene of Crime team coming?' Jessica added. 'It stinks down there.'

'I'm surprised they're not here now to be honest.'

Jessica interrupted the man. 'Matt!'

'Er, no, I'm Ian.'

'No, sorry, I didn't mean you. The tattoo: it could say Matt.' The man looked at her, confused, but Jessica dismissed him. 'Don't worry. I'm going to head off. Don't let anyone else down there until the lab team arrive. Tell them what they're looking for is on the right past the bins and the fire exit. It's in a proper state.'

Jessica got into her car and manoeuvred herself out of the small gap that was left now the police cars had parked either side of her. As she drove back to Longsight, she tried to remember if any of the players from the rugby photo were called either Matthew or Matt. Off the top of her head it didn't ring a bell but the photo itself, as well as the bits of research they had on each person, was back at the station. If either Dave or Izzy had been back there, she would have called them but they were stranded at the CCTV offices.

After parking at Longsight, Jessica called Izzy to tell her the hand had been found. The constable said there were no camera angles that had caught their figure in black emerging from the alley. She made a crack about having to catch a bus back to the station and added that they had a good grab of the person sticking their thumb up to the camera. A digital version of the footage had also been sent off to the police's own labs to be analysed officially.

Jessica thought about going to tell the DCI what had happened but was more interested in the name Matt. She went to her office and shuffled around the papers and files that were, as usual, cluttering her space. She finally found what she was looking for but couldn't see a player whose name matched what she thought the tattoo could say.

Given the possible letter combinations, she was struggling to match anything before it occurred to her the letters could represent someone else, for instance the person's son or daughter. It seemed an odd place to tattoo a different person's name but then she had once arrested a woman who had a tattoo of a fully naked female on her breast, so anything was possible.

Temporarily giving up, Jessica walked through the main floor to find the officers who had been working on the updated list of missing persons. After asking a few people, she was directed to two officers sitting opposite each other in the far back corner of the room. Aside from when she was at either Izzy or Dave's desks, Jessica didn't spend too much time on the main floor but when she herself had been more junior, her own area had been exactly where the two people were sitting.

Jessica had always found the corner hot and stuffy in the summer, cold and draughty in the winter. As she made her way over, Jessica could almost feel herself sweating because of the temperature. She had stopped asking for updates about the state of the station's air-conditioning. The part the refrigeration company were apparently waiting for had gone missing somewhere in Eastern Europe, its replacement impounded by customs officers. No one seemed to know what was going on beyond the fact it was far hotter inside than it was out. Jessica had persuaded the admin department to give her the number for the company supposed to be fixing things but the customer service department had almost left her wanting to cut off various body parts from the clowns who worked there. Twenty-five minutes of having to press 'one' to get through to another set of options where she needed to press 'four' followed by ten minutes on hold, five minutes of someone not helping her and then another ten minutes on hold hadn't put her in a good mood and she'd given up.

One of the two officers was on the phone, the other was typing on a keyboard. Jessica knew their faces but not their names. She sat on the edge of their desk and both officers acknowledged her. The one who wasn't on the phone was a new recruit, a young woman somewhere in her twenties. 'Are you all right, Ma'am?'

'Yeah, don't call me that though. Seriously, "Jess" is fine or "DS" or "Sarge" if you really must.' Some officers preferred the formality of using titles. Jessica did understand it in that it could make it easier to separate 'real' life from the job but, from her point of view, each time anyone called her by anything other than her actual name, it just made her feel old.

'Sorry, the DCI asked us to start working on bits for you but we haven't called because there wasn't much to report,' the constable said.

'How much have you got through?'

'We brought together all the missing persons reports from Greater Manchester, Lancashire, Cheshire and a few others we managed to get. They've all gone onto the list we had to start with and we're working our way through a bit of background to see if any were former prisoners.'

'Have you got a list of names?'

'Only on screen.' The constable pointed at the computer monitor and Jessica crouched over to look.

'Can you search for anyone called "Matt" or "Matthew" please?'

The officer clicked through a few screens and brought up a list. There were only two names and one of them had been missing long-term. The second had disappeared the previous week and Jessica felt a familiar tingle down her spine as the operator brought up the details they had.

Matthew Cooper lived locally and had been reported missing by his younger brother. Not only that but, give or take a couple of months, he was the same age as all the other victims who'd had their hands left around the city.

'Can you find out as much as you can about this guy for me?' Jessica asked, noting the phone number of his sibling.

Jessica went to brief Cole about everything that had happened and then, as Rowlands and Diamond arrived, annoyed at having to use public transport, the three of them called the remaining members of the rugby team who they knew were alive. They also looked over their list of college-leavers but Matthew Cooper wasn't on it.

She let the two constables leave for the day but, not entirely willing to give up her theory, called the missing man's brother, Luke. The details around his sibling's disappearance seemed fairly straightforward – he had gone to the pub one night and not returned. The missing man's friends said he had left as he normally would and, as Jessica had seen from the brief information they had on record, there hadn't been anything the local force to the west of the city had found. Although missing people weren't exactly common, Matthew wouldn't have been the first person to stumble into the canal after having too much to drink.

Because there was no other obvious way to identify who the hand had come from, Jessica asked Luke if an officer could visit to take a mouth swab that would be tested by the labs against the mangled hand. She tried not to give the man any hope his missing sibling had been found but it was a tough situation. Either way, he agreed and Jessica figured they might have a match one way or the other in the next twenty-four hours if they were lucky.

It was as she was about to hang up that Jessica realised she had overlooked the most obvious question. 'Does your brother have any tattoos?' she asked.

'He's got a few on his arms and a big one on his back,' Luke replied.

'Is that all?'

'Why?'

'It could just help us with identification purposes if need be.'

'The one on his back is a dragon while he's got some Chinese bits on his arms.'

Jessica didn't want to give specifics about the tattooed letters she'd seen on the victim's fingers in case it gave too much away. Nothing had been released to the media so far and if it did turn out to be the man's brother, she would want the DNA confirmation first before telling him properly. 'Are you sure he doesn't have any others?'

'I think there's something on his calf . . . oh, and he's

got something on his knuckles too,' the man added. Jessica held her breath as the man finished his sentence. 'I don't know why he got it but it says my name "Luke" on one hand and "Matt" on the other.'

Jessica kept herself calm as she thanked the man for his help and said she would contact him once the DNA results came back. She hung up and took a deep breath.

It seemed likely the fourth hand belonged to Matthew Cooper but, considering he neither played rugby – nor went to school – with the other three victims, she had no idea how he was connected to them.

25

The almost two-day wait to get the identity of the severed finger confirmed had been interminable. It seemed fair that the lab workers had to take their time given the state of the hand but that hadn't stopped Jessica swearing silently at them in the privacy of her office.

Edward Marks, Lewis Barnes and Jacob Chrisp had all gone to the same school together and played in the same rugby team. Matthew Cooper had none of those connections and, apart from being roughly the same age and coming from generally the same area, Jessica hadn't managed to find anything else to link him to the other victims.

After confirmation of his identity, she broke the news to Luke Cooper that his brother was most-likely dead and tried to get as much information as she could about the missing man. The problem was that, aside from an odd taste in tattoos, Matthew simply seemed too normal. He worked in accounts, had a small group of friends, was apparently happily single and, from everything they had found, had no obvious enemies or reasons for people to hurt him.

Jessica didn't know if it was a good or bad thing but January Forrester had also been ruled out of their inquiries. At the time the fourth hand was being left, she was doing volunteer work at a hostel and had half-a-dozen witnesses to say where she was. Jessica was glad in a way as it closed that chapter but, on the other hand, didn't give them much to work with.

While Rowlands and Diamond continued to look into Matthew's background to see if there was something they had missed, Jessica had an up-to-date photograph of the missing man from his brother and was taking a day to visit relatives of the other people who had disappeared.

Vicky Barnes wasn't ready to admit January was innocent and was still angry with the police for releasing the woman. She kept saying she didn't feel safe in her house but, while Jessica had some sympathy, there wasn't really anything the woman had to back her feelings up, other than the fact January had been freed. Either way she didn't recognise the picture of Matthew Cooper and neither did Jacob Chrisp's parents.

Her final call was to Charlie Marks, who invited her over to the house again. Jessica had no problems finding the place second time around and parked at the top of the driveway. The gardens looked as if they had been cut since the last time Jessica had visited and as the man strolled out of the house, it seemed clear he had now moved in properly. He looked like a man of leisure, wearing a different pair of baggy shorts and flip-flops, finished off with a loose-fitting cotton shirt and sunglasses. It was a slightly strange thing to do but, as he emerged into the sun to greet Jessica, he took the glasses off.

If anything his hair looked blonder and messier than before and he smiled as he welcomed her inside. For a moment, she thought he might try to hug her but he simply held out his hand for her to shake.

'How are you keeping, Charlie?' she asked.

'Not too bad. I'm still sorting through some of my brother's papers and I've been in touch with a couple of solicitors. Obviously I'm still hoping you'll find him but there are bills that need to be paid and so on. It's very complicated because Ed is still classed as "missing" rather than anything . . . worse. I don't think he was very good at keeping up with things.'

Jessica nodded, knowing it was hard enough dealing with the legal issues when someone had died, let alone when they had just disappeared. 'I don't really need to stay for long, I was wondering if you might be able to take a look at a photo for me to see if you recognise the person?'

'Sure, but if it's anything to do with my brother, I'm not sure there's much I'll know. You're aware of the . . . problems between us.'

Jessica slid the photo of Matthew Cooper out of an envelope. Charlie scanned it but stuck his bottom lip out and shook his head. 'No idea, I'm afraid.' He handed the photo back and she put it away.

'Do you want a drink? I can sort you a tea or something? Maybe a cold drink?'

Perhaps it was because she didn't fancy an afternoon in the stifling police station but Jessica surprised herself with her answer. 'Sure.'

She followed the man as he led her through the house and Jessica glanced from side to side while they walked. Ed's art was hung throughout the area, a stark contrast to some of the clutter which had simply been left around. Their footsteps echoed from the hard floor until they reached the kitchen.

While the rest of the property seemed a strange mix of being half-finished as well as old and new, the kitchen was impressive. There was a huge American-style fridge on the wall directly opposite the door, with a gas cooker that had six hobs and a huge extractor hood overhanging it pressed against the wall to her right. The rest of the area was taken up with thick worktops. Jessica blinked, trying to take in the difference in the room compared to what she had seen before.

'Do you cook?' she asked, almost feebly.

'A little. None of this was here when I left, I guess my brother had it all put in. I've been playing around over the last couple of weeks though. It would be almost a shame not to, given everything that's here.'

'Why do you think so much effort went into this room?' As Jessica asked the question, a mobile phone started to ring. Charlie at first looked surprised as the sound clearly wasn't coming from his pockets. He tried a couple of drawers before eventually finding the device. Without answering it, he pressed a button to silence it.

'Sorry about that. I have no idea what it was doing in there.'

'Is it yours?'

'Yeah, yeah. I've been looking for it for a couple of days.'

'But I called your mobile not long ago to see if you were around,' Jessica said, a little confused.

'I've got a couple. I had one for work that I never ended up giving back. I should probably send it down to them to be honest.'

Jessica didn't say anything but it seemed odd. He put the phone into his shorts pocket and opened the fridge. 'I went shopping the other day. I've got lemonade, Coke, water, fruit juice . . . ?'

'Lemonade's fine.'

Charlie sat on a stool with his drink as Jessica walked slowly around the room. 'Can I help you with anything?' he asked.

'No, sorry, just being nosy – force of habit. I don't think I've ever seen a kitchen this nice before.'

'I don't know what to tell you. It's not really mine.'

'Can I look around the rest of the house?'

'I guess . . . is there anything you're after specifically? I know where most bits are now.'

Jessica shrugged. 'I'm not sure. You found that rugby picture, perhaps there's something else? People other than your brother have gone missing and it must be for a reason. There's so much stuff here, maybe there's something we've all missed because we've been looking in the wrong place?'

Charlie smiled and downed his drink. 'That's fine. I was going to be around all afternoon anyway, though I've got a few phone calls to make. All I'd say is to be careful if you go into the pool area. I'm still trying to get to the bottom of that. From what I can tell some contractors took the money, did half a job and that was that. Lot of gippos around here, so who knows? I'm getting someone in to do a proper job but he's good so there's a waiting list. He's working on some footballer's house just over the back at the moment then he's going to come here. I need to get a bit of money released before then but it's all with the solicitors.'

Jessica nodded but didn't really have any need to go to the half-built room. She didn't know what she was doing and was acting more on a whim than with any great purpose. After finishing her drink, she asked Charlie if he minded her going upstairs on her own but he was fine. Jessica walked across the hard white-stoned floor of the entranceway then up the carpeted stairs to the wooden landing. The kitchen also had a wooden floor and Jessica wondered quite why it was all so mismatched.

She felt strange about being given such free rein to root through someone else's possessions. It wasn't as if it was the first time she'd done something like it but there was usually a warrant involved. It occurred to her that Charlie didn't mind because so little of it was directly his.

She ignored the room she had identified as Ed's bedroom the last time she had been in the house and instead looked in the ones she had only glanced at before.

The first was in keeping with the rest of the half-finished house. The ground had bare floorboards with boxes stacked in one of the corners. She opened the flaps of the card but it contained only decorating items, with stiff old paintbrushes and tins of paint with logos that looked outdated.

In the second room was a single bed on a clean-looking carpet. It didn't look new as such, more untouched, as if it had been set up for a guest who never arrived. Jessica looked out of the arched window over the back garden where Charlie was pacing, talking to someone on the phone. He saw her and gave a cheery wave which Jessica returned slightly less enthusiastically. She was finding him an odd man to read but there were a lot of strange things in his life. He had not long made up with his brother, only for Ed to disappear. That left him as the sole heir to the house, something he didn't really seem to know what to do with. It seemed pretty obvious Ed was a little eccentric, given the state of the house he had been living in apparently alone since his father's passing.

Jessica had never had money to spare, not that she had struggled financially for a long time either. She earned enough to pay her bills, tried to save a little, then have some left over for whatever she fancied during the course of a month. As she looked around at the vast expanse, she wondered how she would have reacted to inheriting something so large. Maybe it would have been in the same way Ed and apparently his father before him had – by only half-dealing with things. Some rooms, such as the kitchen and Ed's own bedroom, were nicely maintained, others were a shambles. It seemed they had created as much comfortable space as they needed to live in and not much more.

Jessica had looked into the family dynamic as much as possible and couldn't help but feel there was something not quite right. At the same time, everything Charlie said had been verified and it wasn't as if there was anyone else to check the family issues with. She wondered why neither of the sons had any type of relationship. Charlie was apparently single while Ed, who had also been a decent-looking young man with artistic talent and plenty of money, was apparently unattached too.

Jessica knew she wasn't exactly an authority on relationships but it wasn't as if she had found any trace of former girlfriends, or boyfriends, connected to the brothers. When the media got hold of big cases, things such as murders or something akin to what Jessica was working on, people would often contact the police because they knew the victim. It might be a former girlfriend or boyfriend, sometimes distant relatives or old friends. They wouldn't necessarily be able to add anything to the case itself but it might help them build up a picture of who the person was. With Ed, they'd had next to nothing, almost as if he lived in the giant house on his own and didn't have anyone else in his life.

Jessica continued to look through the house. The bathroom was as impressively decked out as the kitchen – one large wet room with a tiled, slanted floor for the water to run into a drain in the centre. The taps and shower unit were made of stainless steel, the sink and toilet the same colour as the shiny black walls. Jessica had only seen a bathroom quite so well equipped once before. On that occasion, she'd had to visit Edinburgh for work purposes and the force had paid for a hotel room. Because the place was oversubscribed, the staff had put her in a suite at the top of the building. It had been so much classier than anything she'd experienced before, she ended up taking two showers and using a remote control to open and close curtains in the bedroom just because she could.

She finally found her way back into the room where Charlie had handed her the picture of the rugby team. She felt drawn to the window again, spending a few minutes watching birds flit into the back garden and chase each other before flying away. There was no sign of Charlie outside and the scene seemed incredibly peaceful. She could understand why Ed had spent his time painting in the room that looked out onto the back.

Jessica eventually turned away, peering towards the clutter of boxes around the room. She didn't know what she was after but started to look through the one closest to her. Even the contents seemed to have no order to them. In the first one was a certificate for Ed from primary school because he had finished fourth in a maths quiz but underneath it was a tin of shoe polish, four wall brackets you would use to put up shelves, an empty glass milk bottle and a board game that had an old television presenter's face on the box, despite the fact he'd been dead for over a decade.

After pulling the items on the floor, Jessica did her best to repack them into the box they had come out of, although she wondered if they would ever be taken out again. The contents of the second crate were just as mismatched as the first. It contained golf balls, some old curtains, a snow globe, some tacky old sunglasses, a few candles and three newspapers from over twenty years ago. Jessica looked through the papers in case they had been kept for a reason but, if they had, she couldn't see it.

As she put all the items back into the box, Jessica was beginning to question her own judgement about what she was hoping to achieve. She opened a third box and took out some wire coat hangers plus four empty tobacco tins. Underneath those were a set of framed photographs.

The first one was of two boys around nine or ten years old building a sandcastle on the beach. One was blond, the other had dark hair. Both were grinning at the camera and Jessica could just about see the resemblance to Charlie. When they were younger, the two brothers were fairly similar, although the brown-haired Ed was a little shorter. Jessica continued to look through the pictures. The next one was of Ed on stage in what looked like a school play. He was a little older, maybe thirteen, and appeared to be giving some sort of sincere soliloquy. Charlie was the subject of the next photo, riding a bike around a park though it could possibly have been the garden. There was also a photo of Charlie fishing, another of him playing football and a final one where he and Ed seemed to be doing their homework. The pair were sitting opposite each other at a table concentrating on separate work books.

Jessica thought the photo underneath those was hauntingly beautiful. It looked as if Ed hadn't even known it was being taken. He was around sixteen years old and sat painting in the room underneath. Light streamed through the windows ahead of him with a misting of rain on the glass. She found the image incredibly compelling and wondered who had taken it. Perhaps confused by the way she had been drawn to that photo, Jessica almost failed to notice what the next picture was showing. She had gone to put it face-down on the other photos before realising its significance.

She turned it back over and stared at the contents. There were six young men, perhaps eighteen or nineteen, all toasting the camera with glasses of beer in their hands. They were all a mixture of tanned brown and burnt red and it seemed clear they were on a holiday of some sort. After studying it the second time, Jessica could clearly see Ed Marks in the middle with a huge grin on his face. Next to him on one side was someone who looked like a younger Matthew Cooper. She had only just got hold of an up-to-date picture of him but felt sure the resemblance was there.

Next to Matthew was someone she couldn't place but, on the other side of Ed, Jessica could see something she had been waiting for since the first hand was found. There was one more face she didn't know but the final two tanned faces grinning out of the photo undoubtedly belonged to Lewis Barnes and Jacob Chrisp.

26

On almost every occasion where Jessica heard or saw something that excited her relating to a case, she would feel her heart racing, ready to leap into action. Instead, she simply stared at the photo of the men. She looked at the hints of blue sky above them, wondering where it had been taken and who had been behind the camera. Was it a barman or a passing stranger? Was it a seventh young person somehow related to whatever the picture was showing her?

Jessica walked back down the stairs still looking at the photo, also holding onto the image of the two brothers doing their homework. She found Charlie in the kitchen. 'Are you all right?' he asked, adding: 'What have you found?'

She handed over the holiday picture. 'Do you know anything about this? When or where it was taken? Who might be in it?'

Charlie stared at the image and then looked back at her. 'Are these . . . ?'

'Four of them, including your brother, are missing. I need to find out who the other two people are, then what happened with the six of them.'

'I don't really know,' Charlie said, slightly stuttering his words. 'I vaguely remember him going to Faliraki when he left college but we had different friends.'

'At least one of these people didn't go to college with him though,' Jessica said, thinking of Matthew Cooper.

Charlie shrugged. 'I don't know. All I remember is that it was the first time he'd gone abroad and he had to sort out a passport. It was the summer after he finished his exams but I guess it didn't necessarily mean they were all people he was at college with. He did this art class thing once a week too. I just don't know.'

'So he would have been eighteen or maybe nineteen?'

'I guess so.'

Jessica took the photo back. 'Can I take this for now?'

'No worries.'

She showed him the other one of the two boys doing their homework. 'I found this. I didn't know if you might want it?'

Charlie took the photo from her and smiled slightly. 'I remember this being taken. It's nice. Dad used to make us do our homework when we got home from school before he'd let us out. I remember him taking this.' He used the support at the back of the frame to prop it up on the kitchen counter.

Jessica indicated towards the photo she was holding. 'Can you keep quiet about this for a bit?'

'Sure, it's not as if I know anyone anyway.'

'I mean from the papers.'

'Whatever you want.'

Jessica drove back to the station trying to think things over but there were no obvious answers. If something had happened on the holiday, the person leaving hands around the city could perhaps be one of the two faces from the photo she didn't recognise – or it could still be someone else entirely. The first priority had to be finding out who the remaining two people were and hoping neither of them had gone missing and that they would be willing to talk. Whether the holiday itself was relevant would be something they would hope to find out in due course – but at least Jessica now knew there was a connection from Matthew Cooper to the other three victims.

After parking at Longsight, Jessica called Charlie to ask if he could look through the rest of the boxes at his house and let her know if there were any others of Ed at a similar age. Two of her leads had already come from him and it would be irresponsible to not finish looking through things. With his agreement, she could have asked officers to go over but the house was so big, it would be easy to miss items and there would be no guarantee they would know what they were looking for. At least Charlie was aware of the type of photos she was after and, regardless of his odd circumstances, he did seem keen to help.

Dave and Izzy had already left for the day, as had Cole. Jessica would usually run ideas past at least one of them but, after looking around the station, she returned to her own office. DS Cornish was sitting at her desk and it was the first time Jessica had seen her in their office for a while.

'How's things?' Jessica asked.

Louise sounded tired. 'Slow and painful. I'm seeing red vans in my sleep.'

'No luck finding out where it came from then?'

'We're getting there but not easily. We thought that

once we had the make and model it would be a fairly small list – but Royal Mail's records aren't great. Instead of having a small list of vehicles it could be, we've got a long list of vans it isn't. The DVLA are their usual shambles too – they really are the most incompetent, useless bunch of idiots I have ever known. We've got a couple of leads.'

Jessica walked around her colleague's desk and sat at her own, turning to face the other woman. 'What about looking into George Johnson himself?'

'I've been left out of that a little but it's fine by me,' Louise said. 'The superintendent has been talking to a few people. We've gone over his bank records and there are a few cash withdrawals that don't seem quite right but they could be innocent enough. At some point we'll interview him about them but there's so much more we want to look at first. We had to jump through hoops but we've got a warrant for certain emails now too. You know we wanted to do it without him knowing? That created all sorts of problems but we've got tech guys looking over things.'

'Expecting much?'

The sergeant sighed, adjusting one of the photos on her desk to make sure it lined up with the others. It was the longest conversation Jessica had had with her since the other woman started working at the station. 'Who knows? Some people think that if they delete emails, there's no trace of them. Some are too stupid to delete them. Others don't send emails at all and our lab teams could spend the next few days looking over the dullest memos imaginable. I think it will come down to the cash that's now not in his account and whether we can prove he's done anything untoward with it.'

Jessica blew through her teeth. 'You'll struggle. It could have gone on secret love-children, mistresses, cocaine, hookers or a giant stuffed teddy bear just for the hell of it. He's not obliged to keep receipts and all we can do is ask the questions.'

'I know. There's a steady amount of cash he takes out every month which might or might not be legit but there was one larger withdrawal last month and one the month before. We'll ask him but only after we've gone over his emails. I think his attitude could turn then too because so far he's been the confused husband. If it gets leaked he's in the frame there really will be a shit-storm.'

Jessica wasn't exactly shocked by her colleague's language but it occurred to her it was the first time she'd heard the woman swear. As their conversation petered out, she spun her chair around to look at her computer monitor, then pulled up the file of the rugby team she was so familiar with to make sure neither of the two faces from the holiday photo matched the other players. They didn't, which left her without an obvious way of finding out who the people were.

As she was thinking, Louise spoke out of the blue. 'I'm sorry by the way.'

Jessica looked across. 'Pardon?'

'I'm sorry for being a bit of a cow. I know you weren't having a go about me working. It was just a bit of a sensitive issue at the time.'

Jessica was a little taken aback as the statement was so

out of the blue. 'No, look, it was my fault. Sometimes I blurt out any old nonsense without thinking and it comes over wrong. It's not a surprise I also have a problem of not being able to control my own facial expressions.'

Louise nodded and smiled. 'I've been wanting to talk for ages but I always miss you; either I'm here and you're not or presumably you are and I'm not.'

'I know; if it wasn't for the morning briefings every now and then I wouldn't know you still worked here.'

'How are things with your case?'

'Moving but not exactly quickly.' Jessica walked over to the other sergeant's desk to show her the holiday photo. She pointed to the four young men. 'I found this at one of the victim's houses. These are the people the four hands came from. I have no idea who these two are. I'm hoping one of the other relatives does or we're going to be stuck with putting it in the papers and our website with an "Is this you?" request.'

'Those types of thing always look pretty desperate.'

Jessica returned to her own desk and phoned Vicky Barnes. Matthew Cooper's brother and Jacob Chrisp's parents could be visited at a later date if necessary but she figured she may as well start with the one person she'd had the most contact with. The woman was pleased to hear from her and invited her around that evening. Jessica was going to ask about visiting in the morning but it wasn't as if she had anything else on.

She didn't know exactly where she was going but the woman's house was in the Abbey Hey district, just a few minutes away from where January and Lewis lived. Given the short distance between them, Jessica thought it was no surprise January was so annoyed at her boyfriend's mother if she frequently came round. It was early evening as Jessica drove but there were still groups of children on the roads of the estate. Some seemed innocent enough as they kicked a football around in the late day's sunshine, others had a more sinister look. If she'd been driving a nicer car, she might have felt wary of parking on the street but someone trashing her vehicle could give her the proverbial kick – and insurance payout – needed to get something better.

After parking a few doors down from Vicky Barnes's property, Jessica thought about leaving the car unlocked, almost willing someone to at least attempt to steal it. Ultimately, she turned the key and walked to the woman's house.

If the Markses' was a mismatched property, this whole area was a disjointed estate. Jessica had driven past some properties with stale old mattresses and other items of furniture dumped in their front gardens, next to immaculately kept houses.

The Barneses' fell somewhere in the middle; there was nothing on the front but the lawn had been allowed to grow out and it looked very tatty. Jessica rang the doorbell and a cheap-sounding version of 'God Save the Queen' played. Vicky Barnes opened the door looking almost exactly the same as the last time Jessica had seen her, wearing a tight cream crop top that was far too small for her and leggings that looked painted on. The biggest difference was that her hair was no longer greying and had been dyed a strange mix of purple and brown that definitely didn't work.

'You all right, love?' Vicky said. 'Come on in.'

Jessica walked into the house, following the woman into a living room. As she sat on the sofa and Vicky disappeared to get herself a drink, Jessica took the room in. Half of the area seemed to be a shrine to Lewis. There were photos of him from all stages of life, as well as various certificates and awards that had all been neatly framed and put on display. Jessica read the words on a certificate that must have been twenty years old and simply said the recipient had completed a ten-metre swim. Jessica was sure her parents had something similar from her childhood but it would likely be in a box somewhere, certainly not on a wall so long after its award.

She was beginning to see January's point more than ever. Jessica knew Lewis was an only child because of their files. There were no pictures of anyone except for him on display and, if you assumed from that the father wasn't present, it was a pretty sad situation for everyone. On the one hand you had a son who wouldn't have wanted to leave his mother on her own but did want to move in with his girlfriend. Then you had the girlfriend who Vicky would never have thought good enough for him, no matter who she was. Finally, you had the mother who was missing her son but was, to be kind, a little overprotective.

With the fact they lived close together, it really wasn't a good recipe for success.

Jessica looked around the rest of the room and there was a mass of trinkets and the types of ornaments people brought with them back from holiday. There were small statues of buildings as well as plate sets, candles and all sorts of other tat Jessica absolutely hated. The only item she ever brought back from a trip abroad was as much alcohol as she could get away with.

When Vicky returned she was carrying a cup of tea and sat in an armchair opposite the sofa Jessica was on. 'Are you sure you don't want one?' she asked, holding her mug up.

'I'm fine, thanks.'

'Do you like all my pictures of Lewis?' Vicky pointed at a particular one above Jessica's head. 'In that one there he was in the school play. He was fourteen but they wouldn't give him the lead role. He was the best one there though – no one could have denied that.'

'Did you know much about his friends, Mrs Barnes?'

The woman took a gulp from her tea then answered. 'Oh yes, he played a bit of rugby and so on. I used to let him have his friends stay over. I know I probably shouldn't tell you this but I'd get them some beer or something on a Friday night. You know what lads are like, don't you?'

'Would you remember the names though? For instance did you know Jacob Chrisp and Edward Marks?'

The woman pursed her lips. 'I wasn't always sure about the rugby boys. Faces I'm fine with, it's the names that don't come so easily.'

'You didn't remember Matthew Cooper the other day,' Jessica reminded her.

Vicky shrugged defensively. 'If he knew Lewis, it must have been a friend of a friend-type thing.'

Jessica took the holiday photo out of an envelope she had been carrying around and walked over to the woman. She pointed at the two young men she didn't know. 'Do you know who these people are?'

The woman looked hard at the photo. 'I know the faces, erm . . .' She looked up to the ceiling as if it were written up there. 'One of them's "Steven" but I don't know the last name. The other one is somebody Newcombe. They called him "Newey". I'd know the first name if you said it.'

Jessica gave the woman time to think things over but Vicky couldn't remember anything else. They made small talk and Jessica listened to another rant about January before she thanked the woman for her help, adding that if she remembered any of the names fully, she could call at any time. Vicky wanted to know the significance of the photo but Jessica didn't reveal too much. She asked Lewis's mother if she could look for any further photos taken around that time of her son with his friends and then said her goodbyes.

After finding the link from Matthew to the other three victims and having at least partial names for the other two, Jessica was going to drive back to the station, log the information on the system and then go home and drink an entire bottle of wine herself. It wasn't something she did too regularly but there were now only a few hours until her birthday and she was hoping no one had remembered.

27

It wasn't often the post turned up before Jessica had to leave for work but, as if Royal Mail somehow knew, a birthday card was waiting in the hallway of her communal block of flats as she was on her way out. She only needed to read the handwriting on the envelope to know it was from her mother. A few years ago, the postman responsible for the round where Jessica lived had been arrested for stealing from the mail. Over ten thousand undelivered items were found in his garage. Somehow, despite that and another year where there was a strike on, Jessica's mother always managed to get a card to her on time.

Jessica had spent her nineteenth birthday in Thailand with Caroline. The two had gone travelling for the best part of a year after finishing college but, even then, the receptionist at the hostel where they were staying had hand-delivered her a card from her mum. She thought Caroline must have been involved somehow, at least in divulging where they were staying, but her friend denied everything.

Before she pulled her car away, Jessica opened the envelope and read the contents of the card. It both moved her and made her laugh at the same time.

'A third of a century. We're so proud of you. X.'

And then came her mother's signature followed by the sign-off:

'PS: Our phone number hasn't changed. Use it!'

Jessica knew she wasn't great at staying in contact with her parents but it wasn't the easiest thing to do. Her dad always wanted to talk about her job but often it was the last thing she wanted to discuss. Her mum would want to know about boyfriends or Caroline or other things that hadn't been going too well. She had never really told them that she and Caroline had been out of touch for a long while and had only just begun to be good friends again. After things turned out the way they had with Randall, Caroline had gone to stay with Jessica's parents for a short while. They frequently said they saw her as their own, given Caroline's parents had both died.

Jessica's mother and father were both coming down for the wedding and apparently looking forward to it. She didn't want to be asked the obvious questions about when it would be her turn to walk down the aisle. That was bad enough but if either of them started talking about grand-children, it really would wind her up.

As she arrived at the station, no one said anything to indicate they knew it was her birthday, which suited Jessica just fine. She had already emailed Cole a few details about the two people in the holiday photo who were so far unidentified. The chief inspector gave her a couple of officers to help find out who they were. Someone was visiting the parents of Jacob Chrisp to see if there were any other photos from the same time and to ask if they knew who the other people in the picture were. A different officer had gone to see Matthew Cooper's brother for the same reason.

While that was going on, Jessica was working from the

station to find out what could be discovered using the names 'Newcombe' and 'Steven'. It was obviously a common first name but they knew roughly what ages the two unidentified men should be, which gave them a start. On the college-leavers' list there was no one with the last name, while the Stevens had all been ruled out, regardless of how they spelled their first names. That meant that, as with Matthew Cooper, they had to look further afield into people who lived in roughly the same area as the other victims, while trying to track down the types of clubs and societies the men might have been in.

It was enormously complicated as they didn't know where to start because the chance of people being friends of friends meant the net had to spread so wide. That left them compiling a list of everyone with the names 'Newcombe' or 'Steven' and then working backwards to connect them to any of the victims. Or, as Rowlands so eloquently described it, 'Trying to find out who's taken a piss in the ocean'.

Jessica didn't leave the station for the entire day but news filtered through that the officers who had gone to see the Chrisp and Cooper families had come back with nothing. Jessica had a long list of people who *weren't* in the photo but nothing concrete to say who was. It was a long frustrating day all around, especially with the air-conditioning still not working. Things were so bad the staff had even stopped complaining about it. People were bringing their own desk fans from home to use, although the temperature had at least dipped a little outside in the past day.

Not a single person asked about her birthday which to Jessica was far more suspicious than people hinting at the subject. She'd had her suspicions but the reason eventually became clear as Rowlands tried to start a casual conversation with her towards the end of the day. 'Do you fancy the pub after work?'

'Are you being serious?'

'What do you mean?'

Jessica raised her eyebrows. 'So it's just us two off to the pub, out of the blue, which is something we've not done in months?'

'It's been a busy few weeks; I figured we could go for a pint and a catch-up. Maybe bring Iz along too?'

'A catch-up? We see each other every day.'

'You know what I mean,' Dave said.

'Yeah, unfortunately I think I do. Right, well, if you do want to do this whole thing then yeah, whatever, pub after work.' Rowlands did his best to look as if he didn't know what Jessica was alluding to but she could see straight through him. 'If you ever get arrested for anything, Dave, make sure you say nothing because the second you start talking you'll give yourself away,' she added.

Her fears were confirmed as Dave and Izzy casually walked her to the station's local, each pretending they were simply after a quiet drink. A smaller team had been left to work on the leads they had and, while Jessica would have preferred to stay herself, she went with her friends. She couldn't even pretend to be surprised as she walked into the pub to find a select group of her colleagues, Caroline and a few other people she knew waiting for her.

There was a token cheer of 'surprise' but a general accept-
ance she would have been one of the worst detectives
going if she hadn't figured out what the two constables
had planned.

Jessica had never been keen on being the centre of
attention, much preferring to sit in the corner and make
sarcastic comments, but she thanked everyone and then
cheered up even more when the landlord said her drinks
were free for the night. She walked around the pub a couple
of times, making small talk with the people that had come
to say hello and then, almost inevitably, ended up in a
booth towards the back with Caroline, Dave and Izzy.

'So which one of you organised this then?' she asked.

'You can thank Dave,' Izzy said. 'Although I did tell him
there was no way he'd keep it a secret.'

Jessica turned to Rowlands. 'I'll give you one thing;
you can definitely organise a piss-up in a brewery. If you
can sort out a shag in a brothel, you'll be up for promotion.'

The constable smiled. 'You really don't do gratitude, do
you?'

Jessica put on a sarcastic voice. 'Thank you very much
for reminding everyone I'm getting old.'

'No problem.'

Although it was early evening, Caroline said she'd left
work an hour prematurely. She was certainly dressed up
for the occasion, wearing a short purple dress the type of
which wasn't seen very regularly in a police pub like the
one they were in. The older male officers had certainly
noticed but her friend seemed oblivious. She told Jessica

that Dave had invited her. They had met on a couple of occasions in the past, although not as embarrassing as this one, and he'd kept her phone number just in case something like this came up. Jessica suspected he had taken her number just in case the woman became single at any point but didn't want to point it out.

'So, presents,' Caroline said, sounding excited. She pulled a large glossy paper bag out from under her seat. Jessica tried to look cool but, even though public parties weren't her thing, presents always went down well and she struggled to hide at least a degree of excitement. There were three items in the bag. She unwrapped the first to find a cook book that boasted it could teach simple culinary methods anyone could use. 'I thought it was about time you learned some basics,' Caroline said. 'It's got all sorts in there just to get you going.'

Jessica had been thinking the same thing for years but had never had the inclination. She wasn't convinced the book would give her that but smiled and thanked her friend nonetheless. She also poked a smirking Rowlands in the leg.

The second gift was some vouchers for a department store in the city but Jessica really felt touched by the final one. It was a framed picture of her and Caroline from the week before they left to tour south-east Asia. They were both teenagers and it was a photo Jessica recognised and remembered being taken but hadn't seen in years. They were cheesily grinning at the camera, wearing each other's clothes. Jessica smiled and gave her friend a small hug. 'This is really nice, thanks.'

Rowlands picked the picture up from the table. 'Christ, you look young here.'

'It was taken before I had to endure the stress of working with you every day.'

The constable ignored her. 'Girls get such boring presents. Us lads get computer games, toy cars, robots and all sorts of cool stuff. You get bloody pictures and all kinds of shite.'

Jessica put on a serious face. 'It's called growing up, Dave. Most people stop wasting their life with games, comics and robots when they hit their teens. If you're still doing that by the time you get to thirty, it might be time to get a proper hobby.'

'All right, all right, enough of this "turning thirty" talk. You know how to kick a man when he's down, don't you?' Dave protested.

'Actually, there's no better time to kick a man than when he's down. I pride myself on being good at it.'

Izzy stepped in to change the subject. 'So, when's the wedding then?' she asked Caroline.

'Just a few weeks now.'

'Are you excited?'

'Yeah, can't wait.'

'It's my wedding anniversary in a few weeks. It only seems like yesterday in some ways.'

'Have you got kids?' Caroline asked.

Jessica winced, realising her friend had asked exactly the thing she shouldn't. Caroline realised it too because of the look on Izzy's face. 'Sorry . . . I didn't mean . . .'

'No, it's fine. I haven't got any children, no.' The

constable stayed calm but the atmosphere was edgy and it was clear it was a touchy subject.

'Who are you taking then?' Dave asked Jessica, obviously trying to lighten the mood.

'What, to the wedding?'

'Yes, who *are* you taking?' Caroline added. 'We've left a place for them at the table but haven't got a name to go on the plan yet.'

Jessica shuffled nervously. 'Just someone. It's all sorted, don't worry about it.'

'A secret boyfriend?'

'No, just a friend.'

'A friend who's a boy?' Caroline pushed.

'Sod off, just a friend. Don't worry about it.'

'Is it someone from the station?' Izzy asked.

'Can we change the subject?'

The other three people looked towards each other and almost collectively made an 'oooh' sound. 'Right, what's the plan for later?' Jessica said, still trying to change the subject. 'Are we staying here or what?'

'It's up to you,' Izzy replied. 'It's your birthday.'

'Right, well, considering I'm on free drinks all night, I vote stay here, then pizza on the way home.'

Dave laughed quietly. 'You're not going to invite us all round and cook fried eggs now you've got your new book?'

'If you fancy a pot noodle, you're welcome. Well, you're not but these two are.'

'I don't really do pizzas,' Izzy said. 'I'm more of a kebab kind of girl.'

Jessica pulled a face. 'I used to be like that but the

problem is the morning after. With a pizza you can have the leftovers for breakfast. With a kebab, it looks as if someone's hurled it up.'

The other three people around the table were united in their reply. 'Eew.'

'Are you telling me I'm wrong?'

Izzy answered. 'No, but there are some things you don't have to say out loud.' Jessica laughed and had to admit that was true. The constable grinned herself. 'If we'd organised this properly we could have gone around town doing the birthday scam.'

'The what?' Jessica asked.

'Way back before I was an officer, me and my friends used to do it when we were teenagers. We'd go to one of the restaurants in town and someone would drop the hint it was someone else's birthday. All the servers would come over and clap and sing this stupid song but you'd get a free cake out of it. Then we'd move on to the next place and do the same thing. There were about five places in town who had that policy so every few weeks we'd be out claiming it was someone's birthday.'

'I'm not convinced we'd get away with that any longer given our oath to uphold the law,' Jessica said.

'Maybe not but you'd get free cake.'

Despite her reservations about any sort of acknowledgement of her birthday, Jessica ended up having a good time. She liked that the two constables kept her grounded.

Jessica found herself getting tipsier as the evening went on. She didn't know if the free wine was courtesy of the landlord himself or because her colleagues had put money behind the bar. By the time she'd got close to finishing her sixth glass of wine, along with the various shots that had been placed in front of her, Jessica knew she was beginning to slur her words. She had always found it ironic how much she and other officers drank, considering most of the crime they investigated, especially officers in uniform, ultimately came down to alcohol. She had always been a good drinker and was more inclined to laugh the night away than get herself in trouble. If anything, Jessica had always thought she was far more likely to say something stupid when she was sober as opposed to after she'd had a bit to drink. Despite that, she decided she had finished drinking for the night, especially as she would have to be back at work the next day.

There were a few mini protests from the constables as Jessica said she wanted to go but Caroline didn't look too bothered as she had gone quiet and seemed to be fighting to stay awake.

Jessica caught a taxi from the nearby rank but it was only after she arrived home, via a pizza shop, that she noticed she had missed calls. Her head felt fuzzy but the takeaway took the edge off ever so slightly. Jessica pressed the buttons on the phone to listen to her voicemail but it took a few attempts to get it to do what she wanted.

She listened through the message once but Jessica's brain wasn't thinking clearly enough to take it all in. It was only on the third listen that she finally realised why she had been called so late. The team working at the station had identified both of the remaining people in the photograph – and one of them was already dead.

28

Jessica felt a little silly as she finally got her head around the message. Firstly, she had somehow managed to miss three separate phone calls from the station. It would have only been one or two people working their way through the list of names who had found the breakthrough and the person wouldn't have been calling because they expected her to go back, simply because they wanted to update her. If Jessica had noticed her phone going off in the pub, even with what she had drunk, she would at least have been only around the corner from the station.

Back at home, there was no realistic way she could get herself back to Longsight and, given how drunk she was feeling, it wasn't as if she could do much good anyway. Jessica thought about calling Cole to see if he knew any more but had enough self-awareness through her drunken haze to know she should probably leave it for the rest of the night.

She lay on her bed still wearing the clothes she'd had on all day and, as she watched the ceiling spin, Jessica thought the pizza wasn't the best of ideas after all. She wanted to think about the two people that had now apparently been identified but it wasn't long before her mind gave up and she drifted off to sleep.

*

After the amount she had drunk, Jessica would have expected to sleep through to the moment the alarm on her phone went off the next morning but surprised herself by instead being awake over an hour before she had to be and feeling just about as alert as she could be, given the circumstances.

Apart from an aching bladder, Jessica felt ready for the day. She listened to her voicemail one more time. The officer who had left the message sounded nervous but excited, a nuance which Jessica had definitely not noticed the night before. They said they knew the final two people were called 'Steven Povey' and 'Barry Newcombe' but that Barry was already dead.

From just that, it was difficult to know exactly what was meant. Had the man already died or had he recently been killed in a way that related to the case? None of the other victims they'd found hands from were confirmed as deceased so something certainly sounded different. Jessica checked the times of the calls she had missed. They were all at a point where she would have been sitting in the booth in the pub and it was only then she realised she had somehow muted the device. It wasn't the first time she had managed to do something similar but it was the only time she had missed something important through doing so. Her one crumb of comfort was that, given the time the calls had come in, she wouldn't have been able to do much anyway.

Jessica again thought about calling Cole but, because it was early, didn't want to disturb him while he might be with his family. Instead she caught the bus to the station, having left her car there the night before. She read her emails and, from what she could tell, the officer responsible for the breakthrough had simply been a little lucky in that they had stumbled across the right combination of names. After they had found the correct 'Newcombe', that had led them to work out who the other person was. It was always likely to be a matter of time before somebody found the right people but Jessica would still make sure the person responsible got the credit they deserved.

It only took a few moments for Jessica to realise the message she had been left the night before was slightly misleading. Barry Newcombe was dead but, if it was down to foul play, then the person involved had been very clever. He had been involved in a head-on collision in a car eight years previously in which he, his girlfriend in the passenger seat and the driver of the other car had all been killed. The reports showed Barry had been almost three times over the drink-drive limit and, given the car's positioning on the road, the only suspicions of anything being untoward related to the man's own decision to drink and drive.

If he had somehow survived the smash, he would have almost certainly been charged with causing death by dangerous driving and the witness reports were pretty damning. He had apparently been drinking at a party with some of his friends and had not even pretended to hide the fact he was going to drive home. A few of his mates said they had tried to stop him but none had called the police. Quite why his girlfriend had joined him nobody really knew but the poor guy he had crashed into left behind a wife and four children.

It wasn't the first story of its type Jessica had read but it was one of the worst. A whole family had been destroyed because of the selfishness of one person.

She found it hard to concentrate on the other name that had been left for her, Steven Povey, but realised he was now the one person in the holiday photograph that was still unharmed. He was the youngest of the six men pictured at twenty-nine, which meant he would have only just turned eighteen at the time they figured the photo was taken. Barry Newcombe was the eldest and would have been twenty. The other four men would have been either nineteen or just about to have their birthdays.

Jessica had already checked with a few well-known travel operators but none of them had records going back eleven years. That meant Steven Povey was her one final link to finding out what the reason could possibly be for what was happening. Although it wasn't quite eight in the morning, Jessica couldn't be bothered to wait and phoned the number the officer had left for him. The man had moved out of the city a few years before and now lived in a village further north in Lancashire. He reluctantly agreed to meet Jessica later that day. Initially he wanted to put her off but she insisted it was urgent and that it had to be as soon as possible. Jessica didn't tell Steven about the holiday photograph or talk about possible links to the other men at first but stressed it was important she was able to speak to him.

Jessica waited for Cole to arrive and told him where things were up to before going to grab either Dave or Izzy to take with her. Both constables were looking a little the worse for wear after the night before – but had clearly caught up on the news about the final two faces from the photo. Izzy looked marginally less hung-over, so Jessica left Rowlands to dig up any other information about the car crash which had killed Barry Newcombe, while the two women went to meet Steven Povey.

Jessica was a fierce defender of her car whenever colleagues wanted to give her stick about its age and the volume of the exhaust but she never trusted it to get her much further than from her flat to the station. She certainly didn't want to risk it on the motorway and so asked Izzy if she fancied driving. The other woman's vehicle was only a couple of years old and was definitely a lot less likely to break down. As it was, Jessica needn't have worried, not that it gave her any comfort. There had been a major accident north of the city on the M60 ring road. A tanker carrying diesel had spilled across the carriageway and not only were large parts of the throughway closed, but traffic was backing up into the city centre.

What should have been a simple forty-five-minute journey up the motorway turned into a two-and-a-half-hour inquest into everything that was wrong with the country, the police force, their colleagues and, eventually, life in general as they sat in largely stationary traffic. After they finally got onto the M61 to take them north, the pair had pretty much come to the conclusion they were the only two sane people left on the planet.

After they left the motorway, it had taken a lot longer than Jessica would have thought to get to their destination. On the online map she'd looked at, it wasn't a long distance to Steven Povey's house but the single-track lanes with high-banked overhanging hedges took a while to negotiate because there wasn't always room for two cars to pass each other and Izzy frequently had to pull over.

As they drove into the village, the scene almost seemed to spring into colour. A large bank of flowers that spelled out the name of the place welcomed them, with baskets of plants hanging from seemingly every house. The properties were all detached, with large driveways and patches of grass around them.

A sign proudly told visitors the village had won a 'Britain In Bloom' award for eight years running, another informing them the village's summer fete would be taking place on the following Saturday.

It was the kind of location Jessica figured people from overseas pictured when they thought of Britain because of the television shows that had been sold abroad through the years. If it wasn't for the smattering of satellite dishes and brand-new cars, it could almost have been as if they had travelled back in time forty or fifty years.

Although it was just a few centimetres on the map, the whole area felt a world away from the city. Ultimately Jessica knew people were prone to the same mistakes and cruelties regardless of where they lived. She wasn't sure whether she preferred the honesty you might expect from residents on a rough estate or the apparent tranquillity you would probably get in a village like the one they were in.

There was only one main road through the village but, without a satellite navigation device, neither of them were entirely sure which of the side roads the house they were looking for was on. Izzy pulled over next to where a man was sitting having a lunchtime pint on his own outside a pub. Although she had lived in the north-west of England her entire life, Jessica found his accent hard to decipher but, between the two of them, they eventually worked out where they should be going.

Back in Manchester, a lot of the buildings were a mismatch of styles as diverse estates had been put up at different times, while other properties had been renovated or built by various people working independently of each other. All of the houses in the village seemed to have been either built at the same time or at least created with an eye on the tone of the rest of the area.

Steven Povey's house was no different and looked strikingly similar to the rest of the surrounding properties. There was a low stone wall at the front, edging onto the side road he lived on. There were tidy neatly trimmed grass areas on either side of a concrete path leading to the man's front door. The house itself was made of grey stone with an old-fashioned authentic-looking wooden edge to the windows and door frames. The door was painted bright red, perfectly matching the shade of the rest of the trims. On the front was a heavy black metal knocker, which Jessica used. A man soon answered. He had black hair swept away from his face with a small amount of equally dark designer stubble. He was wearing a T-shirt, three-quarter-length trousers and a pair of brown sandals.

He looked nervous as they introduced themselves and he invited them in, confirming he was Steven Povey. He asked if they wanted to sit outside and led them through to his back garden. There was a black metal table already set up, with four matching chairs around it. The grass was as tidily cut as it was at the front and went back a lot further than Jessica might have guessed from looking at the front of the house.

Steven was still edgy as he sat opposite them. Aside from confirming his identity, no one had given him the full details of why they wanted to speak to him, except for the fact it related to something from the past. He was clearly trying to force a smile as he looked from Izzy to Jessica. 'How can I help you?'

Jessica took out the photograph of the six men on holiday from an envelope. It was a copy of the original she'd taken from the Markses' house. She had spent the last few days almost memorising the features of the unidentified duo in the photo and it had been clear to her straight away that the man in front of her was one of the two. She pointed to the image. 'Can we confirm this is you, Mr Povey?'

He picked the photo up, staring at it. Jessica carefully watched his reaction and there was an obvious flicker of recognition. 'It was taken a long time ago but it is me.'

'Do you know the other five men with you?'

'I suppose . . . but it's been years since I last saw any of them. I lived next door to Barry and he knew one of the other lads.' Steven pointed to Lewis Barnes. 'This guy is Lewis, I went around his house a few times but I only remember that because his mum was a bit weird. I can't really remember the names of the others. They were only sort of my friends.'

'Where was it taken?'

'Faliraki, I think. It was the first time I'd gone abroad without my parents.'

'Can you remember who took the photo?' The man shook his head, so Jessica rephrased the question. 'What I'm asking is if there were six or seven of you who went away? Was it one of your friends behind the camera or a stranger?'

'Oh, right. No, there were just the six of us. I don't know who took the picture.'

'How long ago was it taken?'

The man shook his head. 'Maybe ten years? Eleven? I think I'd just turned eighteen.'

'Why did you go if you didn't really know them?' Jessica asked.

'It was through Barry. Someone he knew was organising a lads' holiday and they were looking for people to go because it was cheaper if you had more. He asked me and I thought, "What the hell". I don't really remember all the details. It was such a long time ago.'

Jessica nodded as everything he said pretty much backed up what they already knew, or at least thought they knew. The next set of questions was where things would begin to get complicated. 'What happened while you were away?' she asked.

Steven shuffled in his chair. 'What do you mean?'

'Just that. You went on holiday with a group of lads you didn't really know, so what went on?'

The man shook his head a little but Jessica wasn't convinced by his words. 'Well, nothing. The accommodation was awful, we ate, we drank, we came home.'

'Anything else?'

'Like what?'

Jessica slid the photo back across the table. She pointed to Barry Newcombe. 'This is your friend Barry, yes? Do you know what happened to him?'

Steven looked confused. 'He was killed in a car accident years ago.'

'Did you know him then?' Jessica asked.

'Yes, but that was a long time ago too. I don't know what that has to do with anything now.'

Jessica nodded, pointing to the next face. 'This is Edward Marks; a few weeks ago we found his severed hand in the centre of Manchester. Even if you didn't remember the name, you may have read about it or seen it on the news. This man here is Lewis Barnes, while this is Jacob Chrisp and this is Matthew Cooper. We have found hands belonging to each of them. All four of them have been reported missing and we have no idea if they're alive or dead. That means you're the one person left out of these six who is definitely still alive.'

Jessica watched Steven closely. As she had revealed each person's fate she saw his eyes widen ever so slightly. She was clearly telling him something he didn't know. 'Can you think of a reason why four people have gone missing, Mr Povey?'

He blinked a few times. 'It wasn't anything to do with me.'

'I never said it was.'

'No, I know . . . I just . . . I'm sorry, do I need a solicitor?'

Jessica didn't know if he was involved but his reaction seemed as genuine as she would expect. If he was a formal suspect, they would have taken him to the station for questioning but, at least for now, Jessica didn't want to take things that far. She chose her words carefully. 'If you want a solicitor, it's entirely up to you. We can talk to you here or at a station, I don't mind. All I'm asking you is if you know of any reason why four people you went on holiday with eleven years ago might have gone missing.'

Steven was clearly nervous. It was warm and he'd seemed edgy throughout but there was sweat on his forehead. He looked quickly from one detective to the other. 'I'm not sure what you want me to say.'

'It's pretty simple,' Jessica said. 'I believe something happened when the six of you went away together and that is the reason why the people you were on holiday with aren't here. From that, I can make two conclusions. The first is that you are somehow involved in what has gone on with the hands being left. The second is that you are also a target. I don't believe you have kidnapped four people, cut off their hands and driven to Manchester to leave them for us. If you continue to insist nothing happened on that holiday, we won't have many options other than to start looking into your background. If you want to be honest with me, we might be able to offer you some sort of protection.'

Steven listened to everything she said and then gazed away towards the back of the garden. His tone was lower as he spoke again. 'It was such a long time ago now. I've got a wife, kids . . .' Jessica nodded but didn't reply. 'Have

you ever done anything stupid when you were younger?'
he added.

'Lots of things but nothing that's ever made anyone
want to cut off my hand.'

The man said nothing but when he finally spoke, it
didn't take long for the pieces to start to fall into place.

Steven Povey winced as one of the other men slapped him on the shoulder. He had never really burned in the sun before but using sun cream didn't particularly seem like the masculine thing to do when he was surrounded by a group of lads he barely knew. It had only taken a day for his shoulders and arms to turn bright red and, although the other areas of his skin had gone brown in the five days that had followed, his shoulders were still raw and beginning to peel.

The man spun around to see who had smacked him and wasn't surprised to see it was Barry. Back in England the pair lived next door to each other and, despite an almost two-year age gap between them, their parents got on well and they started hanging around together as children. It was easy to cross into each other's garden to kick a ball around and they had grown up together. The trouble Steven had found was that Barry was a completely different person when he had been drinking. At home it didn't create too much of a problem but, in the week they had been in Faliraki, they had drunk a lot, which meant his friend had spent a lot of time being abusive and aggressive.

That was a problem in itself for Steven but had been compounded by the fact he didn't really know anyone else. Matthew and Lewis seemed like decent enough guys and kept their heads down in much the way he did. Ed was very quiet and they'd not seen much of him in the past couple of days but it was Barry and Jacob who seemed to be permanently drunk. Steven wasn't enjoying spending time around either of them but it was hard to walk away considering the six of them were sharing two rooms.

Barry was standing with two empty glasses. 'You want another one, Stevie?'

The young man hated being called 'Stevie', 'Stevo', 'Steffie', 'Stig' or any of the other nicknames which seemed to have appeared on the holiday. He often wondered why it was so hard to simply call him by his name. 'I'll skip this round.'

Barry looked on, disgusted. 'Fellas?'

Of the three other young men sat around the table, only Jacob nodded. 'Same again.'

Barry stared from one person to the next. 'Matty? Lew? You guys in?' The two shook their heads. 'Lightweights,' Barry said, stomping off towards the bar.

Steven exchanged knowing looks with Matthew and Lewis but was grateful they were sticking together in not being forced to drink. The holiday had been something of a learning curve. He had come away largely because of Barry's promise to find him a girl. He wasn't a virgin but it had been a while and the girls back home never seemed interested in him. Barry's promise of 'drunken slags who'll shag anything' wasn't exactly what he had in mind but he thought there would at least be a lot of girls he'd never met before – and perhaps one among them who wouldn't mind hanging out with him.

As it was, the focus of the holiday had largely been alcohol-related and, although there were large groups of girls around, Steven hadn't really had the courage to talk to anyone. Barry and Jacob were the two who had confidence, although they were frequently too drunk to do anything other than leer and shout. Steven hadn't really enjoyed the break at all. He wanted things to do that didn't involve spending most of the day in bed or on the beach, then all night drinking. For some people that inertia would sound like an ideal day but, for him, it was boring.

He was currently in a bar just off the main through street in Faliraki. It was English-themed and the fact they'd flown for five hours to sit in a bar and eat full English breakfasts at five in the afternoon wasn't an irony that was lost on him, even if it clearly was on both Barry and Jacob. On the first night, Matthew had suggested trying a Greek restaurant near their hotel but he had been instantly shot down by Jacob saying, 'I'm not eating that foreign shit'. They'd had either fry-ups, chips or burgers every day since then. The current bar was the one they had started the last three evenings in. St George's flags were pinned along the wooden frames of the structure and a giant television at the back had British sports channels on continuously. When there was no live sport to show, cheesy pop music blared out of speakers over the bar. It wouldn't have been Steven's choice of venue but it was admittedly cheaper than some of the bars in the area.

'Where's Ed?' Jacob asked, not directing his question to any of the other three in particular.

Matthew, Lewis and Steven all exchanged looks to query who Jacob had been speaking to but it was Steven who answered. 'I think he's off with that girl again.'

'Pfft,' Jacob said dismissively. 'What a deserting little prick. It's not as if she's even got any friends for the rest of us.'

Steven was actually a little jealous. On the second day of their break, the six of them had been in a bar on the main street. It was crowded and noisy but, after an hour or so, Matthew noticed Ed was no longer with them. They had found him outside on a raised kerb talking to a girl. According to Lewis, who played rugby with him, Ed was still a virgin and everyone seemed surprised it was him who had been the first to hook up with someone of the opposite sex.

In the days that followed, Ed and the girl, who they had found out was called Sam, had spent pretty much all their time together. Barry and Jacob hadn't taken it too well but it was clear to Steven their jealousy was based around the fact they hadn't had any luck with women since they had arrived on the island of Rhodes. Steven didn't actually resent Ed as they seemed to – he was simply envious because he wanted to find someone of the opposite sex he could hang around with.

The evening progressed much as the previous few had. Jacob and Barry drank constantly while Steven, Matthew and Lewis had just enough to get them drunk without going completely over the top. They moved from the English bar into one of the clubs. Most people went there to dance but the five of them sat in near-silence close to the bar watching the swaying crowd. Jacob would make the odd grab towards girls if any were unfortunate enough to get too near but, aside from that, the night was as uneventful as the rest of the holiday had been.

The next night they would be going home and, for Steven, it couldn't come soon enough. After an hour or so, Jacob made one lunge too many towards a girl and they were thrown out. The places didn't have bouncers like clubs might at home but the threat of the police had convinced Jacob it was time to go. After he hurled a mouthful of abuse at the few security staff, the five of them started to walk towards their apartment block.

Steven found the hotel itself horrible. There was no air-conditioning, which made sleeping at night almost impossible, while sharing a room was something he wasn't overly comfortable with seeing as he was an only child and not used to it. Barry was a bad snorer but at least tended to fall asleep after they got back. Matthew wasn't too bad and the other three were in the room next door. Although they were all clearly struggling to sleep, Steven would at least lie on his uncomfortable bed and try. In the adjoining room, Jacob would put music or the television on and generally make life miserable for all of them. If it had disturbed Barry, he would have probably stopped but Jacob knew the other four were intimidated by him, so did whatever he wanted.

The walk back to the hotel was slow and tortuous with both Jacob and Barry offering to fight bystanders for no reason other than the fact they were there. Steven, Matthew and Lewis kept quiet and walked a few paces behind, trying not to get caught up in things. Over the course of the week they hadn't said too much to each other but had bonded in a silent way because of the way they had been mutually bullied into submission.

Eventually they arrived back at the apartments, making their way up the outside stairs to their rooms on the fourth floor. Steven had the key and opened the door but was hit by a wall of humidity as he walked into the room. The evening was cool but the room was far hotter. He had barely reached his bed when he heard Jacob's unmistakable voice from the next room. Barry had opened the door that connected the interiors and was standing in the doorway cheering before crossing into the other room. Dreading what he might see but feeling inquisitive, Steven followed Matthew into the adjoining room.

It only took a moment to see what the noise had been about. Ed was in a bed on top of Sam. They had clearly just been disturbed while having sex and the look on the woman's face was pure horror. Because the boys had been thrown out of the club, they had returned to the rooms around an hour-and-a-half earlier than they had on previous days.

Sam was holding the thin white sheet across the top of her chest with Ed lying half on top of her, also under the cover. Jacob was still cheering. 'Waheeeeeyyyyy. Have you brought her back for us all to have a go? Good lad.'

Steven could see the disgusted look on the girl's face. Her blonde hair was tangled across her face and he could see thin tan marks on her skin from where she had been wearing a bikini. She looked directly at Jacob then glanced across at the other boys. It was obvious she was associating the five of them together. 'Fuck off,' she said venomously, clutching the cover to herself. Ed looked as if he was going to say something but Barry was now standing next to the bed. Jacob was a little further back in the room next to Steven, Lewis and Matthew.

'Mind your fucking language,' Barry said, snatching the sheet away. Jacob started laughing as there was a brief tug of war with Sam desperately trying to hold onto the sheet. Ed's eyes were wide with fear, Sam's full of fury. It only took a second or two before Barry managed to grab the sheet away, leaving both Ed and Sam naked on the bed. The woman tried her best to cover her body as Barry and Jacob sneered with joyous laughter.

Steven felt sick and ashamed as he took in her thin frame but said nothing. The humid air suddenly felt cold. He shivered as Jacob stepped forward. 'Nice of you to bring your little girlfriend around to give us all a go.'

Ed was reaching towards a pile of clothes on the floor. 'Leave her alone.'

Jacob lunged forward and slapped him across the face with a large crack. Steven heard Lewis gasp next to him and felt stunned himself. 'Do you think you're better than us?' Jacob said loudly. Ed was shaking with what Steven guessed was a mixture of shock and anger. Jacob slapped him again. 'You think you're better than us just because you've got yourself a whore for a week.'

Jacob's words were slurring together, the alcohol in full effect, but Ed seemed unable to speak himself. Steven felt frozen and neither of the other two standing next to him said anything. Sam was staring at Jacob herself, still trying to cover her body. 'Leave him alone,' she shouted.

Jacob picked Ed up and shoved him to the ground then sat on the bed as Sam tried to shuffle away from him. Her clothes were in a pile with Ed's on the opposite side of the bed from where she was. Sam went to stand but Jacob reached across and snatched her hand away so she was no longer covering her top half. 'Why, what are you going to do about it?'

Barry threw the sheet across the room and walked to the door connecting the two rooms, closing it. He then went to the main front door and locked it. Steven watched on, too intimidated to say anything. As the doors were shut he saw the look on Sam's face change from defiance to outright fear.

'Let me go,' she said fiercely. Ed had taken a pair of shorts from the floor and put them on. He stood and tried to hand some clothes to Sam but Barry snatched them away and flung them across the room.

At seeing her clothes being tossed around, Sam repeated her words but it sounded far more of a plea second time around. 'Let me go.'

Steven finally found his voice but it faltered and cracked as he spoke. 'I think we should just leave things.'

Jacob glared across at him furiously, then he used his free hand to point at Steven and the other two standing next to him. 'If any of you fucking move, I promise you won't be getting on that plane back home in one piece.' He then turned to Ed. 'And if you try anything, you'll get the same treatment.'

He yanked the young woman fully onto the bed by only her wrist. She started shouting but Jacob put a hand across her mouth and pushed her hard into the mattress. Steven would never forget his next words. 'Bazza, she's all yours.'

29

As Steven finished talking, he was in tears. Jessica felt a sickness in her stomach that she'd only had on a few occasions and she was furious. 'Did you just stand and watch?' she said, barely trying to control her anger. Izzy looked close to tears next to her.

The man shrugged. 'I tried not to watch.'

'Well, that's all right then. Some innocent girl was attacked by two men while you did nothing but because you were staring at the ground, everything's just fine.'

Jessica rarely lost her temper when interviewing but she couldn't control it. She hadn't thought throughout speaking to Steven that he was involved in cutting off people's hands but they now had someone who had a motive as good as any. There couldn't be many better ways to tell people to keep their hands to themselves than by cutting them off. It was also now obvious why they had been left so publicly – the poor woman wanted the police to know what the men had done.

Jessica realised she was jumping to conclusions but wondered if 'Sam' was the person responsible or if it was someone she knew. An enormous part of her wished the woman luck but there was still a part of her thinking rationally as a police officer, trying to calm herself. Steven hadn't said anything and was still crying gently to himself.

'Do you know her last name?'

'Sam's?'

'Who else?'

'Sorry, I don't remember. I've tried to forget.'

'Do you have any photos or anything from the holiday?'

Steven was snivelling. 'I think I might have a copy of the one you've got somewhere but that would be all. When we got back no one ever talked about it. It was as if it never happened. I didn't really see them after that, only Barry.'

'Could you describe Sam?'

Jacob gave them a vague description of a girl with blonde hair and brown eyes. Jessica said she would arrange for him to see someone who could digitally create an image from his description but she doubted it would do much good.

'Do you think I'm in danger?' he asked.

Jessica forced herself not to say what she was thinking, *'You should be'*, but instead answered professionally. 'I don't know, possibly. We might be able to arrange someone to come around and be with you.'

'What about my wife and children?'

'What about them? We would protect them too.'

'I'd have to tell them why there was someone here.' Steven seemed frightened, his eyes wide and teary.

'That would be up to you,' Jessica said.

'Couldn't you put someone . . . I don't know, like a secret plain-clothes officer or someone across the road or something?'

'It doesn't work like that,' Jessica said. 'Besides, they would have to follow you wherever you went. If you want protection, I can ask and see what we can arrange. It's up to you if you want to explain that to your wife.'

The man nodded dejectedly. 'Am I going to be in trouble?'

Jessica stood and Izzy followed. 'I don't know, we'll come back to you. We've got to get back to Manchester but I'll leave you my card. If you want me to ask someone about sending an officer here, you'll have to let me know.'

The drive back to Longsight was a lot shorter as the motorway had been cleared but the two women sat in near silence. Although Jessica had said she would get back to Steven about whether he'd be in trouble, she knew he most likely wouldn't be. She would check the records but unless a crime had been reported in Faliraki itself, there would be no record of the attack. Not only that but, without a victim or formal complaint, all they actually had was his confession to watching an assault happen. She didn't want to tell him that straight away though. Jessica also doubted he would contact them for any sort of protection because he would want to keep things from his wife and children. If she thought for a moment his family could be in danger, she would have gone out of her way to arrange it regardless but, so far, no one else had been harmed except for the four men.

Jessica thought back to her own meeting with Jacob and the cocky way he had eyed her and Izzy. At the time she had ignored it but she could see it in a different light now and was a little unnerved.

Back at the station she went straight to see Cole, taking Izzy with her and passing on everything Steven had told them. It was tough to know where to go from there because they had so little information on Sam. At some point Steven could be brought in for a formal interview but Jessica doubted he would have much more to add than what he'd told them. If anything, he'd offer less because he'd be more nervous with a tape running.

Izzy left to see if she could find anything from the police in Faliraki. None of them had ever liaised with the Greek police in the past but there were interpreters available if the language proved too much of a barrier. If the crime had been reported, the woman's full name would have been recorded. Meanwhile, Jessica and Cole talked through the few options they had. Steven insisted the girl had an English accent but, because the attack had happened overseas, they had no idea what part of the country she might come from. They couldn't exactly launch a national 'Were you assaulted eleven years ago in Faliraki' media campaign and they had nothing else other than a first name to work with.

Jessica decided she was going to revisit the victims' families to see if any of them had come up with any further photos from the trip. Given the nature of what had happened, she doubted many of the young men involved would have kept too many mementoes but Vicky Barnes was her best bet simply because she seemed to keep a record of everything relating to her son. From what

Steven had said, Lewis had been an onlooker in the same way he had but Jessica doubted he had told his mother anything about what had happened. If that was true and he brought home photos from the trip, Vicky might have kept them for herself.

She went back to the main floor of the station where Diamond and Rowlands were both working. Usually Jessica would have a bit of a joke with them but it was clear Izzy had told her colleague everything and they were both working quietly and determinedly.

'How are you doing?' Jessica asked.

Izzy seemed annoyed. 'I've had to jump through all sorts of hoops to get through to the right person but the head of police on Rhodes actually speaks really good English. He checked the records of crimes reported from eleven years back but there was nothing that suits our case. There were a few sexual assaults and all sorts of violent crimes but the ones caught were fined and deported and a huge majority are unsolved because the people would have gone home. He looked at the sexual crimes but there was nothing reported by anyone called "Sam" and nothing matched the circumstances Steven described.'

Jessica sat on the edge of their desk. 'Bollocks.'

Rowlands looked up at her. 'I've checked outstanding warrants passed from their police to ours but there's nothing on there either. As far as we can tell, the attack was never reported. We don't have a clue what her last name was.'

Jessica stood back up. 'I checked with the holiday companies before and they didn't have records going back that far.'

'What are we going to do then?' Rowlands asked.

'You come with me and we'll visit Vicky Barnes again,' Jessica said. 'Maybe Lewis brought back some photos or he kept a diary? If she doesn't have anything we'll go to Charlie Marks's house to look.' Jessica looked across to Izzy. 'Can you do something else for me?'

'What are you after?'

'It's not nice.'

'Go on.'

'Get an officer and check back through any unsolved sexual assaults from the past thirteen years or so. See if any of the descriptions match Jacob Chrisp. If there was DNA it would have been matched when his hand was identified so look for cases where we don't have that. It might be nothing but, if Steven's account is right, he might well have form for it. We would have to visit the victims with a photo of Jacob if anything does compare but it could at least give them some closure if he was responsible.'

Jessica let Dave drive to Vicky Barnes's house. The Markses' might have been the more obvious choice but it was going to be a big job to hunt through all of the junk and Charlie had already said he would. Vicky was apparently doing the same but Jessica didn't know if she was looking for the right thing. They travelled more or less in silence, Jessica still upset by everything they had found out that day. Asking Izzy to check other unsolved cases had been done on something of a whim but, if Jacob was as sinister as Steven had made him sound, he certainly seemed the type who wouldn't have stopped at one attack. They would probably examine Barry's background at some point too but he had died a fair few years beforehand and would have had a smaller amount of time to be involved in anything.

Jessica had called Vicky Barnes to let her know they wanted to come around again and she'd said that was fine. As she welcomed them in, the woman assured the officers without prompting she had the kettle on. Jessica wasn't bothered by that but let the woman fuss. Dave seemed as disturbed as Jessica had been by the shrine Vicky kept to her son. They whispered in the living room as the woman was in the kitchen.

'This is really weird,' Rowlands said quietly as he looked around at the pictures.

'It might be a bit *unconventional* but it's really a mother who loves her son,' Jessica pointed out.

'I'd be creeped out if my mum kept all these things for me.'

On another day, Jessica might have said that was because he had a face not even a mother could love but she wasn't in the mood. 'I wouldn't fancy being her son's girlfriend like January was. It's no wonder there was a clash between mother and potential daughter-in-law,' she replied.

'Yeah, sod that.'

They stopped talking as Vicky walked back into the room with a cup of tea for her and two glasses of water. 'I've been looking through the photos as you asked,' she said. 'I couldn't see any others of Lewis with those other boys or I would have called.' She sat in the same armchair she had the other day as the two officers leant forward on the sofa.

Jessica spoke next. 'Do you keep photos of Lewis's friends as well as him?'

'Yes but I didn't have any of the two you were asking about.'

'How about Edward Marks? He was one of the ones who played in Lewis's rugby team. Do you have any more of him?'

'Rugby photos?'

'Anything, maybe ones from the same holiday the other photo we were looking at was taken on?'

Vicky pulled a face as if thinking. 'There were a few but they're mainly of Lewis . . .' She took a long slurp from her cup and then stood. 'Everything is upstairs. You can come up if you want.'

On the way up the stairs, there were more photos of Lewis pinned to the walls, along with more certificates. Vicky led them into a bedroom that had Rowlands gasping.

'Do you like it?' Vicky asked, hearing his surprise. 'It's as he left it.'

The room was decorated as if a teenage boy lived in it. There were posters of girls and footballers on the wall, a few toys and a duvet cover of an old cartoon character. Jessica rolled her eyes, knowing Dave's reaction was because this was his ultimate bedroom.

'It's great,' he said.

Vicky crouched and pulled two huge boxes out from

under the bed. 'This is everything I kept. You might have noticed some of it on the walls but I rotate things around.' She pointed to the first box, then the second. 'Everything from when he was born up until eighteen is in that box, everything eighteen to now is in there.' Jessica could see stacks of photo albums as well as small wallets which likely contained loose pictures. Vicky continued to describe the contents. 'He got a digital camera and took some photos on his phone but I had them printed out. There might be some bits on the computer at his flat but this is everything I know of.'

As the woman mentioned her son's 'flat', Jessica realised she could be on the brink of another rant about January so she stepped in before she could start. 'If Lewis went to Faliraki when he was almost nineteen, which box should it be in?'

'Everything's in chronological order, it will be easy to find.' Vicky sat on the edge of the bed and picked a few albums out, skimming the contents, returning them, then taking another. It was less than a minute before she handed Jessica one small album and Dave a wallet. 'Everything is in those. I checked the other day after we'd spoken but there's nothing of the other two; it's mainly pictures of Lewis. I remember because it was the first time he had gone away without me. I didn't want to let him at first but he kept on about it and eventually I said he could as long as he took photos of everything.'

Jessica started to look through the album as Dave sat on the bed and took out the pictures one by one. It was clear straight away Vicky knew what she was talking about.

Every picture in the album Jessica had was of Lewis. In most of them he seemed to be forcing a smile and was either sitting by a pool, on a beach or in a bar. Neither Barry, Jacob nor Steven were in any but there were odd shots with Ed and Matthew in.

Jessica tried to take her time to search the backgrounds of the images but there was nothing. Rowlands was around two-thirds through his pile of photos when he held one up. 'Jess.'

He wouldn't have usually called her by her first name out of the station in anything other than a social situation but Jessica wasn't bothered and could tell from his tone he had something. She stepped across to the bed and took the photo from him. The picture showed two people grinning and holding drinks up as if saluting at whoever had taken the photo. One of them was Ed Marks, the other a young blonde woman with brown eyes.

30

Steven Povey sat in his garden staring at Detective Sergeant Jessica Daniel's business card. He wanted to call her and ask for someone to come and watch him but the consequences of having to tell his wife why the person was needed were something he couldn't face. The police's visit had largely been a surprise as he didn't follow the news too closely and wouldn't have recognised the names of all the victims in any case. He had seen something about a hand that was found in Manchester but hadn't realised it could have any connection to him until the officer had said.

The incident on holiday was something he had done his best to forget. He'd not spoken about it to anyone since and, of the other five, only had contact with Barry after they arrived back in the UK. Even that had only been because they lived so close to each other but Steven had soon moved away. He'd heard of Barry's death in a car crash but had no strong feelings about the man by that point.

After hearing about the possible fates of the other four people, Steven was certainly scared. He didn't know if it was Sam who had been targeting the men who were in the room that day but whoever it was certainly seemed to know what had gone on. He didn't know of any further connection he had to the other five people so it must be related. From what Sergeant Daniel had said all of the men involved were now dead so if it wasn't Sam or someone like a husband or boyfriend, who else could it be?

The only crumb of comfort was that none of the other men's families had apparently been targeted, meaning his wife and children should be safe.

Steven continued to stare at the business card trying to figure out if he was more frightened of the person who might be coming for him or of letting his wife down. The house had been given to them as a wedding present by her father, who loomed heavily over their lives. He was a businessman who owned a string of health clubs throughout the country. To the surprise of his wife and mother-in-law, Steven had been welcomed into the family with open arms.

His father-in-law had never taken to any of his daughter's previous boyfriends but he liked Steven for whatever reason and the house had been an extravagant gift to show that. If Steven were to tell his wife what happened all those years ago, it could wreck everything and, while his family seemed safe, he wanted to do all he could to avoid letting her know.

Steven pocketed the business card and stood up from the table, looking at his watch. The officers had left almost fifteen minutes ago and he had barely moved. He'd been mostly honest with them but hadn't given them one piece of information, thinking perhaps he could find a way to deal with things on his own.

He went to the computer in the hallway and switched it on, waiting for it to boot up then loading an Internet browser window. He had searched for the name a few times in the past, using search engines and, more recently, social networking sites.

'Samantha Weston' was a name he had never forgotten.

He didn't know what he might be able to do if he did track her down somehow but he thought it was a better option than giving the full details to the police and having everything come out.

Steven first tried the social networking site where he had his own profile. As with the last time he had searched, there was no one who seemed to match the woman's details. He didn't know where she came from but, with a name and general age, Steven had an idea of what he was looking for. The biggest problem was filtering out the male 'Sam Weston' matches from the females but, even after doing that, he couldn't find someone who seemed right. There were also far too many general matches through the search engines he tried and he realised the woman could have either emigrated or got married – or both – which would affect his results too.

He tried numerous combinations of 'Sam', 'Samantha', 'Weston', 'wedding', 'married' and 'marriage', eventually finding a couple of combinations of alternative names the woman could have. With that information, he then returned to the social network and did some new searches with the other name. After almost an hour of trying, he settled upon a profile for 'Sam Kellett'. The woman's main picture was of her in a wedding dress. Because of her privacy settings, Steven couldn't see much information about her but he did manage to view the photo in a higher resolution. He wouldn't have said it was an absolute likeness but it had been eleven years since Steven had seen the woman and he thought there was definitely a similarity in appearance. Her hair was a lot darker in the wedding photos but anyone's facial appearance would change slightly over time.

Without anyone else matching the age or likeness criteria, Steven figured this 'Sam Kellett' was the only possible candidate he was likely to find for the woman he had watched being attacked all those years ago. He returned to his previous searches and looked for the wedding notice. It had been placed in a local newspaper in the Harrogate area just across the Yorkshire border eighteen months ago and, from what it said, the woman's husband was called 'Colin'. It was probably an hour's drive assuming they still lived in that neighbourhood but, aside from the name and area, he didn't have an exact address. Steven tried more Internet searches for 'Kellett' and 'Harrogate' but there was nothing that gave him any more information.

Leaning back in the computer chair, Steven wondered what he should do. He could call Sergeant Daniel and tell her what he had found but, if things ended up in court, there was no way he could keep everything from his wife.

The man spent the next twenty-four hours running through scenarios in his mind, wondering if there was some way he could reveal what he knew without tearing his family apart. Would his wife understand he had said nothing during the attack because he was scared himself, or would she have a similar reaction to the officer? He wanted to take the risk of telling her but ultimately he felt more scared of her reaction than he did of whoever might be targeting him.

With that, Steven continued to try to find Sam. He didn't know for sure if what was happening was down to her – or what he'd do if he found her – but he wondered if he might be able to reason with the woman. A voice at the back of his mind told him he deserved everything that was happening. As well as more Internet searches, Steven called directory enquiries, asking for 'Sam Kellett', 'Samantha Kellett' and 'Colin Kellett', none of which returned any results.

Eventually, two days after the visit, Steven felt almost resigned to his fate. He didn't know if someone might end up coming after him but he did start carrying around a pocket knife just in case. His wife sensed something was wrong but he said things were fine. If he left the house, he tried to make sure he had someone else with him. He felt guilty at using his wife and children almost as human shields but tried to blank those feelings out.

After the weekend, his wife went to work as usual and, with his children at school, Steven was alone in the house for the first time properly since the officers had visited. He often worked from home anyway but was edgy about being on his own. He made sure the windows and doors were locked and tried to do his regular work.

Halfway through the morning the doorbell rang. Steven felt his heart rate rise but looked through the side window and saw the postman standing there. He signed for a parcel but, after taking it inside, realised how jumpy everything was making him.

Not long after, the doorbell sounded again. Steven again checked through the side window. A short and fairly slight man in jeans and a T-shirt was waiting but, from where Steven was looking, he had no idea who the person was. He moved around so he was on the other side of the door and shouted. 'Who is it?'

'Gas man, I'm here to check the meter.'

Steven hadn't noticed a van outside his house but decided it wasn't necessarily unusual as the person could have parked at the other end of the row of houses and then walked from one to the next. 'Have you got identification?'

The man pressed a badge up against the window to the side of the door. Steven stared at it, realising that, aside from a company logo, he had no idea what he was looking for. He still couldn't see the person's face either. The identification had someone's name on, as well as a company and a phone number. Steven thought about calling the number to check but figured it was probably a little over the top. He unbolted the door and opened it inwards before stepping back. His hand hovered imperceptibly close to the knife in his pocket.

The visitor stepped into the house and looked up. There was a flicker of recognition between the men and Steven realised he'd made a horrible mistake. 'You?' he said.

'Me.'

Steven tried to grab the knife from his pocket but the other man was quicker, reaching forward and pushing something into his neck. His last thought before his eyes closed and he slumped to the floor was that the police officers who had visited him didn't know how horribly wrong they were.

31

Jessica had worked through the weekend as best she could but the problem, as ever, was that most people in other organisations didn't. She spoke to DCI Cole on Friday but releasing the photo of the woman to the media in a 'Who's this?' way was their last resort. The problem was that Jessica couldn't think of another method to identify the person. They had nothing except for a first name, only a vague idea that Sam was English and no clue where she came from, or if she would still be there eleven years on. Not only that but there was something not quite right about the picture that Jessica couldn't figure out. Jessica looked at it over and over, feeling there was something obvious she was missing but she couldn't see what it was.

She again tried the various travel companies but the people she spoke to repeated that they didn't keep records that went back that far. With no crime reports and no other way to identify who the person was, Jessica spoke to the chief inspector again on the Sunday morning and he agreed the picture of Sam could be released. The trouble was that they didn't actually know if the woman was responsible for everything that had been happening. She was the only suspect they had but it would be harsh to get her photo on news bulletins, potentially reminding the woman of something terrible that had happened over a decade ago if it ended up having no relation to what was going on. If Jessica could have thought of any way of identifying the person without having to do that, she would have done.

Rather reluctantly, the senior press officer came into the station on Sunday afternoon and worked with Jessica on something they could release to the media. The biggest problem was that it would have to be run as nationally as possible. With local campaigns they both knew people they could lean on if they really needed a favour to get something published but it was far harder to do something across the whole country.

The statement they ended with was a mixture of spiced-up language including a recap of the hands found. The comments relating to Sam were toned down and carefully worded to make it clear she wasn't a suspect. She might well be but they couldn't have that broadcast. Instead, Sam was someone who 'might hold key information'. Jessica knew it was the type of nothing phrase the police always came out with but, in this instance, it was as good as they could manage. They hoped the recap of the juicy details regarding the hands might persuade the newspapers to print something, while the television news may have a brief segment with Sam's photo. Everything was also put on the police's own website and the press officer put out alerts across their social network accounts. It was about as much as they could do and Jessica hoped they received phone calls so they could find out who Sam was and, with luck, figure out exactly what had been going on.

On the Monday, there was something on the television

news. One of the two main news channels ignored their story but the other gave them the briefest of ten-second slots where they flashed Sam's photo and a phone number for the public to call if they knew who it was. It wasn't the best result but there was some information on a few news outlets' websites and Jessica knew it was now a waiting game to see if any useful suggestions came in.

The day didn't produce too much but the news story gradually received more attention as it went on. Jessica didn't hurry into the station on Tuesday, partly because she had put the hours in over the weekend but also because there wasn't a whole lot she could do. The calls were being taken by the national Crimestoppers service, with any names suggested being fed back for her team to go over. She had already left Rowlands and Diamond instructions.

As she arrived, Jessica instantly knew something was going on because of the lack of marked police cars in the car park. Usually there would be a couple of rows of vehicles but there were just two. She walked into the reception area, asking the desk sergeant what was going on.

'They've found a body.'

'Of who?' Jessica's first thought was that one of the handless victims had been discovered but she wasn't prepared for the actual response.

'They think it's Christine Johnson.'

'You're joking?'

'Nope. It's been mad in here all morning. Some tip-off had everyone dashing out; even the DCI's gone and some-one said the super was on his way too.'

'Where?'

'Some garage not that far away.' The sergeant wrote out the address for Jessica. She first went to check on Dave and Izzy, who were working their way through a few names that had been put forward that morning but, as yet, no one who had been suggested matched 'their' Sam.

Jessica left them to it and drove herself to the site where Christine's body had apparently been found. She was grateful it hadn't happened a day earlier, else there was no way she would have had any coverage to help find Sam. As she neared the location, Jessica could tell someone had said something they shouldn't. A helicopter belonging to a news station was hovering overhead while vans with enormous satellite dishes were parked nearby, meaning someone had tipped the media off. Jessica shoved her way through a small crowd that had gathered, ignoring questions being shouted at her by the waiting journalists.

The garage was only a ten-minute journey from their station, the type of place that looked as if it had been there for years and was easy to ignore. A sign at the front promised cheap MOT prices with a wide driveway leading towards the working area. The public and media were being penned back at the end of the drive as Jessica walked quickly towards where she could see other police officers in a courtyard, as well as a couple of the Scene of Crime team standing around.

'What are you doing here?' Cole asked as Jessica strode towards him.

Jessica shrugged. 'I don't know. My team are handling

the calls back at the station so I thought I'd come take a look. Have you really found her body?'

The chief inspector nodded towards a set of large doors ahead of them that were closed. 'Probably. It looks as if it could be her but we don't know for sure. The body is a little decomposed and was being stored in the well underneath where they work on the cars.'

Jessica could tell from the placement back and away from the main road that it would be easy to conceal things at the garage. 'Do you mean the pit things that mechanics stand in and then work above them? How were they keeping her down there, they're not exactly deep? Or was it just her body they had dumped?'

'We don't know,' Cole replied. 'You're right about it not being big enough to leave someone, it's not like a mine shaft or anything, it's an area roughly five feet deep. She could have climbed out. It's a mess of oil and diesel so the forensic boys aren't happy. We're assuming it's where her body was dumped.'

'How did you find it?'

'That red van. Someone scrapped a red former Royal Mail van down in the Midlands on Saturday. The guy who was working handed over the money and so on but the scrapyard's owner noticed the transaction this morning and luckily he watches the news. Because you need the DVLA documents, it would be pretty hard to fake an address. He phoned us, gave us this place and, when we came around earlier, there was the body.'

'Has anyone been arrested?'

'No, we're looking for the guy who runs this place but

he's not here and not at his house. We reckon he might have seen the police cars this morning and made a run for it. We know who he is though so I don't reckon he'll be able to hide out for long. Any luck with your woman?'

Jessica hadn't been thinking about her case. 'Not yet. We'd have been screwed if this had happened a day earlier. At least we made the news this morning. Has anyone told George Johnson we might have found his wife?'

Cole pointed at the helicopter overhead. 'Bit hard to keep it from him. He's in London but someone's gone to see him.'

'Do we have anything on him?'

The chief inspector stopped looking at the closed garage doors, peering towards Jessica. He lowered his voice. 'Some of his emails showed he was certainly *friendly* with his PA and there were the regular cash withdrawals but nothing really. All we can do is ask him but we've been delaying bringing him in to see if we can connect any more dots. He's clean though; he'll be able to say the emails were harmless flirting and I'm sure he'll have a reason for the cash. Our best hope is finding the garage owner. If he was acting alone then we'll have our man, if not then hopefully he'll be willing to tell us.'

'Why are you here?'

'The super's on his way so I'm waiting for that. I suspect he'll say something to the cameras. We've got to try to get the garage owner's photo distributed as far and wide as possible so it's going to be one of those days.'

'You wait all year for a manhunt to come along then two pop up at once.'

Jessica hoped Cole would smile but he was unmoving. He looked as if he was about to say something but his phone rang. Overhead the helicopter moved swiftly away from the area, flying towards the city centre. Because of the noise, Jessica missed the first part of the conversation but the second was clear enough and, if she was in any doubt, it evaporated when the chief inspector handed her his phone.

Another hand had been found.

Jessica leant back into her office chair, closing her eyes. She couldn't remember a busier day than the previous one at Longsight. A hand she assumed belonged to Steven Povey had been left not far from Piccadilly train station. Jessica arrived there to find the news helicopter overhead and a handful of officers trying to keep the scene fresh while bemused and annoyed commuters hurried past, oblivious to what was going on.

The appendage had been recovered but tests were going to take a while to confirm the identity because the forensics team were tied up with what everyone assumed was Christine Johnson's body. Jessica had managed to contact Steven's wife, who said she hadn't seen her husband since the previous morning. She had reported it to her local force but not much had happened because it was only a little over a day since he disappeared. Jessica didn't reveal anything specific that she knew but did feel bad about the whole affair. Though Steven had refused protection because he didn't want to talk to his partner. Jessica wondered if she could have forced him to accept protective custody but it was unlikely, especially with their lack of resources.

The hunt for Sam hadn't got much further than where it had been the previous morning, largely because the discovery of Christine Johnson's body had overtaken everything, both at the station and in the media. A few phone calls were coming in relating to the woman in their photograph but nothing that seemed to match their criteria for age and appearance.

If everything happening at the station wasn't already enough, the company had finally arrived to fix the station's air-conditioning unit and had been clattering in and out of reception as confused journalists stood at the front gates wondering what was going on.

Jessica breathed in deeply enjoying the relative quiet and, for the first time in a while, not feeling sweaty in her own office.

'Jess? You awake?'

She jumped, wondering if she actually had dozed off for a few moments. She certainly hadn't heard her office door go. Opening her eyes, she saw Izzy standing in between her desk and DS Cornish's.

'I'm just having a rest after a long few days.'

The constable clearly thought Jessica had been asleep for some time. 'I just wanted to make sure I was fine to get off?'

Jessica looked at the clock above the door and realised she had been sleeping for almost an hour. On most days, it wouldn't have been possible but with everyone dashing around to find the garage owner, people hadn't been bothering her. 'Of course. I take it nothing came in on the phones to match our Sam?' she asked.

'No, but I guess it's going to be over now, isn't it?' Jessica must have had a confused look on her face because the constable followed it up. 'I mean, that's six men from the photo and all of them are either dead or missing.'

It seemed an obvious point but, for whatever reason, Jessica had missed the significance of the find. She was feeling tired after working through the weekend but Izzy was right. Unless they had missed something major, the six men involved in the assault Steven Povey had described were all accounted for in one way or the other. Barry Newcombe had been killed in a car accident but Jessica wondered if the other five men's bodies would ever be found, assuming they were dead.

'I don't know what we're going to do if we can't find Sam,' Jessica said. It was an honest statement but not something she would have revealed to many of her colleagues.

'She's bound to show up somewhere.'

'Maybe, but we've only got a picture that's eleven years old and we can't get too much attention for that at the moment.'

'She won't be able to hide forever though.'

Jessica sighed. 'Don't you think it's a really rough way of doing things? The only thing we've got to connect her to the six men in the photo is the say-so of Steven Povey and he's disappeared. What if it's nothing to do with her at all? What if we're going after someone who's spent eleven years trying to forget everything and we're punishing her for it?'

Izzy paused, thinking it over. 'Do you think Steven was lying?'

'No, you saw him; he was genuinely frightened but I wonder if we've missed something else.'

'Like what?'

Jessica shrugged. The truth was she didn't know. It wasn't as if they had any other suspects or leads but she felt very uneasy with making assumptions about the woman whose face she had been responsible for getting in the papers and on the news. 'I have no idea.'

She had spent the morning going through more CCTV footage. The hand had been left in very similar circumstances to the others. A figure wearing a black hooded gown had dropped it near the train station in the early hours of the morning. With so many people hurrying past, it had somehow been ignored for almost six hours. Jessica wondered how people could be so oblivious but, as she watched the footage, it was clear everyone leaving or arriving at the station was in a rush. As before it seemed clear the person knew where the cameras were and, from what Jessica had seen, they had no clear views of the person. She wondered if it was the sheer amount of time staring at monitors over the past few weeks that was making her feel so tired.

Izzy scratched her chin. 'What about the woman in black?'

Jessica weighed up the question. 'Who knows? It could be Sam. Whoever she is knows the area well. Her photo has been in the local papers so you'd assume she would be recognised but we've not had anything so far. Honestly? I just don't know.'

Another package arrived for Jessica the next day but, once again, she didn't get to see it before it was taken away by the science team. The previous ones had bothered her but Jessica had pretty much expected another finger to arrive. If it was Sam, she wondered if the woman knew who she was because of the media reports.

The biggest development of the day again didn't relate to her case. The garage owner was found hiding in a caravan in a field north of the city. His photo had been everywhere and a member of the public had called the police after spotting him. He had spent the first twenty-four hours no-commenting but there were hints from his solicitor that he might have information to reveal. Jessica thought he might have been more willing to speak given the fact he was likely to be charged with murder but people could do strange things when they were either frightened or felt they could be battling for their life. What had perhaps been telling was that George Johnson hadn't said anything to the media since his wife's body had been found. For someone who had been only too keen to speak beforehand, it really was a turnaround and, from what Jessica could tell, had convinced Cole and Reynolds even further that he was somehow involved.

On the Thursday, Jessica finally got confirmation the hand they'd found belonged to Steven Povey. She'd thought all along that it did but actually getting the test results had her wondering what might happen next. With the final finger also identified, Jessica debated if things really were now over in terms of finding body parts. It was an odd feeling, thinking a killing spree had started and ended on her watch.

Also playing on her mind was the fact it was Caroline's wedding in two days. Jessica had done her best to stay in touch over the past week and gone to the final dress fitting but things had been so busy it was proving almost impossible to be involved. Caroline seemed to be calm but Jessica felt she was neglecting her friend by not having the time to visit her with the day so close. Jessica was due to sleep at the bride's house on the Friday night but hadn't packed anything to take. She was frequently disorganised but had wanted to get everything ready a day or two ahead of time.

Jessica was sitting in her office thinking about marriage when her desk phone rang. The noise surprised her and it was almost as if she didn't know what to do. When she answered, the man on the other end sounded nervous. He introduced himself as an officer from a force somewhere around Nottingham. He waffled for a little bit but, when he finally got to the point, Jessica was left worrying whether or not she would be back in time for Caroline's wedding as there was no doubt she was going to have to travel to see him the next day. A woman named Sam Kellett had handed herself into her local police station, identifying herself as the person in the holiday photo.

32

Jessica made an awkward phone call to tell Caroline she was going to be spending the day before her wedding in Nottingham. Jessica assured her friend she would be back to stay at hers that evening but wasn't actually certain herself. Caroline took it well – they had known each other for long enough for her friend to realise sometimes the police work took over. The final thing Caroline said was, 'Please don't miss it'.

Because she didn't want to rely on trains to get her back to Manchester on time, Jessica called Rowlands to ask if he would drive them down to the Midlands the next day. He was still roaring around in a boy racer-style car but it did at least seem reliable, something her vehicle most certainly was not. Jessica updated Cole with what was happening and was surprised at how much attention he gave her given the break in the Johnson case. He even offered to go to Nottingham with her but she knew he should probably be at their station with the clock ticking on the garage owner.

It was after eleven at night when Jessica finally got around to packing the things she needed to stay at Caroline's.

Rowlands picked her up from her house the next morning. Jessica found the journey relatively stressful, largely because of the motorway traffic jams and the fact she hadn't slept much. Her colleague kept fishing to ask who she was taking to the wedding but she ignored him. Jessica wouldn't have admitted it to him but Rowlands was a pretty good driver. He weaved them in and out of the slow-moving traffic, getting them off at the correct junction without too much hassle before finding the police station as if he had memorised the route.

As they pulled up, Jessica hurried out of the car, leaving her colleague to offer a sarcastic 'You're welcome'.

'You'll get your thanks when you get me back to Manchester in time,' Jessica called, not looking backwards.

The police station was a lot smaller than the one they were used to back at Longsight. It was on the outskirts of Nottingham in a little community of its own. It had just one storey and an unmanned front desk where Jessica had to ring a bell to summon someone to meet them. Sam Kellett had been let go the previous evening and asked to return to be interviewed the next day. According to the officer Jessica had spoken to, the woman was fine with that but was worried about her husband finding out she had visited the police.

Jessica's instinct told her those were the actions of someone shocked to see their own face on the news, not a person who had spent the last few weeks chopping off hands and leaving them in public.

After ringing the bell, nobody came to the reception. Jessica shared a sideways look with Rowlands but wasn't in the mood to be messed around. She started banging the bell with the palm of her hand repeatedly until eventually a red-faced overweight woman bundled into the area behind the glass counter.

'Oi, what do you think . . .' the woman started to say angrily but Jessica took her identification out of her pocket.

'We're down from Manchester to interview Samantha Kellett. I was assured you'd have a room ready for us.'

The woman glanced up at a clock behind her on the wall. 'You're a bit early like.'

Jessica nodded. 'Yep, we're an efficient bunch up north.' She wasn't annoyed with the woman as such and knew the over-zealous ringing of the bell was a little childish given the station was most likely very understaffed. Ultimately, she wanted things sorted one way or the other so she could get back to Manchester.

The officer behind the counter unlocked a nearby door, ushering Jessica and Rowlands through. 'Sorry, there are just three of us in today. We'd love to be as *efficient* as you but we have budgets to stick to and so on.'

Jessica said nothing, knowing she deserved the little dig. The woman led them down a short corridor through a locked door and into an interview room that wasn't too dissimilar to the one Jessica was used to at Longsight. Neither looked as if they had been updated in the past fifteen years with peeling dreary cream paint on the walls and a sweaty musty smell.

The other officer stood in the doorway as Jessica and Rowlands stepped into the room. She gave a big sigh before speaking. 'In our notes it says Samantha Kellett is due to be back here by ten o'clock so you've got half an hour. You can hang around here and make sure every-thing's up to your *standards* or there's a coffee machine just down the hall. We'll make sure she's brought through when she gets here. Is there anything else I can help you with?'

Jessica was definitely feeling a little silly for her earlier outburst and the other officer was clearly annoyed.

'Does your tea machine spit out drinks that taste vaguely of washing-up liquid the way ours does?' Jessica asked.

The woman stared at them for a moment then laughed. 'I guess that's the standard nationwide. Don't risk the hot chocolate either, that tastes worse.'

'Thanks for the tip.'

When they were alone, Jessica checked the recording equipment over and everything seemed in a better condi-tion than theirs, which wasn't a surprise. It didn't take long before there was a knock at the door and a nervous-looking young male officer showed Sam into the room.

Jessica could see a lot of herself in the woman. They were roughly the same age and had the same figure. The woman's hair was black, Jessica's was a dark blonde, but they both had it in loose ponytails and were even dressed similarly. Jessica was wearing a light grey work suit, Sam's was slightly darker.

The woman sat across the table from them and, when the door was shut, Jessica introduced herself and Rowlands and checked Sam's name. 'You do know you're allowed a legal representative with you,' she added.

'I don't need one,' Sam said confidently.

'Are you sure? We can arrange for someone to talk to you for free.'

'It's fine, I haven't done anything.'

'As long as you're absolutely positive.'

Sam looked determinedly at Jessica. 'Why did you put my picture on the news?'

'We're investigating . . .' Jessica started to say but she was interrupted.

'I had to lie to my husband and tell him it wasn't me. He pointed out how similar I looked to the photograph and I had to say I didn't know anything about it.'

'So you admit it is you in the photograph with Edward Marks?'

The woman twitched ever so slightly as if trying to suppress a full-on shiver at the mention of the name. 'What of it?'

'Can I ask you how you knew Mr Marks?'

Sam's eyes narrowed. 'Do you already know?'

'We've been told . . . certain things.'

'So why do you need me to tell you?'

'Because we don't know if what was told to us is true.'

The woman sighed, looking away. 'Why are you bringing this back up? It was over ten years ago. I've moved on.' For the first time her voice faltered slightly.

Jessica wasn't usually nervous in interviews but she knew this one wasn't going to get her anything. Everything about the way the woman had spoken initially and how she had handed herself in indicated she had nothing to hide. 'Do you know what happened to Mr Marks and his friends from that holiday?' she asked.

The woman turned sharply and looked back at Jessica. 'I don't care.'

'One is definitely dead, the other five are assumed murdered.'

'I saw about the hands on the news. What does it matter?'

'Because you're the one connection we have that goes back to the six of them.' Jessica paused and then added, 'And, from what we've been told, you might well have had the motive.'

Sam snorted, looking away with tears in her eyes. 'You're joking, right? I mean, when I read about the picture you'd released I wondered why you wanted me. I thought perhaps you might have thought I was a witness to something, maybe even that you wanted to investigate what happened back then. I should have known you were going to accuse me of, I don't know, whatever. It's like those shit cop shows.'

'We're not accusing you of anything.'

'Why am I here then?' Sam was shouting now, emotional, standing and pushing back her chair.

Jessica was lost for words and surprised when Rowlands spoke. 'It's okay, Sam.' They were the first words he had uttered since the woman had entered the room. The outcome was strange because he had only said three words but it was almost as if hearing her own name calmed the woman. Sam looked at him and regained her composure, sitting and staring back at Jessica.

'We're not out to trip you up,' Jessica said, trying to sound reassuring.

'What do you want to know?'

'I know it's going to be hard but can you tell us what happened on holiday eleven years ago?'

Sam looked sideways to Dave, who gave a small nod. The woman said she had initially enjoyed a holiday romance with Edward but then went on to confirm more or less everything Steven Povey had told them. Her mood veered from anger to upset and back again before eventually finishing calmly.

'This is the first time I've told anyone about this since it happened,' she added. 'My husband doesn't know and we've been together for five years. We've got two kids.'

Sam seemed steady and Jessica made sure she was all right to continue talking. The woman nodded, and said she wanted everything finished with. 'We have got to ask you about your whereabouts over the past few weeks,' Jessica said.

'Can I use my phone? My diary is on there.'

Jessica ran through the dates the hands had been left, as well as the nights before and a few other random times in between. With the exception of one instance, Sam had an alibi for everything. She helped out in clubs for her children and her family had recently been on a week-long holiday with friends. Rowlands took notes of everything and it would be checked discreetly but Jessica knew it would all match up. With her husband also with her on the holiday, it seemed to rule him out too.

Sam asked if they could keep everything from her husband and Jessica assured her they would try. He wasn't a suspect and, although they would check the details of the holiday and make sure he was there, it didn't necessarily mean he had to be informed. The woman repeated she had never told anyone, including her parents, about what had happened, insisting she'd had no contact with any of the men after that night in Faliraki. Jessica believed her and asked for the woman's maiden name, if only for their records.

They released her and Jessica gave the woman her card just in case she managed to think of anything. Jessica phoned Cole to tell him what had happened but the car journey back to Manchester proved to be something of an inquest, the only positive that they would be back in plenty of time for Jessica to get to Caroline's house.

'Poor woman,' Rowlands said.

'It's my fault,' Jessica replied. 'I didn't know what else to do and ended up sticking her face on the news for no reason other than the fact she was attacked eleven years ago. She spent all this time getting over it then I punished her for it.'

'It wasn't your fault,' Dave said but Jessica knew it was. It didn't matter that she hadn't had many other options; it was her who had gone to the DCI and asked to work with the press office. Jessica didn't reply but it wasn't long before Rowlands asked the question she knew she didn't have the answer to. 'What do we do now?'

Unless another hand showed up unexpectedly, they were completely out of leads. 'I really don't know,' Jessica said, not even trying to hide her dejection.

Between the two of them, they went over everything that had happened so far. They still had the CCTV footage of the woman in black but no clue as to the person's identity and, now that Sam Kellett had pretty much been ruled out – although it would take some time to officially check her alibis – no reason why the person was making things so public.

They could return to the lists of college-leavers but everything had already been gone over once and, as the holiday photo had shown, the links between the young men could be widespread and unexpected. Jessica felt deflated and unsure what she should do next.

Because of the light traffic, they had time to go via the station. Jessica went to Cole's office, reiterating what she had told him on the phone. She would arrange for an officer to formally check Sam Kellett's whereabouts but had no doubts it would be accurate.

Cole said the garage owner had started to speak in the Johnson case. The man apparently had text messages that could implicate George Johnson but the chief inspector said that was information that couldn't get out. Jessica felt strange that something so big was going on where she worked but that she wasn't a part of it and even worse that her case had stalled. They agreed to leave things over the weekend, which would give them a chance to think things over, then decide where to go next on Monday. It wasn't ideal but, with Caroline's wedding, Jessica didn't have any better ideas.

Jessica tried to have a fun evening with her friend on her 'last evening of freedom' party as Caroline had dubbed it.

The two women drank and reminisced about their younger days. Jessica tried to put to the back of her mind the feelings of failure and inertia at having her investigation come to a halt. She happily shared bottles of wine and the more she drank, the more she felt able to laugh and join in. Caroline asked who she was bringing the following day but Jessica remained tight-lipped. 'You don't know him,' was all she would say, adding she had arranged to meet the person at the church.

The Saturday morning was a rush of people coming and going from Caroline's flat. The bride-to-be had a small team of her friends and relatives from the groom's side coming round to help her get ready, with Jessica left to sort herself and the other bridesmaids into their light blue dresses. The two younger bridesmaids were relatively co-operative and their parents were also present to help, which was a relief. The girly atmosphere wasn't really to her taste and she was glad when everyone had finally left and it was just her and Caroline alone waiting for the car to take them to the church. The bride anxiously watched the clock on her wall as Jessica tried to assure her everything would be fine.

The car was on time, as Jessica said it would be, and she helped her friend into the rear seat. As the driver set off for the short journey, the two women were sitting next to each other but turned so they could talk face-to-face.

'It's really happening,' Caroline said with a nervous giggle.

Jessica smiled back. 'I wondered what all the dresses and fancy car were about.'

Caroline laughed again. 'What do you think of Thomas?'

'He picked you, so he's got pretty good taste.'

'I've been wondering if I'm on the rebound because of . . . y'know, Randall.' Caroline's voice had dropped at the mention of his name and she paused for a moment before continuing. 'I'm sorry things drifted between us after that.'

Jessica looked into her friend's eyes. 'It's not your fault. Things happened and it's where we are now that matters.'

'Do you think I'm on the rebound?'

Jessica didn't know whether to answer honestly but it wasn't really in her nature to stay quiet, even at what could be inopportune times. 'I don't know, you tell me,' she replied.

Caroline blinked back tears and laughed. 'I wanted you to say "no".'

Jessica could tell her friend was being half-serious. 'Sorry . . .'

'It's all right. I don't know either. He's nice though and he loves me, that's what matters.' Jessica said nothing, letting her friend get things off her chest. 'It's just big-day nerves,' Caroline added. 'I'm not going to make a dash for it when we get to the altar.'

'I don't think you'd get too far in those heels anyway.'

The church was a small building in a little village on the outskirts of the city that had been on the same site for hundreds of years. As the sun shone and the two women stepped out of the vehicle, the photographer rushed in, taking photo after photo. Jessica hated having her picture taken at the best of the times but she gritted her teeth and did her best to smile, knowing this was bad enough but the posed pictures that would be taken after the ceremony would really test her patience.

When he finally left them to enter the church and get into position for the aisle walk, Jessica looked up to see the setting properly. The picturesque church and its green surroundings, along with the bright blue sky, really was like something on the front of a postcard.

'This is lovely,' Jessica said.

Caroline looked a little emotional as they walked the short distance to the church's main doors. They entered a small room just inside where the other bridesmaids were waiting with their parents before the adults went into the main part of the church, leaving just the four of them.

As the church organ started up with the opening chords of the wedding march, Jessica winked at her friend. 'Deep breath.'

They stepped out of the room and began to slowly walk down the aisle. Aside from the organ, Jessica could only hear shuffling as people turned en masse to look at them walking together. Jessica had visions of tripping and wiping out her friend along with the other bridesmaids but kept a careful eye on where she was stepping.

They neared the front and Jessica glanced up to see the grinning face of Thomas and his best man then glanced to her left and almost gasped with embarrassment. The man sitting on the end of the line two rows back caught Jessica's eye and smiled. She could see he was wearing a purple velvet smoking jacket along with dark green trousers. Jessica couldn't see what shoes he had on, if any, but dreaded to think what they could be.

'What *are* you wearing?' Jessica mouthed silently to the man but he shook his head as if to indicate he hadn't understood. She stopped looking at him and continued to walk until the small party arrived at the front and the organ went quiet.

It was clearly a little strange for her to be giving Caroline away but everyone involved must have known the situation. The ceremony went as would have been expected but Jessica felt self-conscious standing at the front.

After it was over and the newly married couple walked back down the aisle towards the outside of the church, Jessica didn't waste the opportunity to slide in next to the man two rows back.

'What *are* you wearing?' she demanded in a loud whisper as the church organ blared again.

'What?' he said.

Jessica looked down to see he was wearing a pair of canvas trainers that matched his jacket. 'You're wearing purple shoes, a purple jacket and green trousers to a wedding. What kind of idiot wears trainers to a wedding?'

The man shook his head as if he didn't understand the point. 'You said "dress smartly".'

'Exactly!'

'These are my best clothes.'

Realising she wasn't going to win the argument, Jessica stood back up, offering the man her arm to exit the church. 'You and I are going to have to go shopping, Hugo.'

33

The other people at the wedding seemed part-bemused, part-amused by Hugo. His real name was Francis but he was a magician who used 'Hugo' as a stage name. Jessica had first met him a couple of years ago and, although not a friend as such, she figured he was as good a person as anyone to take to a wedding. There was no real attraction but her thinking had been he could at least entertain the other guests. She'd overlooked the fact he could also embarrass her but, given this was the first time she had ever seen him wearing shoes that matched, Jessica figured it could have been worse. He did at least look as if he had combed his hair for the occasion, his shoulder-length brown locks as tidy as she had seen them. The one good thing was that Caroline fell in the 'amused' rather than 'bemused' camp.

Jessica tried to pretend she was enjoying herself as she was yanked, sometimes literally, from one posed photo to another. By the end of it, she could quite happily have cut off the photographer's hand to stop him putting it in the air every time he wanted the assembled people to smile and say 'cheese'.

When the organised picture-taking was over, Jessica finally got a chance to catch up with her parents. She had seen them in the church but only to wave to while, before that, she hadn't seen them in a few months. Her dad took the opportunity to tease her about her new 'boyfriend'.

The bride and groom had gone off to their hotel room for a few hours before they were going to return to the party. When the youngest bridesmaid had asked why they weren't just going directly to the reception, Caroline had told her she and her new husband were going to 'rest', completely ignoring Jessica's inadvertent snort of laughter.

'Enjoy your "rest",' Jessica said with a giggle.

With a few hours to kill, Jessica, Hugo and her parents went to a local pub for a chat before heading to the reception venue. Hugo didn't seem to mind the fact he wasn't really involved in the conversations and happily sat around watching people go by. Jessica wondered if he was feeling hot in the velvet jacket but, if he was, he said nothing. After a couple of drinks, she even began to warm to his outfit and, before long, they had to catch a taxi to the reception itself.

The party was being held in a massive conference room at a nearby golf club where Thomas's father was apparently one of the higher-up members. Huge bay windows on one side of the room opened out onto the course itself and it was along there where the long head table was placed.

Jessica saw from the seating plan that she was on the main table with Caroline on one side and Hugo on the other. It was the traditional spot the father of the bride might have had and she couldn't help but feel a little embarrassed. Her parents were on one of the circular tables placed around the room. Each one was named after a different country for a reason Jessica didn't know. Her parents were on 'Canada', which was next to 'New Zealand'.

Although Caroline told her she didn't have to, Jessica had spent some of her free time trying to put together a speech. Despite that, when the moment came after the meal, she just ad-libbed, talking about her friend and telling the story of how they met quite by chance because they ended up sitting next to each other in a lesson many years ago. She ended with a standard 'Congratulations' and sat down, leaving it to the best man to poke fun at the groom.

Just when it looked as if everything was completed, with the staff hovering ready to start moving the tables so the floor could be cleared, Jessica heard someone else tinkling their glass. She looked sideways and saw Hugo rising to his feet, tapping his knife on his champagne flute to get people's attention. Caroline nudged Jessica with her elbow and the two women exchanged the same 'What's going on?' look.

Before Jessica could intervene, Hugo started to speak. 'I would just like to add my congratulations to the happy couple and I hope they haven't dropped too much food on themselves.' He sat back down as quickly as he had stood up and, apart from one person who started clapping at the back of the room before stopping when they realised no one else was joining in, there was silence.

Jessica noticed Caroline look down at her lap, presumably wondering if she had dropped any food. She picked up the cream-coloured satin napkin that was still on her lap and went to put it on the table before squealing slightly and opening it out. Jessica saw there was a beautifully drawn picture of the bride and the groom on the material. She had no idea what had been used to create it but Caroline first showed it to Thomas and then turned it around for the rest of the room to see. It really was a strange piece of art but absolutely compelling because of its perfect likeness of the two people.

'Did you draw that?' Jessica asked Hugo, who shrugged with a vague acknowledgement as people around the room began to applaud the unconventional gift.

Caroline turned it around to have another look and then leant behind Jessica to talk to Hugo. 'This is amazing. Thanks so much. We'll get it framed or something, it's so unique.'

Hugo continued to nod in the way Jessica had seen him do before when he had stunned people with tricks. This was slightly different but equally as impressive, although Jessica never ceased to be amazed by how strange he was. She wondered what else he was good at, given she could now add art to the list of illusion, singing and taxidermy he had impressed her with.

The tables were cleared by staff and a band started playing soft background music. There were plenty of wine bottles still around the edges of the room that hadn't been finished during the meal and Jessica happily drank away. She was feeling nice and tipsy when the first dance finally got under way. The groom's parents were both in tears, leaving Jessica feeling a little uncomfortable as she rarely showed any outward emotion. Halfway through the song,

Caroline beckoned her onto the floor but it was Hugo who dragged her towards the happy couple and put his hands on her waist, initiating a slow dance. Other couples followed and, before Jessica knew it, she was in the middle of a host of people gently swaying to the song.

If anyone else from the station had been present, Jessica would have felt deeply embarrassed but, as it was, she allowed Hugo to lead her around. She stepped in closer to him, letting him hold her and figuring he was a good choice of person to bring. He was definitely odd but at least he wasn't trying to come on to her.

After what seemed like an age, the song finally ended and everyone stopped to applaud the newly married couple. Hugo grinned and stepped away from Jessica almost as quickly as he had pulled her onto the dance floor in the first place.

While some carried on dancing, Jessica trailed her guest back to the children's table. She didn't know why that was where he wanted to sit but followed his lead. A few of the younger boys were racing up and down at the rear of the room but Hugo beckoned them over and showed them a trick where he made a wine glass disappear in front of their eyes. Before Jessica knew what was happening, there was a small crowd of people around them watching the magician go through a routine of making things disappear and reappear, or simply guessing the contents of their pockets after asking a few questions. As she suspected he would have, Hugo also had a deck of cards in his pocket and moved onto card tricks, bringing various 'oooh' noises from the people present.

At one point he borrowed a bracelet from Jessica's mother and made it reappear on Jessica's own arm. Neither of her parents seemed to believe that she wasn't in a relationship with Hugo. 'Oh, he's lovely,' her mum kept saying, while her dad said he couldn't wait for the man to take Jessica off his hands, openly asking how much it would cost him. Jessica didn't have the inclination to tell them Hugo lived above a betting shop and surrounded himself with dead stuffed animals. Luckily for Jessica, her parents left relatively early as her father was feeling tired. She kissed them both and assured them she would call in the next day or two.

The photographer was still hanging around and had moved from taking photos of the couple dancing, cutting the cake and eating the cake to focusing on the other guests. He was particularly taken with Hugo and, as the crowd slowly began to thin with the younger children leaving, he asked for a picture of Jessica and Hugo together.

Jessica wasn't in the mood but had no time to object before Hugo shuffled into the seat next to her, beaming at the camera.

'Can you smile for me,' the picture-taker said to Jessica as if addressing a child. She did her best to not look annoyed. 'Okay, now can you each hold a glass as if you're toasting the camera,' he added. Hugo eagerly picked up his glass while Jessica's was again empty. Someone poured her more wine and she copied Hugo in saluting the camera with her glass, smiling wearily. 'Okay, can you swap hands?' the photographer said, pointing at Hugo then at Jessica. 'You're holding it with your left hand and you've got it with your right. It doesn't look right.'

Jessica swapped and the photographer snapped away. He went to stand up but a thought popped into her head. 'Can I have a look at those pictures?' she asked. The man seemed confused but crouched down, turning the camera around so she could see the images in the viewfinder. In the second set of pictures, she and Hugo were holding the glasses in their outside hands. She had hers in her left, while he was using his right. In the first set, they had the drinks on their inside hands next to each other. The photographer was correct when he said things didn't look right. 'Thanks,' Jessica said, letting the man stand again.

After he had walked away, she turned to Hugo. 'Are you left-handed?' He shrugged in the same way he always did when acknowledging something. 'You are?' Jessica asked again, wanting confirmation.

'Yes.'

'So would you always pick a glass up with your left hand?'

'I guess.'

Jessica thought about herself. Most of the time she would drink using her right hand. On occasion she might use her left but not often. She stood quickly.

'Do you mind if I leave, Hugo?'

'No, I'll come with you if you want?'

'I'm going back to the station for a while.' It was an odd thing to do given it was late on a Saturday evening but the man said nothing, as if her answer was the most normal thing.

'That's fine. I've enjoyed it today.'

Jessica leant forward and kissed him on the forehead. 'Thanks for coming. We should go out again sometime.'

She left him showing off more card tricks and went to find Caroline to apologise for leaving early. She said she had a slightly upset stomach and kissed the newly married couple, warning Thomas he'd better look after his bride. The pair were going on honeymoon for a fortnight the next day, so Jessica told her friend she expected a present and hugged her a final time before walking quickly out to the front of the building.

A couple of taxis were already waiting and Jessica got into the first one.

'Are you "King", love?' the driver asked, half-looking over his shoulder.

'Sorry?' Jessica replied.

'I'm here to pick up someone called "King". I thought it was a couple though.'

Jessica realised the golf club was out of the way and the only taxis would be ones other people had booked. She couldn't be bothered waiting. 'Yeah, sorry it's just me,' she said.

'Where are you off to?'

'This might sound weird but can you take me to Longsight Police Station?'

'Are you sure you're "King"? My note said a couple to go to Stockport.'

Jessica sighed. 'All right, you've got me. My last name isn't King but I am a police officer who's a little bit tipsy and I could really do with getting back to the station.'

The driver turned around and Jessica saw him eyeing her outfit. 'All right, whatever you say, love. I've not seen too many "officers" wearing a dress like that.'

Jessica wouldn't have let too many people get away with looking at her the way the driver had and it was clear he didn't believe who she was. Partly because of the alcohol she'd had but also because he started driving in the direction she needed to go, Jessica said nothing.

The man tried to strike up a conversation more than once but Jessica was pretty adept at giving dull answers to make him stop and he eventually pulled up outside of the police station. 'Are you sure this is where you want to go?' he asked sarcastically. Jessica ignored his tone and dropped some money on the passenger seat before getting out of the vehicle and walking towards the main door.

Most of the officers on duty on a Saturday night would have been in the city centre dealing with various amounts of trouble. Jessica knew the station would only get busy in a few hours when the first van of people arrested for various drink- or violence-related crimes would arrive.

As she walked into the station, the desk sergeant first looked her up and down and then did a double-take when he realised the woman in the blue dress and matching shoes with her hair clean and down was the same person who usually wore a trouser suit with her hair tied back in a ponytail. Jessica ignored his stare, walking around the counter as she would do usually.

'Are you all right?' the sergeant asked.

'Fine. I've just got to check something in my office and

then I'll need a lift home if you can get someone to sort that?'

'I'll see what I can do.'

Jessica walked along the corridor to her office and opened the door. She turned the lights on and headed to where there were the usual piles of clutter on her desk. She sifted through a few things and then settled on a copy of the photo that showed Edward Marks and the woman who had been Samantha Weston.

Something about the photo hadn't seemed right to Jessica when she had looked at the picture before and only now was she beginning to understand what it was. Ed and Sam were holding their glasses towards the camera in exactly the way the photographer had said looked awkward. Thoughts began to swirl around her head as Jessica wrote frantically on a pad the names of people she would have to speak to before the weekend was over.

34

Jessica spent her Sunday partly at the station and partly at home, trying to get hold of the people she needed. By mid-morning on the Monday, she had checked over the final few things from her flat. There had been little point in going to the station as the commute would have wasted time.

Jessica phoned Cole's mobile but it went straight to voicemail so she called his desk phone, which also went unanswered. She then called the station's reception and told the person who answered who she was. 'Is the DCI around?' she asked.

'Haven't you heard?'

'What?'

'They arrested George Johnson first thing this morning. He's been in there with him all morning, it's chaos here.'

'What about Jason?' Jessica asked.

'I've not seen him all morning. I assume he's there too.'

'Shite.'

'Do you want me to take a message?'

'No, I'll be in later.'

Jessica had learned the hard way a couple of years earlier not to go charging in on her own but felt hamstrung by the fact all of her supervisors were unreachable. She could have contacted one of them the day before but didn't feel as if she had the entire picture and figured gathering that evidence before taking it to her bosses couldn't do much harm.

She drove to the location she needed to be at, completed one final task and stood outside of the big front door feeling the rain fall on her hair. As she had struggled to figure everything out over the past few weeks, the sun had shone but now she believed she knew a lot of the answers, the weather had finally turned. The irony of it happening just after the air-conditioning had been fixed at the station wasn't lost on anyone.

After knocking on the door, Jessica waited in the rain for the man to answer.

Charlie Marks soon opened the door wide and waved her in. He was eating a piece of toast, rotating his free hand around in a circle as if to apologise. When he had finished chewing, he smiled. 'Sorry about that, I know we spoke yesterday but I didn't know exactly what time you were coming.' Jessica closed the door behind her as Charlie ate the final piece. 'Was there anything in particular I can help you with?' he added.

Jessica shook her head. 'Not specifically, we're just tying up a few loose ends.'

Charlie was unmoved. 'Do you want to look through the things upstairs again?'

'There are a couple of pictures I was hoping I could borrow for a short while.'

Charlie shrugged. 'That's fine, do you need my help? You're welcome to look on your own if you know what you're after.'

'I've seen them before. They're just upstairs if you don't mind.'

'It's fine. I'll be in the kitchen if you want me.'

Jessica made her way up the stairs in the same way she had done a few times previously, heading to the room where Charlie had handed her the photo of the rugby team and where she had found the photo of the six young men on holiday. She could feel her heart beating faster as she stepped across the threshold, walking towards the window. There was a steady beat of the rain falling outside as Jessica looked out towards the back garden wondering about the specific questions she didn't yet know the answers to.

The serene view was almost hypnotic as she stared into the distance before turning around and walking towards the box where she had previously looked through the photographs. She was partly relieved to see the ones still there from the last time she had been in the room. Jessica had no reason to think they would have been moved and ultimately it wouldn't have altered her theory but it was nice to hold some degree of proof in her hands.

Jessica stood thinking about her next move. Should she return to the station with what she was holding? It appeared Cole was going to be unavailable for most of the day and, although she was confident she knew what was going on, Jessica wasn't completely sure.

After a few moments' thought, she took the photographs downstairs, entering the kitchen where Charlie was sitting on a stool typing on a laptop computer that was on the main counter.

He glanced up as she walked in. 'Did you get what you needed?'

'Yes, here you go.' Jessica held out one of the photos and Charlie took it, looking at the picture then up to Jessica, clearly confused. 'What about these?' She handed him two more photos which he took, glimpsed at and then put on the counter.

'I'm not sure what you're showing me,' he said.

Jessica smiled thinly. 'Is there something you want to tell me, Charlie?'

'Like what?'

There were a few moments of silence which Jessica let hang before continuing. 'Given it was Sunday yesterday, it took a bit of doing but I managed to speak to a couple of your former colleagues at Bennett Piper. It wasn't the first time I'd talked to them but this time I knew the right questions to ask.' Charlie shuffled nervously but didn't move from his stool. 'This time I asked about how you quit your job and I'm sure you know what the reply was.'

The man shook his head. 'I sent them an email, so what?'

Jessica nodded. 'That's right; an email to your boss and a couple of text messages to your other colleagues. If I had known that all those weeks ago, it might have had me thinking straight away.'

'About what?' Charlie reached forward, closing the lid of his computer.

'About the fact no one I can find has seen you in person since you announced you were moving back up north to see your brother again.'

Charlie was silent for a moment, as if thinking how to reply. 'I'm not sure what you're trying to say.'

Jessica nodded and picked up the pictures the man had put on the counter. 'What were you like as a kid, Charlie?' He shrugged as if not knowing what she was getting at. She held up the photos one by one for him to see. They were the same ones she had looked at upstairs a couple of weeks ago before finding the one of the six men on holiday. 'You liked football, yes?' she asked, showing him the one of the young boy with a ball.

'So what? Lots of people do.'

'Were you a good angler? I'm not sure I would have guessed you were a keen fisherman.' Charlie looked at the second photo and shrugged. 'What about building sandcastles with your brother? Do you remember that?'

'I have no idea what you're getting at.'

Jessica picked up a fourth photo from the counter. It was the one of the two boys doing their homework together while sitting across from each other. 'Even your body language since I walked in has told me everything I needed to know. When you were eating as I came in, the toast was in your left hand. When you shut the laptop lid, you did it with your left hand.'

Charlie started to stand but Jessica raised her voice and he almost cowered under it, sitting back down. 'How about this photo of you building sandcastles? The older, blonder child – Charlie – is using his right hand while Ed, the younger, dark-haired kid, is using his left. In the one of you doing your homework, Charlie, the older, blonder child is using his right hand while Ed, the younger, dark-haired kid, is using his left.'

The man shuffled nervously but seemed transfixed by what she was saying. 'How about young Charlie kicking a football with his right foot? Or young Charlie holding a fishing rod with his right hand? And that's where the problem is because, in the photo of Ed having a drink with Sam Weston on holiday, just like the ones from when he was young, he is using his *left* hand to hold his drink.'

The man winced at the sound of Sam's name. 'You know her name, don't you, *Edward*?' He said nothing but Jessica stood, continuing to speak. 'It wasn't Edward's hand we found first of all, it was Charlie's. You killed your brother, then took his identity, acting as if you were only just returning from London. I checked the dates and Charlie's colleagues say he left his job a fortnight before his hand was found. When I spoke to you on the phone, you said you were coming up to Manchester on a train. But you were already here because you're Edward and you never left.'

The man shook his head. 'I don't know why you're saying all of this. I use my right and left hands to do things.'

'It's not about being right- or left-handed. That was just what got me thinking. The hand we've been thinking of as Edward's this whole time was never identified by anyone because we didn't have anything else to match it to – except for when you came along and gave us a mouth swab. But all that proved was that the hand belonged to your brother. You reported "Edward" as missing, even though you *are* Edward. When we matched the DNA and you told us you were Charlie, we made the obvious conclusion we had found Edward's hand. But the DNA was always going to be a match because you *are* brothers. We just didn't know which one had lost a hand and which one hadn't.'

Jessica stopped for a breath before continuing but he didn't attempt to respond. 'From the photos, you look fairly similar,' she added. 'Because Charlie had been out of the area for such a long time, all you had to do was dye your hair and you would easily pass as him as long as none of Charlie's colleagues in London ever saw you.'

The man's voice was level and had a small undercurrent of menace that wasn't lost on Jessica. 'Even if all of this were true, how would you prove it?'

Jessica was feeling a little nervous and wondered if she should have involved officers higher-up from the station. She ignored his question and continued. 'I still don't know everything. I don't know which brother contacted the other about reconciliation but I guess it was you because it was the only way you could make the plan work. I assume the figure in black on the cameras was also you? You're roughly the same size and shape but the same thing always confused us; the way the person walked in those shoes. I've not figured it all out yet but there were women's shoes in one of the bedrooms upstairs at the bottom of a wardrobe. Considering the only people who lived here were you, your brother and your father, I don't know why there would be the need for female things. There were so many random items around it didn't register at the time but there were women's heeled shoes in there plus other female clothes in boxes. When I first came here, your neighbour told me he didn't like to stick his nose into other people's business but, when I visited him this morning and asked what he meant, he said he'd often seen a man in women's clothing coming in and out of the house late at night. He was pretty sure it was the young man who owned the house but didn't want to say anything about it. There's no law about cross-dressing but I can't help but wonder if that's why you were so confident about walking in heels?'

He said nothing, narrowing his eyes but Jessica was on a roll. 'As for why you made everything so public with leaving the hands, I'm not really sure. It was you who gave me the leads from the photographs too. I think maybe you wanted everyone to find out what the other men had done when they'd attacked Samantha. Perhaps she was your first proper girlfriend and you never recovered from it?'

'You don't know anything.' His tone was hard to judge – firm but unthreatening.

'That's what I'm saying,' Jessica said. 'I really don't. I have no idea why you killed your brother but all I can come up with is that it was the only way to make your plan work. You'd fallen out with him over who owned the house so it got that out of the way while also confusing us. As Edward, all you'd have to do is sign the house over to your brother, who you planned to kill, then set the wheels in motion. I don't really know why you sent me fingers but perhaps that was part of the game? I also don't know how you managed to subdue the other men because they are almost all bigger than you.'

'You're so wrong.'

'Am I?'

'Yes and I can prove it.' The man quickly got to his feet, surprising Jessica with his movement. She took an involuntary half-step backwards but he didn't move towards her, instead stepping towards the kitchen door, holding it open for her. 'Come and see.'

Jessica was a little confused. She realised she didn't know everything but felt sure her explanation about which brother was which was correct. Without really thinking, she walked towards the door, ducking ever so slightly under the man's arms and going through it. It was then Jessica realised she had made a terrible mistake as something sharp punctured her neck and the man pushed her to the floor.

Jessica swung violently with her legs as the man lunged down on top of her, sitting across her midriff and pinning her arms to the floor. She heard a clattering noise as something bounced to the ground. He was a lot stronger than she would have thought and no matter how much she fought, she couldn't escape his grasp. His eyes locked on hers; they were fierce and staring, although he seemed completely in control of himself. 'Just go with it,' he said.

As Jessica tried to struggle, she could feel her arms and legs heavy with the effort. Her mind was alert but her body wasn't reacting to her commands. She didn't know how much time had elapsed while he was on top of her but it didn't feel long before he stood. Jessica couldn't move her neck far but saw him crouch and pick up an empty syringe from the floor. She tried to move but her limbs weren't responding.

'I really didn't think that would work,' he said, a mixture of confusion and amusement on his face.

35

Jessica wanted to speak but her lips wouldn't move and she could feel a small amount of drool around the corner of her mouth. The man went into the kitchen then returned without the syringe. He picked Jessica up and leant her against the wall so she was in a sitting position.

'Sorry about that,' he said. 'I don't want you to swallow your tongue or something stupid.'

Jessica's mind was screaming 'GET OFF ME' but no words were coming out.

The man stood back and looked her up and down. 'If it's any consolation, you're right, I am Edward. It's pretty clever figuring it out from those photos. If I'd thought it through, I would have hidden those ones but the left-right-handed thing didn't even occur to me. I wanted you to find the rugby photo and so on. As you say, I wanted people to know what those animals did to Samantha. I was hoping it would get on the news a bit more so they would be exposed but it didn't quite work as I hoped. The problem with this *unfortunate* situation is that it might never come out now.'

Jessica was trying to stay calm and focus on breathing. It wasn't hard exactly but felt slightly unnatural because she found herself thinking about it. She felt so stupid – she had literally fallen for the oldest trick in the book. Someone had said, 'Look over there' and, while she had, they'd seized their chance.

Edward sat cross-legged on the floor a few feet away from her, his head tilted slightly. 'Pancuronium if you're wondering. It's a muscle-relaxing drug. When my father was ill in his later days he was in a lot of pain and his doctor prescribed it. Small doses would help him sleep but I managed to keep plenty of it over the final few months. Larger doses of it leave you in a state, well, like you are in now. As you can probably tell, most of the other men were bigger and stronger than me, so I needed something in my favour. Jacob was a bit different but it was easy enough to spike his drink. This is quite a useful little drug really. It takes around a minute to kick in and then, depending on the person's size, can last for anything up to three hours. I didn't want to take any risks with Jacob because he's a big guy.'

Jessica continued to focus on her breathing. She had never heard of the drug but didn't doubt the things Edward was telling her were true. Her arms felt floppy and useless by her side and she fought to move one of them a small amount. She realised she wasn't totally paralysed but certainly couldn't do much more than twitch her right arm.

Edward scratched his chin, appearing a little unsure. 'As I'm sure you know by now, this wasn't really part of the plan. I don't actually know what to do with you. I've got this storage unit in the city with two big chest freezers. I got them about a year ago from this supermarket that went out of business. After I'd killed them, that's where I kept the bodies before going back for the hands when I needed them. I've never had a live victim in the house so I'm at a bit of a loss because my tools are all there.'

He stood and paced before walking into the kitchen and returning. He sat back down in front of Jessica and started playing with a large kitchen knife, moving it from one hand to the other and staring closely at the handle and blade before looking back to her. 'This is a pretty good knife, you know. I like cooking and I use it a lot. I don't really want to have to throw it out but it's not as if I can use it on you then go back to chopping carrots tomorrow, is it?'

He laughed slightly as he spoke. 'This is like one of those big movie moments, isn't it, where the dastardly crook reveals everything to the plucky secret agent, who is seemingly in an impossible situation but the agent then somehow escapes.' He shuffled forward and poked Jessica in the shoulder. 'You're not going anywhere though, are you?'

Edward stood and put the knife deliberately on the floor close to Jessica, then stepped towards her, picking her up and holding her over his shoulder. She felt sick, her head hanging limply against his back. She bobbed up and down as he walked toward the area where the pool was being built. Edward pushed through a plastic curtain, then placed her gently on the floor, propping her up so she could see the room before he left.

Jessica couldn't do anything other than twitch her arms but it was suddenly obvious what he had done with the bodies of the other men. When she had seen the room before, the whole area was covered in plastic sheeting and she hadn't bothered to look. It was uncovered now, revealing a giant pit in the centre of the room where the pool would go. The surface wasn't level, with some areas far deeper than others and a few sections filled with concrete that had set.

Edward entered back into the area with the knife and set it down on the floor next to Jessica. Instinctively she tried to move towards it but her limbs were incapable of responding. He started to walk around. Plastic sheeting was pinned to the ceiling and shielded the gaps in the walls where the windows would go. Jessica could hear the rain falling but it sounded louder because, aside from the sheets, there was nothing to separate them from the outside. Edward talked loudly as he wandered around the space where the pool would be before ending up back next to Jessica.

'I know you're not stupid so you'll know by now that this is where all those bodies ended up. Charlie, Lewis Barnes, Jacob Chrisp, Matthew Cooper and Steven Povey are all in the foundations of the pool. I've got a company coming around on Thursday to put the sealant in and get a proper bottom down. For obvious reasons I've had to do a lot of the foundations myself; I couldn't really get a company in to help me bury bodies, could I? I don't really know what I'm doing. This other company dug it all out for me and I've just been burying them then pouring the concrete into the space they dug. It was actually a little easier than I thought.'

Edward paused and coughed, kicking a bit of plastic

sheeting before continuing. 'When you were around the other week I was worried you'd take me up on the offer and have a much closer look around here. The covering sheets were all out and luckily you didn't pay too much attention. There were no bodies on show but it was a bit of a mess. I dreaded it every time you came around because, on the second occasion, Charlie's phone went off. I'd been keeping it just in case but obviously forgotten to turn it off. I was surprised the battery hadn't died.'

As he finished his loop, Edward crouched near to the edge of the pit. 'There's still a space at this end and I've got loads of cement left. It'll be a waste of a day and I'll have to do something with your car but at least the driveway's long enough so no one will see it for now. I'm a bit pissed off you spoke to the neighbours actually but I can just say you came and went. I'll think of something. Maybe I'll use your phone to send a text then ditch it?'

Jessica was still trying to concentrate on breathing but panic was beginning to set in. The knife was on the ground mere inches away but her body wouldn't move.

Edward stood and moved to stand directly in front of her. 'Right, to business,' he said, clapping his hands. 'I know it's a bit of a cliché but I figure you may as well go out actually knowing what's gone on, so what the hell. I've got to be quick though because I've got a body to bury and a car to get rid of, though you already know that.'

The man's cheeriness was incredibly unsettling and he continued speaking in the same tone. 'Right, here goes. I am your woman in black. It was pretty funny actually when I saw those headlines. At first, it was just a disguise but then I realised it really had confused you. I was a bit pissed off with those robbers who stole my disguise but I guess it didn't do any long-term harm. Either way, I dress up in women's clothing now and then, so what? I might have to have "words" with my nosy neighbour though. I know the city pretty well and, once you realise where the cameras are, it's pretty easy to get out of places without being spotted.' He paused for a moment, then added, 'Any questions?'

Jessica couldn't have spoken even if she'd wanted to. Edward smiled. 'No, right, well, it was me who reconciled with Charlie. The guy's a complete dick; I bet you didn't know that. I was the one who looked after Dad and he left me the house. Charlie whined on about his share and then pissed off to London. I got in touch a few months ago and gave him a sob story about signing over half the house and making up and so on but it was just because I needed him for this. He was the key one because I wanted the story to come out about what they'd done to Samantha but I couldn't do everything as Edward because you lot would know it was me. So I came up with the idea of killing "me" off and becoming Charlie. That way you'd have no way of knowing I was involved. Well, in theory anyway.'

Jessica found his tone and mood difficult to judge. He spoke about the killings in a matter-of-fact voice with no emotion at all. He seemed almost put out by the entire affair and, although he clearly intended to do her harm, he almost seemed regretful about the whole thing.

He began to speak more quickly, clearly becoming impatient. 'You probably want to know why I sent you the fingers. I should really apologise because it can't have been nice to get something like that in the post, especially when a big package arrives. Whenever the post van turns up, I always get a little excited wondering what's inside. I feel like a kid again whenever something with my name shows up that I haven't specifically ordered. Anyway, sorry about that. It was just because I didn't want you to forget. That was the reason I gave the thumbs-up and waved at the camera too – I wanted you to find the reason for it all so people would know. I figured you might have been struggling to identify everyone and I wanted to keep you interested. I couldn't make it too obvious, which is why I used the fingers and called you over for that first picture. It almost worked out.'

Edward tapped his hand on the floor as if wondering what else he should say. 'Umm,' he muttered to himself, tutting. 'Right, I suppose the only other thing is to tell you why.' He stood, pacing a couple of times before sitting directly in front of Jessica. He moved the knife away from her and made sure her eyes could meet his. She had no choice but to look at him.

He lowered his tone and his voice cracked a couple of times as he spoke. 'I was a virgin, you know. I met Samantha on holiday and we had a really good time. We'd talked about meeting up again when we got back to England. She was the first girl who ever really showed much interest in me. I know you know most of this now about the attack on her. I wanted to tell them to stop but Jacob was so much bigger than me. I didn't know what to do; I was just some scrawny kid.'

Edward looked away, then met Jessica's eye again. He sniffed and then spoke even more quietly; his demeanour had changed completely from being breezy and cheerful to sounding far more solemn. 'I wasn't always like this. You know in "The Shining" when Jack Nicholson goes a bit crazy in a big house on his own? I've felt a bit like that since Dad died. I've got all this space and don't know what to do. I paint and cook but it's only for me.'

He paused for a moment. 'I've not had a girlfriend since Sam. The dressing up is just for show. Manchester's the right place to be for all of that with other men but I don't really know what I am. I started to think all of this through about a year ago. I figured that, if I could make the other men pay for what they did to Sam, maybe I would be able to get over it too? It took ages to find out where everyone was but the Internet's a wonderful thing. After that, I had the problem of it being obvious it was me. That's when I thought of using Charlie too. Believe it or not, after all the planning, it really wasn't that hard.'

Edward stood again, sounding a little cheerier. 'I think that's everything. At least you should be happy now.' He played with the knife before putting it back down and muttering under his breath, 'Bit messy'. He made a 'hmm' noise then began to speak again. 'Sorry about all of this, I've never done it like this before. The men were easy because it all happened in the storage unit which was easy to clean out.'

Jessica continued to try to move but her body refused to respond to her commands. Her arms and legs felt heavy and she couldn't shift them. She didn't know any of the correct medical terms but Edward had clearly gone mad. She could perhaps just about understand his motive but everything had been exacerbated by his isolation. Jessica wondered about the effect of seeing his girlfriend assaulted and how it had changed him. It sounded as if he were just a normal teenager before that but now he had turned into a killer whose moods shifted drastically.

He was clearly artistic and clever, while everything must have taken a huge degree of planning. Somewhere along the way, though, he had lost his conscience. The casual way he was talking about getting rid of her but being unsure how to do it was almost as disconcerting as the fact he was happy to kill an innocent person. Jessica tried to keep herself cool and focused on trying to move her right arm. She could twitch it ever so slightly more than she could before but still nowhere near enough to do anything of note. It was hard to stay calm but she realised getting frustrated would do no good either.

The man was still muttering to himself but quickly stopped pacing, turning to look directly at Jessica. Everything that had happened in the previous minutes almost felt as if it were occurring to someone else but, for the first time, Jessica felt genuine fear at the steel in Edward's eyes. Something had changed in his thought process.

'You do look rather pretty sat there all helpless,' he said. His tone was level and Jessica felt a chill go down her back. It was the most feeling she'd had in a while. 'The others were all men and not for me but it would be such a waste to leave you there.'

Edward reached towards the belt that was holding up

his linen trousers and started to undo it. 'At least we can have a bit of fun before you have to say goodbye,' he said casually. 'Given the reason all of this has happened, it'd be fairly apt, don't you think?'

36

Suddenly realising the horror of what Edward intended, Jessica tried as hard as she could to move her limbs. Her legs weren't responding but her right arm had a tiny amount of motion, although barely enough to lift it. She wanted to scream but no sound came out. The man dropped his trousers and Jessica tried not to look at him, closing her eyes tightly.

While she stared into the darkness of her eyelids, time almost seemed to hang still but her feeling of terror was interrupted by the doorbell sounding. Jessica opened her eyes and looked up at Edward. He was on his knees in front of her and had stopped to pull his trousers back up. 'Bollocks. That had better not be the pool people, I told them Thursday,' he said breezily.

His tone of voice, as if they were old friends and this was the most normal thing in the world, would have been funny if it wasn't so terrifying. He stood, refastening his trousers as the doorbell sounded again. 'I should have told you how pleased I was you liked my art, by the way,' he said. 'I wanted to tell you it was mine of course but it would have given everything away. Anyway, be right back.'

As he left the room, Jessica saw a flicker of movement from her left by one of the plastic sheets hanging from the ceiling. They were clear but translucent but she thought she could see a glimpse of something red. Emerging slowly from behind one was DC Diamond. 'Are you okay?' she whispered loudly. Jessica wanted to say she wasn't but couldn't move.

The constable stepped closer, glancing from side to side before fully emerging into the room. She had climbed through the space where the window should go. 'We were waiting at the bottom of the drive like you said but, when no one came out, we thought we'd see what was going on. Are you all right?'

Still looking towards the open doorway, Izzy moved quickly towards Jessica, stopping to look at the knife on the floor and then picking it up. She leant in towards her. 'Jess?'

She must have realised to some degree what was going on because she reeled back. 'Oh God, Jess. Can you speak?'

Jessica tried to say something and really pushed to move her arm but nothing happened. She could hear faint voices from the hallway. Izzy's eyes widened. 'It's Dave out there.' The constable stood quickly, knife still in her hand and left the room. Jessica closed her eyes and concentrated on breathing.

Jessica took a deep breath and leant back into the seat before downing the rest of her pint. She only drank lager on special occasions but would have probably enjoyed whatever was put in front of her at that exact moment.

'Get 'em in then, Dave,' she said, looking to the constable next to her.

'Isn't it your round?' Rowlands asked.

'Yeah, but I'm still a patient.'

He laughed, before turning to Izzy. 'Whatever. Do you want the same?'

'Yeah, but make it a double.' Dave slid out from the booth in the pub closest to the police station and headed towards the bar. The atmosphere was relatively upbeat and Jessica was trying her best to join in with her friends, even though she had kept so many of the details surrounding what had happened in Edward Marks's house to herself.

It had been a week since the man had been arrested. Between the two constables, Edward had been subdued. Jessica didn't know the entire story as she had first spent time in hospital, then at home. The pub visit was the first time she had gone anywhere near the station. Her doctor had signed her off work for a fortnight but she had avoided all calls from anyone at the station except from Izzy and Dave. It was partly because she didn't want sympathy from any of them but also because she felt embarrassed at charging into a situation almost on her own. By taking the two constables with her, it showed she had learned her lesson from two years ago when Randall Anderson had almost choked her to death. Jessica was still aware she had been just moments away from something awful happening.

It was largely that which kept her away from the station. She had tried to block out the look in Edward's eyes but it was constantly in the back of her mind. Jessica had not said a word about it to anyone and, although it was obvious she had been drugged, no one knew the extent of what had almost gone on – and she had no intention of telling them.

'Are you okay?' Izzy asked.

Jessica tried to speak with a confidence she wasn't feeling. 'Yes, I was a bit unsteady for the first couple of days. The doctor said the dosage of the drug Edward injected into me could send some people into shock or cause permanent damage. I feel all right but I've got more tests tomorrow.' She looked at the empty glasses on the table. 'I probably should have stayed off the booze.'

'Are you back at work the week after next, then?'

'I don't know.'

Something in Jessica's tone must have not sounded quite right because Izzy followed it up, more quietly the second time around. 'Are you ever coming back?'

Jessica looked up from the table to meet her colleague's eyes, feeling vulnerable. She looked away before replying. 'I don't know.'

The constable sighed almost involuntarily. 'Oh God, Jess. I'm so sorry. I know we should have come in quicker. What happened?'

Jessica spoke firmly. 'Nothing.'

Izzy didn't look as if she believed her, tilting her head sideways, her long red hair hanging around her shoulders.

The mood was interrupted by Rowlands returning with their drinks. He was using both hands to push all three glasses into one another so they didn't drop and slowly manoeuvred them onto the table. He must have sensed a slight tension. 'Everyone okay?'

'Fine,' Jessica said before Izzy could speak.

The constable nodded. 'Good, good. So, we make a pretty good team all in all then.'

Jessica put her arm around Diamond's shoulder. 'Well, *we* do. I don't know where you come into it.'

'Hey, I was the one who arrested Edward Marks,' Dave protested.

Izzy nodded. 'Only because I'd taken him by surprise.'

'Exactly. That's what I mean by teamwork.'

Jessica wanted to change the subject away from what had happened. 'Fine, *we* make a good team. So tell me, what's going on with everyone's favourite MP?' The two constables exchanged glances. 'Come on,' Jessica added. 'I know you're not supposed to know but I'm not going to tell.'

Rowlands lowered his voice. 'The DCI and DI are keeping it all pretty quiet but, from what everyone says, they've got nothing on him except hearsay. The garage owner reckons he took cash to kidnap Christine Johnson but none of it can be matched back to the MP. The phone calls and texts the mechanic has records of are only to an unregistered pre-pay mobile number they've not been able to tie to Johnson either. There are all sorts of circumstantial bits and pieces but people are saying the only one going down for it is the bloke who owned the garage. It looks like he did it, of course, but everyone thinks it was Johnson who paid him.'

'Have they got any sort of motive?' Jessica asked.

'I don't know,' Dave said. 'George Johnson's rich enough anyway and there's no life insurance, so it's not that. Apparently he was having an affair, even if he denies it, but he knows we've got nothing on him and so does his solicitor. Jason is furious but what can you do? Someone leaked it to the media saying we'd taken him in for questioning. People are saying it was the DCI himself who leaked. I think they're hoping someone else comes forward with information but no one's holding their breath.' The constable paused to have a sip from his glass before continuing. 'The garage owner should be convicted, which is a result because he's basically confessed to the actual crime. He's not the one they're after though.'

Jessica nodded, thinking it sounded about right. She took a large slurp of her drink before Rowlands continued. 'I take it you know what's going on with Edward even though you've not been in?'

There was a short pause. Jessica had listened to a few voicemails and gone through some emails via her phone. She had also given a statement about everything Edward had told her. 'I've heard bits,' she said.

'Do you know they found the remains of the five men in the foundations of the pool area?'

'Yes.'

Izzy shuffled nervously but Dave seemed oblivious to either her or Jessica's discomfort and carried on. 'They discovered the storage unit too. It was in his dad's name which is why we hadn't found it before. Forensics have been in but we don't know if they have found anything yet. Iz went down to London and went over mug shots with Charlie's former colleagues. They insist our "Charlie" isn't their "Charlie" and we're getting a formal identification sorted. By the time it gets to trial the bleach will have grown out of his hair and he'll be back to dark-haired Edward.'

Jessica already knew most of it but it was good to hear they had evidence building against the man. One of the messages Cole had left her was about giving a more formal statement but she hadn't felt ready.

Izzy leant in and picked up the conversation. 'The biggest issue has been the CPS, although you can't blame them. They've been dithering all week because they don't know what name he should be put in front of court under. "Edward Marks" was classed as missing so it's a bit of a mess at the moment. There was something else though.'

'What?' Jessica asked.

'You asked me to look into unsolved sexual assaults where no DNA had been left. We found one where the victim identified Jacob Chrisp as her attacker. He can't be convicted obviously but at least it's some closure for the victim.'

'Good.'

'How did you figure it out?' Izzy asked.

Jessica sighed, sipping her drink. She didn't want to talk about it but figured she owed her colleagues some explanation. 'A few things,' she began. 'When I did that careers day thing at the school one of the kids asked me about how to get away with a crime. It was just one of those silly things but it had me thinking that the best way wasn't to leave no clues at all, it was to leave signals that pointed to someone else. If you leave nothing, people like us delve further into your background. Edward obviously didn't want that.'

She went on to explain about the left-right-hand connection from the wedding and pointed out it had all fallen into place. 'It was just a guess more than anything,' she concluded.

'Are you going to contact Sam Kellett?' Rowlands asked. 'None of us have but someone probably should before it gets to court.'

Jessica nodded but said nothing, not wanting to commit to any course of action. She remembered promising Garry Ashford an exclusive too and thought he would be pleased after the court case when he got all the juicy details.

She took two more large mouthfuls of her drink. 'I think I'm going to go on holiday,' she said, placing her glass back on the table.

It was a statement out of the blue and the two constables glanced at each other before turning back to her. Rowlands made the obvious response. 'Sorry?'

'I'm going to go on holiday. I'm owed loads of time off anyway and I've not been away properly in years.'

Jessica saw the two constables exchange another look, this time with more worried expressions, then Izzy spoke. 'Are you okay, Jess?'

'I just need a break.'

Dave put a hand on her shoulder. 'I know we arse about but seriously, are you all right?'

Jessica had rarely seen him show genuine concern for her, although she knew most of their mutual teasing was for show. She nodded. 'I'm good.'

Dave removed his hand, seemingly satisfied. 'Are you going on your own?' he asked mischievously.

'Yeah, why?'

'I hear you've been getting a little, ahem, friendly with a certain someone recently.'

Jessica knew exactly what he was talking about. With Caroline on honeymoon, the only person she had kept in any kind of regular contact with over the past week had been Hugo. They had exchanged text messages and he had come to her flat and cooked her tea, showing off yet another hidden talent. As she struggled to bury the feeling of helplessness from when she had been drugged, Hugo's weirdness had helped keep her smiling.

Jessica said nothing but Dave carried on his teasing. 'Don't forget it was me who introduced you.'

Izzy leant in to the table. 'Oooh. Tell me more.'

Before Jessica could speak, Dave cut in. 'Jess has been getting friendly with our mutual friend Hugo. I hear you had a fun time together at your mate's wedding?'

Jessica realised Rowlands didn't know about the contact she'd had with Hugo since then. 'So what? We only went as mates,' she replied, trying not to sound too defensive.

'All right, I believe you,' Dave said, although it sounded strongly as if he didn't. 'You'd make a great couple anyway. He'd be the intelligent multi-talented one, while you walk around bollocking people into submission.'

'Sod off.'

'Detective Sergeant Jessica Patch, it's got a nice ring to it,' Dave said airily.

'His last name is "Patch"?' Jessica asked, struggling to hide the surprise in her voice.

Rowlands raised his eyebrows. 'Didn't you even know that?'

'I guess not.'

'Some girlfriend you are.'

Jessica couldn't be bothered to argue. She took a long drink from her glass before returning it empty to the table. 'Your round,' she said, looking at Rowlands.

THINK OF THE CHILDREN

Jessica Daniel Book 4

One boy is dead. A killer is free. Who is next?

Detective Sergeant Jessica Daniel is first on the scene as a stolen car crashes on a misty, wet Manchester morning. The driver is dead, but the biggest shock awaits her when she discovers the body of a child wrapped in plastic in the boot of the car.

As Jessica struggles to discover the identity of the driver, a thin trail leads her first to a set of clothes buried in the woods and then to a list of children's names abandoned in an allotment shed.

With the winter chill setting in and parents looking for answers, Jessica must find out who has been watching local children, and how this connects to a case that has been unsolved for 14 years.

This is Book 4 in the Jessica Daniel series, following on from *Locked In*, *Vigilante* and *The Woman in Black*.

An extract follows here . . .

ISBN 978-1-4472-2340-5

1

The windscreen wipers on Detective Sergeant Jessica Daniel's battered old car thundered from side to side in an attempt to clear the pouring rain. She leant forward for what seemed like the hundredth time since starting the journey, wiping a thin layer of condensation away from the inside of the front window.

Jessica steered with one hand while continuing to clear the windows, muttering curses under her breath that related partly to her car, partly to the daily commute, but mainly to the weather itself. She had lived in Manchester for over a decade and if there was one thing the natives were used to, it was rain. She shivered slightly as cool air poured out of the car's vents. It was almost five minutes since she'd set the fans to the hottest temperature possible but they still weren't producing anything other than a light but decidedly arctic-feeling breeze.

Glancing away from the road, Jessica looked at the man in the passenger seat. 'If you could stop breathing for a while it would make this a lot easier.'

Detective Constable David Rowlands gave a half-smile. 'Was that one of the selling points when you bought this thing? "Works perfectly as long as you don't breathe when it's raining".'

'You can walk if you'd prefer.'

Out of the corner of her eye, Jessica saw the constable take a half-glance out of the passenger window but it was clear he wasn't thinking about it seriously as the rain continued hammering on the roof of the vehicle. 'You're all right. I can't believe you make this journey every day.'

Jessica sighed, continuing to edge her car forward in the slow-moving traffic. She lived in the Didsbury area, south of the main city centre. In a region that offered everything from high-priced flats at Salford Quays and multi-million-pound footballers' mansions all the way down to some of the most deprived housing estates in the country, it wasn't a bad place to call home. The biggest problem where she lived was the traffic jams on the way to the Longsight police station where she worked. The tailbacks were bad enough at the best of times but with the weather the way it was, everyone was moving even more slowly than usual. She kept tight to the car in front, ignoring the person in the vehicle she knew was trying to cut into her lane.

'You didn't have to stay at mine last night, you know,' Jessica said.

'Yeah, but we had a good time, didn't we?'

Jessica paused and smiled, thinking about the night before. 'Don't say things like that around the station or you'll start rumours.'

'Ugh, yes. You're right.'

'You don't have to be so disgusted at the idea of being associated with me. Anyway, I'm amazed your girlfriend came for tea; I've spent the last four months thinking this "Chloe" was imaginary. At least I've met her now and verified she isn't clinically mental.'

Rowlands sighed. 'Is that an official medical term?'

'Yes.'

The temperature changed almost instantly from freezing cold to searing hot. Jessica's car's fans didn't differentiate between anything other than the two extremes. The shift meant the windscreen did at least begin to clear, although the only thing it revealed was rows of traffic seemingly not moving and a set of traffic lights in the distance, the red light beaming through the misty greyness of the morning.

Jessica shuffled uncomfortably in the driver's seat, trying to stop her legs from cramping, and sighed again. 'It wasn't that long ago I was on a beach for my only holiday in years reading crappy books, drinking cocktails and enjoying the sun.'

'How can I forget? They dumped all your paperwork on me. I can't picture you lying around not doing anything though. In all the time I've known you, you never stop.'

Jessica didn't want to admit it but he was right. She had spent the first morning on the beach with a book trying not to look at an overweight tourist wearing leopard-print Speedos and a sailor's hat. After getting bored and hiring a car, she spent much of the rest of her three-week break driving around the Greek island. She had intended for the holiday to be relaxing, a chance to get some space after a series of murders where the killer had sent her severed fingers from the victims through the post. After almost becoming the final casualty herself, Jessica had wondered what she wanted from her future. Given her state of mind and accrued unpaid overtime, she was given permission to take a longer holiday than most officers got.

She went away not knowing whether this was the job for her and returned none the wiser. So little had changed.

Jessica ignored Rowlands's assessment, slowly moving her car forward as the lights ahead turned green and the line of traffic inched along. The car that had been trying to cut into her lane edged in behind her and Jessica felt a small pang of utterly irrational elation at the minor victory.

Dave started to hum an upbeat tune Jessica didn't recognise, which only added to her irritation. The lights flicked back to red just before she could drive through and, although she thought about not stopping, she slowed before putting on the handbrake, coming to rest at the front of the queue.

'Can you stop doing that?' she asked irritably.

Rowlands turned to look at her. 'What?'

'The humming.'

'Sorry, I didn't even realise I was doing it.'

'You've been doing it a lot recently. This whole domestic bliss, moving in with your girlfriend thing has almost turned you into a normal member of the human race. Albeit one that hums.'

Rowlands laughed quietly to himself. 'It's Christmas in a few weeks. Aren't I allowed to be cheery?'

'No, it's unnerving.'

Jessica reached towards the fan controls and turned them off. She hoped the mixture of cold then hot air would even itself out and make the final five minutes of their journey bearable. To her relief, the thudding rain on the metal roof started to ease. She peered up at the still-red traffic lights, then looked to her left where cars continued to speed across the junction.

The screeching noise was the first thing she heard. It sounded as if it had started some distance away, but it was hard to tell because of the rest of the din going on around her. Jessica quickly looked to her right as a black car squealed across the junction, wheels locked, spinning on the drenched surface. Everything seemed to happen in slow motion, the vehicle twisting a full circle and smashing into a lamppost in the centre of the junction before being hit by a blue car coming from the opposite direction and completing another half-spin.

Jessica blinked, trying to take in what she had just witnessed. For a fraction of a second, it was as if everything had stopped, even the rain. Without thinking, she switched off her engine and got out of the car. She didn't say a word but Rowlands was moving too and together they dashed across to where the mangled car had come to a halt. Jessica headed for the black vehicle, Rowlands towards the blue one.

Jessica could feel her heart beating quickly as she arrived at the wreck. There was a huge crack in the windscreen, the deflating airbag pressed against it. Car horns blared around her and other people were approaching the car. Jessica took out her police identification and shouted for them to stay back, at the same time pointing at a man who had his phone out and telling him to dial 999.

Because of the way the car had spun, it hadn't entangled itself with the lamppost, instead bouncing after being hit by the other car. Jessica moved to the driver's-side door, trying to peer through the cracked glass. The mixture of rain and condensation made it hard to see through the other windows and she took a snap decision to open the door. As she did, a splash of dark red blood from the inside dribbled onto the ground; the cream material lining of the seat was also drenched.

Jessica knew instantly the driver was dead.

The blood-soaked airbag had begun to sag onto the driver's lap as Jessica finally allowed herself to look at the victim. She had seen plenty of dead bodies in her time but this one was a distorted mess. Jessica quickly realised why: the seatbelt clasp hung limply by the door, unfastened. She felt a shiver go through her as it started to rain again, droplets of water streaming down her face as she tried to put the pieces together. Despite the mess, the driver's greying hair made him look as if he was in his fifties. She didn't know for sure but it appeared that his neck had snapped. It could have been him hitting the windscreen or the force of the airbag colliding after the impact. Not that it mattered considering the way the pulped skin, blood and glass made his face look like a warped, dropped pizza. Jessica could not look for more than a second or two. Not wearing a seatbelt had cost him his life.

Jessica shut the door, knowing there was nothing she could do and not wanting to contaminate the scene either through her own presence or by letting rain in.

She again warned members of the public to stay back before walking the short distance to the blue car where Rowlands was crouched, talking to a young woman still sitting in the driver's seat. As Jessica came closer, it was clear the woman was crying hysterically, a seatbelt stretched across her. She reached the car and put a hand on Dave's shoulder, shaking her head slightly to let him know the fate of the other driver before crouching herself.

Rowlands spoke slowly and deliberately. 'This is Laura. She was on her way to work, weren't you, Laura?' The woman nodded, eyes wide with disbelief as tears continued to flow down her face. Jessica knew her colleague was doing his best to keep the woman calm, using her name frequently to keep her attention until help arrived. Outwardly, aside from long dark hair which was tousled across her face from the impact, the driver looked fine, but she was obviously suffering from shock.

'Are you okay, Laura?' Jessica asked. The woman nodded again but said nothing.

Jessica left Dave talking as cars swerved around the accident, sirens blaring in the distance.

She stopped to take a deep breath, swallowing a feeling of claustrophobia despite being in the open. The car horns and engines, the chatter of nearby pedestrians, the patter of the rain: it was becoming overpowering. Jessica felt a few drops of rain slide down her neck, struggling not to shiver as she made her way back towards the black car while tying her long hair into a ponytail.

The vehicle looked much more of a mess from the other side. It was a mid-size four-door model that Jessica thought of as always being advertised with a family sitting inside, as if the machine itself was the key to parenting bliss. A scrape ran the full length of the passenger side, the front headlight a concertina of mangled metal.

Jessica blinked the water away from her eyes as she saw the flashing lights of an ambulance a few hundred metres away, the noise from the siren blaring ever louder. Her eyes were attracted to the rear of the vehicle where the car's boot had popped open ever so slightly. She put a hand on the metal, at first thinking about pushing it shut, but curiosity got the better of her and she opened it instead.

If she'd had to, Jessica would have struggled to guess the contents of her own boot. There might well have been jump leads and possibly a petrol can but she wouldn't have put money on it. She definitely wasn't prepared for the sight that met her in the rear of the smashed-up black car. Thick plastic sheeting was wrapped tightly around an object with heavy-looking tape sealing it into a tight cocoon. Next to the object was a rusting spade with a muddied plastic handle. Jessica felt something in her stomach urging her forward as if she already knew what it was.

She pushed the boot down but didn't lock it in place. As the ambulance drew up, she ran to her own car, opening the driver's door and digging into the well before pulling out a pair of scissors.

Her father had always been good about keeping things in their old family car just in case but Jessica hadn't inherited his forward thinking. She had found the scissors not long after her dad bought her the car second-hand a decade or so ago, left by the previous owner. She dashed across the junction again, silently thanking whoever that previous owner was and feeling justified for never cleaning out her car.

As she arrived back at the black vehicle, paramedics stepped out of the ambulance. Jessica flashed her identification and told them the fate of the driver. One of them went to check on him anyway as another walked to where Rowlands was still comforting the woman from the blue car.

More sirens blared in the distance as Jessica returned to the black car's boot, opening it and moving the spade to the rear of the compartment out of her way. Layer upon layer of plastic sheeting was wrapped tightly around the object and Jessica struggled to force through the blunt blades of her scissors. As she pushed harder, it started to rain more heavily, huge drops bouncing off the tarmac road. Jessica could feel the force of the water smashing into the top of her head. She continued to cut and finally felt the scissors push through the top few layers of the plastic. Reaching in with her hands, she pulled hard to try to tear the material apart. Slowly, it began to give and, with a combination of her hands and the scissors, she opened up part of the wrapping.

With the plastic pulled back, all she could see was a piece of cloth that had a flowery pattern. It reminded Jessica of the curtains her parents used to have at their house when she was a child, a hideous mixture of yellow and brown. Still reaching into the boot, Jessica tugged at the fabric, finally freeing it with a gasp.

Jessica tried to force herself to look away but the pale skin and clamped eyelids held her hypnotically: the haunting lifeless face of a dead child.

extracts reading groups
competitions books new
discounts extracts
competitions
books new
events books
extracts new titles reading groups
interviews
discounts
new books events
events new
discounts extracts discounts

www.panmacmillan.com

extracts events reading groups
competitions books extracts new